A TEMPTING LIFE

LORD HAWKESBURY'S PLAYERS, BOOK 2

C.J. ARCHER

WWW.CJARCHER.COM

CHAPTER 1

London: Autumn 1589

The White Swan Inn was the last place Leo, third Baron Warhurst, wanted to be on a Friday morning. The worst part about it wasn't that he could have been attending court, greasing the palms of London's most influential gentlemen. No, the worst part was that he couldn't even stop for a drink in the taproom. Thanks to the mess created by his siblings, he had gone to the Gracechurch Street inn to speak to a seamstress. A bloody *seamstress!*

He made his way through the archway to the inn's yard where the ostlers and travelers shared the square cobbled area with a theater stage. The raised wooden platform stood towards the back of the large yard. Steps led up to it from the ground and a curtain separated the stage from the tiring house beyond. According to his half-brother, that's where he'd find the woman who might be able to help him with his family's problem.

A problem that had landed firmly on Leo's shoulders like a canker. He needed to remove it before it was too late and any chance of restoring the tenuous respectability of the Warhurst title was lost forever. Since the perpetrator of the problem was not at home that morning, or last night, or the day before, Leo had come here.

To speak to a seamstress.

It would have been laughable if the situation wasn't so dire. He'd only ever dealt directly with one seamstress. A slack-faced woman reeking of cheap wine had accosted him in the street years ago demanding Leo pay for the gown his late father had commissioned her to make for his mistress. The seamstress had threatened to tell Lady Warhurst about the other woman if Leo didn't pay the debt. He'd told her she was welcome to speak to his mother since she already knew, as did the better half of London. The seamstress had curled her top lip, baring broken teeth, and scampered like a rat back to the gutter out of which she'd crawled.

Hopefully the seamstress his brother sent him to possessed more sense and less drink-fueled audacity.

He paused on the bottom step leading up to the stage and squeezed the bridge of his nose. God, he was tired. He'd traveled like the devil for a week to reach London and not been able to sleep since. This woman had better know something other than how to thread a needle. Leo was in no mood for a fool's errand.

He lifted the curtain aside and peered into the room beyond. Several chests, some opened, occupied most of the space. A row of stools dotted one wall and a central bench almost disappeared beneath piles of neatly folded costumes. A massive pair of wings made of feathers hung between two hooks and what looked like a cauldron was slotted beneath the bench. The room was crowded but not chaotic. Someone kept it orderly.

Whoever it was, they weren't there. Another bloody wasted effort. He was about to release the curtain when he heard the swish of lush fabric, velvet perhaps, coming from behind what appeared to be an unhinged door propped up in the middle of the tiring house.

"Damnation!" The voice, a woman's, came from behind the door screen. With language like that, she must be the woman he sought.

"Hail!" he called out. "Is someone here?"

A pale, heart-shaped face topped with a tall hat popped out from behind the door. "Oh! I didn't know I had company."

"I'm sorry to startle you," he said.

"You didn't. I'm simply surprised."

He failed to see the difference and was about to say as much when she stepped out from behind the door and his words were sucked away along with his breath. He'd been wrong. She couldn't be the seamstress. This lady wouldn't have been out of place at court with her tall, slender frame, striking cheekbones and a firm, almost imperial set to her shoulders. She was a lady used to speaking her mind if her direct gaze was any indication. He had no doubt she usually got what she wanted too. A lifetime of experience with such women had taught him to identify the species. Unfortunately, it had not taught him how to deal with them.

"Madam, I am Lord Warhurst." He bowed.

She stepped forward and the swish of her crimson gown was soon drowned out by the drumming of his heartbeat in his ears. Her simple movement had caused the exposed flesh above her too-tight bodice to wobble most...ah, delightfully.

"Perhaps you could step a little closer," he said when she hesitated. "I would like to have a better look at your...face."

She did, with hands firmly on her hips, and stopped directly in front of him. "My face is *above* my neck, my lord."

He glanced up and got an icy blast from a pair of pale blue eyes. He bowed again, partly to hide his embarrassment and partly because it afforded him another view of her bounteous flesh. If God gave her a pair of luscious breasts like that, surely He meant for man to gaze upon them. Otherwise why create such low-cut gowns?

But on second glance, the gown seemed a little too low-cut for this lady's, er, jewels. Although exquisitely made from what he could see, and certainly beautifully—and expensively— embroidered in gold thread, it was a poor fit.

"If you are looking for the players then I'm afraid they're not here," she said.

He looked up again. Although her glare was still cool, her

mouth seemed to be smiling—and yet not. How did she do that? It was quite intriguing. And certainly alluring.

"You are all alone here, my lady?" He could have bitten off his tongue after the words tumbled out. He sounded like a villain assessing the likelihood of having his wicked way with a defenseless woman.

"Lady?" She blinked at him. Then looked down at her sleeves, the crimson velvet slashed to reveal the gold of the lining beneath. "Oh."

He frowned. She had not seemed to grasp the crude yet unintentional meaning of his question. Thankfully. But...why *was* such a woman as this alone in the tiring house? What gentleman would allow his wife, sister or daughter to fend for herself at, of all places, an inn and a theater at that? Guilt twisted his stomach at the similarity to his own situation, but he cast it off. It was too late for guilt. Besides, his sister's pregnancy was not his fault.

"Madam, I am—."

"Mistaken." Her laughter seemed to rise up from deep within her and burst forth like a sudden gust of air.

He tried not to notice how the laugh made the flesh above her bodice jiggle. "Mistaken?"

"Quite, quite mistaken. I am not a gentlewoman. It must be this dress..." She caressed the velvet of her gown as if it were her lover's skin. "It used to belong to Lady Dalrymple. She and I are of a height which will suit Freddie, but the similarity does not extend to the chest area." She smiled that smile again, the one that wasn't quite a smile. This time it was accompanied by a wicked gleam in those clear eyes. "As you noticed."

He felt like he was walking on a different path to her. Whatever was she talking about? "Freddie?"

"Freddie Putney, the company's boy actor. He plays the lead female roles."

At least her path was within sight now. "And that gown once belonged to Lady Dalrymple?"

"As I said." She looked at him as if he were a half-wit.

His limbs tensed. He had a bad feeling about this. "And you are wearing the gown because..."

"Because I'm adjusting it of course." She shrugged and the

gown slipped off one shoulder. He stared at the smooth, white skin and wondered if it felt like silk because it certainly looked silken.

She fixed the gown and he was once more running along the path in an attempt to catch up to her.

What had she been saying? Adjusting it... Adjusting...the gown!

The bad feeling slammed into his gut with the force of a hammer blow. "You're Alice Croft," he said heavily. "The seamstress for Lord Hawkesbury's Men."

She nodded. "And you're Lord Warhurst, brother to Robert Blakewell."

"Half-brother," he said without thinking.

"What can I do for you, Lord Warhurst? I assume you're looking for me since you know my name. Did Blake send you?"

She didn't seem in the least surprised or in any way alarmed by his presence or by the prospect of being sought. Women of her station usually lowered their eyes and spoke only when he asked a direct question of them. Unless they were whores or drunk. This woman certainly wasn't a whore—readjusting the gown to cover her bare shoulder was proof of that—and she didn't seem drunk.

Then why was she so different to all the others?

The fact that he was wondering disturbed him.

"Blake did send me," he said in an attempt to keep his thoughts on the task at hand. "He said I should seek you out and that I'd find you here."

"As indeed you have."

He cleared his throat. "I'll have you know this goes against my better judgment."

Her eyes narrowed. "You haven't told me what 'this' is yet."

"If there was anyone else, I'd ask them first. I'd rather not involve someone else in our family dilemma, but Blake assures me you'll be discreet."

"Discreet?" She shook her head. A frown furrowed her pretty brow. "My lord, is this about making a gown for your mistress? Because if it is—."

"No!" He shouldn't have come. Whatever was Blake thinking

to send him to such a woman? How did he even know she could be trusted? He was wasting his time. Leo pulled back the curtain leading out to the stage.

"My lord, wait!" The seamstress placed a hand on his arm. There was no pressure, no attempt to halt his progress, yet he stopped anyway. There was something compelling in her touch, something far more forceful than mere strength. "If Blake sent you then it must have something to do with Lord Hawkesbury. And," she cleared her throat, "and your sister."

He half-turned to see her and was struck once more by those eyes. Of the palest blue, they were almost colorless, and yet they seemed to see right into him. He recoiled. The bad feeling returned like a vengeful warrior.

"You're right," he heard himself say. "I've come to ask you for help."

"Help?"

He focused on the tiny crease between her brows because he had the disturbing sensation that if he continued to look into her eyes, she might see too much. "Yes. Help with the business between Lord Hawkesbury and my sister, as you said."

"But how can I possibly be of service?"

"I have need of someone who is capable of finding out information. Blake suggested you because you are associated with Lord Hawkesbury's Players, and they have a tendency to hear and see a great many things when in their patron's presence. Well? What say you?"

Alice had been told many times in her twenty-six years that her curiosity would be her downfall. As a child she would sneak around the house listening to the adult conversations or explore the narrow lanes near her home—the ones she was strictly told not to venture down. Not even a whipping from her father and a near-escape from a brothel-keeper seeking fresh girls could keep her curiosity and thirst for knowledge in check. Although she kept away from the worst of the lanes after that instance.

Childish curiosity was one thing. Spying on Lord Hawkesbury, a peer of the realm, was entirely another.

"Why not ask one of the players?" she said.

Lord Warhurst gave her a rueful smile, one that sparked a

gleam in his green eyes. She'd never seen eyes quite like them, bright one moment and fathomless the next but never revealing too much of what the man was thinking. They reminded her of the emeralds she'd once seen in a grand lady's rings. With a start, she recalled they'd been worn on the hand of his mother.

"The players were not recommended by my brother," Lord Warhurst said. "You were."

It had been only days since she'd last seen his brother the pirate, Robert Blakewell, and Blake's bride-to-be, Minerva Peabody. They'd informed her that much had changed prior to their betrothal, including Blake ceasing his pursuit of Lord Hawkesbury over the relationship the earl had had with Lilly Blakewell.

It seemed Lord Warhurst was taking up the reins dropped by his brother to save their sister's honor.

Yet it didn't quite make sense. Why all this brotherly fuss over a simple affection? Why the forbidding presence of the brooding Baron Warhurst darkening her tiring house? And why did he need the help of a seamstress?

"My half-brother and I don't get along," Lord Warhurst said, crossing his arms over a broad chest. "But I trust his judgment. If he thinks you would make a fair and discreet information gatherer, then I believe him. I also think you have the look about you of someone who would go unnoticed, something which will be of benefit in this endeavor."

The old, familiar pang stabbed her in the ribs. She'd once thought it was jealousy of prettier girls, the sort who turned heads just by walking down the street. But she'd learned, eventually, that that wasn't the case. Jealousy it might be, but it was the jealousy of a girl who simply wanted to be someone else, someone who *would* be noticed, not for her beauty but for...what?

If she knew the answer, she could perhaps make steps towards changing herself, but all she really knew for certain was that she didn't want to be seamstress for Lord Hawkesbury's Men day after day until her death.

She may be aware of the pang and all it implied but it still hurt to have her plainness in looks and occupation pointed out so baldly.

"That is hardly a convincing argument," she said, perhaps a little too caustically.

He arched one eyebrow in question.

"Telling me I'm too ordinary to be noticed."

"I didn't say ordinary, nor is that what I meant." He huffed out a breath and rolled his eyes Heaven-ward. "I simply was stating the fact that people do not always see those whose presence they take for granted." His words were measured, careful.

"Like servants," she said flatly.

"Like seamstresses." He shrugged, as if what he'd said was obvious and not open to questioning. That it was nothing of importance.

That *she* was nothing of importance.

It was a wonder he had even deigned to speak to someone like her at all let alone ask for help. Her throat burned as she swallowed back a tide of emotions, ones she thought she'd conquered.

"You must hate it," she said with a lightness she certainly didn't feel.

"What?"

"Asking me for help. A seamstress."

He opened his mouth but shut it again. His stare faltered and he looked away. It was all the answer she needed.

"Which means the task you require me to perform must be important," she went on. A little voice within her warned her not to test this man, not to push him into a corner because he would fight. He was a baron and an imposing figure, standing well above her and she was no sprite. Yet she couldn't help herself. She wanted to find out as much as she could before she said yes. About the task, and the gentleman.

That she would say yes was a certainty. She needed an intrigue to break up the endless tedium of her days.

"Why do you want Lord Hawkesbury to marry your sister? Does she really love him so much that she would have her brother force him into marriage against his wishes? Or is there another reason? One more...scandalous?"

He lifted his gaze to hers without lifting his head and glared at her beneath long black lashes. The effect was devilish.

So much for backing him into a corner. She hadn't even budged him in the slightest. What she'd done was potentially far worse—awakened a beast with more anger boiling inside him than she could ever know.

"I think," he finally said through a clenched jaw, "that my brother was mistaken. You are of no use to me. Good day." He spun round and shoved the curtain all the way to the side.

"Wait! I can help you."

But he was already half-way across the stage and he didn't look like stopping to hear her. Not the reaction she'd expected. Hot outrage at her impertinence would have been better than this cool dismissal. But at least she now knew her assumption was correct—Lilly Blakewell was carrying Lord Hawkesbury's unborn child.

"I know where Lord Hawkesbury will be tonight," she called after him.

She might as well have flung her words at a wall. He either didn't hear them or didn't care. He simply jumped off the stage and strode towards the arch leading out to Gracechurch Street.

Well. Good riddance. The man was rude. It was a miracle he'd even lowered himself to speak to her.

Nevertheless, she watched him go with a sinking heart. He and his family's troubles had been a bump on her otherwise flat week. No, make that year. Now even that distraction was gone.

She sighed and returned to the tiring house, letting the curtain fall back into place. There was no point dwelling on what might have happened if she hadn't opened her mouth. There was still much to be done to prepare for the troupe's transfer to The Rose. Henslowe, The Rose theater's owner, had given them permission to perform there on the days Lord Strange's Men weren't using it. The bigger crowds at the dedicated theater would ensure more money for Lord Hawkesbury's Players and for Alice's father, their tiring house manager. But as his assistant and daughter, she would see none of it. Moving to The Rose would simply be more of the same. Mending costumes, cleaning the tiring house, listening to the actors' complaints and gossip.

She looked down at the clothing bought from Lady Dalrymple. The ensemble of bodice, skirt and over-gown was several years out of fashion, but it was the most exquisite thing Alice had ever worn. The softness of the velvet, the vibrancy of the colors and the workmanship that had gone into the embroidery were nothing like she'd seen before. She simply had to try it on. Just for a few minutes she wanted to pretend she was someone else, someone important. A duchess or an heiress or even a wealthy merchant in her own right. Anything would be better than this...nothingness. The clothes had beckoned to her like a lover and she couldn't resist. Besides, no one had seen.

No one except Lord Warhurst and she was not likely to see him again. She doubted he cared enough to tell her father or Roger Style, the company's manager. If Style had caught her wearing the costume that had cost him a week's profit, he'd have dismissed her without hearing her excuses and perhaps dismissed her father too. It had been a risk but a risk she'd been prepared to take.

With another sigh, she removed the hat. She was about to step behind the door used as a screen for privacy when she heard the swish of the curtain opening behind her. She knew without turning around that Lord Warhurst had returned. She couldn't say how she knew it, she just did. Perhaps it was his brooding presence, so powerful that it surged ahead of him like a flood.

"Why do you want to help me?" he said.

She turned and shrugged. The ill-fitting sleeve slipped off her shoulder. She adjusted it but not before she saw Warhurst's lips purse. In disapproval? Irritation? Or suppressed desire?

"I liked your sister," she said. "And your brother."

His eyebrow forked again. "That may be the case, but I doubt it is your sole reason. There must be more for you to risk your livelihood. I'm sure you are aware that Lord Hawkesbury could have you removed from his company if he discovers your involvement in this scheme."

She nodded. "That's why I want something from you in return."

"Money?"

"Not quite." She chewed the inside of her lip, thinking fast. Should she ask him? Would he agree? If she didn't ask, she would never know his answer. And such an opportunity would never arise again, of that she was certain. She *had* to ask.

She lifted her chin and stepped towards him, the better to gauge his reaction. But his only reaction was a lowering of his gaze to her breasts bursting over the top of the bodice. She cleared her throat but refused to cover herself. Let him look. She wasn't ashamed.

"I cannot take you on as my mistress." He looked up, face flushed, eyes hooded.

"Pardon?"

His flush deepened. "I, er, isn't that what you were asking of me?"

"No! Good Lord, what sort of woman do you think I am?"

"I...I'm not entirely sure. To be honest, I've never encountered a woman such as yourself before."

"That is quite obvious."

He bowed. "My humble apologies, Mistress Croft." He blinked rapidly and looked away, pretending to study a Roman shield leaning against the wall.

An awkward silence ensued until she could stand it no longer. "What I do want from you is your patronage, or sorts."

That got his attention. "So you do want money?" He said it without a hint of disapproval, as if he expected it, almost welcomed it.

But what she wanted wasn't quite as simple as an exchange of coins. "I want you to establish me as a seamstress with a shop of my own in a respectable part of the City."

"You want *what*?"

"In essence, you will be my patron but only until such time that my earnings cover the rent. I have some money set aside to purchase the tools I need. You could also use your influence with certain merchants so that I can buy cloth and other materials at a good price. It would be to your benefit," she said quickly when his mouth dropped open. "The more money that remains in my coffers the faster I will be able to support myself and you can wash your hands of me. Oh, and there is one other thing."

"I don't doubt it," he muttered.

"If you could send some elegant ladies of your acquaintance to my shop, I would be most grateful. You would benefit—."

"Yes, yes, so I see." But he shook his head and she thought she heard a low chuckle, but he didn't smile so she couldn't be sure. "First of all, Mistress Croft, you over-estimate my influence in elegant circles. As you can see," he stretched out his arms, "I am no gallant."

"True, but your clothes are well made and suited to your...demeanor."

He frowned. "Meaning?"

"They are serious." She thought it wise not to mention she'd seen puritans wear less bleak clothing. There wasn't a hint of embellishment in his doublet, even the buttons were covered in the same black material. No slashing, no embroidery, no pinking, and yet the doublet was silk and from what she could see, the tailoring superb. It fit him to perfection, without needing any padding across shoulders or chest. What lay beneath the clothing must also be perfection. The thought made her heart skip.

"I have seen your mother and sister," she forged on, "and they are both women with exceptional fashion sense. If I provide them with some gowns, free of charge of course, to prove my skill then perhaps they could send their friends to me. You could give them the gowns as a gift."

He nodded thoughtfully. "A reasonable plan. And my brother's new bride would require something to wear for her wedding feast. Could you do it?"

"How soon?"

"In a month or two I would imagine."

If she started as soon as possible she should be able to make Min an outfit to rival the queen's. "I should like to make her something special anyway. We have become friends of sorts."

He nodded. "But I'm afraid you mistake my position in this City. I am rarely here and I do not know any merchants. As to renting a shop..." He drew in a breath. "I shall see what I can do."

"I'm sure your brother knows many merchants from his privateering jaunts. Perhaps you could ask him since Mistress Blakewell is his sister too."

He acknowledged this with a curt nod. "You have a solid understanding of business, I see."

"Then we have an agreement?"

"We do, on one condition. That you do not mention this to anyone. We shall rent the shop in your name and in no way will any transactions between us be known. I cannot afford for our connection to be discovered."

"Because you don't wish Lord Hawkesbury to know?"

He hesitated before saying, "Quite."

She chewed her lip again. He wasn't telling her the entire truth. Not that it mattered. The anonymity of her new patron suited her needs too. Her father knew she had some money set aside; she would simply inflate the amount when he asked how she could afford to set out on her own.

"Only my half-brother will know," he said, "but if pressed, he'll say he does not."

She was about to ask why when she realized she already knew the answer. "He wishes to keep Min happy and to do that he needs to ensure her plays are performed. Upsetting the patron of the company performing them would be a poor move. At least until she is able to sell them to another company."

The green eyes briefly flared and she thought she saw a flicker of surprise in them. Surprise that she could think for herself?

The man grew more pompous by the minute.

"Furthermore," he went on as if she had not spoken, "I think it best that you do not give up your position here with Lord Hawkesbury's Players until our task is complete."

"Agreed. Shall we shake on it?" She held out her hand.

He didn't take it, didn't even acknowledge it with so much as a glance. "You do not wish to know how I want you to gather the relevant information before agreeing?"

"My lord, unless you are asking me to whore for you then I will do whatever is required."

"What makes you think I am not asking you to whore for me?"

She shrugged and lowered her hand. "You seem far too prudish to ask that of any woman. Even a seamstress."

He tilted his head back as if struck. Then, unexpectedly, he smiled. Just a slight lifting of the corners of his mouth at first, then a few twitches until finally a wide grin broke out, as if it had escaped despite his attempts to smother it.

"I can assure you, Mistress Croft," he said, capturing the grin once more and hiding it away, "that I am no prude." He picked up a fine lawn partlet from the top of a pile of clothes stacked on a closed chest. "Nor am I immune to your...charms." His gaze dipped once more to her breasts and this time it was her turn to blush as heat prickled her throat, her face. He closed the space between them until he was so near she could smell him, a pleasing mix of fresh air and man. "So I would appreciate it if you kept those charms covered when next we meet." He tucked the edge of the partlet down the front of her bodice. His long finger grazed her skin, just above the nipple.

She let out a breath and dared not draw in another as it would cause her chest to rise, bringing his finger closer. Closer. Even though that was exactly what she suddenly, desperately wanted. For this man to touch her. Everywhere. The need throbbed within her like an ache.

But some very deep part of her kept her from drawing the breath that could start something. Or stop it.

Then his finger was gone, leaving the partlet covering the rapid rise and fall of her chest as she sucked in breath upon breath. Their gazes locked and heat flooded her, sliding through her like warm sunshine.

She thought she understood this man from the moment he'd walked in with his conservative clothing and crisp aloofness. Now she knew she did not.

"You said you knew where Lord Hawkesbury would be tonight," he said, voice low and rough.

"I..." She nodded and stepped away, out of reach of his powerful presence. "He's commissioned a performance from the troupe to entertain his betrothed and her family at Hawkesbury Hall."

His brows rose. "The Enderbys?"

She nodded. "I don't usually attend private performances, but I can devise a reason for my presence tonight. I might be able to learn something, if you tell me what it is I need to look for."

He blinked slowly. Then he straightened and put his hands behind his back. "Our task is to find out why Lord Hawkesbury is marrying Patience Enderby when neither he nor the girl wants the marriage."

"He doesn't love her?"

"He says not."

"Nobles marry for reasons other than love all the time."

He gave her a tight smile. "I am well aware of that."

Alice knew Lord Warhurst wasn't married, but was he betrothed to some influential heiress he didn't love? Would he care if his potential wife didn't love him? What about his own heart's desire? Did he even have one? A desire, not a heart— although she couldn't be sure he possessed either.

"From what my half-brother tells me," Lord Warhurst said, "Hawkesbury is being forced into the union by the girl's father, Lord Enderby." He put a sneer into the name that was so slight she almost missed it. "From the little I know of Hawkesbury, it would take a shifting of the earth for him to agree to something he didn't want to do. He lacks neither money nor power so it must be something else."

"A secret. A very grave one."

"Precisely." He gave a nod, as if impressed that she had grasped the situation. "It is my understanding that the secret Lord Enderby possesses could harm Hawke's loved ones if discovered."

"Who are his loved ones?"

"He has a sister and mother still living."

Alice huffed out a breath. "You have a difficult task."

"Learning the secret will not be easy, I grant you. But with your assistance, I believe we will prevail."

She shook her head. He hadn't quite understood her. "Discovering the secret is only one hurdle."

When she paused, he said, "Go on."

"The more difficult problem will be ensuring the secret is no longer a threat to Lord Hawkesbury. You must somehow silence Enderby without letting the secret out." From the grim set of

Lord Warhurst's mouth, she knew he was aware of that fact, as he was no doubt aware that Hawkesbury would have already tried purchasing Lord Enderby's silence with something other than a betrothal to his daughter.

"We'll cross that bridge when we discover what Enderby knows," he said.

Alice wasn't so sure ignoring it before they even began was a good idea, but she didn't say so. She was being paid to help discover the secret, not concern herself with events beyond that.

Lord Warhurst raised his hand to silence her. The *clip clop* of hooves on the cobblestones echoed around the inn-yard. The rider called for an ostler and their brief exchange was followed by the sound of the horse being led away. The door to the taproom opened and a lively tune strummed on a lute drifted out to the tiring house along with the trickle of laughter and voices.

"I must go," Lord Warhurst said. "We should not be seen together. Not here. There's a small inn called the Golden Lion near St. Mary le Bow. It's out of the way and not likely to be frequented by either Hawkesbury, Enderby or your players. Do you know it?"

"No but I'll find it."

"Good. Dine with me at midday there tomorrow." It was an order and Warhurst seemed used to giving them and having them obeyed.

She nodded because it wasn't in her interests to refuse him. "Until midday then, my lord."

He turned but paused at the curtain. "Thank you, Mistress Croft," he said without fully facing her. His profile was strong with the hard lines of his jaw and straight nose. Alice felt the odd little flutter in the pit of her stomach again and tried very hard not to stare. "I appreciate your assistance," he said. "I will ensure that your safety will not be jeopardized by anything I request of you."

"Your words are noble, Lord Warhurst, but I assure you I am capable of taking care of myself." She wasn't sure why she said it. Perhaps it was a need to assert herself with a man who thought her so far beneath him he was almost too embarrassed to speak to her.

He turned to her fully and his direct, unblinking gaze held hers. She swallowed. "Nevertheless, you are now working for me and I take my responsibility to those in my employ very seriously."

"I am not one of your servants," she tossed back.

His nostrils flared but he said nothing. He opened the curtain and walked away.

She let out a long breath and slowly began to remove the gorgeous costume, beginning with the lawn partlet he'd so deliberately and deliciously tucked into her bodice.

CHAPTER 2

*I*t was as if Leo had been walking about in his sleep for years and now he'd been shocked awake. Shocked by Alice Croft. An absurd observation but an accurate one, nevertheless. He dodged the traffic rumbling along busy Gracechurch Street then glanced back at the grand half-timbered inn on the corner. Its sign swung in the breeze and another weary traveler rode through the arch to the courtyard and theater stage beyond. A flash of crimson caught Leo's eye. He stilled. Watched. Waited for the vibrant color to reappear. But it did not. An ostler sauntered out to the street, looked right and left and spat into the gutter before ambling back into the yard again. No crimson about his grubby person. No crimson anywhere.

Leo snorted softly at his own foolish imaginings. He'd spent too much time around all those ridiculous theater props and costumes and now his mind was seeing things that weren't there. He shook his head but couldn't quite shake off the strange mood that had wrapped around him since meeting the seamstress.

There was something about her that scratched at his nerves, made them raw and sensitive. Something he couldn't put his finger on.

Perhaps it was simply the oddity of finding a quick wit within such a person. He knew many women with a mind as clever as a man's—he lived with two of them!—but they had been educated and came from the best stock. Alice Croft was a seamstress but even after their short meeting, he already knew there was something that set her apart from other women of her trade.

A shout drew him from his thoughts but not in time to side-step a thickset man falling out of an open tavern doorway. Leo caught him by his jerkin and righted him on unsteady feet. The man belched his thanks in Leo's face.

"Unhand him, he's mine," said another man, emerging from the same doorway. It appeared to lead to a tavern.

"With pleasure," said Leo, holding up his hands in surrender.

The newcomer was about his own age or younger with a soft face and hard eyes. He drew his sword. "Move aside, sir, this has nothing to do with you."

"True," Leo said. "But I don't think your opponent is in any state to fight back." He nudged the drunkard who swayed dangerously before Leo caught his arm and held him upright.

"Then he should capitulate. What say you, *Swine*?" The man pressed the point of his blade to the drunkard's throat. The oaf belched again.

"I'm not sure he's capable of saying the word capitulate at the moment," Leo said, keeping an eye on the blade. The gentle-man's fight may not be with him, but he was under no illusions that it could swing his way. London's streets were notorious for brawls. He wasn't inclined to become involved in one that didn't concern him. Not today.

However, he couldn't allow an incapacitated man to become victim to someone who seemed to have his full wits about him. It wouldn't be a fair fight by any stretch.

"What is your issue with this man?" Leo asked. "Perhaps it can be resolved without swords."

"Who do you think you are, a justice of the peace?"

"Not here."

The swordsman's sneer vanished. He gave Leo a more thor-ough once-over and couldn't have failed to notice that he dealt with a gentleman. "Ah, a meddler then." He lowered his sword from the drunkard's throat and pointed it at Leo's chest instead.

"Since your friend is not fit to fight, perhaps you wish to draw on his behalf?"

Leo gently shoved the drunkard and he stumbled back through the door into the tavern. Although Leo's hands were free, he didn't draw his rapier. "We are not friends, as you well know. I am simply passing by and do not wish to kill you or anyone else today."

"Kill *me*?" The man chuckled and pressed his sword against Leo's doublet. "Cock-sure as well as meddlesome, I see."

Leo could feel the point against his chest, but it didn't scratch and wouldn't have even cut the fabric. The application of even the merest pressure would quickly change that.

But he was certain he was faster than the other man. Years of sword fights with his half-brother, some playful, others not so, had ensured he was quick on his feet. Speed and a good measure of skill were imperative when faced with the pointy end of Blake's blade.

Leo shrugged and kept his gaze fixed on the other man's eyes for any tell-tale signs that he would do something foolish. Very foolish. There were at least a dozen on-lookers and it must be clear to them that Leo was not only a gentleman, but he was not going to draw. Attacking him would be a hanging offence, unless the man could evade them all and lose himself in the crowd.

The door to the tavern swung open again and another man of solid build stepped out. "There you are, Kit, what—." He spotted the drawn sword and gasped. "God's wounds, Marlowe, what are you doing! I thought you came out to claim what that drunkard owed you but when I saw him come back in, I thought you must have got yer money and went home."

The swordsman—Marlowe—humphed. His lips, quite feminine in their plumpness, curled into a most unfeminine sneer. "He still owes me, but this man chose to be his champion."

Leo sighed. He really didn't have time for this. "I suggest you go inside, find the man who owes you and get your money. If he doesn't have it, make him sign an I.O.U. in front of witnesses."

"He's right, Kit," the companion said with a deep frown. "This isn't worth it. You don't want to be sent back to Newgate again so soon. The jury might not put it down to self-defense this time."

So, the swordsman had a history of violence? It was probably only a matter of time before his temper got the better of him and he was either swinging from a Tyburn gibbet or lying dead in a ditch.

Marlowe lowered his sword. "Another day, perhaps."

Leo resisted the urge to roll his eyes at the melodramatic tone. "I doubt it. Good day to you." He waited until Marlowe and his friend had re-entered the tavern, then turned to go. The eerily silent crowd parted to let him through, and he went on his way. The scene that had just played out was nothing compared to what he was about to face at home.

As if she'd read his mind, Lady Warhurst was waiting for him when he arrived at his family's Dowgate Street house. He'd hardly shut the door when Greeves the steward met him with the words, "My lady requires your presence in her chambers."

Leo sighed. She must have another candidate.

"You summoned me, Mother?" he said on entering her private withdrawing room.

"Ah, there you are," she said without looking up from her writing desk. Autumn sunshine speared through the window, brightening the room which didn't need any more brightening. The emeralds set into his mother's rings clashed with the red and gold of the cushions scattered across every surface from chairs to daybed. The effect was dazzling.

She signed her name on a document, blotted the ink and folded the parchment. He waited, not very patiently, while she dripped red wax onto the letter and sealed it with her stamp. He knew from experience that his mother couldn't be hurried.

When she finished, she stood and handed him the document. It smelled faintly of the lavender water she liked to sprinkle on all her correspondence. "Take this to Lady Norwich at your earliest convenience."

He arched an eyebrow. "You want me to run an errand for you?" He huffed out a breath. Clearly his mother was in one of her strange moods, the sort that her children had long put down to eccentricity. "Why not send one of the servants?"

"Do stop scowling, Leo. You frown so much of late. Your face will set permanently if you're not careful and no girl wants to wed a cantankerous old man."

Perhaps he should have taken that Marlowe fellow up on his challenge. It would have been fun compared to this. "Thirty-four is hardly old."

"It is to a fifteen-year old." She waggled the letter at him—the letter to Lady Norwich, mother to a young girl who could very well be about fifteen.

Forget Marlowe, perhaps he should stab himself with his own blade now. "No," he said, stepping away from her and the letter as if it was poisonous. "Mother, she's a child."

"Have you seen any fifteen-year olds lately, Leo? I can assure you, Elizabeth is hardly a girl anymore. She's a woman in all the...obvious areas."

An image of another woman's obvious areas came to mind. He tried to shove aside the picture of Alice Croft spilling over the top of her ill-fitting gown but couldn't. There was certainly nothing of the girl in her. She was very much a woman.

"Nevertheless, she is unsuitable," he said. "Lady Norwich's daughter, I mean."

It was his mother's turn to frown. "Were we speaking of anyone else?"

He cleared his throat and took the letter. "I'll have someone send this to your friend." She began to protest and he held up his hand. Surprisingly, she stopped talking and simply sighed. "As to the Norwich girl..."

"Elizabeth."

"Yes, Elizabeth. As to her, she is too young, Mother. I require a wife nearer my own age. Someone with good sense, a sweet nature and a clear conscience." He paused, thinking of Alice Croft and the easy way in which her thoughts followed his. A mind like hers would be an asset in a marriage. He shook his head and almost managed to dislodge the image of her from his mind. "A quick wit would be welcome too."

"You're only allowed one wife," Lady Warhurst muttered.

He rolled his eyes ceiling-ward and huffed out a breath. Having a sensible conversation with his mother was like raking fingernails across skin lately. A little painful and very irritating. "Shall we add obedient to the list too?" he said, more to annoy her than anything else.

She gave him a tight smile. "I hear Whitby's bitch has just had a litter of pups," she said. "Perhaps one of those would suit."

He ignored the jibe. "And my wife must be strong enough to survive my family."

She linked her hands in front of her and rubbed a thumb across the largest of her emerald rings. It had been a wedding gift from his father, the second Baron Warhurst, before he'd squandered all the family fortune. She'd continued to wear the ring even after he died and she remarried. Her second husband, Leo's stepfather, had bought her the other rings to match it.

"You forgot the most important characteristic," she said.

"That she must come from impeccable stock? No Mother, I had not forgotten. It goes without saying."

"At least we agree on that. But Son..." She came out from behind her desk and took his arm, squeezing it in an uncharacteristically maternal gesture. "Do you think you could lower your expectations a little? I've already exhausted all the eligible young women of my acquaintance and you've not liked a single one. Why, pray, are you being so particular?"

It was a question he'd often asked himself. His mother had presented several suitable candidates, but after meeting each of them in turn, he'd not been able to go through with the contracts. None had measured up to his idea of a wife. They'd all been too silly or too dull or too shrewish. "Am I being particular?" he said. "Do you honestly think I would be happy with any of the women you've tried to marry me to?"

She sighed again and her entire body seemed to deflate. Suddenly the tall, proud woman appeared smaller, older, weaker. Three words he'd never thought he'd associate with his mother. "I'm sorry your father did not leave the Warhurst title and estate in good standing for you, Leo. But what is done is done and it is now up to you to fix it."

"By marrying well." He took his mother's hand and brought it to his lips. She rarely spoke of his father but when she did, a transformation always came over her. Usually she bristled with anger or frustration, but this weariness was new. He didn't like it. Didn't know how to deal with it. "Don't worry, Mother. I know what I must do and that is exactly why I must choose my wife carefully. I too want to see the title returned to good favor. I want my children to inherit one of England's jewels, not a decaying country residence clinging to poor land and a title with nothing, but scandal attached to it. I want them to be proud to bear the Warhurst name."

As he'd never been.

She patted his cheek. "Take the letter to Lady Norwich and see the girl for yourself. She may surprise you."

He doubted it. But if it would appease his mother then his life would be marginally easier, at least in the short term. "If you wish." He left her.

It wasn't until he reached Lilly's apartments that he began to wonder if he'd just been manipulated by the grand dame of manipulation.

With a rueful smile he knocked on his sister's door. She bade him enter. She reclined on her daybed at the far side of her withdrawing room, her feet tucked beneath the folds of her skirts. He was shocked by how colorless and small she looked amidst the mountain of pillows. She'd always been so bright herself, like a vibrant gem, the glory of the family with her glossy black hair and her dancing green eyes. Now her hair was dull and her eyes flat. There was no dancing in their depths.

"Ah, Leo." She held out her hands and he took them. They were cold and as fragile as icicles. "Where have you been?"

"Greeting friends, I've not seen since I was last in London."

"Reacquainting yourself with your old haunts, no doubt," she said with a hint of her famous smile.

"I have no haunts in London unless you count the archery butts in Finsbury Fields. And the palace of course." The palace, always the bloody palace. It was where he should be now, finding out what had changed since his last visit to the City. Who was the new favorite? Who should he avoid? Who had control over which duties? Whose back should he scratch until his fingers bled?

God, he hated court.

"I find that very hard to believe," she said. "I seem to recall you cut quite a swathe through the City's better inns for a time."

And some of the worst ones too but he saw no point in reminding his half-sister of the fact. The days where he would drink to excess were over. Youthful anger coupled with cheap wine had resulted in too many aches in the head. When he grew older and wiser, he'd realized an aching head wasn't going to get back what his father had lost.

He suddenly smiled. "I'd much rather be here talking to you, Lilly."

She eyed him suspiciously. "Why are you smiling at me like that?"

He shrugged. "I'm happy."

She made a sort of grunting sound, albeit a delicate one. "Where *have* you been this morning?"

He picked up a candied fig from a trencher that she'd not touched. "Looking for Lord Hawkesbury." He opened his mouth to pop the fig in, but she snatched if off him before he had the chance.

"Those are for me." She took a bite and glared at him defiantly.

"I see I've hit a raw nerve." He'd not meant to wound her. Indeed, how was he to know she cared enough for the cur that the mere mention of his name would turn her into an angrier version of their mother. To his half-brother's credit, Blake had warned him that Lilly loved the earl.

Foolish, blind girl. And she used to be so sensible too.

"Those are also mine," she said, dragging the trencher of sweetmeats onto her lap.

Until she said it, he hadn't been aware he'd been staring at them. His stomach growled. Lilly's smile was all childish petulance.

"Good," he said. "You should eat them. You're fading away." He pulled a chair closer to her and sat down. "I don't like seeing you this way."

"You mean carrying a bastard child?"

He winced. "I mean ill. Like a shadow. You sit here in your rooms day after day." He indicated the books piled up beside her needlepoint. "All you do is read or embroider. You never go anywhere anymore."

"That's because I don't wish to vomit in front of our friends."

He rubbed a hand across his face. It seemed she wanted to make the conversation difficult. Very well. He would bite. "I hate what Hawkesbury's done to you."

"You and Robert are obviously cut from the same cloth," she muttered. "I seem to recall him also forgetting that I had something to do with my condition."

He sighed. "Lilly—."

"No! No, Leo!" She returned the trencher to the table, stood and went to the oriel window. She stared down at the central courtyard below, crossing her arms over her waist as if holding onto her unborn babe. "Leave Lord Hawkesbury alone." She sounded as faint as her complexion. "He will not marry me, no matter how hard you try to force his hand. He's going to be wed to Patience Enderby who is also carrying his child. He made his choice."

"Blake says Hawkesbury assured him the girl's babe is not his. You don't believe him?"

She lifted one shoulder. "I don't know. But what I do know is that it is better for everyone that you accept Hawkesbury's decision. It's better for all of us if you get on with your own business."

"My own business!" Hot, sharp rage spiked through him. He picked up the chair he'd been sitting on but had enough composure to put it down again without throwing it into the fireplace. "My business is to create the best future for my family. A secure, happy future where they are admired and respected. Your...state is an impediment." He regretted it as soon as he said it, but he couldn't take the words back. That would only lessen their impact. Lilly needed to understand that her actions had a far-reaching impact.

"You speak of a family you don't yet have, Leo." He had to step closer to hear her, but then he was sorry he did. The sorrow in her words stripped him to the bone. "But what of your current family? What of your brother and sister? Do we not matter in this future of yours?"

He stood utterly still and stared at her back. Sunlight picked out the deep green hues of her gown, the luster of the pearls in her earrings, the pureness of the white ruff at her throat. It warmed his skin and melted his anger. "Of course you matter." He touched her arm, tentatively, and felt her shudder beneath his fingers. She didn't pull away. "Forgive me?"

She hesitated then turned into him and buried her face in his chest. If she cried, she didn't make a sound. He held her and considered ramming Hawkesbury through with his blade or letting her have her way. Since neither was a viable option, he tried to steer her away from her woes by mentioning their brother's luck.

"It seems Blake will be the only one of us to find happiness this year."

"He doesn't have to be." She looked up at him with her huge green eyes. "Why can't you be more like Robert?"

"You wish me to become a pirate?" He knew it wasn't what she was suggesting but he wanted to return to their familiar, and safe, bantering.

"I mean find a sweet girl and fall madly in love with her."

"Ha! You wish me to take leave of my duty and my senses?" Blake should have sorted out the whole bloody mess between Lilly and Hawkesbury in the days after his return to London but instead he'd fallen in love and dumped the burden onto Leo. If that's what love did to a man, then he wanted none of it.

"I am aware that Min is not the sort of girl you can marry, Leo. Her family is hardly reputable but that was not important in Robert's case. What I am referring to is their happiness, their suitability and their deep affection. Min has transformed him."

"And you want a woman to transform me?"

She sighed. "I simply want you to be happy. We all do. You're such a tyrant lately."

"And you think falling in love will make me less of a tyrant? Make me happy?" He scoffed. "I am hardly a poetry-reading, soft-headed youth."

"Neither is Robert and yet Min makes him happy." She smiled wanly and wiped his doublet where her face had been moments ago. "Spend more time with him and you'll see."

"Now that we are both in the one place together, spending more time with him will be inevitable. But if he spouts poetry at me, I shall be forced to shut his mouth with my fist."

"I'd like to see you try," said a familiar voice behind him.

"Robert!" Lilly let go of Leo and ran to her other, full-blooded, brother.

Blake caught her face between his hands and frowned. "You've been crying." He turned on Leo. "What have you said to her?"

"Nothing you shouldn't have already said before my arrival in London."

Blake's eyes narrowed. He looked like he wanted to knock Leo's head off his shoulders.

Lilly placed a hand on her brother's arm. "Robert," she warned. "Not here. My maid has just changed the rushes."

Blake seemed to relax, just a little, and Leo almost smiled at his sister's technique for diffusing potentially explosive situations.

"My study," he said to Blake. "Now. We have business to discuss."

Lilly rolled her eyes. "Very well, go and talk about me behind my back. Everyone else will be soon enough," she added, patting her still flat belly.

"Oh, Lil," Blake said, kissing the top of her head.

"No they won't," Leo said, brushing past them both. "They'll be praising you on your fortunate marriage. Come, Blake."

"Yes, my lord," he mocked, "as you wish."

Leo waited for Blake to take his leave of Lilly then together they strode to Leo's study in silence. When they reached the sparsely furnished room on the south side of the house, Leo indicated his brother should sit. Blake remained standing.

"I spoke to Alice Croft this morning," Leo said, sitting at his desk. If his brother wanted to stand, so be it.

Blake's face lightened a little at the mention of her name. "How is she? Still giving her father headaches?"

"I wouldn't know." Leo pulled out a sheet of parchment. "But I'm sure she is. A woman like her..." He trailed off, aware his brother was watching him with a sardonic smile.

"Yes?" Blake prompted.

"She is entirely too clever for a woman."

Blake tipped his head back and laughed so hard his shoulders shook. "I'm not sure there is such a thing as a woman being too clever, but that's where you and I differ. I like a woman with wit."

"It's not the only thing we disagree on. Will you bloody sit down! My neck is aching having to look up at you."

Blake sat, still smiling. "Did Alice agree to spy on Hawkesbury for you?"

Leo nodded. "For a price." He told his brother about the arrangement he'd forged with Mistress Croft including Blake's own role to play with London's merchants and his betrothed's wedding dress.

Blake listened and agreed. "She's thought of everything. It'll be a good arrangement for her and I've no doubt she'll make a success of any venture she takes on. But you're a fool, Leo."

"For agreeing to her terms?" He'd been wondering the same thing. What if the seamstress decided it wasn't enough and demanded more from him to keep her silence?

"For spying on Hawkesbury at all. Our sister doesn't want the union."

"So she says," Leo said. "But you know as well as I do that she's lying. Despite everything, she still loves the cold-blooded cur. Would you deny her that love?"

Blake snorted softly. "You speak of love as if you know what it is. But I can assure you that you do not. Not yet." He leaned forward and regarded Leo with sympathy. Sympathy!

Ha! Blake was the poor fool who'd fallen victim to soft-headed tendencies, not the other way around.

"Our sister does love Hawkesbury," Blake went on, "but that is precisely why she cannot marry him. Not unless he wants the union too. Wholeheartedly."

Leo shook his head. His brother was talking nonsense again. Falling in love had a lot to answer for. "She needs to marry him, or she will be ruined."

"As will your chances of returning to the fold at court if she does not?" Blake scoffed. "This isn't about you, Leo."

Leo shot to his feet, rounded the desk and grabbed Blake by the front of his doublet. He would have hauled Blake to his feet, but his half-brother rose of his own accord, his arms outstretched in surrender. Damn him. Leo could do with a good fight. At least if he fought Blake there'd be no repercussions afterwards. Well, not as many as if he fought a stranger in the street.

"I am well aware of that," Leo said, shoving Blake away. "How can I not be in this family?"

"Leo—."

"Are you going to help me or not?"

"I've already said I will."

Leo returned to the desk and retrieved the quill from the inkstand. He handed it to Blake. "Write a letter of introduction for Mistress Croft to one of your cloth merchant contacts. Then go and tell Minerva that the seamstress will be making her a gown for her wedding feast. Don't mention anything about our arrangement."

Blake took the pen and dipped it in the ink. "I will mention everything to Min whether you like it or not." Leo began to protest so Blake stopped writing. "We have no secrets between us."

"How sweet." Sickeningly so.

"Min can be trusted."

If Blake believed it then it was probably true. He was a good judge of character no matter what other faults he possessed. "Just write the letter."

Blake signed his name and replaced the pen in the inkstand. "Now, as to the rent for Alice's shop."

"What of it?"

"How will you pay for it?"

Leo didn't detect any note of sarcasm in his half-brother's tone but still, the question grated. "I will find a way."

"You have no money."

"I have land in an area known for its coal."

"But you have no mine, and no capital to start one or even investigate the viability of one."

"I'll find the capital," Leo said. "Someone at court will be willing to sink their funds into a partnership if it might make them even richer."

"Do you truly think so?" Blake folded the parchment and reached for a stick of sealing wax. "A partnership with the son of the last Baron Warhurst who infamously fleeced half the court in exactly the same way that you plan on making money?"

It was true. Leo's father had petitioned several noblemen—Hawkesbury's blackmailer, Lord Enderby, among them—for money to invest in a mine on his land. He never dug a single hole, however, and instead spent the money on his mistress. That was over thirty years ago, just before he died. Leo had been only a babe at the time but those who'd lost heavily to his father never let him forget it after he came into his majority.

"I paid back their debts as soon as I could," he said.

"And bankrupted the Warhurst estate in the process." Blake pressed the seal on his signet ring into the wax then returned it to his finger. "Hardly a good business brain you have there, Brother. I'm not sure anyone would be flinging their money into a mine on land which may or many not yield anything let alone coal."

"Do you have a point or do you simply like reminding me of the stain attached to my name?" Not that Leo needed reminding. He was all too aware of the tarnished blood that ran through his veins.

Blake leaned heavily on the desk and lowered his head. "I'm sorry." He straightened and turned. "I shouldn't have said that. I wish I could help you but—."

"Don't say it."

"I have enough—."

"Don't be a fool, Blake! You'll soon have a wife and father-in-law to care for, as well as Mother and Lilly. When her baby and your own babes come into the world, even your copious funds will be strained." Leo held out his hand. "The letter, if you don't mind."

Blake handed it to him but didn't let go so that they performed a kind of childish tug of war. "Let me pay the rent on Alice's shop at least."

"No. I'll sell Father's sword if I have to."

Blake gasped. "But it's a beautiful piece of workmanship! The queen herself gave it to him."

"Too beautiful to be of any use to me. I prefer a blade to be functional, not covered in pearls and fancy engravings."

Blake finally let go of the letter. "Very well. I can't stop you selling the only thing of worth he ever gave you."

For some reason, Leo found that funny. "You don't think the Warhurst estate and title are worthy?"

Blake gave him a crooked grin. "Apart from those." He sobered. "Are you sure I can't give you the money?"

"No. Lilly's burden is ours to share. I'll not let you pay for everything."

"I have enough—."

"Christ, let *me* do something for her at least."

Blake shrugged. "Very well. But your pride will be your downfall, Leo, if you're not careful."

"Full of pithy wisdom today, aren't we?"

Blake held up his hands and strode towards the door, Leo following close behind. "Let me know how you and Alice get on," Blake said. "And be nice to her. She has a good soul. She deserves to be treated with respect."

Leo opened the door for his half-brother. "I'll give her all the respect she's due."

Blake left, scowling and shaking his head. Leo was relieved to shut the door on his back.

CHAPTER 3

*A*lice's father didn't need any convincing to allow his daughter to accompany the troupe to Hawkesbury Hall for their evening performance. Afflicted with a sore throat, dripping nose and a fretting wife, he was ordered to remain abed. Since Roger Style, the company's manager, would not risk any last-minute costume faults destroying his opportunity to shine, he readily agreed to have Alice join them instead.

The sun sat low over London's pitched rooftops as the troupe's cart rumbled through Ludgate's arch and over the Fleet River bridge. Edward Style, sitting with his back against one of the chests filled with Roman togas, sang a soft ballad and soon the other actors, Henry Wells and Will Shakespeare, joined in. Freddie Putney accompanied them with a series of tuneless snores from the corner. Alice, who had no singing voice, tapped her finger on her knee and smiled at them. She would miss their cheerful companionship when she moved on.

Although if she was being honest, these contented moments were rare. Perhaps their good humor had something to do with the prospect of expanding their audience numbers with the imminent move to The Rose theater. Or more likely it had something to do with Roger Style sitting up the front with the driver out of the way. His scowling presence rarely inflicted a happy mood over the group.

For her part, Alice's smile was due entirely to the agreement she'd struck with Lord Warhurst. Her future was suddenly looking interesting. Oh to be the mistress of her own shop! To be commander of her own fortune! To meet people of the most esteemed sort, people like Lord Warhurst and his family. Her smile grew.

Lord Warhurst. A most intriguing man with his solid, unyielding countenance, his conservative appearance and a wicked streak as wide as the Thames. The way he'd tucked the cloth down her bodice was proof of that. Yet he hid that wickedness and hid it well. He'd been rude and condescending and arrogant, but he'd cast aside his prejudices long enough to ask her for her help. He must have very strong reasons to do so—somehow, she didn't think his sister's reputation was all that was at stake—and Alice wanted to know what those reasons were.

The cart halted at the stables in the extensive grounds of Hawkesbury Hall and she hopped down onto the gravel. The enormous house stretched before her. Built in brick in the shape of an E to honor the sovereign it was a grand testimony to the wealth and position of its owner. The last rays of sunshine flooded the many glass windows of the three storey mansion in shimmering light and bathed the stone birds perched on the gables in golden splendor. Crenellated turrets reached into the sky and the two wings of the house embraced the terraced garden like a lover's arms. It was a house fit for a princess.

Alice breathed deeply as if she could capture the moment, the feeling, of being that princess. "Magnificent."

"Isn't it."

She spun around. "Lord Warhurst!" She knew it was him even though he wore a black cloak with the hood pulled low over his face. His clear, deep voice hummed across her skin the way it had done on their first meeting, and there was no mistaking the broad chest and shoulders. The hood wasn't low enough to shield his lips either. She hadn't noticed how curved they were, like a bow, but now she couldn't stop staring at them.

"What are you doing here?" she whispered. She glanced around but no one seemed to be taking any notice of them. Roger Style directed the players and servants in unloading the cart and soon everyone, including the belligerent Freddie, was busy carrying chests and props up to the house.

"I wanted to warn you to be careful," Lord Warhurst said.

"Perhaps I should give you the same warning," she said. "It is unwise for you to be seen here, my lord."

"I'm perfectly safe. The servants assume I'm part of the troupe and the troupe assume I'm a servant." He watched a groom unhitch the horses from the cart and lead them into the stables. "Be careful, Mistress Croft."

"You already said that."

His lips flattened. "If you feel you are in any danger of discovery, then forget our plan. I'll find another way."

"Trying to get out of our agreement already, my lord?"

"I don't want any misfortune to befall you. I already have enough on my conscience."

"Thank you," she said wryly, "that was almost kind." His gentlemanly sense of honor had come a little too late. If he'd been at all concerned for her safety, he shouldn't have asked her in the first place. "Blake put you up to this, did he?"

He crossed his arms and regarded her. Or at least she assumed he did—it was difficult to tell beneath the hood. "I came here of my own will, if you must know. I wanted to assure you I would be nearby if you got into trouble."

"Oh. Well. Thank you. That is reassuring." She nodded in the direction from which they'd come. "But what about the gates? We've been given special dispensation to return after they close but how will you get back into the City tonight?"

One side of his mouth twitched into something close to a smile. "Never mind that." There it was again, that mischievous quality which she'd detected lurking beneath the surface on their first meeting. It only served to enhance the mystery of the gentleman. And heighten her interest.

"'Lo! alice!" Roger Style bellowed from the path leading up to the house. "Stop lazing about and come do your job. Freddie's hem has come down."

"Coming!" she called back. To Lord Warhurst she said, "I must go. Be careful."

Again the twitch of lips. "I think that's my line."

She nodded a farewell and joined Roger who stood waiting for her, his foot tapping on the gravel. "You are here to work," he said through gritted teeth, "not flirt with every servant who puts himself before you." He strode ahead, muttering about men being more reliable than women. "That's why we don't have girl actors," she heard him say before he disappeared through the servants' door.

Alice poked her tongue at his back then glanced towards the stables before entering the house. The hooded figure in black was gone.

* * *

ALICE WAS QUITE sure the play would be a success without her presence. Shortly after the second act started, she told Style she'd left a spool of thread in the cart. Whether he heard her or not she couldn't say, but his nod was sufficient enough to dismiss her.

Instead of heading outside, she crept through the shadowy mansion, hugging the walls and holding her breath. She soon realized caution wasn't necessary. No one was about. The master of the house, his family and guests were all safely watching the performance of *Marius and Livia* in the great hall. The servants had retreated to the kitchen at the back to enjoy their supper while their betters were occupied. Alice was free to go where she liked.

She walked quickly through a prettily furnished parlor and another sitting area to a staircase. Grabbing a lit candle from the nearby table, she ascended to the first floor and located Hawkesbury's study. It was a more masculine room than any she'd come across in the house. Dark wood paneling surrounded the walls, a solid desk and chair faced the window and three ornately carved coffers squatted on the rush-covered floor. Two slender candlesticks stood sentinel on either end of the massive oak mantelpiece and there wasn't a tapestry or worked Turkey carpet to be seen.

Alice rifled through the books and papers scattered across his desk but found nothing useful. She didn't know what she hoped to find but she was certain she'd recognize it if it presented itself.

Nothing did. Not on his desk or in the unlocked drawers or coffer. Unfortunately she found no key to open the two locked ones.

She was preparing to leave when the sound of light footsteps running up the stairs made the hairs on the back of her neck rise. She sank behind the desk, shielding the candle's flame with her body. The scent of cloves from the rushes mixed with the stink of tallow from her candle, and the overpowering blend clung to the back of her throat. She gagged and the sound seemed louder than a thunderclap in the thick silence.

The footsteps stopped right outside the study door. Alice stilled. Her breath caught. For one agonizing moment she thought she was discovered, that the steward or Hawkesbury himself would flay her for trespassing. Or worse, tell Style.

But the footsteps started again and grew fainter until they finally disappeared altogether. She blew out a measured breath in an effort to calm her furiously beating heart then emerged from her hiding spot. At the door, she glanced left in the direction of the footsteps. Silence. The other person was gone.

She ventured towards the stairs and considered her next move. There was no time to search the house when she didn't even know what she was looking for. She could question the servants. Perhaps they'd heard rumors connected to their master's marriage. But why would they divulge them to a stranger? The more she thought about it, the more hopeless her situation felt. How could she, a seamstress attached to a company of players, learn the secret behind Lord Hawkesbury's marriage to Patience Enderby? If the gentleman himself didn't want the secret discovered then surely he would have buried anything that might jeopardize the union. To think that she could find out anything of use to Lord Warhurst was a joke.

As if to emphasize the point, the audience's laughter trickled up to her, followed by the jaunty sounds of the fiddle. It was the final jig. The play was about to end and she would soon be missed.

Beneath the audience's applause she heard another sound, coming from a closed door nearby. The stomach-churning heave of someone retching. The person who'd run up the stairs moments before had headed in that direction. The retching stopped, replaced by sobbing.

Before she could think too much about what she was doing, Alice pushed open the door. In the middle of the bedchamber knelt a woman, her blue skirts spread about her like a pond, one hand flattening her ruff to her chest, the other gripping a chamber pot in her lap.

She looked up at Alice's approach and gasped. "Who are you?"

"Alice Croft. I'm with the players. You're Mistress Enderby aren't you, Baron Enderby's daughter?" She'd seen her in the audience at The White Swan once. The woman, younger than Alice by a few years, had been sitting in the gallery with Lord Hawkesbury that day but had barely acknowledged him. Hawkesbury had seemed unperturbed by his betrothed's lack of interest. From that moment on, Alice had been sure there was no affection between them.

Patience wiped her mouth with the back of her hand and rose. She placed the chamber pot in a livery cupboard and closed the door. "What are you doing up here?" she demanded, turning around. "This is a private room." Although she'd been vomiting only moments earlier, she was now composed, albeit a little pale. Even in the poor light Alice could see that.

Alice could think of no good reason to explain her presence so she said nothing. She glanced around the chamber. It was sparsely furnished with only a bed, the cupboard and a stool near the hearth. The fireplace was swept clean and there were no rushes covering the floor. The bedchamber was perhaps a guest room but was not being used at the time.

So why was Patience Enderby there? To throw up in the chamber pot in the cupboard? Had it been set there specifically for her use? By her betrothed?

Too many questions and from the brisk way the girl swept past her, she wouldn't get any answers. Not easily anyway.

"Can I find your mother for you?" Alice asked. "Or direct Lord Hawkesbury to send for his physician?" Patience shook her head. "But if you're ill—."

"I'm not ill." She pressed a gold filigree pomander hanging

from the end of her pearl studded girdle to her nose and breathed deeply.

Alice indicated the closed livery cupboard door. "I'm neither deaf nor blind."

"I'm *not* ill." Patience picked up the candelabra with its trio of candles from the mantelpiece where she must have placed them on her entry. The light cast deep shadows over her features—features which had been soft and flushed with the vigor of youth when Alice had seen her in the White Swan's audience, but now seemed wan and pinched. Patience was ill and had been for a few days at least.

Alice must have looked shocked because the girl tensed then lowered her head, but not before Alice saw tears filling her eyes. Patience dropped the pomander and pressed a hand against the point where skirt met bodice at her stomach.

The small gesture said a lot. She was with child. Lord Hawkesbury had got both Lilly Blakewell *and* Patience Enderby pregnant.

"That flea-bitten swine." Alice hadn't been aware she'd spoken aloud until Patience glanced up, blinking back her tears.

"Who?" she said.

"Hawkesbury." She nodded at Patience's flat middle. "It all makes sense now."

"What does?" But then Patience shook her head and clicked her tongue in irritation. "You theater people are all the same. So dramatic."

"I'm a seamstress."

Patience made for the door. "Whoever you are, you shouldn't be up here."

"Wait!" Alice wasn't prepared to see her potential source of information leave. There was too much at stake to let her simply walk away. She caught Patience by the elbow and stopped her. "Is that why Lord Hawkesbury is marrying you? Because you carry his child?"

Patience looked horrified. She snatched her arm away. "What do you know of this? Get away from me."

"No, don't go. Please." Alice had only one chance to find some answers, any answers. She couldn't afford to destroy this opportunity. She thought fast. If Patience didn't love Hawkesbury and he didn't love her...then perhaps the child wasn't his at all. And perhaps she was in love with the father of the unborn babe.

"On behalf of the woman who does love Lord Hawkesbury," Alice said, seeing an opening and heading directly for it, "I need to know why he's marrying you and not her."

Patience stared at Alice. Slowly, slowly, her jaw went slack and her mouth fell open. "He loves someone else." She didn't say it with any hint of anger, or even surprise. She probably already knew. Her eyes filled with tears again. "Tell her...tell her I'm so sorry...but I can't... My father..." She bent her head and the tears flowed freely.

Alice put an arm around her shoulders and held her close. She let the girl cry then drew her away when her tears subsided. "But why is he marrying you if your child is not even his?"

The girl's face crumpled but she didn't start crying again. "I don't know. I truly don't. I never asked." She bit her lower lip and shook her head. "My father must be forcing him somehow. He made me accept Lord Hawkesbury's proposal..." She broke off with a sob.

"But your babe's father?" Alice prompted. "Why couldn't you marry him instead?"

Patience dashed away her tears with the back of her thumb. "He was the land steward on our country estate and when Father learned who I'd been with..." She pressed her hand to her stomach again and drew in a steadying breath. "He removed Richard from his position and forced him to work as a simple farm hand. But he shouldn't be! He's too good for that." Her voice became a shrill wail, but still she didn't cry. "Richard is educated and clever and I thought Father could sponsor him for Cambridge or Oxford and he could become a lawyer. But Father refused."

Alice shushed her lest someone hear. "Tell me his name and where he's working and I'll get a message to him if you like."

Patience's face lit up. Hope sparkled in her eyes where before they'd been empty and flat. "Will you? For me? But...why?"

"I told you. I want to help the woman who loves Hawkesbury. That means finding out why he's been forced to marry you." She wasn't sure why she told Patience but she sensed she could trust the girl. Or it could be that she had little other choice. "I won't lie to you. Our plan is for him to break his engagement to you and marry her."

The girl nodded and gave Alice a watery smile. "I understand. Without Lord Hawkesbury's betrothal, my father will be forced to marry me to another before I begin increasing. I can only hope he'll choose Richard out of desperation if nothing else." She squeezed Alice's hand but broke off at the sound of her name being called by someone downstairs.

"My mother," Patience said. "I must go." She gave Alice another smile. "His name is Richard Farley and he's working on my father's estate at Crouch End. When you see him, tell him...tell him to not give up hope."

Alice nodded. "Now go. I'll follow in a few moments."

Patience left and Alice counted slowly to a hundred before descending the stairs. She returned the candle to the table at the base of the staircase then peered into the great hall. The performance was nearing its end.

"Off exploring?"

Alice jumped. "Good lord, Will," she said on seeing Shakespeare still dressed in his Roman costume at her shoulder. "You shouldn't creep about like that. You scared me."

"I wasn't the one creeping about," he said with a gleam in his dark brown eyes. "So what were you and the young lady doing upstairs all this time?"

"Mistress Enderby? Was she upstairs too?"

He chuckled. "She came down before you looking somewhat pleased. She certainly hadn't gone upstairs with the same demeanor. More like she was about to lose her supper. Don't worry," he added with that familiar twinkle, "I don't think anyone else saw you. In fact, I doubt anyone even noticed you were gone except me."

Hardly a flattering thing to say to a woman. However since her anonymity was precisely why Lord Warhurst had asked for her help, she shouldn't be so surprised by the fact. Still, it hurt.

"You really are entirely too observant, Will," she said. "Especially for an actor. In my experience they're usually more self-absorbed."

"And seamstresses don't usually go wandering about mansions. I don't think either of us can be defined by our current professions, do you?"

Alice liked the player. She really did. She just wished he wasn't so clever. His mind was as sharp as a blade. He would be able to detect a lie as easily as a hound scented game. So she'd best tell him the truth. Or some of it. "I was just seeing what a big house looks like from the inside." That was partly true. She'd never been inside a house with so many rooms before and certainly not one with the amount of servants Hawkesbury retained. Now that the performance was over and light refreshments were being served to the guests and players alike, the house was crawling with them.

"Find anything?" Shakespeare asked, adjusting his toga over his shoulder.

"Just a lot of dusty rooms. He doesn't even use half of them!"

He laughed. Henry Wells came up to them and handed Alice a cup. "Wine for the happy wanderer," he said with a wink.

Alice blushed and took the cup. It seemed people took more notice of her than she thought.

She spent the next hour packing the costumes and props into the traveling chests and helping the troupe carry them back to the cart. She searched the shadows for Lord Warhurst but he was nowhere to be seen. Perhaps he'd already left, but she didn't think so. He was out there somewhere, watching her, waiting to help if she needed it. She was certain she could feel his enigmatic presence in the darkness.

She shivered, but not from the cold, and smiled into the murky depths of the stable building. "Until tomorrow," she murmured.

CHAPTER 4

$\mathcal{E}$ ven though the Golden Lion was filled with diners whose mouths were occupied by slices of meat or pie, it was still a noisy place. It also stank. The smells of ale and sweat weren't quite erased by the aroma of roasting pork coming from the kitchen. Alice had been to other inns before of course, but the Golden Lion seemed rougher than those. The mostly male diners appeared to be merchants and apprentices, but not of the respectable sort. Clothing was simple and grubby, faces pinched and grim. A few heads swung Alice's way when she entered, appraised her openly, then raised their tankards in salute.

"Lookin' for someone in partic'lar, wench?" one of them asked. IIe patted the empty stool beside him and grinned. A chunk of meat hung from between his crooked teeth. "I can be that someone."

"I'm sure you could," she said oh-so-sweetly. "But my lover is the jealous sort and he'd beat you if he saw us together."

The man curled his top lip in a snarl. "Lucky for you, you ain't worth my trouble," he said, turning back to his food.

A hand curled around her arm. It was attached to the very solid frame of Lord Warhurst. Without speaking a word, he pulled her through the crowd to a booth in the far corner of the room. He gently pushed her onto a bench seat and slid into the one opposite.

"You're right," he said, signaling to the serving woman.

"About what?" Alice said.

"I am a jealous man."

"But—." *We're not lovers.* "I'll keep that in mind."

The look he gave her was guarded but a seething power emanating from him punched her square in the gut. It hurt to breathe. He didn't take his eyes off her despite the serving woman's approach, and for an uncomfortable moment Alice thought he would tell her he wouldn't become her lover for the queen's entire fortune.

"I'll have whatever stew you've got today," he said to the serving wench, "and ale. Mistress Croft?"

"I'm not eating," she said, forcing herself to look away and breathe normally.

"She'll have the same," he said and the servant nodded and left. "You need to eat," he said to Alice. "You're too thin."

She cocked her head to the side. "I wasn't going to eat because I'm expected back at my father's table. As to being too thin, you didn't think so yesterday. Not certain parts of me at least."

To his credit he didn't dip his gaze to those parts, safely covered by her gown and cloak. He kept his narrowed green eyes on hers until she was squirming in her seat.

"My apologies," he said stiffly. "I shouldn't have assumed you were lacking good food. I'm sure your father provides for you adequately."

What an odd thing to say. "Of course he does. And for my mother and my two sisters. We're neither destitute nor street rats, my lord, no matter what you think."

"I don't think—." He cut off his own words by pressing his lips together. "I apologize. Again. Now can we get to the business at hand?"

Gladly. The sooner she was out of his presence the better. He was playing havoc with her judgment. She didn't know what to make of him. He was insufferable one moment and disconcerting the next. And utterly compelling. Those eyes made her feel unbalanced when he regarded her so intensely.

"Patience Enderby is with child," she said, getting to the point straight away.

"I know."

She blinked at him. "You *knew*. How?"

"Blake learned that much from Hawkesbury himself. The Enderby girl's child isn't his apparently."

She placed her palms flat on the table and leaned towards him, not near enough to be sucked in by those emerald orbs but close enough to make her irritation obvious. "You knew and you didn't tell me!"

His steady gaze faltered. "I didn't think it was important."

"Not important! Not *important!*" She blew out a measured breath. "How am I supposed to help you if I don't know everything? If I'd known she was with child before I began, I could have asked her directly for the father's name instead of waiting for her to tell me."

"You spoke to Patience Enderby?" It was his turn to lean forward. He closed the gap between them considerably. Alice should move away, back to where it was safer. She didn't. "I admit I'm impressed by your endeavors," he said. "Perhaps you should become an interrogator for the Privy Council."

"I befriended her. It wasn't difficult. I think she's in need of a friend at the moment."

"What else did you learn?"

"That the father of her unborn babe is working at Enderby's Crouch End farm. I told her I would give him a message."

He said nothing and seemed to be waiting for her to continue. When she didn't, he said, "Is that it? Did you question the other players? The servants?"

"The players knew nothing of interest to our investigation and the servants were all too busy to stop for a little chat. I'm sure they'd be too loyal to tell me anything anyway. Worse, they'd probably warn Lord Hawkesbury I'd been asking questions. It wouldn't take long for him to connect me to you, or to your family at least."

Leo had to admit she was right. Again. She was also right in that he should have told her about Patience's state—yet she'd still learned that piece of information on her own. Confirmation that Alice Croft was an astute woman and a valuable asset. One he planned on using more.

"So the name and place of work for this lover," he said, "is the only solid thing we've learned."

"Yes." She sounded defensive.

"Then we'd best go speak to him."

"We?"

He smiled. "Have you got something better to do this afternoon?"

"There's no performance for a few days. We're moving to The Rose soon so there's much packing to be done." She chewed her lip and he had the ridiculous urge to lean over and press a thumb to it to stop her. It was far too delectable a morsel to be mauled like that.

Fortunately for her lip their food arrived. He pulled out some coins to pay the serving woman for both meals.

"No," Alice said, digging into the folds of her skirts and producing a leather pouch. "I'll pay for mine."

"Allow me."

"No." She handed a ha'penny to the serving girl. "Our arrangement is clear and simple and doesn't cover meals. Let's keep it that way."

"As you wish," he said, paying for his stew. "But I want to assure you I can afford it."

She laughed, a surprisingly husky sound that seemed to come from deep within her. It lit up her face and made her shoulders shake. He couldn't help smiling along with her. He liked her laugh.

"I am aware of that," she said, still chuckling as she picked up her spoon.

His smile froze. So she thought he was wealthy. It was perhaps a logical conclusion from her point of view. He was a baron with an estate and his family had a lot of money—money that belonged to them, not him. His stepfather's fortune had gone to his heir, Blake, who'd set up a generous annuity for their mother and a sizeable dowry for Lilly. He'd offered the same arrangement to Leo on more than one occasion, but Leo always rejected it. He didn't want to be in anyone's debt, especially

Blake's. His own father—a man he barely remembered—had taught him that harsh lesson. The late baron had borrowed funds from several noblemen. When he failed to invest it in the search for coal on his land as promised, they'd torn him apart. He became more than an outcast—he was a hunted man. It was that hunt that had caused his heart to give out, leaving all that debt and guilt in his infant son's lap.

Leo felt the weight of that burden in everything he did.

He became an even poorer man after paying off all the debts once he came into his majority, but he was damned if he was going to let a seamstress find out exactly how poor.

They ate their meals in silence. Someone struck up a tune on the virginals and the noise level in the inn rose as everyone spoke louder to hear each other over the music. Leo was glad to get out of there when they finished eating. In hindsight the Golden Lion had been a poor choice of inn to take a woman to with its mostly male patrons, and miserable ones at that. But when he'd suggested it, he'd not been able to think of any other places away from people they might know. Alice didn't seem to mind. In fact, she treated the occasional leers in her direction with disinterest. Either she didn't notice them or she believed the men were beneath her.

They were.

The thought trickled through his mind, unbidden and unwanted and he shoved it away. What she *believed* and what was fact were two entirely different things.

He watched her walking in front of him out of the inn and into the courtyard. Her woolen skirt swayed with the gentle roll of her hips. A breeze blew her pale hair against the nape of her neck and she absently flicked it away with slender fingers. She held her back straight, her shoulders square and took long strides. The overall effect was one of confidence and...grace. Yes, that was it. Grace.

She stopped to speak to one of the inn's lads leaning on a broom near the stable doors. Leo arrived in time see her press a coin into the boy's palm and to hear her give directions.

"To my house," she said for Leo's benefit as the boy ran off. "The lad has instructions to say he's come from the White Swan, not here. I told him to tell my father that I've decided to dine with the troupe and plan on remaining there all day. He'll assume I'm helping them pack."

"And the players? Won't your manager wonder where you are?"

"Style? Probably not. They're moving everything to The Rose today. I've packed the props and costumes so it's just a matter of transporting the trunks across the river. He'll probably think I decided to stay and help my mother at home. Father can be a bear when he's unwell."

"Good. I don't want you to get into trouble." He paused. "Did anyone notice your disappearance at Hawkesbury Hall last night?"

"Not really," she said, turning towards the stables. "Do they hire out horses here?"

"Yes." He signaled to a nearby ostler and ordered him to saddle two horses. "How well do you ride, Mistress Croft?"

"Poorly," she said with a shrug. "But I'll manage."

"Perhaps you should stay behind after all," he said. "I don't want to be caught traveling in the dark. The roads in and out of London aren't safe."

"Meaning I'll just hold you up." She crossed her arms beneath her breasts and he was reminded of their first meeting. Although she had less flesh on display today, the effect was still distracting. "I've already sent the lad," she said. "It's too late to change your mind now."

"No it's not."

"I will *not* be left behind." She all but stamped her foot.

He sighed. He knew a determined woman when he saw one. Arguing with her would be a waste of breath. Besides, some company would break up the monotony of the journey. *Her* company. "A gentle hack for my companion," he instructed the ostler. "One that follows instructions would make a nice change."

* * *

THEY RODE out of the City through the great archway of Aldersgate and soon left the noise and bustle of London proper behind them. Less traffic didn't help Alice to relax. She held onto her plodding mare's reins with a white-knuckled grip and kept her gaze pinned to the road ahead. Every time a cart drew too close, she whispered soothing words into her horse's ear. She'd heard it helped to keep them calm.

"I don't think the horse is the one who needs reassuring," Lord Warhurst said from the saddle. His gelding walked beside her and slightly ahead, sometimes breaking into a restless trot before Warhurst slowed it down again.

He sounded amused but she didn't want to take her eyes off the road long enough to see if he was laughing at her. "I can manage," she said, easing up on the reins a little to prove her point.

"Then you won't mind if we pick up the pace. I'd like to reach Crouch End before my hair turns white."

He was a horrible, horrible man. "Of course I don't mind. But it's too late for your hair. It's already speckled with gray."

"If you think insulting me is going to make me ease the pace then you're wrong."

"I never assumed you'd do such a thing."

He clicked his tongue and his gelding kicked into a trot ahead of her. He cut a magnificent figure on the horse. Powerful, composed and at one with the animal. Drawing in a deep breath, Alice flicked the reins and her mare followed. She held on tighter, wishing she could look as comfortable as he did. It was as if riding was as natural to him as walking. She, on the other hand, must look as awkward as a baby taking its first steps.

"Try to move to the rhythm of the mare's gait," he said, glancing across at her. "That's it. Feel her body through your own. The best riders move in unison with their animal."

"I don't want to be the best I just want to survive this journey in one piece." But she tried to do as he said and think of herself and the mare as a single entity. It worked, in a sense. She didn't feel as awkward although her rear was getting a pounding against the saddle.

"Want to go faster?" he said, an edge of excitement in his voice.

No! "Yes. Why not."

"Are you sure?" His horse danced around her, as if goading her mare.

"Of course." After all, he was too polite to go really fast. Even if he did, her docile mare probably couldn't keep up. She certainly wasn't falling for the gelding's teasing antics, keeping to her own steady pace. Clever animal.

"We'll make a horsewoman of you yet."

He took off and her mare followed instinctively. Traitor. Alice tensed and she gripped the reins so tightly her fingers soon throbbed. When she didn't immediately fall off, she forced herself to relax. As long as she held on, she'd be all right.

She chanced a glance away from the road to Lord Warhurst up ahead. He and his horse moved with graceful symmetry. It was beautiful in a way and she couldn't take her eyes off them.

Suddenly her mare darted to the side and reared. Alice grappled with the reins and pulled back as the horse reared again, the front legs hammering at the air. Her first instinct was to scream but common sense quickly overrode it.

"It's all right," she cooed into the terrified horse's ear. She should pat her neck the way she'd seen Warhurst do but she dared not let go while the animal was still rearing. "There's nothing frightening here. I'm not going to let anything harm you."

Lord Warhurst pulled up alongside her and put a large hand over Alice's, taking her hand and the reins together. "Easy girl," he said gently. "Easy."

The command could apply equally to Alice as to the horse. Her heart had ended up in her throat and was thumping out a wild beat. The combined actions and words of Warhurst seemed to calm the mare and she returned to her previous docility with only a twitching of her ears.

"Are you all right?" Warhurst's hand still covered Alice's. Like the man, it was solid and big and felt capable of a great many things. Calming women and horses being just one of them. She included his own horse in that. His gelding seemed the more skittish of the two and must have wanted to rear along with its stable mate, but he'd kept it under complete control the entire time.

"I think so," she said.

His thumb rubbed across her knuckles, the gentle strokes soothing her even further. It was as if he was trying to infuse some of his composure into her with his touch. If that was his aim, it was working. Wonderfully.

She smiled at him. "Thank you." The ends of his fingers had curled around the side of her hand and she squeezed them. Their gazes locked and in that moment, she felt a connection with him, something tender yet bold and profoundly deep.

But it was all too brief. His hand whipped away from hers and he stiffened. His head tilted back and the muscles in his jaw worked the way they did when clenching teeth. He'd made it clear the connection was not only severed but he'd stuck it on a pike and left it to rot in the sun.

"Did you see what scared her?" he said, turning his horse around, away from her.

It took her a moment to gather her frayed nerves and find her voice. "No," she finally said. "I was watching...something else."

"I admire your courage, Mistress Croft," he said without looking back at her. "Not many women with so little experience would have been able to hold on let alone stay as calm as you did."

"Is that a veiled slight against the entire female sex? Because I can assure you, I didn't feel calm. I wanted to scream. Loudly."

"But you didn't. I admire your spirit." There was no admiration in the sideways glance he shot her. More like curiosity and something else beneath, something that simmered with heat and desire. Definitely desire.

So he'd felt it too.

Except he didn't seem at all interested in exploring it. In fact, not only did he avoid looking at her again but that hard determination had settled onto his face once more. If he had felt anything for her in that moment, he was more likely to be disgusted by it than prepared to act on it.

"Perhaps we can go fast again," she said in a bid to distract herself from the man who both irritated and intrigued her.

One side of his mouth crooked up into what she now thought

of as the only smile he was capable of mustering. "Soon. We can't keep up that pace or the horses will tire."

They rode slowly for a while without talking until Alice could stand it no longer. She needed to fill the silence. The alternative was to dwell on both the near-accident and the alarming direction her thoughts had taken regarding Warhurst. Her hand still tingled from where he'd touched her.

"Hawkesbury Hall was magnificent," she said, picking a safe topic. A discussion about architecture was a sure way to quell the riotous thoughts racing through her mind. "What is your Northumberland estate like?"

"Smaller," he said curtly.

"Is it in the modern style?"

"No."

"So it's old then?"

"Somewhat."

Good lord it was harder getting answers from him than from Freddie in one of his drunken slumbers. "Sounds mysterious. Tell me about it."

"Why?"

Why was he so reluctant to discuss his home with her? "Well, because it must be interesting running your own estate all the way up there in Northumberland. I've never been further than Surrey."

He said nothing.

"Do you have deer in your woods?"

"What makes you think I have woods?"

"Don't all estates have woods?"

again he made no response.

She tried a different line. "What do your tenants farm? Sheep? Corn? Or do you have coal? I believe Northumberland is known for its coal mines, is it not?"

"How do you know that?"

She snorted softly. "I'm not completely ignorant, my lord. I may be only a seamstress but I have ears and I listen to conversations. Occasionally I even join in," she said, not caring to hide her sarcasm. "It might surprise you that I have an opinion on one or two subjects."

"No, Mistress Croft, it does not surprise me in the least. In fact I would be disappointed to learn that you held your tongue when you felt strongly about some point or other."

"Oh? Why?"

He shrugged and seemed genuinely unsure how to answer. "I just would be, Mistress Croft."

"Call me Alice," she said suddenly. "Mistress Croft is too formal for business partners."

He shifted in the saddle and made a great show of patting his gelding's neck. "I prefer to keep things formal."

For Heavens sake! "May I call you Warhurst for simplicity?" she ventured.

"No."

She rolled her eyes. "So why do you not want to answer my questions, Warhurst?" she said, dispensing with the 'Lord' part anyway. He may not like to admit it, but they had definitely moved beyond the need for titles. "They are innocently meant."

"Because they are personal and you and I are not on personal terms."

"No? It's going to be an awfully long ride if we can't discuss anything personal." He said nothing, simply stared straight ahead. What a pompous prig! Well, he might not want to speak about his life but she had no such qualms. And just because she felt like irritating him further, she made it as personal as she could.

"I'm the eldest of three girls," she began. "There's a ten-year gap between Elizabeth and I because my mother miscarried four times."

"I'd rather not know any of this."

"Then you can stop listening."

She told him about her father's occupation, first as a tailor then as tiring house manager for Lord Hawkesbury's Players. She detailed how her parents met, where they came from and what little she knew about her grandparents. He didn't interrupt once. On the other hand, he didn't ask questions or change his expression from the grim arrogance he'd perfected.

"Did I tell you about the time I was almost captured by a brothel-keeper?"

He swung round in his saddle and his mouth dropped open. She smothered a smug smile. If she'd known capturing his attention was so easy, she'd have mentioned the incident earlier.

As if recalling he was supposed to be the stoic lord, he returned his focus to the pot-holed road ahead. "No. You did not."

It was all the encouragement she needed to launch into the tale.

By the time she finished he was staring at her again. "What were your parents doing letting you wander unsupervised around the stews?"

"It's hardly their fault."

"I beg to differ."

"They warned me away from the worst areas near our home but as a child I had a natural tendency to flaunt instructions that began with the word Don't."

"Not only as a child," he muttered.

"Your turn," she said cheerfully.

"To what?"

"Tell me about yourself. You can start with how your parents met."

"They met on their wedding day," he snapped. "The uniting of two great families was a cause for much celebration for everyone involved, except the actual couple. They spent five miserable years together and somehow managed to beget me. I was one when my Father had the good sense to drop dead. Mother then married Sir Nicholas Blakewell in what is widely regarded as a love match. They had two children whom you've met and we all lived happily ever after."

Alice doubted that very much. His short account was not only brisk in the telling but held an edge of bitterness. "That is a short version of what I have an inkling is a very long story," she said.

He pulled his horse to a stop. "I see no reason to go into excessive details."

She stopped her hack alongside his. "Too personal?"

"Not enough time." He nodded at a hedgerow of hawthorn running alongside the road. "We're here."

"But this can't be Crouch End. It's not even a village."

"The village itself is another half mile down the road in the valley. This is the estate of Lord Enderby. You said Richard Farley works on his land."

"How do you know this is his estate without asking at the village? Do you know him?"

"Not very well. I've only visited Enderby here once and that was a few years ago now." He directed his horse towards the gatehouse.

"Why didn't you tell me you knew him?"

"As I said, I don't *know* him. Anyway, it's none of your business whether I do or not."

She'd gritted her teeth and stopped alongside him, prepared to tell him she needed to know everything about Enderby if she was to be of help, but then she saw the house through the archway of the solid stone gatehouse and could do nothing but stare. It was enormous and looked like it had once been an abbey in the days before old King Henry abolished the Catholic institutions. It came complete with buttresses, a steeply pitched roof and a vine-covered ruined wall.

"What a fine house," she said on a breath. "I'll wager it's just as fine inside."

"Is that all you can think about?" he growled. "Fine things?"

"No, of course not," she said without taking her gaze off the impressive façade. "I'm simply curious. I wonder what it must be like to be surrounded by such magnificence every day."

"Flaunt yourself before Enderby if you want to find out," he spat. "I believe he's on the hunt for a young mistress and he's generous with his gifts I hear, although God knows what you'd have to do to earn the trinkets."

What *had* come over him? Bitterness twisted his words and face so that he was no longer the handsome baron but a stranger. She couldn't deny that his attack stung. If that was his intention then he'd succeeded. "I am not in the habit of becoming the mistress of any gentleman let alone one like Enderby." She could have told him she'd had an opportunity to become the mistress of a gentleman she cared about some years ago, but she wasn't prepared to be *that* personal with Warhurst. Besides, he seemed too disturbed by the prospect of seeing Enderby again to notice how insensitive his words were. "He did something quite awful to you, didn't he?" she asked softly, her irritation suddenly gone.

His brows drew together. "What are you talking about?"

"Your tirade just now. You seem to have a lot of anger directed at Lord Enderby."

He glanced away.

"Why?" she pressed. If she didn't ask, she'd never find out. It was worth a try at least.

The bow of his mouth drew into a flat line and she knew she wouldn't get her answer. "I think we already had a discussion about your personal questions, Mistress Croft. Kindly desist from asking any more."

"And kindly call me Alice. I believe that's a discussion we also already had." She clicked her tongue and urged the little mare forward. "If we want to find Richard Farley today, we'd better go and ask one of Enderby's retainers."

He trotted up beside her. "I suppose if I ordered you to remain here while I went in, you'd ignore me."

She grinned. "See how beneficial our personal discussions have been already, Warhurst? You now know enough about my nature to not give me orders."

He grunted. "That part of your nature I already knew."

CHAPTER 5

The farm on which Richard Farley worked turned out to
be far enough away from the main house that Leo
didn't feel he had to cover his face with his hood, as he'd done
the night before in the grounds of Hawkesbury Hall. Even so, he
still kept his eyes peeled for the old prick. He didn't want a
repeat of their last meeting years earlier where Enderby had told
Leo to take his "thieving arse" off his land. That had been *after*
Leo had come to Crouch End to pay back the money his father
had defrauded from Enderby. So much for wiping the slate
clean.

The farmer on one of Enderby's tenant farms pointed to
Farley, a broad-backed youth mucking out the stables. He
stopped and joined them when the farmer beckoned to him.

Leo dismounted. "I'll speak to him," he said gruffly to Alice.
He was still angry with her. He couldn't explain why, and he
wasn't completely convinced that what he felt was anger
although it twisted his gut the way anger did. All he knew was,
it came as a direct result of her obsession with property—first his
and now Enderby's.

He'd not thought her avaricious until now. Ambitious, yes,
but only to have a shop of her own. It seemed she had a duplici-
tous nature—he'd been completely duped by her openness. And
by her other charms, if he was being honest with himself.

She began to dismount and he instinctively caught her round her waist. Her middle was firm and slight beneath his over-large hands but above them, covered by her cloak and too many other layers for his liking, rose her breasts. He'd seen their voluptuous roundness the day before at the White Swan and God help him, he wanted to see them again. The need made his groin ache.

"My feet are firmly on the ground now, Warhurst," she said, a gleam in her eyes.

His fingers let her go like a released trap. *Christ.* Being distracted by Alice Croft was becoming a bad habit. He could attribute his desire at the White Swan to the way the ill-fitting gown enhanced her obvious features, but he couldn't dismiss the desire he'd felt for her today so easily. First on the horse when he'd steadied her hand on the reins and now this. He was turning into a desperate fool. Perhaps he should think about finding himself a lover while in London. He obviously needed the distraction that only a woman could provide.

"You're looking for me?" said Richard Farley, stepping aside so a stable boy could lead the horses to a trough. Farley was a tall, handsome youth of about twenty-five with fair hair and a strong jaw. It was easy to see how a young woman could fall for him.

Leo glanced at Alice. She smiled at Farley. Farley smiled back. Leo stepped between them, forcing Farley to look at him instead.

"I'm Lord Warhurst and this is Alice Croft," Leo said. "Are you the father of Patience Enderby's unborn child?"

Farley's oversized jaw dropped. Must be too heavy. "I, I..."

"What Lord Warhurst is so subtly trying to say," Alice said, stepping around Leo, "is that we are friends of hers."

Farley's eyes narrowed. "If that is so, why has she never mentioned you before?"

"Because we are new friends," Alice said, unperturbed. "She told us how to find you. If we were her enemies, do you think she would give us your whereabouts?"

Farley's gaze flicked between them before finally settling on Leo. "You could have been sent by Lord Enderby."

"Then we wouldn't bother mentioning his daughter's name at

all," Leo said. "We'd simply come here and do whatever it is you think he wants to do to you. Answer my question, Farley. Are you the babe's father?"

Farley's fingers tightened around the rake. "You already know I am."

"There is a way for you to still be with her," Alice said.

He grunted. "There is no way."

"Of course there is," she said. "She loves you. And if you still love her, you'll fight for her."

Farley closed his eyes and tapped the end of the rake against his forehead. Alice stood still, watching him, her own eyes glassy from pooling tears.

Love—ha! Leo huffed out a breath. Farley needed a man's reasoning for a man's problem not love talk. He'd not bedded Patience Enderby because he *loved* her, he'd bedded her because he wanted to relieve an itch. If they wanted something from the youth, it was best to acknowledge that rather than complicate the issue.

"If you help us," Leo said, "then we can help you." There. Direct and honest. No need to muddy everything with soft-bellied *feelings*.

Farley drew in two deep breaths and opened his eyes. They looked no clearer than Alice's. "How?" he rasped. "What can you do for me? Put me to work on your own farm, my *lord*? I'm surprisingly good at mucking out stables."

Leo ignored the jibe. "By destroying Enderby's plans. Perhaps amidst the wake of the destruction, you can take your own revenge upon him."

"Or capture his daughter's hand in marriage," Alice said. She gave Farley an encouraging smile. "You must at least try and do something. For her sake. She's miserable."

He returned her smile although his was decidedly weaker. "Then I will do as you say and try. For her sake. What do you need to know?"

So the youth was indeed in love with the girl. Another good man wasted. At least Alice had secured his cooperation with her astute observation. She'd certainly been worth bringing along on the journey, despite the very distracting nature of her presence.

"Enderby is blackmailing Hawkesbury into marrying Patience," Leo said. "If we learn why he's being blackmailed then perhaps we can stop the union."

"How?" asked Farley.

"That depends on why Hawkesbury's being blackmailed."

"It might be as simple as exposing the cause for the blackmail," Alice said, "or helping Hawkesbury to bury it deeper."

Farley, still leaning on the rake, shifted his gaze from one to the other. "Why are you doing this? And don't tell me you're friends of Patience's. New friends, no matter how kind, do not go to such great lengths to help."

"Our motivation is not your concern," Leo said.

"Lord Warhurst's sister is in love with Lord Hawkesbury," Alice said.

"Mistress Croft," Leo warned. He took it all back—he'd been a fool for inviting her along. In future he would curb his spur of the moment decisions where she was concerned.

"And we believe her love is reciprocated," she went on as if he hadn't spoken. "We would like them to be together." At least she hadn't mentioned his sister's predicament.

"Then I think I can help you," Farley said. "As Enderby's steward, I saw a great many comings and goings in his household, not all of them through the front door."

"Who struck you as a person of interest?" Leo said.

Farley rubbed his jaw. "Sir Francis Walsingham."

"The queen's adviser?" Alice said at the same time Leo said, "The spymaster?"

Farley nodded. "It was late at night so it wasn't a social call either."

"But he's reportedly very ill," Leo said. What could possibly drag such an important man out of his sick bed?

But he knew the answer. Affairs of state. Spying.

"Oh," Alice said. She stared wide-eyed at Leo. He could see the path on which her thoughts were running. The same as his. Enderby was a spy in Walsingham's network and he'd possibly learned something about Hawkesbury, something that would prove very dangerous to the earl if revealed. Perhaps he'd kept the information from Walsingham and used it instead to black-mail Hawkesbury.

It was a very likely possibility.

Bloody hell! If that were indeed the situation, it was going to be damned hard to extricate Hawkesbury from the mess with his reputation intact.

"Thank you," he said to Farley. "You've been most helpful."

"But that's not all," Farley said. "On one occasion, Sir Francis arrived with another gentleman. A Christopher Marlowe."

"Kit!" Alice cried.

It took Leo a moment to place the familiar name. And then it hit him. Kit Marlowe was the belligerent gentleman he'd almost had to maim because he wouldn't leave a drunk alone. Why would such a hot-headed fool be involved with the calmly ruth-less Walsingham?

And how did Alice know him?

"Good lord, how is Kit involved in this?" she said to no one in particular.

"Who is he?" Leo asked.

"A playwright." She shrugged. "I've met him only a few times but some of our company know him quite well. He has a reputa-tion for making trouble. He was recently in Newgate for killing a man but it was ruled self-defense and they let him go."

Leo looked to the sky and drew in a breath and the scents of the country. He missed the smells of grass and horses and the sweetness of the air. He wanted to go back to Warhurst Hall but he couldn't do that until this business was sorted. And, as he was acutely aware, until he'd secured himself both a good reputation and a wife. He had obligations to the future of the Warhurst title after all.

But for now, he needed to return to London before the gates closed at nightfall. "Thank you," he said to Farley again. "Come, Mistress Croft." He strode over to where the horses were munching on hay. The stable lad had given them a good brush down and they looked refreshed enough for an easy journey back. Leo turned to help Alice up onto the saddle but she wasn't there. She was still with Farley.

"Patience had a message for you," she said.

The youth straightened and his tongue darted out to lick his top lip before disappearing again. "Is she well?"

"As well as can be expected given her condition and her melancholia. She wanted me to tell you not to give up hope."

Farley's cheek twitched and he bobbed his head in thanks before ambling over to a plough that stood near the stables. He appeared to be tinkering with it but from what Leo could see there was nothing wrong with it.

Alice joined Leo and swiped at a tear sliding down her cheek. "Let's go," she said.

Leo curled his fingers around the reins. If he didn't do something with his hands he might just reach out and smooth away the second tear. He wanted very much to feel her silky skin against his, kiss the saltiness off her tear-stained cheek. Touch her. Hold her.

But instead he ground his back teeth and turned away. That's when he saw the fat figure of Enderby settled like a lump of lard on top of an approaching horse. He was flanked by two other mounted men and they were all laughing at something. The tenant farmer emerged from the nearby cottage to greet them and the stable boy trotted alongside the horses, waiting for the reins to be tossed to him.

Enderby need only look Leo's way and he would be seen. He didn't want to alert the old cur to his presence, simply because it might cause problems for Farley, so he sank into the stables, pulling his gelding with him.

"In here," he whispered to Alice.

She must have recognized Enderby too and complied without asking questions. A minor miracle in itself.

The sound of Enderby's voice grew louder not softer and Leo realized with a sinking heart that he was heading toward the stables. So he did the first thing that came into his head—he circled Alice's waist, pulled her close and turned her round so his back was to the stable door.

Then he kissed her.

"Who are they?" he heard Enderby ask.

Alice's mouth opened to him and she kissed him back. Her fingers pressed against the nape of his neck and her body sighed into him. Her breasts were soft and round and...hell. He wanted her. Wanted to take her, make her his. He could feel his control unraveling, his wits seeping away as his skin burned with raw need.

He had just enough sense to acknowledge he was losing control. Right in front of Enderby.

And he didn't care.

"Travelers passing through," came Farley's voice.

"With no baggage?" said Enderby.

"Maybe they didn't stop long enough to pack any," Farley said with a laugh.

Enderby grunted, snorted then coughed. The cough turned into a wheeze which slowly faded. He must have left.

Leo could stop kissing Alice. He *should* stop kissing her. But she tasted too good. Felt too good. He wanted her to stay right where she was, in his arms, against his hardness.

Farley cleared his throat. "They're gone," he said. "But don't let that stop you."

Alice sighed and withdrew just enough to take her deliciously swollen lips away. God but she was beautiful with the blush of desire flooding her cheeks and her usually cool eyes smoldering beneath half-closed lids.

"Well," she said, tasting her top lip like a drunkard after consuming the last drop of wine. "That was—."

"A mistake." Leo pulled away and turned his back on her. He pressed the heel of his hand to his eye to grind out her image. But it was useless. She was still there, passionate and beckoning.

Christ. He was the biggest damned fool in all England. And he was going to pay for that kiss.

CHAPTER 6

$\mathcal{A}$lice hadn't thought it possible to travel alongside someone for nearly two hours without speaking. It seemed it was quite possible when the other person sat like a forbidding statue upon his horse and didn't even look at her. The only time he spoke was when he informed her, they would ride to her house. It was said with such decisiveness that she dared not disagree with him.

"We should discuss what happened in the stable," she said when they approached Gracechurch Street. They only had a few minutes left in each other's company and she wanted him to say *something*. Parting on uncomfortable terms didn't do justice to their kiss. Their delicious, heady kiss. Her heart still pounded wildly and her lips hadn't stopped tingling even after riding for hours in the cool autumn air.

"There is nothing to discuss," he said. "I told you, it was a mistake."

"It didn't feel like one. Not to me and I suspect not to you either. You certainly responded—."

"I did no such thing!"

"I could *feel* your response, Warhurst. Not only from your kiss but from your...well, you know where."

His back stiffened. "That was a natural reaction to kissing a pretty wench. It happens to all men."

He thought her pretty? Tears stung her eyes. He thought she was pretty.

Yet their kiss meant nothing to him. He was completely unmoved by it, except in the, er, obvious area. She, on the other hand, was in turmoil. Her thoughts were a jumbled mess and all she knew for certain was that she wanted to kiss him again.

"Then I have to ask," she persisted, "why did you kiss me in the first place?"

"If Enderby had recognized me, he wouldn't have rested until he learned the nature of my visit. I'm not sure Farley could stand up to one of his interrogations. It was easier to not show my face."

"You could have hidden behind your horse," she said. "It was as close to you as I was and wouldn't be pestering you with questions now."

He shifted in his saddle but still didn't look at her. The lead roof of the old mansion used for Leadenhall Market rose ahead, overshadowing the surrounding buildings. Most of the shops had already closed for the evening and people hurried in all directions, heading home for supper before dusk became night and settled like a blanket over the City. She'd wager none of them felt the way she did. Full and yet empty at the same time.

She hated Warhurst. Hated that he thought her beneath him, hated that he could shut her out so thoroughly after sharing something as thrilling as that kiss.

Hated that he'd made her want him despite everything.

"I live down this street," she said, reining her horse to a stop. "We'd best part here so no one sees us." She dismounted and handed the reins to Warhurst.

"I'm sorry," he said, focusing on her shoulder, not her face. "My actions were unforgivable." He gave her a curt nod. "Goodbye, Mistress Croft."

"Goodbye?" She held onto the reins. "Not yet, Warhurst. Our business is not complete."

"Your participation is, Mistress Croft."

"For God's sake, call me Alice!" They shared a kiss and still he wouldn't unbend enough to call her by her first name. He was an infuriating man. "And my participation has *not* ended. You need me to speak to Marlowe. I know him."

"You said you don't know him *well*."

"Better than you."

He tugged on the mare's reins and she let them go. "You are not coming with me. Our association has ended. I will send you the details of our financial arrangements when they're settled." He turned the horses around and left.

She scrunched her hands into fists and just managed not to scream at his retreating back.

* * *

Leo somehow reached the Golden Lion without concentrating too hard on the route. It was sheer luck that no one got in his way and that the weary horses didn't baulk at the late afternoon traffic. They at least gave the journey their full attention. *He* couldn't stop thinking about Alice.

And that kiss.

He could no longer pretend it hadn't affected him. His complete absorption in it proved it did. She'd got under his skin with that kiss, and she was still there. Extracting her was going to be difficult. But he was determined to do it. So much relied upon him forgetting her.

He returned the horses to the ostler at the Golden Lion then trudged back home. By the time he arrived at Blakewell House, he realized he'd made another mistake where Alice was concerned.

She was right. He needed her. Marlowe wasn't going to speak to him thanks to their confrontation outside the tavern. The playwright was more likely to draw his sword and run Leo through.

Leo definitely needed her.

And not just to deal with Marlowe.

Christ. He shouldn't have kissed her.

"You look a little dazed, Son," his mother said as he joined her in her private withdrawing room. She was embroidering yet another cushion by the rapidly fading light coming through the window and the flame of a single candle.

"That's because I'm hungry," he said.

"Supper will be soon."

"I can't wait that long. I'll go down to the kitchen." It was easier to avoid his family there.

She pricked her finger with the needle and hissed. "Light me another candle, Leo. I want to finish this."

He lifted the silver candelabra off the mantelpiece and lit all three candles from the flame of the one she was already using. "Your eyes grow worse, Mother," he said, placing the candelabra on the small table beside her.

"I can see perfectly well, thank you." She sucked the blood off her finger. "It's these new candles Robert bought. They don't throw nearly the same amount of light."

He shook his head and sat on a chest, its sides elaborately carved with the faces of classical heroes and heroines. "How is Lilly today?" he asked.

"Fine," she said without looking up from her embroidery. "Why?"

He lifted one shoulder. "I was simply wondering."

"You never *simply* wonder about anything, Leo, so what is going on?"

"Nothing."

While her needle worked, she peered at him out of the corner of her eye. "Where were you today?"

"Nowhere!"

She cocked her head to the side to peer at him. "I'm no fool, Leo."

He sighed. "I went for a ride out of the City." He was trying to help Lilly for Christ's sake. He shouldn't be made to feel guilty. He shouldn't *feel* guilty.

"A ride." She dropped her cushion to her lap and fixed him with a stare that could freeze the sun. "A *ride*. You went for a ride when you should have been paying your attentions to Elizabeth!"

"The queen? Wh—?"

"Lady Norwich's daughter." She shook her head at him. "Leo, did you leave your wits behind on your ride?"

Most probably. "Mother I have no idea what you are talking

about. There was no arrangement to meet any Elizabeths today, either of the Norwich variety or the Tudor."

"Have you forgotten the letter I charged you to deliver to Lady Norwich?"

"No. I gave it to one of the servants to deliver. I didn't think I'd have time for paying calls today."

"A servant! Oh, Leo," she said on a sigh. "Do you even want to get married?"

He thought about it a moment then said, "No."

A low growl came from her throat as she picked up her embroidery again and stabbed the needle into the fabric. "You need to get married."

"I didn't say I don't *need* to, I said I don't want to. Different things." He stood. This conversation was heading into familiar territory where danger lurked beneath treacherous waters. He'd better flee while he could. "But I will not wed a fifteen-year old girl." He held up a finger to silence her when she opened her mouth. "Not even a pretty, nubile Norwich one."

"That's a pity," she said, holding her embroidery alarmingly close to the candelabra for light. "Because she's coming here tomorrow with her mother."

"What!" If he wasn't careful, he might find himself betrothed to this Norwich girl without having even met her. It wouldn't surprise him if his mother had devised an arrangement with the girl's parent. "What have you been scheming behind my back?"

"If you were here, I wouldn't have to do it behind your back, would I? I could scheme in front of you." She screwed her eyes up and completed a stitch. "Not that you'd notice. You men tend not to see the things that are prodding you in the nose. Especially when it comes to women. Look at Lord Hawkesbury."

"I believe he did notice Lilly," he said wryly. "That is the problem. Speaking of Lilly, I need to see her."

"She's in her rooms as usual."

He took his leave and made as quickly as possible for the door. Not quick enough.

"Lady Norwich and her daughter are coming tomorrow morning," his mother said without looking up from her embroidery. "Make sure you're here."

"I have something else—."

"Please," she said, lowering the cushion and blinking rapidly at him. "Please, Son. For me. Just this once."

"Very well," he said on a sigh. "I'll meet the chit. But I'll not marry her."

She said nothing but started humming a wedding tune.

He made his way to Lilly's rooms on the other side of the landing. He drew in several breaths before knocking on her door then entered when she called out.

"Leo," she said, rising to a sitting position on her daybed. He kissed her cool cheek and covered her cold hands with both of his.

"Were you sleeping?" he said.

"Resting."

"You do a lot of that lately."

"The early stage is tiring."

His gaze rested on her belly. There was really a baby growing in there. His little sister was going to become a mother. He would be an uncle. He didn't feel ready for the responsibility and there would be a great deal of responsibility if Hawkesbury was not made to marry Lilly.

"You look well today," he said, although in truth it was diffi-cult to see. The only light came from the fire in the grate which had been allowed to die down. "Where is your maid?" he said, adding wood from the log box to the low flames. "She should have tended to this long ago."

Lilly answered him with a wave of her hand. "So what can I do for you, Leo? I assume this is not a social call."

He watched the fire crackle around the wood. "Why do you say that?"

"You don't do social calls. Everything you do has a purpose."

He stood and blinked at her. "I can be sociable."

"When you *have* to be. That's the point."

"I came to see how you are," he said, defensively.

"Don't pout, Leo. I don't mind if you're here for something specific. I'm used to your ways."

He wanted to disagree with her but then he'd have to follow that up with proof he could be sociable. Since that involved small talk about the weather or some other dull subject, he decided he might as well get on with his business.

"Do you know of any reason why Hawkesbury might come to the attention of Walsingham's spy network?"

Her eyes widened. She stared at him as if he'd grown another head. "Please tell me this is a joke."

"No joke. I met a man today who used to work for Enderby. He claims to have seen Walsingham leave Enderby's house on more than one occasion."

"What does this have to do with Lord Hawkesbury?"

"Nothing directly. But it proves that Enderby is a link in Walsingham's vast spy chain. He might have come across something that implicated Hawkesbury—."

"In what?" she spat. Her face had turned ominously dark in the same way his brother's did before they fought. It wouldn't surprise Leo if Lilly leapt at him with her fists closed and her aim true.

"In something treasonous. That is what Walsingham is interested in."

"Lord Hawkesbury is not a traitor. He is loyal to his queen, his country and the Protestant faith. Now leave. Take your accusations with you and shove them somewhere unpleasant."

He sat on a chair near her and she clicked her tongue at him. "Perhaps not treason then," he said. "But something that might still damage Hawkesbury's reputation if revealed."

She huffed out a breath. "No. There's nothing."

"Think about it for a while. You might remember something."

"I remember that he's a good man," she snapped, rising from the daybed. The folds of her glossy black skirts swished around her and settled into place. It was remarkable how like her hair the material was. She tilted her chin at Leo and suddenly she looked like the defiant and beautiful Lilly of old, the girl who could make her suitors jump to do her bidding. "I also remember that I love him. Now go."

He rested his elbows on his knees and steepled his fingers against his lips.

Lilly crossed her arms. "What is it now?" she said, sounding weary again.

He tapped his fingers against his lips and tried to think of a way to form his question. But there was no other way. Only bluntness. "How do you know that you love him?"

Her arms dropped to her sides then she sat with a plop on her daybed, her skirts billowing about her like clouds. "You're asking me to define love?"

"No, I'm asking you to tell me how to recognize it."

She cocked her head to the side and her black hair slid over her shoulder. "Does this have something to do with the Norwich girl? I hear she's remarkably pretty."

He suddenly laughed. He hadn't been thinking about the Norwich girl. He'd been thinking about Lilly and Hawkesbury and wondering how she could possibly know she loved him despite everything the cur had put her through. Surely, she must at least hear angels singing every time his name was mentioned.

"I wouldn't know what Elizabeth Norwich looks like," he said. "Nor do I care. No matter what Mother thinks, I'm not marrying a fifteen-year old. Not even a remarkably pretty one."

She grinned, her earlier anger apparently forgotten. Quick to flare and equally quick to forget and forgive, that was Lilly. "You'd think Mother would know by now that you need a woman equal to you in cleverness."

"And equal in other ways too."

Her gaze locked with his and there was no trace of her momentary humor. "Don't pursue Hawkesbury," she said gravely. "I trust him. If he says he can't marry me and must wed Patience Enderby instead then he must have a very good reason."

"You are a forgiving woman," he said. "Of Hawkesbury anyway."

"Because I love him. As to how I know that, well, you'll just have to learn for yourself how to recognize love. Believe me, it's like nothing you've ever experienced before. It lifts you up and carries you on wings."

"It sounds precarious."

"I suppose it is." She thought for a moment. "Flying must be both terrifying and exhilarating if one is not a bird."

He leaned over and kissed her cheek. It was much warmer

now. He liked to think his company had put the heat back but it was more likely to be from the fire.

"She doesn't love him," he said.

"Who?"

"Patience Enderby. She loves Richard Farley."

"Who?" she repeated in a whisper.

"Her unborn babe's father. He was the Enderby's land steward. They want to be together still."

"Oh." It came out more a breath than a word. "Thank you," she said as he rose to leave. "I needed to know that. Very much. But please, Leo, I'm begging you. Leave Lord Hawkesbury's secret in his own hands. No good can come of chasing it." A flicker of pain crossed her face but it was gone so quickly he wasn't sure it had even been there at all. "I have come to terms with our separation. I wish you would too."

He couldn't look at her anymore. Lilly never begged. She never asked anyone for anything, especially Leo—they'd not been very close as youngsters, not as close as she and Blake. It made his heart tighten to hear her voice crack and see her eyes pool with unshed tears. Especially when he couldn't promise her what she wanted to hear.

Without giving her an answer, he turned and left, closing the door behind him. Something soft, a cushion perhaps, hit the thick oak. He smiled. *That* was more like the Lilly of old.

CHAPTER 7

The tiring house at The Rose theater was a sight to behold. Built over three levels, it could easily store all of the costumes and props belonging to Lord Hawkesbury's Men as well as those of Lord Strange's Men, the theater's premier company. One entire floor was used as a dressing room so Alice didn't need to pretend to turn the other way when the actors changed, and her father didn't have to scold them every time they failed to disrobe behind the screens. She could simply go to another room.

The stage was just as magnificent. Two beautiful classical columns painted to resemble red marble held up the Heavens and matching smaller ones propped up the gallery directly over the stage that was used by the orchestra or for balcony scenes. Sometimes lords and ladies sat there—those with the money and a high opinion of themselves who wanted to see and be seen. None sat there tonight but the three tiers of gallery seating skirting the arena were full of paying customers looking down upon the stage and the unfortunate groundlings crammed into the area just in front of it. They would all be the first to see *The Fantastical Lives and Loves of Barnaby Fortune*, Minerva Peabody's latest play.

"Have you ever seen so many people?" Henry Wells said,

coming down the tiring house stairs to join Alice and her father. He wore a green and gray servant's livery, the first of many costumes he would don for the performance and an outfit Alice had made herself specifically for the play. He looked very handsome in it. "I've just been up to the balcony to have a look. The audience is piling in!"

"About two thousand of 'em," Edward Style said, rubbing his gloved hands together. Dressed in the somber robes of a learned gentleman of the law he didn't quite look the part yet.

"Your beard, Aquinus," Alice said, holding up a flowing white false beard made from real hair. She positioned it carefully then attached it with pins to his own hair. "That's better," she said, standing back and admiring her handiwork.

Will Shakespeare came down the stairs wearing the livery to match Henry. Unlike the others, he looked out of place in costume. Although a middling actor, it wasn't his preferred occupation, but Roger Style refused to put on the play he'd written, saying it wasn't sophisticated enough to please the type of audience Lord Hawkesbury's Men catered to. Alice couldn't help wondering if Style had ever seen the groundlings pissing where they stood or starting fights to liven up a dull plot. His reluctance to buy Will's play probably had more to do with Style's prejudice against playwrights who'd not received a university education.

Will shot Alice a friendly smile as Roger Style himself stormed into the tiring house from the stairs leading directly out to the street. His face was flushed, his ruff askew and his eyes bright as he scanned the room. "Is Freddie here yet?"

"He's upstairs getting changed," Henry said, eyeing the troupe's manager with caution. Alice couldn't blame him. Style looked to be in one of his unpredictable moods. She couldn't be certain if he was going to shout at them all or clap them on their backs.

"Where in God's name have you been?" Edward, the younger of the two Style brothers, said. "You look like you've been tumbling a Winchester goose." Unlike the rest of the troupe, he had no qualms when dealing with his brother. Perhaps he thought Roger wouldn't fire a family member. Alice didn't think Edward should be so cocksure.

"Keeping an eye on the gatherers," Roger said, removing his hat. The feathers attached to it—rust in color to match the fine new doublet he'd purchased for opening night—brushed her father's nose and he sneezed. "A few of them are Henslowe's men and I don't trust them. He ropes in his fat-headed whore masters and probably tells them to pocket what they can. Course he'd make them declare the extra to himself but not to me." He shook his hat at no one in particular but the feathers tickled her father's nose once more before he shoved it away.

"He's devious that Henslowe," Edward agreed.

"I wonder who's watching out for the whores," Alice said. They all looked at her. She shrugged. "Well, someone should be. Those poor wretches have enough to worry about without having to take care of their safety too."

"I see your point," Will said.

Her father clicked his tongue. "You do say some odd things, girl." He shook his head and his long, white beard—the real thing—swung from side to side. Roger had asked him to shave it off for the good of the company when he saw the exorbitant prices the wig makers charged for false beards but had been met with a firm refusal.

"You'd best get ready," Edward said to his brother. "The trumpet will blow soon and we don't want to be late."

"Croft, with me," Roger ordered Alice's father. "Help me change."

"Father's still not feeling well," Alice said, frowning at the steep stairs. Her father had wanted to come for their first performance at The Rose despite his wife's attempt to convince him he wasn't well enough. Although he hadn't been deathly ill, Alice didn't think he should over-exert himself by traipsing up and down stairs all day. He'd already moved between the three levels several times.

"I can help," Henry offered.

"I asked for Croft!" Style stamped his fists on his waist above his wide trunk hose. "If he's too ill to work then perhaps he shouldn't be working for me at all! The role of tiring house manager demands soundness of mind *and* body and I know several men who'd beg to be in his position. They don't come with daughters who want to be sons either."

A flash of red behind Alice's eyes momentarily blinded her. Her blood grew hot in her veins and her face even more so. Then everything went quiet. Unnaturally quiet. That pompous little pizzle!

"I'll go," her father said quickly, watching Alice out of the corner of his eye. He grabbed Roger's arm and steered him towards the stairs. "I might be needed to make final adjustments."

Style put a foot on the first step only to be knocked back on his rump by Freddie barreling down them in the other direction. He was wearing the beautiful crimson gown Alice had worn the first time she met Lord Warhurst at the White Swan's tiring house. She'd decided not to alter it too much and the lad looked quite fetching in it with the addition of a blonde wig. But then he spoiled the effect by hiking up all his skirts to re-tie his garter and farting.

Alice giggled. Her anger vanished and suddenly the atmosphere in the tiring house didn't seem so cloying. Edward, Will and Henry also smothered smirks. Her father glared at her, putting as much of a warning into it as he could while trying not to laugh.

"You imbecile!" Roger shouted at Freddie. He stood and slapped his hat against his thigh. "Any more of this behavior and you'll have your apprenticeship canceled!"

Freddie held his hands up in surrender and the crimson velvet skirts swished back into place around his hairy legs. "But I haven't done anything! I'm even ready before you are."

Style's eyes narrowed and he looked like he wanted to argue but Alice's father ushered him past the lad and up the stairs. "No time for this now, we'll be on soon." They disappeared but their footsteps could be clearly heard clomping across the floorboards overhead.

"Will, a word if you please," Alice said to Shakespeare as he passed her. The others dispersed throughout the tiring house, practicing lines or chatting to the hired actors who weren't permanent members of the troupe.

"You may have more than one word if *you* please," Will Shakespeare said. "Or if one will suffice, then so be it."

She rolled her eyes. He was always playing with words, whether his own or someone else's. "You drink with Kit Marlowe on occasion, do you not?"

"I do. And with other playwrights too when they consider me worthy of their company. What's the devil done now?"

"What makes you think he's done anything?"

"Would you be asking about him if he had done nothing?"

A fair point. "What can you tell me about him?"

Will shrugged. "He's tall, quite handsome—."

"No, I mean what's he *like*? Where does he come from? Who are his friends?"

"Ah." Will accepted the sword Henry handed to him and sheathed it in the scabbard strapped to his hip. "You've heard about his recent jaunt in prison?" Alice nodded. "Well, that event sums up the enigma that is Kit Marlowe. He's hot-headed. His temper flares at a moment's notice. I've seen him start a dozen brawls and not hesitate to draw his blade when outnumbered."

"So he's violent."

"Yes, but he also has the devil's luck. Not only was he released from Newgate with a speed not usually associated with our legal institutions, but he was given his M.A. at Cambridge after long unexplained absences, and what some said was a poor application towards his studies." He shook his head. "The devil's luck and a God-given talent."

Alice nodded solemnly. "His plays are good."

"They're masterpieces! Better than Mistress Peabody's plays in my opinion and you know how highly I think of her. I wish I had half the talent he has, and the luck, or at least divine intervention."

"I don't believe in luck," she said, watching Edward pace backwards and forwards in front of the curtain, muttering his lines to himself.

"What do you mean?" Will looked at her askance. "Everyone believes in luck."

"Not I. Perhaps it wasn't luck that he was bailed so quickly from Newgate, and perhaps it wasn't luck that got him his M.A."

"What else could it be?"

She shrugged, unsure of how much she should tell him. But if she wanted his help, she'd have to divulge a little of what she knew. "What if I told you I've spoken to someone who has seen Marlowe and Sir Francis Walsingham together?"

Will's eyes widened. "What are you talking about?" He leaned closer and whispered, "Are you insinuating that Marlowe works for the Crown?"

"I'm not insinuating anything, I'm simply stating a fact. They've been seen together. What do you think? Is it possible Marlowe is a spy?"

He sucked in his top lip then released it with a *pop*. "Anything is possible but...why would Walsingham employ such a tempestuous and unpredictable person as Kit in a profession that requires a cool head?"

"I don't know." She shrugged. "Marlowe *is* clever."

"Aye, and silver-tongued and brazen into the bargain." They exchanged glances but before either could say what they were thinking, Roger Style trotted down the stairs dressed in a fine green and silver doublet with slashed sleeves and silver buttons.

"Someone alert the trumpeter," he announced. "We're ready to start."

One of the hired men dashed outside and moments later a trumpet sounded three times. The audience hushed and Edward cleared his throat.

"Here we go," he said to the troupe then bounded through the curtain and onto the stage. His clear voice could be heard announcing the play to raucous cheers and applause.

Henry beamed and looked every bit the handsome servant who would bring about Barnaby Fortune's downfall. "They'll love this one as much as *Marius and Livia*. Mistress Peabody's a genius."

Roger cleared his throat. "Her betrothed has certainly helped take her writing to new heights."

Alice clamped her jaw down until her back teeth ached and her irritation subsided. Style simply didn't like to admit that a woman could succeed at something as well as a man, sometimes better. Thank goodness he'd not known Min had written her first play before he bought it or it would never have been performed.

"Don't mind him," Will said with a wink. "You'll not change his opinion even if women graduated from universities and became chief advisers to the queen."

"He'd probably think our heads would explode from all that masculine knowledge," she agreed. Her father came down the stairs looking a little hotter than when he went up. "Can you tell me where to find Marlowe?" she asked Will.

"What?" He'd been grinning but it vanished like a sunken ship beneath the waves. "Are you going to try to learn more about the Walsingham connection?" When she nodded, he shook his domed head. "You're mad. After what you've just told me, I'd tread carefully around that subject if I were you. Besides, Marlowe doesn't particularly like women."

She slid her gaze to Roger Style who was studying the prompt book. "I think I'm used to that."

"Then if you insist upon meeting him..."

"I do."

"Tell me why, and I'll tell you where to find him."

She'd expected the question and had an answer ready. "A friend wants to petition Walsingham on a family matter and thought Marlowe might introduce them. My friend has met Marlowe but knows not where he lives."

If he didn't believe her, he didn't let on. "Why would Kit help your friend?"

"I cannot say specifically but I have been assured my friend is in possession of information of a...personal nature regarding Marlowe." Everyone involved in London's theatrical scene knew about Kit Marlowe's preference for manly love and the necessity to hide it. Sodomy was still illegal.

"Ah," said Will, blushing a little. "I see. Very well." He hesitated a moment longer then shrugged, evidently making up his mind. "He has a room in a house on Bishopsgate Street Without facing the pillory at the corner of Hog Lane."

"Thank you, I appreciate your assistance."

Edward's introductory narrative ended to loud applause and cries of "Get on with it" from the groundlings.

"Good luck with the performance," Alice said to Will.

He caught her arm before she could move off to join her father. "I hope your friend does not take you along with him. Kit can be unpredictable, especially when drunk. And he's almost always drunk."

She'd been in two minds about whether to let Warhurst go with her to visit Marlowe—he'd made it clear he no longer wanted to see her—but Will's warning had settled that decision for her. She wasn't such a fool that she would not heed it. However, nor was she fool enough to be left out.

"Shakespeare, we're next," said Henry, beckoning Will to join him at the curtain.

Will nodded. To Alice he said, "Be careful. Kit has a prodigious talent and I admire his plays immensely but I wouldn't trust him, especially after what you've told me." He squeezed her arm then let it go to join Henry. Together they drew their swords and burst through the curtain.

"Why don't you get some fresh air," she said to her father.

He shook his head. "Think I'll rest in here awhile. You've organized things well in my absence, girl, so there's little for me to do now." He patted her hand and gave her a smile. It seemed to infuse him with some color. "You go. Watch the play if you can find room."

"Are you sure you'll be all right without me?"

"Yes, of course. Go."

She left via the back stairs then made her way to the side of the stage. Henry Wells and Will Shakespeare, dressed as servants, were listening to their master—Roger—lament his lover's recent abandonment of their affair after her husband became suspicious. The audience listened too, enraptured.

Minerva Peabody did indeed know how to hook them and Alice had to admit that Style reeled them in with his brilliant acting. She searched the sea of faces for the woman playwright and her betrothed and easily found them seated in the front row in the middle of the first level. On Blake's other side sat his mother, known as Lady Warhurst because her first husband outranked her second so she had kept the higher Baroness's title as a courtesy. But it was none of these three that caught Alice's attention. It was the fourth member of their party, sitting on the end beside Minerva, who Alice couldn't take her eyes off.

Lord Warhurst.

And he was staring straight at her.

CHAPTER 8

She stood out from the rest of the audience, that's why Leo noticed her. There was something other-worldly about Alice Croft, so tall and luminous among the grimy sameness of the groundlings amassed around the stage. She resembled an angel, or at least his image of what an angel ought to look like—all pale skin and golden hair, and eyes the color of a clear winter sky. She looked ethereal and fragile from his vantage point, as if the loud cheers from the audience might shatter her. But she wasn't fragile in the least. In fact, he was beginning to think she was one of the strongest people he knew.

All that explained why he noticed her; it didn't explain why he couldn't stop staring at her.

Or why she stared back at him.

He should break the connection, look away. But he couldn't. Watching her was like watching a sunrise, totally fascinating and always changing.

"She's a beauty," Min said softly into his ear.

"Who?" he said, shifting his gaze to the stage and the players romping about on it. He felt a twinge of guilt that he'd not been following Min's new play but searching the audience instead. He'd been looking for Kit Marlowe but he'd found Alice and there his gaze had remained.

"You know who, my lord," Min whispered, a smile in her

voice. "The seamstress, Alice Croft. You've been watching her, and she you."

"I admit I find her face intriguing, but she's no beauty." He applauded something one of the actors said because everyone else was doing so.

"Ah, but she is," Min went on. She didn't seem as interested in the play as everyone else, perhaps because she knew how it ended. Like Leo, she seemed far more interested in the audience. "She has a sort of subtle beauty," she said. "You don't notice it at first but when you really look at her you realize nothing else compares."

Exactly. "I suppose you're right." He had to explain why he was staring at Alice so he might as well acknowledge that he found her appearance interesting. It didn't mean anything after all and it might shut Min up. "Her face never seems to have exactly the same expression every time I look at her. No," he shook his head, "that explanation isn't right." He searched for a better way of describing his fascination to Min and in so doing, shifted his gaze back to the source. But Alice was gone. He sighed and turned to Min.

She blinked at him and offered him a warm smile. "Blake doesn't understand you at all, my lord. Nor does your sister, I believe."

"Oh? Did they tell you I eat small children for breakfast?"

She laughed. "They said you're too proud to allow others into your life. Others who love you and wish to help you."

Leo turned back to where Alice had been standing but she was definitely gone. "You think they are wrong?" he said, so softly he wondered if she'd heard him. When she didn't answer immediately, he assumed she hadn't.

Then she finally spoke in tones as equally hushed as his. "I think even the straightest, strongest flower in the garden will bend towards the sunlight. But only when it is ready."

He crossed his arms and thought about what she'd said. Eventually he gave up. He had no idea what Min was talking about although he was quite sure she was calling him a flower. Bloody playwrights with their convoluted words. He was *not* a damned flower.

He settled in to watch the rest of the play and actually enjoyed it. Min had a unique talent and the players weren't too bad, although the boy in the main female role was lacking any feminine qualities that Leo could see. He much preferred the way Alice filled out that crimson gown.

"We're going to the tiring house to congratulate the players," Blake said once the customary final jig had ended and the applause died away. The groundlings quickly emptied out the arena, leaving behind apple cores, nut shells and dark patches of spilled ale. Those seated in the galleries slowly made their way down the staircases around the theater, but Leo and his party remained in their seats.

"Will you come?" Min asked him. "I'm sure there'll be one or two people you might find interesting."

Blake snorted. "My brother doesn't find anyone interesting, my dear. That's his problem."

Leo ignored him. "No, thank you, Minerva. I have business to attend to." He hadn't seen Marlowe in the audience, but he did know the tavern where he drank. Perhaps he would find him there.

"Ah, here comes Lady Norwich and Elizabeth," his mother said, stretching her neck above her enormous ruff to peer over the sea of heads. "She said she would seek us out once the performance was over."

"Perhaps I should congratulate the players after all," Leo said quickly, moving in the opposite direction to the Norwich woman and her daughter. He'd spent an hour in their company that morning and he didn't particularly want to spend any more time with them that day. Or any other day. It wasn't that they were unpleasant. Indeed, the girl spoke remarkably well on many pleasant subjects, like embroidery, dolls and her dancing instructor. By the time the hour of their visit was over, Leo had endured enough pleasantness to last him a lifetime and told his mother so after their guests left.

Apparently, she had not understood him when he'd said, "I wouldn't marry her if she looked like Helen of Troy and had the fortune and pedigree of the Queen of England. There must be someone else," because she was trying to throw the girl into his path again.

Leo made his way through the crowd and down the stairs where he waited for the others. They arrived a few moments later without a Norwich in sight.

"That was rude," his mother said, smacking him on the arm with her fan so hard one of the bone spines snapped. "I had to tell Lady Norwich you were feeling unwell." She strode ahead into what was left of the audience, leaving her sons and future daughter-in-law in her wake.

"Did you also tell her I don't want to marry her vacuous daughter?" he said to her back.

"Elizabeth is not vacuous," she said over her shoulder. "She's young." She deftly stepped around a half-eaten pie mashed into the compacted dirt floor, sweeping her skirts aside to avoid the worst of the mess. "You could have molded her into anything you liked but I doubt she'd have you now."

"She's not clay, Mother, and I'm not a sculptor. I like my women fully formed, thank you."

She made a low growling sound which he took as acquiescence. Perhaps now Elizabeth Norwich could be forgotten.

They entered the tiring house through the back entrance behind the stage. It was bigger than the one at the White Swan and not as crammed with props. Two men stood chatting and laughing in the corner while another swept the wooden floor. Yet another man whom Leo recognized as one of the players came down the stairs and, on seeing the newcomers, approached, a broad smile on his oval face.

"Mistress Peabody, what a triumph!" The player kissed her hand then acknowledged Blake with a friendly nod. "You must be thrilled!"

Blake introduced the player, William Shakespeare, to Leo and their mother then made more introductions when another two players joined them. They talked about the play and its fantastic reception—all except Leo who couldn't remove his gaze from the stairs. Everyone seemed to be coming from a room up there. Perhaps Alice would too.

When he realized what he was doing, he promptly turned his back to the staircase. The last time he'd spoken to her he'd been abrupt. He must be so again if they met. She needed to know that the kiss they'd shared had meant nothing. It was simply a kiss.

He closed his hands into fists and dug the nails into his palms. "I have to go," he announced.

"No!" Min said, taking his arm and anchoring him in place. She was surprisingly strong for such a small thing. "Talk with us awhile longer."

"I can't."

"Stay," Blake snapped. Everyone looked at him and he shrugged. "Please."

Leo gently pried Min's fingers off his arm. "I must go. Sorry," he said with a curt bow. "Your play was marvelous, Minerva, and I thank you for inviting me. Enjoy this glory," he said, indicating the players who'd come up to congratulate her. "It's richly deserved."

"Aye," said Shakespeare.

One of the youths in the corner cupped his hands to his mouth and shouted, "Who's up for an ale or several at the Two Arrows?"

"Freddie!" said the square jawed blond player who'd been chatting to Lady Warhurst. "Do you have to shout?"

Freddie. Wasn't he the boy who was supposed to fit into the crimson gown? So this loud, spotty-faced lad had played the main female role? Leo shook his head. A real woman would make a better, well, woman on stage.

"How else will I be heard up there?" The youth stuck his thumb at the ceiling. "This place is bloody huge!"

That's when Leo saw her. Alice. She stood at the bottom of the stairs, smiling.

But not at him.

She smiled at Min and Blake. Not once did she look in Leo's direction, even as she moved towards them. It was as if he wasn't there.

"I knew it would be a success," she said to Min, holding out her hand. "Right from the moment I read it."

Min took the proffered hand and beamed. "Thank you. Your opinion means a lot to me. The opinions of all of you."

"Who cares what *we* think," Freddie said. "It's them out there that matter."

The big blond clapped the boy on the shoulder. "Finally you actually said something intelligent."

Freddie's brows rose and the white makeup still edging his face cracked. "I did? Huh. That deserves a drink." He plucked a hat off a hook, slapped it on his head then strode out of the tiring house.

"Weren't you also about to leave, Leo?" Lady Warhurst said.

"Yes." Best get away. Now. Before he suddenly found himself alone with Alice. He wasn't sure how that would happen but he was quite sure it would.

He almost got to the door when Alice brushed past him. She didn't stop or acknowledge his presence but made her way to a pile of costumes dumped on a table. Leo left and when he was finally clear of the tiring house, he opened his palm and flattened the piece of parchment she'd pressed into it.

I know how to find Marlowe. Wait for me.

He walked off. Then stopped with a sigh and looked to the gray skies. Damn.

He waited.

* * *

Alice easily recognized Lord Warhurst despite his back being turned to her. A back like his stood out in a crowd—broad across the shoulders, straight as a flagpole and shaped like a perfect V. She took a moment to admire it, and the confident stance of the man, before sucking in a breath and crossing the street to meet him.

He turned before she reached him and inclined his head in a nod. "Where is he?" he asked without so much as a greeting.

"It's a long walk," she said. He forked a brow and waited for her to elaborate. "I'll show you," she said and headed off.

"Just tell me how to find him."

She didn't stop but kept walking along the narrow street leading to the Bankside and a set of waterstairs.

He fell into step beside her and caught her arm, abruptly swinging her to a halt. "Mistress Croft, this is not a debate. You are *not* coming. Marlowe is an unpredictable and dangerous man and I don't want you there when I question him."

"How do you know he's unpredictable and dangerous?"

For a moment it looked like he would lie but he must have thought better of it. "I've met him. More or less."

"Which is it, more or less?"

He sighed and let her go. She felt an unexpected disappointment at the loss of his touch. "I stopped him brawling with a drunkard at a tavern," he said. "If he sees me again, he may want to kill me."

"I'm sure he's not the only one," she snapped and continued walking. It was a silly thing to say but it had just tumbled out. She was still angry with him. Furious. He'd taken advantage of her with that kiss and refused to acknowledge it. Warhurst was a coward and a blackguard. Hopefully Marlowe would draw his blade and give the baron's pride the poke it deserved.

She didn't want to miss that. Fortunately for both of them, he didn't try to stop her again and they made their way past bear baiting pits and brothels, avoiding as much of the muck festering in the gutters as possible. Thanks to the location of the area known as Southwark—on the south side of the river and therefore *outside* the jurisdiction of the puritan City authorities— entertainments of the baser kind, including the Rose playhouse, had made it their home. Whores plying their trade from beneath the jutting upper levels of the brothels lining the Bankside—the street that followed the south bank of the Thames—tried to catch their attention. No doubt they appreciated the extra trade generated by popular performances at the nearby theater, as did the watermen. Alice ignored them. Warhurst didn't appear to hear them at all.

They hired a wherry from the Bank End waterstairs with several others who must have come from the performance. Their excited chatter about the play provided a lively backdrop to Alice's and Warhurst's petulant silence. Not only did she not attempt to speak to him, nor him her, she managed to avoid looking at him until they alighted at the waterstairs on the other side of the river.

"Head north," she said, moving off towards Dowgate Street.

"Not that way," he said quickly. "It's steep."

She could easily cope with the steep incline, and he looked sturdy enough to not be particularly bothered by it, but she said nothing and followed him into the spider's web of narrow lanes instead.

"Are you going to be in trouble for this from your parents or the manager?" he asked.

"Do you mean for leaving when there was still work to be done at the tiring house or leaving with a gentleman I hardly know?"

"Both."

She shrugged. "Style wouldn't care as long as the tiring house is clean and the costumes locked away. I left Father with only light work to do and told him I had an errand to run for Mistress Peabody. He knows I'm making her a wedding gown so he wasn't suspicious."

"And if he finds out you lied?"

"Why the sudden concern?" He'd not cared a whit about kissing her in view of everyone and yet he was concerned about her small lie to her father!

A muscle in his jaw pulsed. "It's just that I don't want him whipping you."

She laughed. "Father hasn't laid a finger on me since I was a child and even then, it was only because I was always wandering off without telling anyone. I used to get up to all sorts of mischief and Mother worried so."

"She won't worry now? If she found out?"

"If she finds out that I'm wandering about London with a baron?" She laughed again. "She would probably kiss me then run to tell our neighbors."

The muscle in his jaw worked harder. She was beginning to think it was a sign that he was struggling not to say what was on his mind. She smiled to herself. There could be some fun to be had in shaking up his rigidity.

"If Mother found out, she would encourage me to use all my feminine charms on you," Alice said, putting as much teasing into her tone as she dared. She didn't want to completely exasperate him—she still needed him after all.

"I doubt that," he said flatly. "I'm sure your mother knows that is an impossibility."

"What is?"

"You using feminine charms on someone. You have none." He turned to her, a twinkle shining in his eyes although his face was as serious as ever. Was he laughing at her?

Well. He *was* right. No one had ever accused her of being charming or feminine. She certainly didn't act demure like other girls, and she wasn't very good at flirting. She smirked then grinned then burst into loud laughter.

"You have me there," she said through tears.

His mouth twitched but she didn't get to see if it became a full smile because he strode on ahead. She had to run to keep up with him. By the time she caught up, they were at the point where he'd fared her well after their long ride to see Richard Farley.

"You live there?" he said, nodding at the narrow street down which she lived. It stretched away from Gracechurch Street between the White Swan inn and a leather seller's shop. Her house was situated about halfway down in a long line of identical two-story timber buildings. Her mother would be inside preparing dinner with Alice's two younger sisters helping.

"Aye," she said, hurrying on. She didn't want him dwelling on the meagerness of the houses on her street, the way they all leaned against each other as if propping one another up. Perhaps they did, they were so old and poorly built. But he couldn't have failed to notice the children playing in the shadows of the overhangs, their clothing well-worn and their toys fashioned out of whatever they could find. Two boys kicked around a ball made from something soft, perhaps feathers, stuffed inside a small hempen sack and a little girl sat in the dirt with a rag doll.

"Will you move now that Lord Hawkesbury's Men will be performing at The Rose on a permanent basis?" If he'd been comparing her home to his own then he made no sign of it. She was thankful for his gentlemanly upbringing in that regard at least.

"Father thinks so, although Mother is not keen. She remembers when we lived close by the Theater and the Curtain, not far from where we're heading now. She doesn't want my little sisters to do what I did."

"Be kidnapped by a brothel keeper?" he said. "I hardly blame her for that. Southwark is little better than Norton Folgate."

"I'm surprised you remember that conversation, even though you remember it incorrectly. It was an *unsuccessful* attempt to kidnap me."

He gave her a wry smile. "I'm not completely self-absorbed. I do listen to you. I mean everyone. I listen to everyone."

"You refused to listen to me yesterday when we parted." It was perhaps foolish and fruitless but she had to try one more time. She had to know if that kiss affected him the way it affected her. Did it keep him up all night? Did it make him hot just thinking about it? *Did* he think about it?

She certainly did. Constantly.

"Don't," he said, an ominous note beneath the word. "I already apologized for what occurred in the stables. Please be kind to both of us and do not mention it again."

Not a chance. "I liked it." If she wanted answers, or at least a response, then she would have to unsettle him. He was far too settled within himself anyway, to the point of arrogance. "Did you?"

The very tips of his ears went red. Nothing else about him changed, however. He continued to put one foot in front of the other, his strides long and steady. His face remained hard and expressionless, he didn't blink or glance away from the road ahead. Even when a dog darted past his feet he didn't flinch. It was as if he were a walking, breathing statue. Although she wasn't so sure about the breathing part—his chest neither rose nor fell beneath his black doublet. Perhaps he wasn't human.

She smothered a giggle at the ludicrous thought. "Well," she said, "since you are not going to speak then I will. I must warn you, Warhurst, that although I liked the kiss, and I suspect you did too, I do *not* like you. So it cannot happen again."

He stopped suddenly and she had to double back. He stared at her with those sea-green eyes and blinked slowly. "You can rest assured it will not."

Well. Good. As she'd suspected, that exercise had accomplished little. Except that she had declared her own intention to forget the kiss had ever happened.

She could not forget. Not if she lived to be a hundred. Kisses like that only happened once in a lifetime. She should know. She'd been kissed before by a lover, but it did not compare to the one she'd shared with Warhurst. Not in the least.

She spared a thought for Charles Grayshaw and the fun they'd had in the stables at the White Swan two summers ago. With the memories came the painful stab, never far from her heart. Not for Charles—she didn't miss him at all—but for what he'd done to her. Oh, he'd been kind and generous, but he'd never included her in his future plans. As easily as he'd wandered into her life, he'd walked out of it, shattering her dreams and worse—her sense of self-worth.

It had taken a long time to rebuild her confidence again. She practiced her reading, writing and speech to the point of exasperating her parents and the players and playwrights who'd helped her. To them she must appear to be that young woman again, certain of herself and of her place in the world.

But she wasn't. Not quite.

She still longed for what Charles could have given her. He was a gentleman and a well-connected one, like Warhurst. So like Warhurst. Charles had wanted to kiss her too, and more, but wanting her wasn't enough. He could not abide her for what she was—a seamstress in a company of players—and that overrode everything else in the end.

But unlike Warhurst, Charles had kissed her more than once, taken his liberties, and let her believe he truly cared for her. In that respect, Warhurst had more honor. If his declaration and dour demeanor were any indication, he had no intention of taking the sort of liberties that Charles had.

Good. Such behavior made keeping Warhurst at a distance much easier.

CHAPTER 9

eo and Alice waited in the entrance hall for the landlady to produce Marlowe from the upstairs rooms of her small two-storey house. Leo was having second thoughts about bringing Alice along. Not because Marlowe was a disagreeable character—he'd seen her ably deal with men like him—but because she was a distraction. He couldn't concentrate. Especially since she'd made her bold declaration about their kiss right in the middle of one of the busiest streets in London. He'd only just managed to school his reaction.

Hell. That's what it had felt like listening to her tell him she liked the kiss. Then to have her declare she knew he'd liked it too! She was the devil's maiden. She must be to have know that.

He *had* liked it, but he wasn't going to admit it out loud.

The landlady came down the stairs alone. "Master Marlowe says he's too busy writing and you're to come back later."

"Go back up there and tell him I insist." Leo patted the hilt of his rapier, hanging at his hip.

The landlady's eyes grew wide and she nodded quickly. "I don't want no trouble," she muttered, turning to climb up the stairs again.

"Never mind," Alice said, going after her. "We'll tell him ourselves. Which door?"

93

"Third on the left," the landlady said, puffing and holding her side.

Leo had to walk fast to catch up to Alice. "Thank you," he said to the landlady. "You may remain here." To Alice, he said, "Perhaps you should too."

She clicked her tongue and continued up. He sighed and followed. The third door on the left was closed so Leo banged on it with his fist.

"Go away!" said a voice from inside.

"Open up or I'll push the door in!" Leo called back.

"I'd like to see you try!"

Alice turned the handle and the door swung open. Marlowe looked up from the desk where he sat, a deep frown marring his youthful features. "What the devil—?" His gaze narrowed at the sight of Leo. "You! Come to settle our score?"

"I'm Lord Warhurst." Leo shut the door. "This has nothing to do with that incident outside the tavern. I need to speak to you."

"I'm busy. Get out."

"This will only take a moment," Alice said.

"Who are you, Wench? You look familiar."

"Alice Croft, daughter of John Croft, tiring house manager for Lord Hawkesbury's Players."

Marlowe swore and slapped his pen on the desk. Ink splattered over his page which made him swear again. "Bloody Hawkesbury's Players! Bloody Style! Bloody Peabody witch!"

"Call my future sister-in-law a witch again," Leo warned, "and I'll be forced to teach you some manners."

Marlowe's full lip curled and he changed from a somewhat feminine looking creature to a purely masculine one. "That *witch* stole my audience."

Leo whipped out his sword but pointed it away, unthreatening. "Mistress Peabody may have bad taste in men but she has a good soul and I will *not* listen to you disparaging her! Draw!"

"Gladly." A grin twisted Marlowe's mouth. "Then we'll take this outside." He reached for his sword, sheathed and leaning against the wall beside the unlit fireplace.

"In front of witnesses?" Leo shook his head. He wasn't letting the cur get away with the insult, and there were still questions he needed answering. Having a crowd around would only cause problems and ruin his fun. "No. Let's settle this here and now. I'll be careful with the furniture." Not that there was much to break. Marlowe's study appeared to double as a sitting room but contained only a small table, two chairs, the desk and a solid chest with three locks. The only adornment came from the pages spread over everything, including the floor.

"Gentlemen!" Alice said, stepping between them. "Put away your blades and your tempers for a moment. This is achieving nothing."

"Move aside, Mistress Croft," Leo said. "Let me solve this."

"Yes, out of the way, Wench," Marlowe said. "Your lord and I have more than one score to settle."

Alice groaned. "Oh for goodness sake. Put the blades away this instant!" When neither man complied, she stamped her foot. "Warhurst! Show some of that single-minded reason I know you possess in abundance and sheathe your sword. If we fail to get satisfactory answers then you can do as you please."

A laugh bubbled inside Leo but he suppressed it. Reason? She thought he had *reason*? Hadn't their kiss proved he did not? He sheathed his sword and watched Marlowe do the same. He would give Alice a chance to do it her way, but when it didn't work, he would use his rapier. He had a feeling it was the only thing Marlowe respected.

"Thank you," Alice said. She smoothed down her skirts which didn't appear at all ruffled. "Now, Master Marlowe, Lord Warhurst and I are here on another's behalf to discover what information Lord Enderby holds against Lord Hawkesbury."

Marlowe's brows rose. Clearly the direction of the question took him by surprise. "Why not ask Lord Enderby?"

"We cannot."

"And what makes you think I know anything of it?"

"A guess," she admitted with a shrug. "We know that both of you work for Sir Francis Walsingham. We know that Enderby has information that he's using to force Hawkesbury to wed Patience. We suspect that you handed this information to him."

Leo wanted to applaud. Alice spoke calmly, with the sensible reasoning of a man, and a clever one at that. It was obvious from the way Marlowe looked at her that his sneering condescension had disappeared and she now had his full attention.

"This is a matter for the Crown," Marlowe declared. "Not you."

"I think not," Leo said. "Or Hawkesbury would have been arrested. In fact, I do not think the matter is an offence to the Crown but rather one that may smear the Hawkesbury name." He took a step towards Marlowe and crossed his arms. "And I think you, sir, have just admitted that you know something of it."

"I, I...I admitted no such thing!" Marlowe glanced from one to the other.

"Come now, Master Marlowe," Alice said. "This is not your concern. Tell us what you know."

Marlowe shook his head. "I can't. Enderby will destroy me if I do."

"*I'll* destroy you if you don't," Leo said, hand on hilt.

Marlowe snarled and withdrew his blade again. "Just try it."

"No!" Alice shouted.

"Get out and shut the door," Leo said to her. "Now!"

She backed up, out of his sight, but he did not hear the door open or shut. He half turned to order her again but Marlowe lunged and Leo had to jump aside or be sliced apart.

"Both of you leave my rooms now," Marlowe said, "or I cannot be responsible for my actions. If you choose to stay then you both stay. Your woman can bear witness that this is a fair fight."

"I'm so glad you agree to a fair battle," Leo said, watching his opponent's wrist for a warning that he was about to lunge again. "A sword fight is just what I need right now." For the last few days he'd felt restless, like an itch that refused to be scratched had spread across his skin. A good fight might work it out of his system.

"Oh lord," Alice muttered from somewhere behind Leo. "Men."

He smiled and flicked at Marlowe's blade with the point of his sword. The teasing move drew another snarl from Marlowe and he lunged again. Leo stepped aside and found himself up against the heavily locked chest. He climbed up on it. The small room would make the fight more interesting, but more dangerous for Alice.

"Mistress Croft," Leo said without taking his eyes off Marlowe, standing a blade's length away. "Get out of this room and wait for me downstairs. I won't be long." When she didn't move, he shouted, "Now!"

He glanced at her and Marlowe took the opportunity to lunge once more. Leo jumped over the sweeping blade just in time and landed on the floor, the thin covering of rushes not dampening the thump.

"Go!" he shouted at her again.

She opened the door but Marlowe reached around her and pressed his hand to the solid oak, shutting it before she could leave. "Witness," he hissed.

Alice pressed back against the door. She didn't look afraid, simply wary. Good. If she was to stay, she would need to be alert to keep out of harm's way. He would do what he could to keep the fight on the other side of the room.

But the other side of the room held most of the furniture. Marlowe thrust wildly again and Leo stepped aside, sending Marlowe reeling into the small table. The flimsy thing collapsed under his weight.

"Get up," Leo said.

Marlowe did. He adjusted his grip and shook his shoulders. His next lunge was more skilled, more controlled and therefore more accurate. Leo parried the blade only inches from his chest.

Alice's gasp filled the room. He dared not look at her.

He parried Marlowe's next thrust and the next but found himself backed into the desk. He leapt onto the chair Marlowe had been sitting in earlier and grabbed a hold of the roof beam when Marlowe struck at his legs. Leo swung one-handed off the beam and landed on Marlowe's other side.

Spinning around, Marlowe growled and lunged. "Stand still! Fight like a man not a monkey."

Leo laughed. "Where's the fun in that?" God, it felt good to stretch his muscles again, practice skills he'd not used in a long time. The last sword fight he'd had was against Blake and that hadn't been altogether serious. While they'd been quite intent on doing some damage, neither would have killed the other. Leo couldn't recall who'd won although he did remember they both ended up covered in horse shit as the fight had taken place in the stables.

A lot of things seemed to happen to him in stables. He glanced at Alice. She stood watching from the door, her eyes wide but unafraid.

Then they widened further. She screamed.

"Warhurst! Watch out!" Alice closed her eyes as Marlowe's blade plunged towards Warhurst's head. But there was no sound of a skull being cleaved, nor the squelching of blood. She opened them again.

Warhurst was alive although he was now hatless and his small ruff had come unpinned. He ripped it away and threw it at her feet. She picked it up and clutched it to her chest.

That had been close. Too close. What was it with men and their need to fight? Why couldn't they have been civil and had a decent discussion like sensible adults.

Warhurst jumped on a chair and kicked out, dislodging Marlowe's blade. It tumbled to the floor and Marlowe scrambled to pick it up. Warhurst could have won the fight in that moment but he remained on the chair and waited for Marlowe to retrieve his sword and resume the fight.

"Warhurst!" she said, hands on hips. "What are you doing? End it!"

"Not yet," he said.

Dear God, he was *enjoying* himself. His usually dour, staid countenance had been shed like an outer skin, allowing this fresher, happier one an airing. He looked alive. No, that wasn't right. He looked *real*. For the first time, except during their kiss, Alice felt like she was seeing the real Baron Warhurst.

And she liked him.

After a few more minutes in which the fight seemed to become more and more like a choreographed scene from a play, Warhurst leaped onto the desk again. "*Now* it's time," he said. He kicked off some of the papers scattering the surface, perhaps to ensure he had a stable footing.

"No!" Marlowe shouted, scrambling to pick up the pages. "My play! You'll ruin it."

Warhurst continued to kick them off the desk. "Come up here and stop me," he taunted.

Marlowe's face darkened. His knuckles went white around the hilt of his sword. He looked like he wanted to kill. But instead of going for Warhurst, he went straight to Alice and pressed the blade point against her throat.

"Get out of here or I slice her open."

Warhurst stilled and the last page he'd kicked fluttered to the floor. "Don't move," he said, but whether to Alice or Marlowe it wasn't clear. "Walk away from her. It's me you want. Mistress Croft is innocent."

Marlowe snorted. "I doubt that."

Alice wanted to run him through herself. "Put the swords away and let's talk sensibly," she said.

"Enough talking! I am not going to answer your bloody questions! Wench, open the door." He shifted so she could do as he ordered while keeping both her and Warhurst in his sights.

"Do not touch a hair on her head," Warhurst said, inching closer.

"Stay back!" Marlowe held up his free hand as if that could stop Warhurst.

Warhurst didn't obey. What was he doing? Marlowe would panic if he drew any closer and...

Then she realized Warhurst wasn't drawing closer he was moving around so that it became more difficult for Marlowe to keep both of them in his line of sight. When Marlowe shifted again and turned to see Warhurst, she took the opportunity to lunge at him. Using every bit of her strength, she pushed him while he was distracted.

It was almost enough.

His lightening quick reaction caught her by surprise. His sword lashed out, striking her forearm. The blade sliced through material and flesh and she cried out as pain ripped from fingertips to shoulder blade.

In the instant it took for her cry to tear from her throat, Warhurst was at her side. He shoved Marlowe to the ground and pressed a boot against his shoulder, pinning him and his sword to the floor. His blade point pricked the skin above Marlowe's ruff. A trickle of blood seeped into the starched fabric, staining it.

"Give me one good reason why I shouldn't ram this through your black heart," Warhurst said in a voice that sounded so unlike his own.

"Because we need him," Alice said. Her arm felt like a thousand bees had stung it. Blood, warm and sticky, tracked down to her fingertips, soaking her sleeve. If it hadn't been for the thick wool of her coat and the thinner fabrics of bodice and smock beneath, the wound would have been a lot worse. Nevertheless, all wounds could fester.

"Yes," Marlowe said, looking up from where he lay flat on the floor. His chest rose and fell with his hard breathing and sweat beaded at his hairline. "You need me my lord."

Warhurst didn't take his eyes off the man under his booted foot. A look so ferocious, so dark and frightening, masked his features, twisting them until he wasn't the handsome baron anymore but someone else entirely. For one chilling moment, Alice was unsure if he really would plunge his blade through Marlowe's throat.

Marlowe must have felt the same. "It's something to do with his father," he blurted out.

"What?" Alice said.

"Hawkesbury's secret, the one he doesn't want anyone to find out. I was investigating a rumor about an old plot to assassinate the queen and uncovered a missive addressed to the previous earl of Hawkesbury."

"Assassinate Her Majesty," she whispered. It was too awful to say aloud.

"What did the missive say?" Warhurst asked.

Marlowe shrugged. "I don't know. It was in code. I couldn't read it."

"Then how do you know what it contained?"

"Because it was in code. Who writes in code unless there's something dangerous contained in the message?" Marlowe laughed. When he saw that no one laughed with him, he shrugged again. "Enderby decoded it and told me that much."

"Did he also tell you the last earl of Hawkesbury was involved?"

"He didn't need to. It was addressed to Hawkesbury so of course he was involved."

"So you gave the message to Lord Enderby?" Warhurst prompted.

"He was my contact. He reports directly to Sir Francis Walsingham."

Alice didn't understand. If Walsingham knew, then why hadn't Lord Hawkesbury been investigated? As the son of a nobleman plotter, surely he would now be considered a person requiring scrutiny. People had been thrown in the Tower for less.

"Then why—?" She stopped at the small shake of Warhurst's head.

He removed his foot and withdrew his blade but didn't sheathe it. "Landlady!" he shouted.

The door opened immediately and the woman poked her head around. She must have been hovering on the landing or listening at the door. She took in the three occupants, the broken furniture and scattered pages, and clicked her tongue. "Any damage will be added to your rent," she said to Marlowe.

"Get me warm water and two clean cloths," Warhurst said. "And I mean clean." To Marlowe he said, "Get up. You may pick up your papers but leave your weapon here. One attempt to do myself or Mistress Croft harm will result in your death."

Marlowe's Adam's apple bobbed beneath his bloodied neck. He nodded quickly and scampered towards his desk and bent to scoop up his play.

Warhurst gently took Alice's arm and inspected the cut through the torn fabric. Then he looked up and his gaze locked with hers. Where fury had distorted his features before, they were now soft with concern. "Are you all right?" She nodded. "Does it hurt?"

"A little."

The landlady returned with a basin of water and the cloths slung over her shoulder. "Just washed 'em this mornin' and they've been dryin' by the kitchen fire," she said, handing the cloths to Warhurst. "Want me to do that, my lord?" she asked, nodding at the wound.

He shook his head and sheathed his sword. "Take off your coat and sit," he ordered Alice. She did. He knelt in front of her and rolled up the sleeve of her bodice and smock. She winced as it grazed the wound. "Sorry," he said and continued rolling until the entire oozing, puckered gash was revealed. He used one of the cloths to wash away the blood drying on her skin. It stung but Alice bit down to stop herself from making a sound.

"It appears to have stopped bleeding," he said and blew out a breath. He continued to wash her arm, his strokes surprisingly gentle for such a powerful man.

Marlowe peered over Alice's shoulder, a bunch of papers under his arm. He sniffed and wiped his nose with his sleeve. "It's just a scratch."

Warhurst bared his teeth. "Get away from her."

Marlowe scurried back to his desk and re-stacked his papers.

"Do you have a horse?" Warhurst asked the landlady.

She stood over the broken table, a splintered leg in one hand. "What would I need a horse for round here?" she asked, waving the leg.

"Servants then?"

"I have a girl helps me out in the kitchen."

He pulled out a leather pouch from his doublet and handed her a coin. "Send her to the nearest traveler's inn to hire a horse. A gentle one. Tell her to be quick."

The landlady left, grumbling about theater people and finding good tenants these days.

"What's the horse for?" Alice asked, inspecting the wound.

"For you to ride on." He folded the second cloth into a rectangle and positioned it over the cut.

"I don't walk with my arm," she said.

"You're not walking."

"I can—."

"You're not!" He wrapped the cloth around her arm. "Marlowe! A ribbon."

Marlowe found one on his desk and handed it over somewhat reluctantly. It was red and looked new. Perhaps it was supposed to tie up his latest play.

Warhurst gently tied the ribbon around the cloth, secured it then rolled her sleeves back down. "We'll wait outside for the horse." He took her hand and drew her to up then settled her cloak around her shoulders. At the door, he turned to Marlowe. "If you have lied to us, I will make your life hell." The threat hung like dense fog in the room. Marlowe nodded quickly.

While Warhurst's back was still turned, Alice bent and picked up his ruff which she'd dropped in the commotion. She stuffed it down her bodice.

Outside, they waited in the fading light of dusk until the maid brought the horse. Warhurst helped Alice to mount then he took the reins and walked alongside the plodding animal. The poor mare seemed weary or perhaps just old and it trudged along Bishopsgate Street Without towards the City gate as if it had made the journey a thousand times before.

"I'm not sure how I'll explain this at home," Alice said, more to herself than Warhurst. He'd been silent ever since they left Marlowe's rooms. Not that she minded. The silence helped her to think.

The fight, the cut, the new information...there was so much to take in. It had all happened so fast. It hadn't helped that her mind had become further scrambled by Warhurst's display of tenderness. It had quite literally stripped her of her wits and she no longer knew what to think.

On top of that, there was the rather alarming realization that she actually liked him.

"Then you can't go home," he finally said. His voice was low and gravel-deep, seeming to resonate from the depths of him.

"Then where am I to go?"

"Home with me."

CHAPTER 10

hen they arrived at Warhurst's house, Alice understood why he'd avoided Dowgate Street after they alighted from the wherry. He lived on it. His avoidance of the street must have sprung from not wanting to see anyone he knew. And not wanting them to see Alice.

It was a sensible decision considering their business arrangement and the delicate nature of their investigation. But it still hurt.

Not quite as much as her arm. The stinging had subsided, replaced by a dull throb. He directed the horse to the stables at the rear of the residence which stood almost opposite the Skinners Guild's Hall. Even in the semi-darkness she could make out the house's grand brick and timber façade, twin gables and at least six chimneys soaring into the sky. Even more amazingly, it was detached from its neighbor on the south side so that, positioned as it was on the hill, anyone looking out of the oriel windows jutting from the upper levels could see over the rooftops down to the river.

Warhurst led her inside from the courtyard. He seemed not to care who saw her, a complete switch from earlier in the day. A tall, serious servant met them and silently took Warhurst's hat and sword. He did not glance at Alice although he must have been curious about the plainly dressed woman his master had brought home.

"Who is here, Greeves?" Warhurst asked.

"Lady Warhurst and Mistress Blakewell are supping together in Mistress Blakewell's withdrawing room," Greeves said. "Master Blakewell is supping at Mistress Peabody's tonight. Shall I send someone to inform Lady Warhurst of your return?"

"God no." He inclined his head at Alice. "This is Mistress Croft. She has injured her arm and the wound requires attention. Send for the wise woman Mother uses. We'll be in..."

"The Rose Parlor?" Greeves suggested.

"I think the kitchen. It's out of the way."

"Very good, my lord." Greeves hesitated, his gaze flicking to Alice's. She lifted her chin.

"Yes?" Warhurst prompted the servant.

"May I ask how long Mistress Croft will be staying? Do I need to direct one of the maids to prepare a guest room?"

One of the maids? Just how many were there? Alice swallowed. Of course in a house this size there must be several. There would be too much work for just one.

"Do so," Warhurst said. "She's staying overnight."

Alice's pulse jumped. She'd suspected that was his plan but had not really believed it until now. The thought of staying in this grand house, under the same roof as nobility, sent a prickle of excitement along her spine. Not to mention the close proximity to Warhurst himself.

"We'll need to send a message to my father," she said.

"I know." He sounded grim. "We don't want to alarm your parents. If we assure them that you are well chaperoned here then perhaps they will not be concerned, but...what excuse can we offer?"

Alice had a thought. "Tell them I'm staying at Mistress Peabody's tonight, not here. They will think she and I were sewing her gown and it simply grew too late to wander home in the dark. They know she lives alone with her elderly father so they might not question that."

Warhurst frowned and looked like he wouldn't agree so Alice simply gave Greeves directions to her house.

"You'd better wait until it has grown darker," she said. "To make it more believable."

Greeves left and Alice turned to Warhurst. "Why are you not informing your mother?" Wouldn't it be wiser to tell her before one of the servants did?

"I need time," he said.

"What for?"

"To think up a story to explain this." He waved a hand at her arm.

"Why not tell her the truth?"

"Because..." He huffed out a breath. "Because sometimes the truth makes simple things more complicated."

She had no idea what that meant but didn't feel like pressing him. Her arm really hurt. "I suppose you'd better tell me where the kitchen is. Or have your manservant take me."

"I'll take you." He put a hand to her back and gently shepherded her down a corridor. "And Greeves is my half-brother's steward not mine. He's the most important servant in the house so if you require anything during your stay, he's the one to ask."

"Your brother's steward? Is this not your house?"

His hand dropped away. "It's Blake's," he said flatly.

"But you are the older brother. Did your father leave this house to him and another to you?" These were impertinent questions but she'd earned the right to ask him. In addition to which, she was simply curious. It was one small way to find out more about this enigmatic man.

"This was my step-father's house not my father's," he said. "Blake was his heir."

"Oh." She knew they were half-siblings of course, but she'd assumed the house belonged to Warhurst and they'd decided as a family to live together for the time being. A happy thought. But she knew the brothers didn't get along, so it couldn't be that. So why didn't Warhurst find a house of his own in London?

She caught a whiff of cinnamon and the question was forgotten as he led her down a corridor past the buttery and pantry. The scent grew stronger and her stomach growled in hunger. They entered the kitchen and two women kneading dough at the large central table immediately curtsied. Alice felt like an imposter. They should not be curtseying to her.

The older of the women suddenly dropped her formality and beamed at Warhurst. "Ah, my lord, you smelled my apple pie, I'll wager. You never could stay away from it as a boy." She wiped her flour-covered hands on her apron and shooed the younger maid away. "Go get some pie, Meg, and bring it here for his lordship." She indicated a bench seat running along the wall-side of the table. "Sit, my lord, sit. You too," she said to Alice.

Alice smiled and slid into the seat. Warhurst sat beside her. "I can never refuse a slice of your pie, Cook," he said, rubbing his hands together.

"More like two or three slices," Cook said with a hearty chuckle that made the web of red lines on her cheeks stand out more. "Come on, Meg." She flapped her apron at the young maid. "Don't want to keep his lordship and his lady waiting."

"Mistress Croft," Warhurst corrected.

Meg placed the pie on the table and handed him the knife. He cut two triangular slices and pushed one in Alice's direction. She watched him eat his slice in four bites and nibbled at her own.

"Eat up!" Cook said, pushing the pie closer to Warhurst. "You could do with some fattenin', Mistress Croft, if you don't mind my sayin'. I think there's some beef left somewhere."

"No thank you, this is good," Alice said between bites. "Delicious. I always thought my mother made the best apple pie in all London but it's nothing like this."

Cook beamed. Meg, standing beside her, seemed to relax. Warhurst cut himself another piece of pie.

If the women thought it unusual that their master's noble brother had brought a woman—one whose mother cooked for her family—into their kitchen, they didn't let on. Perhaps it was a common occurrence. Or they'd been warned ahead by Greeves and they were very good at covering their thoughts.

"Excellent," Warhurst said, dusting the crumbs off his fingers.

"There's more," Cook said, pushing the pie closer again. It bumped Alice's wounded arm, resting on the table.

She sucked air between her teeth as pain flared. She snatched her arm back and cradled it against her body.

"Are you all right?" Warhurst asked, gently taking her arm. "Let me see."

"What's happened?" Cook asked, leaning closer as Warhurst rolled up Alice's sleeves and untied the ribbon that held the cloth bandage in place. "Ooh, that looks nasty. Knife?"

"Sword," Alice said without thinking, earning a narrow glare from Warhurst.

"That why Greeves sent my boy to fetch Sweet Mary?"

"Sweet Mary?"

"The wise woman," Warhurst said. "Mother uses her for everything."

"No fancy physicians here," Cook said. She made a huffing sound and wiped her hands on her apron again. "They'll just check your piss and send you to Sweet Mary anyway. Charge you six quid for the tellin' too." She thumped her fist into the dough she'd been kneading. "Might as well go straight to Sweet Mary first and save yourself the coin."

Warhurst inspected the wound, his warm hands cradling Alice's arm. Her insides danced a little jig and her skin tingled all over. To be touched with such gentleness by a potent, powerful man...it was almost too much for her poor overloaded nerves.

He removed his hands and the spell broke when Greeves entered, a woman of middling age with smooth skin and gray hair behind him. Sweet Mary. She went to work quickly, first washing the wound in water and vinegar then applying a poultice from a pot she'd brought with her. It stank. "Marigold paste stops it festering," she said. She reapplied a new cloth around the wound, from wrist to elbow.

"Don't use the arm," Sweet Mary said, tying off the cloth ends. "And don't take that bandage off for two days." She packed her jars, cloths and other implements into her satchel and tucked it under her arm.

Warhurst thanked her. "Greeves will pay you on your way out."

She waved a hand. "Pay me when I check on your sister later

in the week," she said, already out the door. Greeves followed her.

"Wait," Cook said, wiping her hands on her apron and striding after them. "I've got a complaint needs seein' to. So's Meg, haven't you, Meg."

Meg frowned. "I don't—." Cook grabbed her arm and pulled her out of the kitchen.

Alice found herself alone with Warhurst. He sat on the bench seat beside her, so close their shoulders almost touched. Their knees too, under the table. She swallowed and tried to think of something to say.

"Thank you for taking care of me," she said. It sounded so pathetic considering all he'd done for her, and how tenderly he'd done it.

He slid out from the seat and strode across to the yawning fireplace. Small flames licked a single log of wood, keeping the pot suspended from a hook above warm.

Warhurst stood with his back to the hearth, his hands behind him out of sight. "How does your arm feel now?"

She looked down at the new bandage. "It hurts less."

"Sweet Mary's potions work better than anyone else's, so we've discovered."

She nodded. "That's good." Lord, what a dull thing to say!

He nodded too and that was the end of that conversation. She waited for him to say something else, perhaps show her to her room, but he did not.

"We'll wait here until your room is ready," he said as if reading her mind.

So that was it. He wanted to keep Alice out of the way until he could usher her into a room and shut the door on her, the Problem. He didn't want his mother and sister to stumble across her, didn't want them to see the *seamstress*.

Surely he knew he couldn't delay the meeting forever.

"What did you think of Marlowe's discovery?" he suddenly asked.

"You want my opinion?" It sounded bitter. She didn't care. She'd never felt more like an outsider, like she didn't belong. Before, when his servants surrounded them, she'd felt as if she was accepted but that was perhaps because she was one of *them*, the hired help. She was not good enough for the likes of Lady Warhurst or Lilly Blakewell. Not outside the theater at least.

She desperately wished she was home, warming herself in her mother's kitchen, listening to her sisters' idle chatter.

"Of course," he said, incredulous. "I value it."

"Really." She pretended to study the bandage on her arm but in truth she was avoiding looking at him so he would not see the tears welling.

"Yes," he said. She did not see him shrug, but rather heard it in the word. "I thought you knew that."

"I do not pretend to know anything of your thoughts, Warhurst."

He drew in a breath and let it out slowly. "It's been a long day and your arm is sore. As soon as your room is ready you must retire."

Must she? She sat back and crossed her arms then uncrossed them when the bandage reminded her she needed to be careful. "I think he told the truth."

"Marlowe? So do I."

"But do you think the missive will reveal that Lord Hawkesbury's father was a plotter like he claims? The current earl doesn't seem like a Papist."

"Perhaps he's not," he said. "Or perhaps he hides it well. Many do."

Every plot to overthrow the protestant queen could be traced back to Catholic dissidents. Her majesty was rightly suspicious of anyone who practiced the faith of the Roman Catholic church, issuing steep fines to those who didn't attend a Church of England service on Sundays. But it hadn't stopped the plotters. The execution of her cousin, Mary Queen of Scots, only two years before was still fresh in everyone's minds.

If the previous Lord Hawkesbury had been involved in a plot, then his son would naturally be someone the queen would want watched—whether he was guilty or not.

"Regardless of his faith," Warhurst said, turning to the fire, "I don't think he is involved in anything treasonous."

"Why not?"

"Because Lilly is an excellent judge of character and I don't believe she would fall in love with a murderer, of royalty or otherwise."

She'd not thought Warhurst naïve before. Not when it came to matters of the heart. He might respect his sister but surely he knew that love could be blind. As could lust, infatuation and desire. She was considering whether to disagree with him on the point when Lady Warhurst and Lilly Blakewell entered the kitchen.

"Ah, there you are, Leo," said Lady Warhurst, sweeping through the doorway in a cloud of black skirts. Her gaze flicked from her son, facing the fireplace, to Alice sitting at the table, her bandaged arm resting on the surface near the abandoned dough.

Alice rolled her sleeve down and quickly stood to bob a curtsy, an awkward thing to do while hemmed between seat and table.

"Hello," said Lilly with a warm smile. "You're from the theater, aren't you?" Warhurst's half-sister was a little paler and thinner than the last time Alice had seen her some weeks before at the White Swan. She'd been accompanied by her mother then too and had met Lord Hawkesbury who'd been backstage encouraging his players after what had been a mediocre performance. Despite her lack of good health, she was just as beautiful as she had been then with her dramatically dark hair and vibrant green eyes. So like Warhurst in that respect, only Lilly's features were pale and touched by serenity whereas her brother's were as hard as rock.

"I'm Alice Croft, daughter of the tiring house manager." There seemed to be no need to mention which company. The name Lord Hawkesbury was on everyone's mind if not their lips.

"Ah, yes, I remember now," Lilly said. "Min tells me you will be making her wedding gown?"

"Yes."

"Welcome to our home. You have an injury?" She nodded at Alice's arm, now covered by the sleeve.

"A small cut. Nothing of concern."

"Enough to call Sweet Mary here," Lady Warhurst said without looking at Alice. Her sharp gaze was aimed directly at her son who returned it with an equal glare that stamped him as the noble baron. "Greeves informed us that you were hiding down here with Mistress Croft and that the wise woman had been summoned to tend an injury done to the...girl." Had she been about to say seamstress? Or whore? Whatever she thought of Alice, she kept her opinions to herself. Much like her son. The two of them wore identically severe expressions that gave little away.

"We are not hiding," was all he said.

His mother made a sound of disbelief in the back of her throat. "I've also been informed that you have had a room prepared for her."

"This house was closer than Croft's. It made sense to tend to her injury here. I wasn't sure if Sweet Mary would travel to a strange house late in the day but I knew she would come here and not ask questions."

"Does her family know?"

"A message has been sent." It wasn't exactly a lie but nor was he telling her the entire truth—the message stated that Alice was at Min's. Warhurst's gaze remained fixed on his mother's. There wasn't a hint that he'd not been honest with her.

"Thank heaven you at least thought of that." She turned to Alice for the first time since her entrance and let her gaze sweep down the length of the younger, taller woman. But only once and then she turned away. "Welcome, Mistress Croft. If you'll be so kind as to come with me."

Lilly took Alice's good arm and together they followed her mother out of the kitchen. The dowager baroness's black silk skirt rippled like a stream over pebbles and a hint of rosewater drifted back to Alice, walking in her wake. Warhurst brought up the rear as they made their way down the corridor to a wooden staircase. Alice didn't dare look back at him but she was all too aware of his presence, solid and near at her back.

"I hope your arm doesn't trouble you," Lilly said.

"Not so much anymore," Alice said. "Sweet Mary's poultice has soothed it."

"Is my brother treating you well?"

The question startled Alice, particularly since he must have heard it. Lilly's odd little smile implied that she knew he'd heard it too, and that was as it should be.

"Like the gentleman he is," Alice said.

Lilly threw her head back and laughed. "Well said."

"I'm right here," he ground out. "I can hear everything."

"I know," his sister said lightly. "That is the point."

He made a low growl but said nothing.

"This is our best guest room," Lady Warhurst said, opening a door at the top of the stairs. "The last person to use it was Lady Calthorpe. She thinks she lost a pearl earring in here, so if you find it, we would be most grateful."

The little account wasn't really about the earring, Alice was certain. Its purpose had been to point out that guests to their home were not—and should not be—seamstresses. "I will be sure to keep my eyes open for it," Alice said with a gracious curtsy as if she were addressing the queen herself. "You're very kind for allowing me the use of this room for tonight. I promise I will be out of your home before sunrise."

"You'll do no such thing!" Lilly said. "Tell her, Leo."

"You need to rest," Warhurst agreed. "Your arm..." His voice trailed away and he looked around as if searching for an escape in the wood paneled walls. He appeared awkward and out of place, as if he were the guest and not her. But then something happened, he must have come to some conclusion, and he drew himself up to his full height. He strode to the fire and placed another log on it. "You need to be warm," he said simply. "Mother, a word if you please. Lilly, have your maid see to Mistress Croft's needs."

"Of course," Lilly said. Lady Warhurst stepped back out of the threshold so her daughter could pass.

"Good night, Mistress Croft," she said, returning to stand in the doorway. "I hope you find our accommodations to your liking." She spoke without maliciousness but Alice felt the sting of the barbed comment, nevertheless. Lady Warhurst would surely have guessed that Alice had never experienced the luxury of having a bedchamber all to herself, and such a luxurious one at that with its tapestry-covered walls and thick green bed cover.

Warhurst gave Alice a brief nod without meeting her eyes

then left too. Alice was alone. She lay on the large bed, her hands clasped over her stomach, her head resting on the fluffy pillows, and stared up at the tester. How had she got here? It felt like a dream in which things happened to someone else and she was simply watching from afar, an audience member at the theater. It all felt so strange.

And then there was Warhurst, gentle one moment then clamped as tight as an oyster shell the next. She didn't understand him. She wasn't sure she wanted to.

* * *

LEO KNEW he was in for a difficult night when his mother refused to sit upon reaching her withdrawing room. The lack of any emotion on her face, in her eyes, was another good indication that she was heartily displeased. It wasn't too difficult to guess why.

Most likely it was for the same thing that concerned him. Alice Croft was in a room not far away and he couldn't stop thinking about her. Was she resting on the bed or was she washing herself with the warm water from the basin, dragging the cloth over her bare skin...?

He cut the image out of his mind. Perhaps he and his mother weren't thinking of quite the same thing.

"You surprise me," she said, clasping her hands in front of her. Even with only the light from the fire and a single lamp, the emeralds in her rings sparkled like green stars against the black of her skirt.

"Really?" he said idly. "I thought very little surprised you these days, Mother. You seem to have everyone's situations organized."

Her lips tightened and he thought he'd gone too far, but then she said, "Except yours."

"Except mine. But I expect it won't be long before you've taken care of it as well."

She crossed the room to her small desk and picked up a piece of parchment. "I have a letter from my dear friend, Lady Finchbrooke."

"And how is my near-neighbor?" Lord Finchbrooke owned considerable lands to the south of Warhurst, and although their estates didn't meet, they were within spitting distance of each other. His son and heir, George, was Leo's closest friend. They'd hunted together, got drunk together, discussed crops and politics and women all night. Leo wished George was in London with him now. He needed to get drunk with someone he trusted who didn't talk of love all the time like Blake.

"They are all well, however her daughter has been unexpectedly widowed. The girl's husband, Sir William Something-or-other had a riding accident and died a few days later from his injuries."

"How awful." He accepted the letter his mother held out. "Poor Catherine. It says here she is holding up. I hope so, she is a kind-hearted girl." He folded the letter and handed it back to his mother. He did not let go when her fingers took the paper. She raised an eyebrow at him. "I suspect you have already written to Lady Finchbrooke about a possible union between her and I," he said levelly.

She nodded. "As always, I can keep nothing from you, Leo."

A dull ache hammered the back of his head and his mouth felt dry. He needed a drink. A strong one. "That's because you and I are cut from the same cloth. We both want what is best for the family."

"Do we?" She tugged harder on the letter and he let it go. She returned it to a small coffer inlaid with mother of pearl on her desk and closed the lid.

"Of course," he said smoothly. "However you could have let poor Catherine grieve a little, Mother. It is only decent."

"Decent?" She shook her head. "There is no time for decency. If we don't act now, we'll be too late. There'll be a dozen other eligible men making their way to her father's home right now. Widowhood has turned kind-hearted Catherine into a highly desirable woman. Not only did her father settle good land and a house on her at her marriage, all of which will return to her, but she's entitled to a portion of the income from her late husband's lands which by all accounts are quite profitable. I sent a messenger with a letter to Lady Finchbrooke this afternoon. In it I said you would soon return to Warhurst—."

"You did what! Mother!" Leo rubbed his forehead. God it hurt. "Mother, I have business to attend to here. I can't go."

"Not yet, that's true. You must secure your financial position here first before you ask for the hand of someone as valuable as Catherine."

"That is not—."

"Tomorrow morning you'll go to court and petition anyone who will listen." She was as ceaseless as a cow chewing her cud.

"There is the first flaw in your plan," he said. "No one will listen to me. I am the son of the man who defrauded them. They are hardly likely to hand over more money. That's what you want, is it not? Money so that I may go to Catherine, cap full of coin, and offer it to her?" He barked out a harsh laugh. "It won't work."

"Of course it won't work! Not if you don't try!" She snapped her skirts flat and sat down on the window seat. "It is time you stop running about the City with that seamstress and start doing something for your family, your title."

Everything inside him went cold and rigid. The blood drained from his face. He closed his fists against the anger, hot and sharp, and forced them to remain at his sides. "Everything I do is for this family and this title. To hold it together. To keep it safe. To raise it higher." He held his hand up when she opened her mouth to speak and she closed it again. "Alice Croft is doing more for this family than you, Lilly and Blake put together. She is helping me find out what Enderby has on Hawkesbury and when we know, we can force him to wed Lilly. *That* will save me from ruin and only that. Because," he said, tapping a finger against his chest, "who would want a tarnished baron after an extra layer of scandal is thrown upon me? Well? Not Catherine, not the Norwich girl. No one."

"But at what cost is her help?" his mother said quietly. She sat on the window seat, not resting her back against the vast number of cushions. The calm center of a tempest.

"A few favors, the payment of some rent. Nothing more." Anger would not get him far where his mother was concerned. It was like throwing feathers into the wind. He drew in a breath and felt the air flow through his body, cooling his temper.

"Are you quite certain?" She twisted one of her rings and rested her gaze upon his. "It seems to me she may cost you far more than that, Leo."

He scoffed. "What are you talking about?" Before she could answer, he waved a hand in dismissal and turned away. "Write to Lady Finchbrooke. Ask what their terms are for Catherine's hand and state my position. Hopefully she's too far from London to have heard the rumors surrounding Lilly's withdrawal from court before I can lay them to rest for good." He paused at the door and turned back to her. "*With* Mistress Croft's help."

She said nothing nor did she move, but simply sat there watching Leo through eyes that appeared softer. It was the way she used to look at him as a boy, with love and affection and a great deal of concern.

He shut the door and strode towards his room. He needed to lie down, his head was aching like the devil. He got as far as the guest room. Through the door he could just make out two voices, Alice's and Lilly's. Hopefully his sister wouldn't stay long. Alice needed her rest. As did he.

But he knew before he even reached his rooms that he would not get much sleep. There was only one way to ease the ache in his head, in his limbs, his groin.

And she was now only a few rooms away.

CHAPTER 11

lice didn't know what time Lilly left her chamber but it must have been late. The fire had become nothing more than a pile of glowing ashes and their supper of cold beef, cheese and bread had gone hard. Neither felt like eating. The mulled wine fared better—Alice had drunk two cups of it. It made her feel lightheaded but deliciously warm all over. Despite the lateness of the hour, Alice had been sorry to see her companion leave. Lilly was sweet and interesting and didn't seem to care that she was engaging in conversation with a seamstress.

They'd talked about the upcoming wedding and Minerva's dress, where to buy the finest fabrics and the cheapest threads. Lilly told Alice about the queen and Raleigh, and described Whitehall and Greenwich palaces, while Alice imparted the latest gossip about the players which made Lilly laugh. Neither mentioned Hawkesbury or the baby Lilly carried, or Lord Warhurst.

It didn't stop Alice from thinking about him though. Something had happened today. Something wonderful yet deeply troubling.

She was beginning to like him.

No, more than that. The surface of his fierce exterior had been scratched, revealing the baron's softer side. A side that intrigued her. And when Alice's interest was piqued, she was not the sort to ignore it and walk away.

She lay awake beneath the bed covers, listening to the silence. She fancied she could hear the creak of the boats moored on the river not far away, but perhaps it was only her imagination playing tricks. She tossed and tossed again, trying to get comfortable, but the bed was too large and cold without one of her sisters at her back, and the room was too quiet without their soft breathing. She wondered if they too tossed without her in their bed but doubted it. They still slept the deep sleep of innocent children. She smiled sadly into the darkness. She'd not expected to miss them so much.

The squeak of a floorboard outside her room wiped the smile from her face. She sat up. Listened.

Nothing. The house was probably sighing after a long day. Her father's house groaned all the time.

But then there was another squeak, and another, right outside her room. She got out of bed and threw the housecoat Lilly had left for her around the borrowed nightshift. She tip-toed across the floor and flung the door open.

"Warhurst!" she whispered loudly.

He stood holding a single candle, staring at her as if *her* presence was unexpected even though he'd known she was sleeping there. His white shirt was unlaced and a few dark hairs curled at the opening. The hair on his head was tousled as if he'd run his hands through it over and over. Dear God, but he was handsome.

"I...I should go," he said. The candle flame danced sensually between them, the only moving thing. Warhurst remained where he was.

Alice held her breath.

"Is everything in your room to your liking?" he asked huskily.

"Yes."

"Can I...?" He cleared his throat. "Can I get you anything?"

Their gazes locked. Her pulse throbbed in her throat. "Yes," she said on a breath.

He brushed the back of his fingers down her cheek, the touch oh-so tender, as if she were a fragile piece of glass to be admired. Her throat ached at the gentleness. "Tell me," he said. "Whatever it is you desire, just tell me and it will be yours."

She could still untangle herself from him and from the situation she'd found herself in. He'd left it open for her to ask for something, anything—a cup of wine, an extra candle. All she had to do was ask and he would leave her and end the foolishness.

Not a chance!

She fisted her hand in his shirt and pulled him into her room. "Kiss me," she demanded.

He closed the door and set the candlestick down on the top of a chest but too close to the edge. It nearly fell onto the rush-strewn floor but he caught it and pushed it further into the middle where it was safer. It was all done by feel. He didn't take his gaze from hers.

A beat passed. Two. She thought she'd perhaps read him incorrectly, that he really was checking on her comfort.

Then he pulled her to him so hard their bodies slammed together. He kissed her. There was nothing delicate in it, nothing tentative or teasing. It was as if all the hunger and need and deep, deep desire that had been swirling beneath the surface since the day they met had suddenly burst from its banks. It was a gushing torrent, fierce in its intensity, and Alice wanted to wallow in it.

He devoured her. His hands moved from her shoulders to the small of her back and pressed her to him so that her breasts crushed against his hard chest. His mouth was everywhere, on her lips, her cheeks, her eyes, her throat and back to her mouth again. He tasted like wine and felt hotter than a furnace.

She wanted to feel his heat against her skin and tugged on his shirt. He pulled it over his head, breaking their kiss, and she removed her house coat so that she stood before him in nothing but the thin nightshift. He threw his shirt away and she marveled at the muscular planes of his chest and shoulders. She stood on her toes and pressed her lips to the hollow of his throat.

"Delicious," she muttered against his smooth skin. She kissed her way down and took his nipple gently between her teeth.

A small groan rumbled from his chest and he tilted his head back. She turned her attention to his other nipple, licking and sucking until his fingers dug into her shoulders.

"No more," he said thickly.

She let him untie the laces of her nightshift then helped him remove it. It went the same way as his shirt, discarded somewhere in the shadows near the bed. He bent his head and took her nipple in his mouth and sucked and licked until she was on fire and melting at the same time. She dug her hands into his hair and held him at her breast but pulled him away when she felt the first throb between her thighs.

"Bed," she said, hurrying to it.

He removed his hose and netherhose and she took in his hardness—long and thick and ready. He was magnificent. A god, so exquisite to look upon that she wanted to pinch herself to test if she was dreaming.

But she wasn't. He was in her chamber and he was going to make love to her.

"Lie down," he said. She did and his gaze raked over her, taking in every inch of her nakedness. "So beautiful," he murmured.

She blushed. She suddenly felt shy, unworthy. No one had ever called her beautiful before, not even Charles, her first and only lover. She pressed her thighs together and covered her breasts with her arms, the bandage rough against her swollen nipple.

In the dim light she saw him flinch, a mere twitch of muscle. He put a hand up against the bedpost at the foot of the bed and turned from her. "What am I doing? This is madness." He shook his head and rubbed a hand through his hair. He swore. "I shouldn't be doing this to you. I can't..." He bowed his head. "You need to save yourself...for..."

Is that all? She almost laughed with relief. She knelt up on the bed, circled his waist and pressed her cheek to his back. "Don't concern yourself. It's too late for that."

He stiffened and lifted his head. "Who?" It came out half-bark, half-grunt.

"His name is not important. It was just the one, and it is long over." She took his shoulders and gently turned him to face her. His eyes were shrouded in shadows, his mouth turned into a frown. "For tonight," she said, pulling him onto the bed, "I am yours." She reached down and caressed the smooth, sleek hardness of his manhood. It bobbed at her touch and he moaned and dipped his head, bringing his lips to hers. "All yours," she murmured against his mouth.

And you are mine.

Leo was gone. As soon as she wrapped her long, agile fingers around his cock he knew only one thing—he could not stop. So she wasn't a virgin. Part of him was glad. Hell, *all* of him was glad! Especially his conscience. And his cock. His cock was really, really glad.

He lay her gently on the bed and sat back to look at her. Exquisite. Her long, slender limbs and pale hair and those full, round breasts...perfect.

He kissed one nipple then the other until she squirmed beneath him. She took his cock again and guided him to her opening but he somehow found the strength to resist and pull away.

"Not yet," he said. "I want to see your eyes glaze over with pleasure. I want to hear you cry out."

She smiled and he thought his chest would burst to see her happiness. *He'd* put that smile on her face. God, but it was going to be near impossible to resist her for much longer.

"I want that too," she said. "But you need to enter me for it to happen."

Her other lover had not been very good then. "Trust me," he said, settling beside her on the bed. "I don't need to enter you. Not yet."

He caressed the swell of her belly, her hip, her thigh and her inner lips. She opened up for him and her eyes fluttered closed. She was hot and wet and his fingers slipped in easily. Her mouth formed a silent "Oh" and soon she was rocking to his rhythm. His thumb found the swollen, tender nub and he rubbed until she threw her head back and clenched her fists in the bed covers.

Her body shuddered, once, twice, and the muscles in her jaw worked and he knew she was trying not to call out. Even in the poor light cast by the single candle flame he could see that she was flushed all over. He waited, his cock throbbing at the sight of her. He picked his shirt off the floor and laid it on her other side. Then he waited some more because he wanted to watch her as she rode the final waves of her pleasure. He waited until her breathing went from ragged gasps to a more even tempo. He waited until she opened her eyes and smiled up at him with a languid curve of her lips.

Then he kissed her. She dug her hands into his hair as he rose above her. He pressed against her opening and she bucked as his cock brushed her sensitive nub. Slowly, carefully, he slid into her all the way. He gritted his teeth against the sensations filling him up and pressed his forehead to hers. Like that he could watch her, read every note of pleasure etched on her face. Her beautiful, interesting face.

He picked up the rhythm, or perhaps she directed their pace, he wasn't sure. He wasn't sure of anything except that he wanted her so much the house could fall down and he wouldn't notice. He was mad. Mad for her.

And he didn't care.

Her hands pressed against his rear, her breasts were two soft pillows beneath his chest. He tried to slow the pace, make it last, but his cock had other ideas. Faster. Harder. Deeper.

She gasped and arched her back into him, thrusting her breasts out and up. He felt the first shudder of his climax and pulled out, spilling his seed into his shirt.

Afterwards, he wrapped it up and threw it on the floor and lay on his back on the bed, one leg over hers. She curled into him, a warm, soft bundle. Her hair smelled like smoke from the fire that had long ago died down. He kissed her forehead and listened to her breathing until it became even. She was asleep.

He carefully extricated himself from her limbs and stood. Before he drew the covers over her, he took a moment to admire the sleek lines of her body, the curve of hip and breast, the way her hair tumbled over her eyes. He dressed in his hose and netherhose and bundled his shirt up under his arm. At the door, he looked back at her, half hoping she would stir and beckon him back to bed.

But that was his cock talking. His head was telling him to get out while he could, before his cock woke up properly and demanded to enjoy her again.

He shook his head, wishing he wasn't running away like a coward. But it was the only choice he had. To stay would be a monumental mistake, and he'd already made enough of those.

He closed the door and left.

CHAPTER 12

One of the maids woke Alice when she came to relight the fire. Alice cracked open an eyelid and pulled the covers up to her chin. The other side of the bed was cold and empty. Warhurst had not stayed. She wasn't at all surprised.

"Would you like breakfast in your room, Mistress Croft?" the maid asked, returning the flint stones and fire steel to the tinder box.

"What does the family usually do?"

"Eat in their chambers, miss."

"Then I'll do the same."

The maid left but Alice remained in bed, staring at the flickering flames. She'd not expected Warhurst to stay in her room all night but she had hoped for something from him—a kiss, a goodbye or at least an indication of how he wished to proceed. This silence was so palpable it was painful.

She missed him. Missed his strong body pressed against hers, the smell of his skin, his arms wrapped tightly around her.

Best not to think about it. It would only lead to heartache.

She cast off her melancholy, rose and dressed. By the time she'd finished, the maid returned with bread and ale for breakfast. Alice ate alone, sitting at the little table near the window. When she finished, she fixed her hair, donned her hat and opened the door.

Warhurst was standing there as if he'd been waiting for her to emerge. The similarity to the previous night when he'd gone to her room struck her immediately. Unlike then, he was fully clothed in the most exquisite indigo silk doublet embellished with silver buttons and an intricate silver pattern embroidered down the sleeves. The richness of his dress drove home the point that he was one of the nobility, a rare commodity who dined with royalty, attended balls at palaces. And married other members of the nobility.

"You must be going somewhere important," she said, steeling herself for the awkward conversation they were no doubt about to have.

"I have business at court this morning," he said without meeting her gaze. "May we speak, Mistress Croft?"

So it was Mistress Croft again, not Alice, despite everything. She bit the inside of her lip until she tasted blood. The sting took her mind off the other, sharper pain stabbing at her heart.

She stepped aside and he swept past her into the bedchamber. She closed the door, clasped her hands in front of her in an attempt to look as serene as possible and waited for him to turn around and face her. It was several moments before he looked away from the window, and when he did, his face was a mask.

"I'm sorry I seduced you," he said.

"I don't think the seduction was entirely your fault."

His face remained impassive. "Even so, I blame myself. I came here to assure you that no one knows, not even the servants. Your honor and reputation remain as they were."

She gave him a tight smile. "We both know my honor wasn't as pure as fresh snow before last night."

He looked away again and she wished she hadn't reminded him of her previous lover. Men could be odd about things like that. But she would not pretend Charles Grayshaw didn't exist. He had been a part of her life and his actions, both good and bad, had shaped her into the woman she was today. Denying that was foolishness.

"Even so, I am sorry," he said heavily. "I want you to know that it won't happen again." She felt the color drain from her face. "I will not be ruled by my passions," he went on, "you can be sure of that."

The room tilted and she pressed back against the door to steady herself. So he didn't care for her. It had all been about uncontrollable passion, nothing more.

Nothing more.

Of course. What had she expected from a peer of the realm? Gushing declarations and love tokens? To a seamstress? That was the stuff of fairytales and Alice had been around theaters and players too long to believe in such artifice. Real life rarely had happy endings.

She swallowed past the lump in her throat and gathered her wits. "You regret making love to me?" she managed to ask. Her voice shook, her body trembled. She felt both hot and cold. It was like having the ague except that her heart pounded so hard her ribs hurt.

He looked out the window and back again but his gaze settled on her shoulder, not her face. "I should not have seduced you last night, but I did. It happened because I couldn't control myself."

"I seem to recall being overcome by passion too, so don't blame yourself."

A hint of color infused his cheeks but it was gone as rapidly as it had appeared. "I should have used more restraint. I should have employed reason, but I did not. I was ruled by my desire for you and I am sorry for it."

"I can see that," she snapped.

He huffed out a breath. "I am *trying* to apologize."

"No, you are trying to dismiss what happened between us as something dirty. Something to sweep under the bed with the dust motes and forget." She clenched her fists and tried hard to will herself not to cry in front of him but the tears pooled in her eyes, nevertheless.

He took two steps closer to her before stopping in the middle of the room. "What did you expect? I have apologized, what more do you want?"

She hugged herself. Despite the fire in the grate, she felt cold to her bones. "Recognition that last night had been...special."

"Yes," he hissed. "It was." He turned his back to her and hung his head. "Don't you see, that's why it can't happen again. That is why I have to forget it. Forget you."

She blinked back tears. "If I was not a seamstress, you wouldn't be apologizing now, would you?"

Time stretched before he finally spoke, but what he said answered nothing. "Do you think I'm proud of my actions? Do you think I *like* being ruled by desire?" He gave a short, sharp laugh. "I can assure you, Mistress Croft, I do not. But I can't make the same mistake again. Do you understand me?" He looked suddenly haggard, drawn, years older.

"Yes," she said through a rigid jaw. "I understand that I'm not good enough for you, Lord Warhurst. But I also understand that you are rude and selfish and arrogant." She wasn't hugging herself for warmth now, although she still felt very cold, she was trying to hold herself together, as if her arms could stop the shaking, stop the tears, stop the overwhelming sadness that seemed to spill out of her very skin. "I hate you," she said quietly. This wasn't the man she'd made love to. That man had been sweet and gentle, attentive and utterly unselfish.

He inclined his head in a slight nod as if he understood her hatred and accepted it. Welcomed it. "I have responsibilities," he said. "A reputation to maintain. My family and the future of the Warhurst title depend on my good character. I can't allow this to continue. Someone will find out and scandal will erupt all over again. You cannot be my mistress."

She almost laughed at that but the sound came out a strangled choke. "You are right on that score at least." She could not be his mistress. Making love to him then watching him return to his wife would remove a little piece of her heart each time. Eventually there would be nothing left except bitterness and regret.

"I'm sorry," he said again, lifting a hand as if he would touch her. But he was not close enough and he dropped his hand to his side again.

"Tell me one thing," she said, picking up her scattered thoughts. "Why did you bring me here to your home when I am an embarrassment to you?"

Leo couldn't answer her. Not because he didn't know the

answer but because it might finally unravel him. He was only just holding himself back from going to her, taking her in his arms and telling her... What? That he wanted her? God knew, he still did. But that was all, and it would pass. Desire always did.

"I have to go," he said but he stayed where he was. She was blocking the door and he didn't trust himself to remain impassive if he got any closer to her.

She stepped aside and tilted her chin. The tears had vanished from her eyes, thank God, and she looked composed once more. He breathed out a sigh. "What are we to do about Marlowe's information?" she said.

A return to a safe topic at last. He wanted to laugh with dumb relief. "I will make some enquiries at court today. I went to Oxford with a Charles Grayshaw, one of Walsingham's clerks, he might know something."

Alice gasped. At his raised brow, she quickly said, "Oh?"

"We need to know if there is information on Hawkesbury and if the coded missive remained in Enderby's possession or was handed over to Walsingham. If it is still with Enderby we might be able to retrieve it."

"Do you think...Grayshaw will help?"

"He might if I appeal to our friendship." Grayshaw was also one of the only people at court who didn't hold a grudge against the Warhurst name, but even so, getting him to co-operate could prove difficult. Grayshaw, like anyone at court, rarely did something for nothing and nothing was all Leo had to offer.

"Well then," she said tartly. "Goodbye, Lord Warhurst." She bowed formally, as she had done to his mother the day before.

His chest constricted as if a hand clasped his heart and squeezed. He moved past her and laid his hand on the door handle. "If your arm continues to trouble you, see Sweet Mary immediately. Greeves will tell you how to find her." He opened the door, checked that the landing was empty, then left. His words of farewell stuck in his throat.

CHAPTER 13

The court was at Whitehall, one of the queen's favorite palaces, for the approaching winter. Leo joined the scores of other courtiers and gentlemen vying for Her Majesty's attention in the presence chamber. They were like baby birds opening their beaks for their mother to drop a morsel into their mouths, only to swallow it and immediately re-open their beaks and demand more. She must hate it. Leo would if he were in her place, never knowing who her true friends were and who only wanted favor and advancement.

Leo knew who his friends were. There were precious few of them so he should. His neighbors the Finchbrookes, some of his old Oxford pals, Charles Grayshaw among them.

And Alice Croft.

No, not her. Not anymore. She must want to forget him after the way he'd treated her.

He certainly wanted to forget *her*. So far he'd had no success in that endeavor despite last night's attempt to exorcise her from his mind and satisfy the ache in his cock. A very thorough attempt.

He searched the cavernous room for Grayshaw's amiable face among the familiar, less friendly ones. He nodded at an acquaintance but was ignored. Two other gentlemen pretended they didn't see him even though they bumped into him. Another courtier openly sneered in Leo's direction. These were the very men he'd repaid upon gaining his majority years before. Everywhere he turned he was met with cool stares and even colder shoulders. Only one elderly gentleman nodded civilly but he moved on before Leo could speak to him.

"Well, well, if it isn't the prodigal son returned," a voice mocked.

Leo turned to see the ruddy face of Lord Enderby. The pockets of flesh at his jowls wobbled into a supercilious grin revealing yellow-gray teeth.

"Lord Enderby," Leo said, mustering as much politeness as he could without vomiting up his breakfast.

"I'm surprised you dare show your face at court," Enderby said, adjusting his black doublet over his grossly protruding waist.

If Leo put a fist into Enderby's pug nose he'd probably be thrown out, or worse, end up in Newgate. It might be worth it. Thankfully, before he had to think of an inane retort, Charles Grayshaw approached and clapped Leo on the back.

"Finally you've returned to bask in the glory of Her Gracious Majesty like the rest of us, you old dog!" Grayshaw turned to Enderby. "Please move, sir, you are getting in the way of my basking."

Enderby spluttered so hard spittle stuck to his moustache. He looked like he wouldn't move an inch but then the queen herself lifted her golden head, covered with a cap trimmed with pearls, and smiled in their direction. Enderby bowed but it was shallow thanks to his lack of a waist. When Grayshaw bowed, he touched one knee to the floor, swept his hat along the flagstones and remained that way until the queen laughingly told him to rise.

Grayshaw smiled back and there was a collective sigh from all the women. He took a step forward, as if the queen had beckoned him. But she had not and he stopped and waited. Her Majesty looked past him to Leo.

She beckoned him with her fan. "Lord Warhurst isn't it?" she said as Leo approached. She held out her hand for him to kiss. Leo wasn't surprised to see that his mother wore more rings than the queen. "It has been some time since you were at court, my lord."

"Almost a year, Your Majesty," he said. "Too long to be away from your glory."

She laughed a high, girlish laugh and covered her mouth with her fan. "Pretty sentiments, my lord. I suppose you are about to tell me I have changed for the better in the year's absence, that I am looking more radiant, more beautiful than ever. That is the customary thing to say if you want my favor. Ask anyone." She swept the fan in an arc to include all the men and women in the presence chamber. "They'll all tell me that very thing after an absence of a week, a day, a minute!"

"Then I am an ignorant man," Leo said, "because I was not thinking such a thing. Forgive me." Behind him someone— Grayshaw?—drew in a sharp breath. Conversations that had been going on around them dried up. The entire room seemed to strain to listen. "I was going to tell you that you have not changed in the least, Your Majesty. If that isn't the customary thing to say then I apologize. My northern country manners need some refining."

It was a blatant lie of course. Up close, the thick white face paint couldn't quite hide the new pock marks, and the jewels in her wig, dress, fingers and ears didn't dazzle enough to detract from the extra wrinkles around her eyes and mouth. For all that, she was still a remarkable looking woman, not a beauty but certainly striking.

"It is not the customary thing," she agreed, "but I like it better." She tapped him on the arm and leaned forward although her voice didn't drop. What she said in this room, this theater, was said for the benefit of any who would listen. The queen was the best player Leo had ever seen. "As to your country manners, perhaps it's time you sought a wife to teach you more refined ways. I'm surprised your good mother and my dear friend, Lady Warhurst, has not found you a bride yet."

It wasn't for her lack of trying. "It's my greatest wish that I obtain a wife soon," he said. The trio of ladies' maids sitting in the window embrasure stopped talking and like sunflowers, turned their heads toward him.

"See," the queen said with a satisfactory nod to the women, "already you have garnered some interest with your handsome face and country manners, my lord." All three of the women blushed on cue. It was like watching that boy player in Alice's troupe—*Hawkesbury's* troupe—smile and say his lines exactly as they'd been written for him.

"Unfortunately that is all I have to offer a wife," he said. "That and an estate in Northumberland."

"That might be enough for some if it comes with a face as favored as yours. You have your father's looks, sir, but it appears you lack his charm. Let us hope you also lack his fickle nature."

Leo swallowed and acknowledged her pointed comments with a nod.

"It would please me *greatly*," her voice rose on the word so that even those courtiers in the far corners of the presence chamber could hear, "to see you make an advantageous match, my lord."

One of her advisors approached and whispered in her ear. She nodded. "Very well, let us not keep the ambassador waiting." She rose. The room hushed except for the rustle of gowns and cloaks as everyone bowed. She left with her advisors and ladies in waiting in tow. As soon as she was gone the noise level rose again as most people filed out.

"Not you too," Grayshaw said, remaining behind with Leo.

"Not me what?" Leo asked.

"Getting married." Grayshaw made a face.

"Mother has someone in mind."

"A mother like yours would be an advantage in the negotiations. Unfortunately I have to navigate the dangerous waters of betrothals alone." Grayshaw had been an orphan for as long as Leo had known him. A modest inheritance had allowed him to purchase a house in Blackfriars after completing his Oxford education. His uncle, a lawyer, had obtained him the position at court and after a few years, Grayshaw was made assistant to Sir Francis Walsingham. It was a solid position for a gentleman in his situation.

"You may borrow my mother at any time," Leo said. "Don't be in a hurry to give her back."

Grayshaw laughed. "If only you'd stayed in Northumberland, you could have avoided your mother and pleased her at the same time."

"How so?"

"The Finchbrooke girl is widowed. You know her brother well as I recall."

Leo nodded. "The Finchbrooke estate is not far from Warhurst."

Grayshaw turned serious. "What's she like?"

"Kind. Pretty but not in the way of these court beauties. She has a...quieter sort of beauty that radiates vibrancy and wonderment. She's got a sharp wit and she laughs—." He bit off the rest of the sentence. The person he'd just described wasn't Catherine, daughter of Lord Finchbrooke, but Alice Croft. He tried to conjure up the memory of what Catherine looked like but couldn't. The only picture in his mind was of Alice, her face soft, her eyes closed in ecstasy, her hair sprayed like a fan across the pillow.

Christ.

Grayshaw watched him with a curious expression. Leo cleared his throat. "My mother is opening negotiations with Lord Finchbrooke for a betrothal," he said.

"Oh."

Leo narrowed his eyes at his normally jovial friend. "Oh?"

Grayshaw sighed. "I too have opened negotiations with Lord Finchbrooke." He tugged on his lace cuffs. "I'll bow out."

"You will not. Catherine deserves to have more than one man vying for her affections." He held out his hand. "May the best man win."

Grayshaw shook it then shook his head. "We both know that will be you. You have the title, I have only a modest income."

"You have favor here at court and some influence with the queen's advisors. You could rise even higher and who knows, wealth and a knighthood might come to you. Don't give up."

What was he saying? He should be encouraging Grayshaw to look elsewhere for a wife. Catherine would be the new Lady Warhurst. She had to be. She would bring enough property with her that Leo could use it as surety against any loans. He needed the loans to sink some mines and he *really* needed those mines. His people, scratching out a pathetic living on his barren lands, needed them.

They all needed Catherine. Together they would care for his tenants, mine the coal and extend the simple tower of Warhurst Hall and build something grand. Something to pass down to his heir. Far away from London.

Far away from Alice.

Leo's stomach tightened as if it had been tied into a knot and someone was pulling the ends.

"Are you ill?" Grayshaw asked, taking Leo's elbow. "You look pale."

"I just need a little air. It's stifling in here." He moved toward an open casement window and peered out onto the formal terraced gardens below. Grayshaw followed him. "Charles, I have a favor to ask of you."

"Anything. We see little of each other these days but I like to think we are still good friends."

Leo wasn't sure the friendship would stretch to giving away state secrets but he had to try. Today more than ever he was determined to succeed. If he didn't wed Catherine then everything rested on Lilly marrying Hawke—everything he'd worked for, everything he dreamed for his tenants and himself.

He must forget Alice and conquer his lust or he'd never be able to concentrate on the more important task of securing his future.

He told Grayshaw about his investigation without mentioning Lilly's state, although from the look on his friend's face he'd probably guessed she was carrying Hawkesbury's child. "I need to know if there is anything in Walsingham's files on Hawkesbury's father," Leo said after he repeated Marlowe's admission without naming the playwright.

Grayshaw shook his head. "I'm sorry, my friend, I can't. Not even for you. If I get caught reading files I'm not authorized to search then I could lose my position."

"I understand, but—." A new arrival into the presence chamber caught Leo's attention.

Lord Hawkesbury.

His gaze settled on Leo then shifted to Grayshaw. The smile on his lips froze, the dark eyes narrowed. Leo could see the pieces falling into place in his mind—Leo's presence at court for the first time since his arrival in London, his quiet conversation away from everyone else with the assistant to one of the most powerful men in the country.

Even from a distance Leo could see him swallow heavily. Hawkesbury inclined his head in greeting then made his way to a group of courtiers and joined in their conversation.

Lord Enderby was nowhere to be seen.

CHAPTER 14

lice thought lying to her parents about her whereabouts the night before would be easy. It *had* been easy to send them a message but now that she was face to face with them and her sisters in the kitchen, she felt horrible. She almost wished they didn't believe her. She deserved a tongue-lashing, not their enthusiastic attention.

"What was it like?" her youngest sister, Jane, asked. Her huge eyes regarded Alice with wonder, as if she'd been to Heaven and back.

"What was what like?" Alice said, sitting beside her other sister, Elizabeth, near the fireplace. A large pot hung over the low fire and delicious smells of stewing meat wafted up with the steam. Why her mother still bothered to cook so much food, Alice didn't know. Since the company had moved to The Rose on the other side of the river, it was too far for Alice and her father to return home for their midday dinner every day so they mostly dined out with the rest of the troupe. Her mother made them eat another hearty meal at supper time simply so none went to waste.

"Mistress Peabody's house!" Jane said in exasperation. She hopped from foot to foot until her father growled at her.

"Be still, child," he said.

"I can't." Nevertheless, she stopped hopping and plonked

down on a stool, put her elbows on her knees and her chin in her hands. "So?" she said to Alice. "How big is the house? It must be enormous! Her father is a gentleman, is he not?"

"Jane," their father scolded. "Don't pry." He popped a pin in his mouth and poked another through the hem of the doublet he was mending. The pale blue cloth spread over his knee and the lace edge touched the newly laid rushes. It was a costume worn by Edward Style in their latest play.

Alice frowned, searching for Minerva's father's name. She smiled through sheer relief when she remembered it. "Sir George Peabody is a gentleman scientist, but that doesn't make him rich." She didn't know what degree of wealth the Peabodys had so she decided to give answers that said as little as possible.

"He must be," Jane said with absolute certainty. Her restless, ten-year old body began to wriggle again and her father shot her another scowl but with a pin in his mouth, he remained silent.

"How many servants do they keep?" her mother asked, dipping a wooden spoon into the pot.

"I'm not sure," Alice said. She too squirmed in her seat but not for the same reason as Jane. In contrast, Elizabeth, her grave thirteen-year old sister, sat almost still. Only her fingers nimbly worked at trimming an old hat of Alice's.

"Not sure? What were you doing there all that time?" her mother pressed. She tucked a strand of gray hair behind her ear and regarded Alice with pride. "Just think, my beautiful girl making friends with gentle-folk. How you do rise, Daughter."

Alice blushed. Sink was more like it. Today especially. Last night she'd risen on emotions so high, so sweet, she'd been flying. But today her heart felt like it was weighted down with a pile of bricks. She looked at her lap until she'd blinked back her tears. She must not think of Warhurst, of their night together, and of his subsequent coldness.

Unfortunately it was all she *could* think about. It made lying even more difficult.

"I didn't see all the maids," she said. "Just the one assigned to me."

"You had your own maid!" Jane exploded with a whoop.

"Jane," their father warned, removing the pin from between

lips overhung with whiskers. "Calm yourself. Let's hear what your sister has to say. And quickly for we must go, Alice."

"Yes, tell us more, Alice," Jane said. "What was the bed like?"

"Cold without you and Elizabeth," she said truthfully. Elizabeth looked up from her work and smiled prettily. Jane shook her head and said, "That's not what I meant."

"Big," Alice said. "And soft."

"Was there a lot of silver plate on display?" her mother asked. "What did you sup on?"

Alice told them as much as she could, blending actual events from her night at Blakewell House with what she guessed might have occurred had she been staying with Minerva. The lies grew easier to tell as her family listened ravenously. She even included a tale to explain how she cut her arm involving a pair of scissors and a clumsy maid.

"Come, Alice," her father said, rising from the table. "We must go or Style will lose his temper."

"He's always losing his temper," Jane said crossly.

"Hush, child." Their mother frowned at her. "You shouldn't say such things, not even to us. Without Roger Style, your father would not have work."

Jane pouted. "That may be so but he's still a horrid man."

Alice smothered a smile then kissed both her sisters on their foreheads. "I missed you two. Be good and help Mama. I'll see you both later and you can help me with Minerva Peabody's wedding gown."

Elizabeth's eyes lit up. "Oh, *can* we? Alice, you are so good to us. To work on something so fine would be a joy."

"Yes, you must make something fit for a grand lady like Mistress Peabody," Jane said.

Their father snorted softly. "Might I remind you that Mistress Peabody is a playwright, not royalty. And might I also remind you that you are my assistant first and foremost, Alice. The wedding gown can wait."

It was time to tell him, tell them all. There'd never be a better opportunity. Alice blew out a breath. "I am your assistant for *now*, Father, but not forever. I have different plans for my future."

Everyone stared at her for several minutes—at least that's

how long it felt. "Plans?" her father finally spluttered. "What plans?"

"To open a shop and make fine clothes. The very finest. Minerva's gown will be my first."

More staring. Beside her, Elizabeth swallowed loudly.

"But," her mother began. She held her wooden spoon up in the air and the juices ran unchecked down the handle. "But why?"

Alice knew they wouldn't understand but she had to try and explain it to them somehow. She owed her parents that much. "Because I can't be Father's assistant forever—."

"Why not?" he bellowed. "What is wrong with being my assistant? It is an admirable occupation for a girl such as yourself."

That was the crux of the issue. *A girl such as herself.* It wasn't enough. It never would be. "I want something more," she said. She shook her head. That wasn't quite right. "I want something *else.* I want to do things I've never done before. Things that others take for granted."

"Who?" her mother asked.

"And what *precisely* are they doing?" her father said. He looked like a thunder cloud about to unleash a storm on a picnic.

"No one in particular," she quickly said. "And they aren't doing anything bad, simply...adventurous. I find I'm a little bored of late, that's all. I wish to—."

"Bored! Bored!" Her father loomed above her, his flowing white beard trembling with his rage. Elizabeth shrank back. Jane stayed mercifully silent and still for once. "What has got into you, Alice?"

She bowed her head. "I knew you wouldn't understand."

"How can we?" her mother said, plopping down on a stool and slouching as if she were an empty sack. "You say you want to be something more, but how is opening your own shop going to achieve anything? It sounds like a great deal too much work for one girl."

"Not something more, Mama, something *else.* I want to be something other than the seamstress who works for Hawkesbury's Men."

"And what is wrong with that?" her father snapped. "It's nothing to be ashamed of." He eyed her critically. "You haven't become one of those woeful Puritans, have you?"

"No!" She sighed. This was hopeless. "You don't understand. I am not ashamed of who I am, I am simply bored with it. I associate with the same people every day, most of them men, and not a single one of them really notices me. I am not Alice Croft but John Croft's daughter."

"That is nothing to be ashamed of," her mother said, pointing the wooden spoon at Alice. "I am very proud of your father. You should be too."

Alice sighed again. "I am." It was useless to go on. They didn't understand how she felt and never would.

Her mother rose and returned to the pot over the fire. "You are who you are. That will never change no matter what you do."

"Come, Alice," her father said quietly. "We must go."

They donned their cloaks and headed off to The Rose on the other side of the river. Her father grumbled most of the way about the extra distance and the pain in his knees. Alice, plunged into melancholy, didn't respond. First Warhurst's cold treatment and now this.

That the two were connected struck her when they were halfway across the bridge. Warhurst's behavior was simple to explain—she was a seamstress, daughter of a tiring house manager. She worked for her father and she would never earn enough to rise above the station she was born into. Perhaps if her shop ever became successful she might one day be mistress of her own life, but until then she was reliant on others' whims. Either way, it would never be enough to satisfy Lord Warhurst.

But to be fair, her dissatisfaction over her lot in life had begun many years ago. She wasn't quite sure when but ever since becoming a woman, she'd felt out of sorts with the rest of the world. She wasn't allowed to do anything interesting. She couldn't wield a sword, she couldn't go about at night, she couldn't even walk down certain streets without an escort. The amount of money her father gave her for her work was entirely at his discretion and everything that was hers was really his, including her clothing. The only thing she could safely say belonged to her was her mind and she might as well not have one of those either. It would certainly make life easier if she didn't think all the time, and wonder.

"I'm growing too old for this," her father said as The Rose loomed into sight above the other buildings. "Are you quite sure you want to have this shop?" he asked suddenly.

"Yes," she said. "Arrangements are already under way."

"Remarkable," he muttered. "But it's not really about the shop is it?" He didn't look at her but stared straight ahead at the street already packed with drays, carts and people from all walks of life. A goose girl herded her flock towards the bridge and two men had to step nimbly aside to let the gaggle pass.

Alice touched her father's arm and she felt him lean into her a little. "No," she conceded. "It's about being...somebody. Do you understand?"

After a moment he shook his head. "I concede I do not." He patted her hand. "You're a good girl, despite everything."

"Thank you."

He didn't appear to notice her dry tone. "Perhaps if you got married, you wouldn't be so concerned with all this shop nonsense."

She stopped walking. "Married!"

He stopped too and shrugged. "Yes. Don't you think it's a good idea? Marry a respectable man in a solid trade and you'll feel much better about everything. Trust me, marriage can fulfill a person. Now, do you know of any men that you might care for?"

She blinked at him. He was serious. Good lord! If only she'd kept her mouth shut about the shop until the last minute. "The only men I know are theater people," she said. Or, more to the point, they were the only men she knew who'd *marry* her. There were others—or one in particular—who'd *had* her.

He made a face. "Don't concern yourself, my dear. You are young yet and most men your age are still completing their apprenticeships. In a year or two they'll be in need of a wife as capable and pretty as you. You'll see. I'll ask around the guild. Someone will turn up, perhaps even a man who wishes to have a shop. Or if you prefer someone older—."

"No!"

He chuckled into his snowy beard. "Very well." He patted her hand. "A young husband you will have. In the meantime, you'll remain my ever-efficient assistant. No lad could match you as a tailor!"

She sighed. It's not that she had an aversion to marrying, she just didn't want to think about it at that moment. Not when her thighs quivered at the memory of Warhurst thrusting between them and the ghost of his kisses warmed her throat, her breasts.

She was so grateful to arrive at The Rose she didn't even care when a green-faced Freddie ran into her, failed to apologize then barely managed to reach the gutter before he added the contents of his stomach to the already stinking ditch.

"You're putrid!" Roger Style shouted at him from the back door that led to the tiring house. "Don't come back in here until you've finished. I don't want my gowns ruined."

"Too much drink again?" Alice asked Henry Wells and Will Shakespeare when she got inside. They sat side by side on stools, blonde head and dark bent over the only complete copy of the play.

"Aye," said Wells.

"Care to read his part?" asked Shakespeare. "I dare say you'll do an admirable job of acting the role of a woman."

Alice smiled at the twinkle in his gentle brown eyes. "Alas I have work to do," she said.

"That she does," Style said, striding past them to the stairs. "Get one of the hirelings to read."

"I can spare her for a while," her father said.

Style paused, his foot on the bottom stair. He raised an eyebrow and Alice thought he would argue with her father but he nodded instead. "Very well. She's your assistant. But I'll wager she does a poor Isadora. It requires a man's skill to understand the nuances of a character like her."

"A man?" Shakespeare muttered quietly so that only his two companions heard. "It's a wonder he thinks Freddie is capable then."

Alice smothered her smile but Wells wasn't quite so discreet.

He barked out a laugh and received a narrowed glare from Style before the manager disappeared up the stairs.

She spent the remainder of the morning practicing lines, mending costumes alongside her father and setting up the tiring house for the afternoon's performance. Just as the company prepared to dine at a nearby inn, Alice made her excuses and left.

It was time to pay Warhurst a visit and find out if he'd spoken to Charles Grayshaw. Having the name of her former lover said by her current one had been a shock at first but she was no longer surprised they were acquainted. It made sense that the two gentlemen knew each other—they both frequented court after all.

It was odd that she'd been attracted to both, although Charles held no interest for her anymore. They were nothing alike. Charles was charming and funny and Warhurst was so forbidding and serious. Yet they were equally matched when it came to their treatment of her. Neither considered her a suitable marriage prospect. And both had hurt her deeply because of it.

CHAPTER 15

$\mathcal{A}$lice crossed the river over the bridge to save the expense of a wherry and made her way to Dowgate Street where she tapped on the servant's door near the kitchen and asked the maid if Lord Warhurst was home. He was not.

She thanked her and left but only got as far as the nearby lane. Safely hidden in the shadows, she could see everyone coming and going from Blakewell House. But after a few minutes she began to feel like a coward for spying and was about to return to the house and tell the maid she would wait after all when Warhurst rode past.

"My lord!" she called out.

He turned in the saddle, his beautiful green eyes wide. "Mistress Croft!" He dismounted faster than a blink and was at her side. "Are you unwell? Your arm..."

"My arm is unchanged."

He rubbed the horse's nose and turned his face away from her. "Then what are you doing here?"

She bristled at his bluntness. So it was to be like that between them now. He couldn't even muster a polite tone let alone look at her. The man really was the heartless creature she'd pegged him to be on their first meeting.

"Two things," she said crisply. "First, I wish to know when our business arrangement will be finalized."

The sudden turn of his head made his horse take a jittery step. Warhurst held it steady, all the while looking at Alice. Glaring more like it, with his top lip curled. She'd never seen him look so...cruel. She swallowed then tossed her head.

"Well?" she prompted. She would not be intimidated nor would she apologize for their lovemaking. It had been wonderful. But that was in the past and with a different man, a man who liked her for herself and didn't see her as a base-born seamstress hardly better than a whore from the Bankside stews.

"You will get your shop in due course. All is not yet in readiness."

"And the fabrics."

"I haven't forgotten our agreement. The second thing?"

"How did you fare with Charles Grayshaw?"

He went back to patting his horse's neck. "This is no longer your affair, Mistress Croft. Thank you for your—."

"No!"

He lifted an eyebrow. "Pardon?"

She thrust her hands on her hips and took a step towards him so she could speak low and not be overheard by passersby. What she had to say was not fit for strangers' ears. "I said no. I will not be shut out from this, not like you've shut me out of the rest of your life so very thoroughly. I may be only a seamstress, Lord Warhurst, but I have as much pride as you. You will not treat me like a whore and use me then discard me. Not in this."

"I didn't—."

"You *did*."

His Adam's apple jerked with his hard swallow. "I'm sorry," he said. "I didn't think..." He shook his head and huffed out a breath. "What do you want from me?"

"I want you to allow me to continue to help your sister. I like her and I can see how much she's hurting. I want you to treat me like a partner, an equal partner, in this investigation."

"I'm not sure it's for the best." He studied the daubed wall behind her. "Not after last night. Not after..." He took his horse's bridle and began to move off. "It's a bad idea."

Alice blocked him. "Tell me what Charles Grayshaw said."

"Nothing! He couldn't help. Now move aside."

"Couldn't help or *wouldn't*."

"What does it matter? Grayshaw is in a delicate situation. If he's caught helping me, he may lose his position. I can't ask a friend to risk his livelihood over this."

"Charles? Lose his livelihood?" She snorted. "I doubt it. That man could charm his way out of a situation ten times worse than what you're asking him to do."

Warhurst's face went from white to gray to red and back to white again. "Grayshaw," he said flatly. "You know him."

"He was my previous lover, yes." She shrugged. "What of it?"

He went very still. "You could have told me."

"Why? Would it have mattered?"

"He's my friend."

"Oh lord." She rolled her eyes. "I suppose there's a gentleman's code of honor about sleeping with the same lover even though two years has passed between you. Well I hardly think honor has played a very big part in any of this, do you? And since it has been made pointedly clear that neither of you *gentlemen* plan on returning to my bed, I don't care what either of you think."

He had the decency to look sheepish at least, although his chest rose and fell with his hard, ragged breathing. It was only a hint of anger but it was better than the cool disinterest of earlier. At least it meant he was capable of feeling.

She was too angry to say goodbye so she simply turned and walked away. But Warhurst caught her arm, her uninjured one.

"Where are you going?" he snapped.

"To see Charles."

His grip tightened. "Why?"

"I might be able to make him see reason where you could not."

"How?" The word was more snarl than speech.

She squared up to him and tilted her chin. "How do you think?" She wasn't sure why she said that. It only seemed to fuel his anger. But she was angry too! Furious. She'd vowed never to allow a man to undermine her again after Charles Grayshaw had unwittingly chipped away at her self-confidence, but it was happening anyway. Two lovers, twice discarded because she wasn't good enough to be anything more than their forgettable plaything.

And being angry suppressed the hurt, just a little, and made her feel strong again, whole. She would need that strength if she was to get through the bleakness enveloping her and come out the other side.

His nostrils flared and his gloved fingers flexed, firming their grip. Alice refused to wince. "Unless you want to render this arm an injury as well," she said, "then you'd better let me go, my lord."

His hand dropped to his side. "I'm sorry," he whispered. "But I forbid you to see Grayshaw."

"You have no authority to bid me to do anything. Charles Grayshaw is—."

"Is a popular person right now." It was Lord Hawkesbury, mounted on a gray. Alice had not seen him approach. She'd been much too intent on Warhurst. There could have been a brawl on Dowgate Street and she'd not have noticed it.

Hawkesbury dismounted. "Care to tell me what you and Grayshaw were discussing at court this morning?" he asked Warhurst.

"That was a private conversation," Warhurst said. "As is this one." Even as he said it he faced up to him. They were of a height, both dark and broad shouldered, but Warhurst rippled with fury.

"Then you should have conducted both in a more private place," Hawkesbury said cheerfully. "I cannot help it if I happen to be wandering past and overhear you." He bowed to Alice. "It's Mistress Croft, isn't it? My seamstress?"

"She's not *your* anything, Hawke. Go away."

"Now that's not a very nice way to speak to someone who only wishes to be your friend."

"You and I will never be friends. Not after what you did to my sister."

Hawkesbury's good humor vanished so quickly Alice wondered if it had been there at all. "Have a care, Warhurst," he said. "Anyone can hear you."

"Then let's proceed further into the lane."

"Gladly."

They tied their horses to a nearby post then sank further back. The jutting upper levels of the houses on both sides of the narrow lane almost met overhead, casting the two men in deep shadow. Alice followed them.

"So, you and Charles Grayshaw..." Hawkesbury said. "Care to tell me why you were discussing me?"

"No."

Alice held her breath. They were like two big bears in the baiting ring but without the chains tethering them. Anything could happen.

"You're going to deny you were talking about me?" Hawkesbury asked calmly.

"No." Warhurst clenched and unclenched his fists at his sides. "But I won't tell you the nature of our conversation."

Hawkesbury removed his riding cloak and threw it over a crate lying upturned on the dirt. One by one, he undid the buttons on his dark blue velvet doublet. His movements were slow, deliberate, and he didn't take his eyes off Warhurst. "I'll give you one more chance," he said.

"Warhurst!" Alice cried. Both men turned to her as if they'd just remembered her presence. "He's going to hit you! Just tell him for God's sake. What does it matter if he knows? It changes nothing."

"Go home," Warhurst ordered her. "This is men's business."

"Then men are dolts! This can be resolved without the use of fists." She turned to Hawkesbury. "He was asking Charles Grayshaw if Sir Francis Walsingham's office has a file on your father. We have reason to believe—."

"Mistress Croft!" Warhurst took a step towards her but Hawkesbury grabbed hold of his cloak to stop him. Warhurst snatched the cloak away, swung his fist and punched Hawkesbury on the chin. Hawkesbury's head jerked to the side but otherwise he didn't move.

"Go home, Mistress Croft," Warhurst said. His tone was low, ominous, as he stared at the other man rather than Alice.

"Let me guess," Hawkesbury said. He didn't rub his chin, didn't back away from the tower of anger seething before him, but spoke levelly. "You've heard some nasty rumors about my father and you wanted to find out if they were true."

"The truth doesn't concern us as much as knowing whether Walsingham is aware of the rumor or not," Alice said. She half expected Warhurst to punch her on the chin too to keep her quiet but he didn't. He now had his back to her and it was as unyielding as an ancient oak. "Grayshaw was supposed to help us find out," she went on. "But he refused."

A flicker of something she couldn't identify passed over Hawkesbury's face. "Thank you, Mistress Croft." He gave her a brief bow. "Now if you'll kindly leave us, I have some business to discuss with Lord Warhurst in private."

She crossed her arms. "I'm staying here."

He bowed again. "As you wish, but kindly move back a few steps." Frowning, she did as he suggested. His gaze shifted to Warhurst and even in the poor light Alice could see his eyes gleam like cold metal. "Leave my family alone," he said. "That includes those who've passed on."

"My sister is sitting in our brother's house on the other side of Dowgate Street carrying your child," Warhurst said, pointing past Alice and down the lane towards the main road. "They are also your family whether you like it or not. You should be fighting for *them*, damn you, not letting someone like Enderby dictate—."

"You want me to fight for them?" Hawkesbury said, a vicious, mocking smile on his lips. "Good. Because I've wanted to do this ever since I met you." He punched Warhurst on the cheek, sending him reeling backwards into a doorway.

Alice gasped. She ran to Warhurst but halted when he re-emerged, fist swinging. Hawkesbury ducked but Warhurst's other fist was lightning fast and smashed into the earl's face.

Hawkesbury fell backwards. Warhurst removed his cloak and doublet and threw them onto the crate. He then withdrew his sword and a scream caught in Alice's throat. But instead of thrusting it through Hawkesbury's heart, he set it aside too.

"Get up," Warhurst growled.

Hawkesbury rose and removed his sword. He just finished leaning it against a wall when Warhurst landed another blow then another. Hawkesbury almost fell again but was saved by the wall. He pressed a sleeve to his lip. It came away bloody.

"Stop it!" Alice cried.

Neither man seemed to hear her. They stared at each other as if there was no one else in the world.

"Stop it or I'll fetch Lady Warhurst!" she shouted in exasperation. She couldn't think of anyone else who either man might respect enough to cease their ridiculous argument.

But her plea had no effect. She might as well have been a thousand miles away. Like two deer locking horns, they lunged at each other, landing blow after blow on faces, shoulders, chests, wherever they could find an opening. Their hard breathing turned to barbaric grunts. Blood splattered their elegant white shirts and their handsome faces bore cuts and the beginnings of bruises.

Foolish, ox-brained *men*! Why did they always resort to violence? If she didn't stop it soon no one would recognize them and it would achieve absolutely nothing.

She could strip naked but she wasn't sure either man would notice, they were so focused on hurting each other. Passersby had stopped to watch and a man leaned out of a window above. He shouted directions down to the two fighters before a woman joined him and told them all to keep quiet.

Alice tried another tactic. "Since you seem to have no need of me here, Warhurst," she called over the grunts, "then I think I'll go speak to our mutual friend." She didn't want Hawkesbury to know where she was going but she wasn't sure Warhurst understood the veiled reference to Charles Grayshaw either in his state. He certainly took a long time to respond.

But it eventually must have filtered through his punch-drunk haze because he half-turned and said, "Don't—!"

He never finished the sentence. The distraction gave Hawkesbury an opening and he landed a blow to Warhurst's nose, sending him to the dusty ground.

She ran to him and crouched down. "Are you all right?" She tilted his chin to inspect his nose and breathed a sigh of relief to see it only bled a little. Hawkesbury must have eased back before his fist connected.

Warhurst wiped the blood with his sleeve. "You distracted me," he said. But there was no malice in it, just simple statement of fact.

"I had to stop you two somehow." She cast a glare at Hawkesbury, standing to one side, breathing heavily and watching them with undisguised interest. Alice stood and crossed her arms. "You are both fools," she said to Hawkesbury. She no longer cared who he was. He might be an earl but he was behaving like a common tavern brawler. "Lilly will be horrified to learn you beat up her brother."

"He did not beat me up," Warhurst said, getting to his feet. "He landed a lucky blow because *you* distracted me."

Hawkesbury pulled at his cuffs in a useless attempt to straighten his disheveled appearance. "Unless you tell her, she'll never know. I doubt Warhurst will want to inform his sister of his humiliation."

"I am *not* humiliated! It was a lucky blow! Next time you see me get into a fight," he said to Alice, "please do me the courtesy of leaving the scene before you get me killed."

"You seemed to be well on the way to achieving that without my help."

Warhurst grunted. Hawkesbury, unexpectedly, chuckled. "You appear to have your hands full, Warhurst. And since I can't seem to knock any sense into you without doing some real damage, I shall tell you only one more time—cease your investigation. It will achieve nothing except great heartache. Understand?" He picked up his sword, cloak and hat which had come off during the fight. He clamped the hat on his head but carried the other items. "Good afternoon, Mistress Croft. I'm sorry you had to witness that but if you insist on associating with Lilly's mulish brother then you probably understand why such action was necessary." He bowed to her then walked off down the lane, a slight limp hampering his usual grace. He untied his horse and walked it down Dowgate Street out of sight.

Warhurst strapped his sword belt to his hip and swung his cloak around his shoulders to hide the blood splatters on his shirt.

"You might want to go to the kitchen and have Cook clean

you up before your mother sees you," she said. "You're quite a mess."

"Thank you," he said wryly. He headed down the lane to his horse, without limping she noticed, and untied it from the post.

"Do you need help?" she asked.

"I'm not an invalid."

She shrugged and moved past him. "Very well." She walked off, determined not to glance back at him. If she did, she knew the sight of his battered face would melt her resolve. It was only a small step to go from there to kissing his wounds better.

"Wait!" he called after her. "Tell me you are not going to visit Grayshaw."

"I am not going to visit Grayshaw," she repeated dully.

"Mistress Croft!" he shouted. "I forbid you!"

She did turn around at that. As she suspected, her heart skipped erratically at the sight of his emerging bruises but she managed to stay firm and not run back to him. "You cannot forbid me to do anything. Charles is an old friend. If I wish to see him then I shall."

His expression was one of anger, dismay or pain. It was difficult to tell beneath all the cuts and bruises. Perhaps it was all three. She sighed, spun on her heel and left him. The heat of his gaze burned into her back.

CHAPTER 16

*A*lice was met at Charles Grayshaw's Blackfriars house by his manservant who peered down his long nose at her, sniffed, and asked her to state her business. If he remembered her then he made no indication.

Alice gave him what she hoped was a dazzling smile. "Is your master at home?" she asked. Hopefully Grayshaw had returned there to dine and wasn't conducting business elsewhere.

The servant cast a critical eye over her again, frowned, then disappeared into an adjoining room, leaving her standing in the modest hall, wondering if she was doing the right thing.

Of course she was. No matter what concerns she had over the reaction she'd get from her ex-lover, this was one of those occasions when pride had to be set aside. It seemed pride was to always be the victim where Charles was concerned. He'd ended their relationship unexpectedly and Alice had been surprised and hurt. Her feelings for him had been strong and it wasn't until many months later that she realized what they'd shared wasn't love but something more akin to deep friendship.

Still, the reasons he'd given for ending the relationship stung. They were the same reasons why Warhurst didn't want to see her again. Today of all days she felt she had some justification for her bitterness towards both men. But if she wanted Charles's help she must swallow her bitterness and smile.

"Alice?" Despite the turmoil of old memories, the smooth, modular voice lifted her spirits instantly and turned her smile into a genuine one. "It is you!"

Charles Grayshaw hadn't changed at all. He was still the dashingly handsome young man whose cheeks dimpled when he grinned. "Charles. May I still call you that?"

He took both her hands and drew one to his lips. His kiss lingered slightly longer than was polite. "Of course you can. How are you?"

"The same," she lied. In truth, nothing was the same. Not since she'd last seen him and especially not since last night. It never would be again. "And you? You look well."

"Is that your way of saying I've aged and my looks are fading?" He grinned and she couldn't help laughing.

"Of course not. You are as handsome as ever. I'm sure you have all the court ladies swooning every time you walk into a room."

"Only my share," he said, "and unfortunately the heiresses have been warned away."

It should have pained her to hear that but it didn't. All she could do was smile at him. It was so lovely to see him and talk to him but not care for him. It would seem she was cured.

She had Warhurst to thank for that.

Warhurst. Always bloody Warhurst. Damn him.

"Alice, there is an alarming shine to your eye," he said with mock seriousness. "I haven't done anything to put that there, have I?"

"Of course not. It's simply nostalgia at seeing you again."

"You are a sweet girl for saying so although I know you're not the type to look back and regret." He took her hand again and pressed it to his cheek. His face grew soft as he regarded her through heavy lids. "It's good to see you again. Come into my study and we'll talk. I'd invite you into the parlor but there's no fire lit." He made a face. "I'm economizing."

He led her down a corridor past a series of domestic rooms to a large study with no adornments on the wood-paneled walls to soften its masculinity. He pulled two straight-backed chairs to the small fire and bid her to sit.

"So what can I do for you, Alice?" he said. "Anything that is in my power to do, I will."

She thought he would add "because I owe you that much" but he didn't. Whether it even occurred to him, she wasn't sure. The amiable smile certainly didn't leave his face, but that could be because he was aware of how handsome his smile made him. Charles Grayshaw had never doubted his appeal to the opposite sex.

"That's good because what I need to ask you is a little out of the ordinary, but I believe it's within your powers to bestow."

He forked an eyebrow. "Intriguing. Go on."

"You spoke to Lord Warhurst this morning at Whitehall, I believe?"

His other brow met its mate high up on his forehead. "Ye-es. Now I'm even more intrigued. Do you mean to tell me you *know* Lord Warhurst?" The way he said it left her in no doubt he was asking if she knew Warhurst in an intimate sense.

"We're acquaintances." She'd promised Warhurst she wouldn't link their names in public but this was an instance where that promise needed to be broken. Besides, she could trust Charles.

"Well, he never told me," he said.

"Should he?"

He shrugged. "I suppose not. But I'm not sure I like it. I mean he and I are friends and you and I were..." He coughed. "And now he and you..."

"I said *acquaintances*, Charles. I'm helping him with something and in turn he'll help me establish a shop."

His face cleared. "Ah. I see. So...a shop of your own? Extraordinary. Although if any woman is to succeed at such a venture it would be you. You always had too much spirit to remain working for your father forever."

She smiled and remembered why she liked him so much. He understood her. "Thank you. Am I to believe you did speak to Lord Warhurst then?"

"I did. And if the business he and I discussed has anything to do with your business with him then I must caution you to be careful." She rolled her eyes and he laughed. "Forgive me, I forgot who I was speaking to for a moment," he said. "Asking you to be careful when you have the scent of adventure is like asking a hungry cat to not chase the mouse."

"I like to think these last two years have taught me some sense on that score. But perhaps you're right. So, may I ask if he told you everything?"

"You can and he did." He briefly recounted Warhurst's tale. "And I'll tell you what I told Warhurst: my hands are tied. I can't help I'm afraid."

"Of course you can. We're not asking to see the letter or the file, simply that you tell us whether it exists or not. We want to know if Enderby passed on the knowledge to his superiors." She leaned forward, as did he, so that their heads almost touched. "And do not try to tell me you will lose your job over something so trivial. You, dear Charles, could talk yourself out of any sort of scrape if you set your mind to it."

He roared with laughter. "Is that what you truly think of me?"

"Well?" she said, ignoring him. "Will you do it? For me? For..." *For what we'd once meant to each other. For the hurt you caused me.*

He must have been thinking the same thing because his sparkling eyes dulled and his dimples vanished. "Of course. Indeed, it's already been done."

"Really?"

He nodded. "After Warhurst left I looked for the file." He shrugged. "I have a key to the storage room where the paperwork is kept so it was easy enough when no one was looking."

"You told Warhurst you could lose your job!"

"Ah. Yes, so I did. And I could if I was discovered, or if the file had been a sensitive one. But I wasn't discovered and Hawkesbury's file is painfully thin and hadn't been looked at in years. It was quite dusty. I was deciding whether to inform Warhurst or not when you arrived. Now you've saved me the trouble of a visit." The two dimples returned to his cheeks. "And given me the pleasure of your company."

"So there was nothing in it?"

"Nothing to cause any Hawkesbury, living or deceased, to

quake in fear." He waved his hand in the air. "A few vague rumors, never proved, but that's all. There are hundreds of files like it in our storeroom. Indeed, it's a measure of a noble gentleman's status to have a file. It shows he is an important man in the realm and worth watching, rather like having an ancestor's head removed for treason and stuck on the bridge's southern gate tower. It's a point of pride for some."

She grimaced. "I see your point. So there was no coded missive?"

He shook his head.

"Well, it's a relief to know it hasn't reached your superiors."

"I suppose you'll go to Warhurst and tell him now?"

"Of course. This is his affair. I'm simply helping where I can."

He nodded, thoughtful. He rested his elbow on the arm of the chair and propped his chin up with his fingertips. "I hope he appreciates you, Alice. More than I ever could."

"It's not like that," she said quickly.

He sighed and gazed into the flickering flames of the fire. "No, I suppose it's not. Not for someone like Warhurst."

"You mean stubborn, proud..."

He chuckled. "I mean someone as poor as, well, as me. And worse, he's got the scandal to smooth over."

Poor? Scandal? Her shock must have been evident on her face because he paled a little. "I think I've said too much."

"Not nearly enough. He's a baron, isn't he? He has lands up north."

He chewed his lip and rubbed his short beard. "I suppose I won't be telling you anything you can't find out from more biased sources," he said with a shrug. "Warhurst has a moderate estate and a rather barren one I believe. That's the problem. He needs money to determine if there's coal on his land but no one will lend it to him. That's where the scandal part comes in. About thirty years ago his father wanted to do exactly the same thing. Or so he said. He borrowed heavily off just about everyone in his circle, high and low born. However he never used the money on improvements to his estate, but rather on his mistress."

"Mistress!" Oh. Poor Lady Warhurst.

"From all accounts she was a gold-digger who ran him ragged and sent him to an early grave. She followed soon after, which must have been some consolation to the family."

Good lord, what a terrible time it must have been for those close to him. "And those people he borrowed money from still take their anger out on the current Lord Warhurst? Even after all this time and when it wasn't his fault?"

"Exactly. Most are of the opinion that the apple doesn't fall far from the tree. Bloody Warhurst in his pig-headedness rarely comes to court so none of them see what a fine gentleman he is. He's paid the debts off of course, but it hasn't changed matters. Indeed, that only served to impoverish his estate more."

"But his brother is wealthy, can't he lend him money?"

"Have you ever seen the two of them together? It's a marvel they haven't killed each other yet."

"I see," she said on a sigh. She rubbed her aching head. So much to take in. Charles's information explained a great deal about Warhurst's behavior.

Perhaps. Or perhaps not. Oh, how was she to know if any of this was connected to his coldness towards her?

"If I had any money I'd lend it to him myself," Charles said. "I know he'd find a way to repay me if the mines didn't produce."

She smiled weakly. "You're a good soul with much to offer the realm, Charles. I hope you will one day find happiness."

"Much to offer the realm but little to offer a wife," he said with false cheerfulness.

"Are you thinking of marrying?"

He regarded her with such intensity she had the awful sensation that he was going to say something he may regret. But fortunately the moment passed and his genuine smile returned. "Warhurst and I are pitted in battle over the hand of a wealthy widow. I'm afraid his title beats my position at court easily."

Alice's heart skidded to a halt. Her throat closed, her mouth went dry. Somehow she managed to mutter, "Oh."

"Yes," he said hollowly. "My thoughts exactly. Not sure I'm ready for marriage but if the right woman presents herself then I must put forward my suit. And this woman is infinitely suitable."

"You've met her?" she said in a voice barely above a whisper. "What's she like?"

He shook his head. "I've not seen her but Warhurst told me only this morning that she was pretty and gentle and good-natured."

She looked down at her hands, clasped in her lap. They were trembling. "She sounds perfect."

"Perfectly dull." He laughed again and took one of her hands. "Warhurst is welcome to her. I prefer a girl with spirit." He rubbed his thumb across her knuckles.

The action helped shepherd her scattered thoughts. She withdrew her hand quickly and he sat back suddenly. She'd wounded him.

So be it. He'd wounded her two years ago.

"Are you sorry for what...for what happened between us?" he asked, staring unblinking at her.

"Sorry? No, not at all. You were an experience I shall never regret."

His smile was sad. "I'm relieved. Only...I've never quite forgiven myself."

She squirmed in her seat. She'd wanted to say so many things to Charles since he'd left her. She'd wanted a chance to hurt him in return, to tell him that she thought his actions cowardly. She'd wanted him to come back to her on his knees so *she* could then walk away from *him*. But now that she had the opportunity, she found she no longer cared enough to do any of those things.

All she cared about was that Warhurst was getting married. To a pretty, kind, rich lady. A lady who probably came from a noble lineage, who knew her place in the world and always said the right thing at the right time. A woman who could lift him higher, not drag him down further.

She swallowed past the lump in her throat and closed her eyes against a wave of dizziness.

"Are you all right, Alice? You've become even paler and that's no mean feat."

"A slight ache in my head. I should go."

He walked her down to the hall. At the front door, he bowed

over her hand, kissed her cheek and wished her well. "I'm glad we had this meeting," he said.

"So am I. Goodbye, Charles." She turned and walked unsteadily down the street. Once she was out of sight of the house, she stopped and pressed her back against a brick wall and closed her eyes against the weak autumn sun.

He's getting married.

* * *

LEO'S KNUCKLES may have been split and bruised but he could still mess up Grayshaw's pretty face. Even from his position across the road, half obscured by a conduit, Leo could make out the look in his friend's eyes as he kissed the back of Alice's hand. Desire. The dog turd wanted her, despite their separation of...how long had she said? Two years? Not nearly long enough to forget her.

Clearly Grayshaw hadn't forgotten. But had the silver-tongued rat tried to remind her of their past during their little reunion?

More to the point, how far was Alice willing to go to get information?

The door closed and Alice paused as she leaned against a wall. A few heartbeats passed then she made her way down the street, passing Leo without seeing him. Nor did she see the muddy puddle until she stepped in it. She quickly hopped out, shook her soaked hem and swore at the puddle.

"It's hardly the fault of the puddle that you trod in it," he said.

She gasped but when she saw it was him, flicked the drops more vigorously in his direction. "It isn't my fault you are here and yet here you are to torture me once more."

"It is your fault," he said, trying for levity when all he wanted was to sit her down and make her tell him what had occurred in Grayshaw's house. "You practically threw down the challenge to me to meet you here as I sparred with Hawkesbury."

"I did no such thing. I was simply trying to stop him from killing you."

"Ha!"

"He may not have succeeded but at least he gave that proud nose of yours a few dents. Pity." She walked off and he was left wondering if she was referring to his damaged nose or the fact that Hawke failed to kill him. "Don't worry," she said when he caught up to her, "it hasn't marred your handsome face over-much. Indeed, I wouldn't be surprised if you attract more attention from the ladies. I'm sure they'll want to kiss your wounds better."

There was venom in her tone if not her words and it stung but the sting was lessened by one throw-away observation that made him want to smile, despite everything. "You think I'm handsome?"

She toyed with the stray wisps of pale hair fluttering at her cheek but not before he saw her blush. "When it comes to you, Warhurst, I try not to think at all. It makes my head ache and often leaves me with a feeling of emptiness afterwards."

He stopped, she didn't. Indeed, her strides lengthened. "What does that mean?" he called after her. When she didn't answer, he ran up and caught her by the arm, pulling her a little too roughly to a halt. "Enough of this nonsense. Tell me what happened in there."

She winced and too late he remembered it was her wounded arm. "Hell, I'm sorry. Does it hurt?"

"No," she said, but he suspected it was a lie.

"Allow me to inspect for myself." He went to take her arm but she put it behind her back. God's wounds but she was the most infuriating woman! "Mistress Croft, I hurt you now let me see."

"Don't distress yourself, you did not hurt me. Marlowe did."

He looked towards the sky and wished there was some advice amid the clouds about dealing with this woman. "I just want to see for myself that I did not add to your injury." It took every ounce of patience to speak calmly but it was worth it to see her body relax and a small smile soften her mouth.

"No."

Damnation! "Mistress Croft, I—."

"Why would I let you inspect my person when we are not

even on a first name basis?" She tilted her pert little chin, turned and walked off.

"I'm going to—." He bit his tongue before he attracted too much attention from the passersby and once more found himself walking quickly to catch up to her. "I'm going to strangle you," he said quietly when he reached her. "And I'll thoroughly enjoy every minute of it."

"If you do, you'll not find out what I learned from Charles."

Charles. It seemed she was on a first name basis with *him.* "Finally! I thought we'd never get to this point."

"Do you want to know or not?"

"Yes!"

She shot him a sideways glance then neatly stepped around a small puddle. She was no longer distracted it would seem. Leo apparently had the affect of sharpening her wits rather than muddling them like Grayshaw did. That comparison only made him want to hit something again, preferably Grayshaw's face and that was uncharitable considering he liked the man.

So, apparently, did Alice.

"Charles told me he went in search of the old earl of Hawkesbury's file after he spoke to you at court this morning."

"So much for losing his job," he mumbled. "And?"

"And there was nothing very interesting in it. There were certainly no coded letters that might implicate him in a plot."

"So either Marlowe lied or Enderby never passed it on to Walsingham's people."

"You think Marlowe lied?"

"No, I don't, because he knows I'll return to his rooms and ram my rapier down his throat if he did."

She gave him another sideways glance. "You are in a violent frame of mind today."

You don't know the half of it.

"So Enderby still has it," she said decisively.

"I'd wager he does." They walked side by side in silence while he tried to think what they should do next. But all he could think about was how Alice had learned that piece of news from Grayshaw. How far had she gone to get it?

As far as she'd gone to get what she wanted from me?

But that was absurd. Leo had already agreed to pay the rent for her shop *before* they'd bedded. There'd been no avaricious motives on her part that night. Of that he was certain. She'd asked for nothing and he'd promised her the same.

What else could she want from him then?

"Why are you looking at me like that?" she said, cutting off his thoughts.

He hadn't realized he'd been watching her. He quickly looked away and signaled a waterman on the river. They'd reached Paul's Stairs. Water slapped against the steps and the sides of a wherry just leaving with a gentleman passenger on board. It passed another wherry preparing to dock, the waterman steering with expert precision into the landing area. His two passengers alighted and he called out "Eastward 'ho!" with his inquiring gaze firmly on Leo.

"I was going to use the bridge," Alice said. She was still watching him, a deep frown drawing her brows together.

He resisted the urge to smooth it away with the pad of his thumb and instead stepped lightly down to the waterman. "This way is faster," he said. He could see the top of The Rose's polygonal roof directly across the river. It only covered the galleries and tiring house, of course, but it was prominent, nevertheless. Taking the bridge would add extra time to her journey. Time which might alarm her father or Style. "I'm sure they're beginning to worry about you."

"Hardly," she said on a sigh as she came up beside him. "I could miss the entire performance and no one would realize. Not even Father if he was busy."

He took her hand to help her into the wherry. The fingers were long and slender, like her, but held surprising strength. "Then they're all fools." As soon as he said it, he wished it back. He also wished he hadn't been holding her hand.

Her fingers tightened around his. Then, as if she'd been bitten, she suddenly let go. "Thank you." She settled into the bench seat and pulled out her leather pouch. Before she could pay the waterman, Leo pressed a penny into his callused palm.

"No, I'll pay," she protested.

The waterman simply chuckled and pushed off the stairs with his oar.

She twisted to look back at Leo standing on the landing. "What now?" she called out.

"Now you return to the theater and I return home." No, not home. Not yet. There was something he needed to find out first.

"That's not what I meant." Leo was sure he could hear the click of her tongue in annoyance, despite the splashing of the oars and the distance.

"We'll sleep on it," he shouted to her, "and discuss our thoughts tomorrow."

He couldn't quite make out her face anymore but he suspected she was scowling. Perhaps she didn't trust him to come to her. Or perhaps she thought sleep was out of the question. Whether it was for Leo depended greatly on what Grayshaw had to say.

CHAPTER 17

"**W**arhurst!" Grayshaw said upon Leo's arrival in his study. He indicated Leo's bruised and cut face. "Haven't you and your brother grown too old for that?"

Leo fingered his swollen lip. "This isn't Blake's handiwork. Some other fool got in my way."

"When will you learn that your fists will only get you so far? It's wit and charm that achieve the best results."

"When wit and charm lay an opponent flat, I'll consider employing them. For now, I prefer a solid punch."

"Wit and charm can lay the *women* flat, I assure you." Grayshaw chuckled and bade his old friend sit. Leo hesitated then sat on the only spare chair, situated to one side of the desk. "You just missed Mistress Croft." Grayshaw picked up a pile of papers and began to shuffle them over and over. "I believe you two are...acquainted."

"As I believe are you," Leo shot back.

Grayshaw returned the papers to his desk upside down and finally met Leo's gaze. "We were once. Acquainted I mean." He laughed nervously. When Leo didn't join in, he tried to cover it by clearing his throat. "Can I ask how well you are...acquainted with Alice?"

"No."

Grayshaw's brows rose. "I see."

166

"No. You don't. I hardly know her. She's helping me with information gathering, as you know. We aren't even friends." None of which was a lie. It wasn't quite the truth either but Leo wasn't prepared to dwell on that.

"Oh." Grayshaw's dimples appeared with his sudden grin and he leaned back in his chair. "Good to hear. She did assure me there was nothing between you but..." He shrugged and left the sentence unfinished.

"What? Are you jealous?" Leo tried to make it sound flippant, as if he were teasing, but it was hard when the words felt like sand on his tongue.

Grayshaw scoffed. "Certainly not." He ran his hand absently along the edge of the desk. "What a ridiculous notion."

"Then tell me, what is the nature of your relationship with Mistress Croft?"

Grayshaw's hand stilled. "I'm not sure that's any of your affair." The boyish good humor was gone and for the first time since they'd met many years earlier, he looked like he wanted to smash his fist into Leo's nose. So much for wit and charm.

Leo shrugged. "I like to know about the people who work for me."

Grayshaw smiled again. "I was under the impression she was working *with* you, Warhurst, not *for* you. Alice doesn't take orders well from anyone, not even her father I suspect. It's a good thing she'll have her own shop soon. I commend you for helping her in that endeavor, by the way. I wish I could have done something like that for her." The smile remained on his face but it turned sad, distant.

A clamp closed around Leo's heart and squeezed. "You haven't answered my question. What is the nature of your acquaintance with Mistress Croft?"

Grayshaw drew in a deep breath and crossed his arms. "If I fail to answer will you leave it alone?"

"No."

"I didn't think so." He sighed. "We were lovers. It ended two years ago."

"I said what *is* the nature of your acquaintance, not *was*."

"There is no is. Today was the first time I'd seen her in two years and all we did was talk. She asked me about Hawkesbury, the same as you did this morning. There's not much in his file, by the way."

"I know. I spoke to Mistress Croft just now. Thank you," he added as an afterthought.

"If you saw her then why didn't you ask *her* about the nature of our relationship?"

Leo didn't speak for a few heartbeats then said, "I thought you'd give me a more honest answer."

"Alice isn't dishonest, Warhurst. Indeed, she's one of the most trustworthy people I know. And kind too. So if you hurt her..." He wagged a finger at Leo but must have seen the look on his face and withdrew it before Leo snapped it off.

"The way you hurt her?" Leo finished for him. He wasn't sure what prompted him to say it. Alice hadn't given him any real indication that her relationship with Grayshaw had ended badly, and yet...and yet...

"She never loved me." Grayshaw spoke quickly as if he'd wanted to say it for some time. "Despite..." He shook his head. "The feelings between us were not equal. I knew that, although I'm not sure she did at the time." He waved his hand. "Besides, it wasn't a relationship that had a future. You of all people should understand that."

Leo knew. God how he knew it.

"If she never loved you, why was she with you?" Leo's voice sounded overly loud cutting through the thick silence that shrouded them. But he had to slash through it, had to know more. Had to. "What did she want?" Grayshaw shrugged. Leo leaned forward. "Tell me. What did she want from you?"

"Nothing." Grayshaw buried both hands in his hair and shook his head. "I don't know. I offered her nothing. I had nothing to give!"

Leo rose and looked down at his friend, his head still in his hands. He wasn't sure if he felt sorry for Grayshaw or not. He did know he no longer wanted to wring his neck. "You could have given her your name," he managed to say. The clamp around his insides tightened, squeezed like the devil.

Grayshaw barked out a laugh. "Don't be absurd." He stood

and met Leo's gaze with a steady one of his own. "You of all people should know the impossibility of someone like her marrying someone like me. Like us. I may not have the title like you, Warhurst, but I have just as much pride and ambition."

"I don't have ambition," Leo snapped. "What I have is duty to my family, to my tenants and my lineage."

Grayshaw's mouth twisted. "Same thing."

"It doesn't matter anyway. We're not talking about me. My relationship with Mistress Croft is based on a financial arrangement, that's all."

Grayshaw rolled his eyes. Leo wanted to reiterate the point but kept his mouth shut. Protesting more would only dig the hole he'd stumbled into deeper.

Grayshaw walked him to the front door. They shook hands on the threshold but there was no warmth in it. "Good luck," Grayshaw said.

"With what?"

"The Finchbrooke widow."

Christ. Leo had forgotten about Catherine. "You too."

Grayshaw shook his head. "I have no chance with her. Not now."

"Why not now?"

Grayshaw shrugged. "It doesn't matter. Anyway, I'm not sure I can marry someone I've never met."

"Lucky you're not royalty then," Leo said. It was an attempt to lighten the mood between them but it failed pathetically. Melancholy seemed to have settled on Grayshaw's shoulders.

"Sometimes I wish I was a simple tailor," he said. "Someone with no ambition beyond being good at my trade. Someone who didn't have to resort to desperate measures to satisfy his desires."

Leo swallowed and looked down at his boots, then forced himself to look up at his friend. "So you could be with Mistress Croft?" he said.

Grayshaw shrugged. "The irony is, I don't think she'd be interested in me if all I could offer her was the life of a tailor's wife."

Leo said nothing. How could he when his friend was right?

Alice wanted more than the life she was born to. She'd tried to get it from Grayshaw.

And now she was trying to get it from him.

He left Grayshaw standing in the doorway and headed home on feet that felt like they were made of clay. He wanted to find Alice, wanted to shake her until she admitted the truth, admitted that she'd slept with him to get more from him than rent and some fabrics.

Or until she denied it.

He pressed the heel of his hand to his eye but that only made the bruise there throb. Confronting Alice would be a stupid thing to do. Especially now while he couldn't think straight and he was liable to say something he later regretted. Best to wait until the blood pumping through him had settled and his heartbeat steadied.

That meant not thinking about her at all. An impossible task considering his mother took one look at Leo's bruises when he arrived at Blakewell House and said, "Did you incur those over that seamstress?"

Leo had wanted to avoid his family until he could inspect the damage Hawkesbury had caused but the ever-present Greeves had met him at the door and insisted Lady Warhurst needed to speak to him. Delaying the meeting would only delay the inevitable lecture so Leo went straight to her withdrawing room where he found her sitting at her desk.

He kissed her on the cheek she raised to him. "Do you mean Alice Croft?" he said.

"Have you been spending time with any other seamstresses lately? And before you try to tell me you haven't seen her since she left here this morning, I should warn you I saw you two speaking a short time ago."

He strode to the window and peered at his reflection in the glass. A half-closed black eye, cut lip and bruised cheek looked back at him. "Been spying on me again, Mother?"

"Gazing out my window on occasion is not spying. I saw you together across the road, just before you and Lord Hawkesbury disappeared down that lane."

He switched his focus to the far side of Dowgate Street. Just his luck that his mother would be looking out her window at the wrong moment.

"My disagreement with Hawkesbury had nothing to do with Mistress Croft. It was over Lilly, of course."

"Of course." Her pen scratched across the paper as she signed her name with a flourish. "I hope he knocked some sense into you, Son."

He swung around to face her. "I'll not end my quest, Mother, if that's what you mean. I will make him marry Lilly. I'm not sure why you keep insisting I leave it alone."

She returned her pen to the ink stand and regarded him with her shrewd, narrowed gaze. "Because Lilly assures me it is fruitless. I believe her. And that's not what I meant."

He cocked an eyebrow. "Ah. You were speaking of Mistress Croft again."

Her lips flattened at the mention of Alice and her gaze darted back and forth across his face, as if she were searching for something there. "Yes," she said. "I am." When he said nothing, she rose and came toward him. She linked her fingers in front of her skirts and regarded him openly. "What is she to you?"

He sighed. He was tired of explaining. Or attempting to explain. What Alice meant to him defied any reasonable explanation. He didn't entirely understand it himself. She was more than an acquaintance. His conversation with Grayshaw had taught him that much and now that he was calmer he could see a little more clearly. He cared about her. Cared that she wasn't going to get her heart broken by Grayshaw. Cared that she was going to find happiness with her shop.

But that was all. Absolutely, definitely nothing else.

"She's my friend, Mother. Nothing more."

She stared at him so long he worried that she could see into him, see what he was feeling. Perhaps he should ask her to interpret what she saw there because he couldn't.

"Good," she said emphatically. "The last thing we need now is a scandal. Even a whiff of something inappropriate could waft up to Northumberland and create a stink. Catherine's father wouldn't tolerate it, not with those puritanical tendencies of his."

A prick of heat swept up Leo's spine and flared before his

eyes. "Don't," he said but it was drowned out by the pounding in his ears.

His mother turned away as if she didn't hear him. "It might be best not to speak to your *friend* until the betrothal with the Finchbrooke widow is sealed." She sighed and sat at her desk. "Let's hope it's settled before Lilly's condition becomes obvious. Perhaps you should also stay away from Lord Hawkesbury too before someone grows suspicious about your constant bickering. Is that clear?" She looked up at him and frowned. "Good lord, are you unwell? You've gone quite pale."

"Don't tell me what to do, Mother." He strode across the room, pulled open the door with a jerk, walked through and slammed it so hard the walls shook.

"Ah," said Blake, lounging on the landing. "In one of your tempers, I see."

Leo grabbed him by the front of his doublet and shoved him back into the wall. "You puss-ridden scum!"

Blake held up his hands in surrender but he looked anything but contrite. The fool smiled. Leo punched it off.

"What the hell was that for?" Blake said, shoving Leo away. "Just because someone used your face as a punching bag doesn't mean you have to make mine match. I have to go see Min later." He suddenly smiled. "If I get some sympathy out of it, I won't make you pay next time I see you."

Leo grunted an apology.

Blake rubbed his chin. "So who'd you offend?"

"No one." He strode past Blake but his half-brother followed him down the stairs.

"I find that hard to believe."

"Believe what you like. It's none of your business."

"Speaking of which, how is your business proceeding with Hawke? I assume it's your pursuit of him that resulted in your face getting rearranged."

They reached the bottom of the stairs but Blake kept following him into the main hall. "He asked me to stop pursuing the matter. I refused. We settled the disagreement with our fists."

"I see. So Hawke won and now you have to leave him alone."

Leo stopped and his brother halted alongside him. A couple

more bruises, one on each eye, wouldn't look amiss on Blake's smug face. "You have so little faith in my ability to fight that you think I lost?"

Blake had the decency to appear apologetic. "You could best almost anyone, Leo, except me and perhaps Hawke. He's good with a sword and as capable with his fists so I hear. Does that answer make you feel better?"

Leo snorted. "You think I can't beat you? Your memory is short, Brother. Have you forgotten the time I made those womanly lips of yours bleed?"

Blake rocked on his heels and shook with laughter. "How could I? Mother made us both muck out the stables for a month. The grooms thought it a great joke. But that was years ago. I've improved since then."

Leo took a step closer to his brother. "Care to test that theory?"

"You want to fight me? Here?" Blake held out his arms, inviting his brother to take another swing. Leo didn't think it would be as easy as the last punch. No matter what he said to Blake's face, he knew his brother was a tough fighter and now he was prepared for the blow.

"God knows I want to hit *someone*," Leo ground out, clenching his fists. "And you're already here."

Blake laughed but kept a close eye on Leo. "This endeavor to uncover Hawke's secret is sending you mad. I'll have to warn Alice to stay away from you. It's not safe."

"Do that. I'll be grateful." As would his mother. And possibly Grayshaw.

"Ah. I see." Blake's smile turned sly.

"See what?"

"Nothing."

"Tell me!"

"Very well," Blake said. He looked like he was enjoying himself. "She's got to you, hasn't she?"

"What's that supposed to mean?"

"It means you slept with her last night while she was here, and now you can't get her out of your mind."

Leo snorted and stalked off down the corridor to the kitchen.

Blake followed him. Again. "What makes you say that?" he asked when his curiosity became too much to bear.

"The mere mention of her name makes you flinch. As if you can't decide if you *want* to hear it or would rather eat hot coals."

"Now you're the mad one," he said over his shoulder. The corridor was too narrow for them to walk side by side. "Being in love is going to your head and turning it soft."

"I'd rather be soft-headed than soft-bellied. You can't even own up to how you feel about Alice."

Leo stopped and rounded on Blake. The two stood only inches apart, their gazes locked. Blake's eyes danced with amusement. "I have no feelings for Mistress Croft," Leo said under his breath. "She and I are friends. We have a business arrangement. You know that."

Blake cocked an eyebrow. He wasn't in the least afraid of Leo or his temper. He was one of the few people who never had been. "Then how do you explain last night?"

There was no point denying he'd slept with Alice. Blake always knew when Leo was lying. "A momentary lapse of concentration on my part. She's a pretty wench under the same roof as me—it was inevitable."

Blake scoffed. "A pathetic excuse. And it doesn't explain it from her point of view."

"What do you mean?"

"Why did she let you into her room? Her bed? Was it a momentary lapse on her part too? Or something more?"

Leo pressed his palm to the wall to steady himself. He didn't want to hear this, not from Blake. He'd already had the same conversation with himself after his visit to Grayshaw. If he drew his sword now he could avoid it, but the narrowness of the corridor made a sword fight impossible.

"Perhaps she had another motive in mind," Leo said, taking control of his breathing with effort. "She's not the sort of woman who does something without a good reason."

"True. But I think we'll disagree on the reason." Blake crossed his arms and ankles and leaned one shoulder against the wall. "Why do you think she did it, Leo? God knows it's not because you charmed her."

Leo took a moment to gather his thoughts. "Alice Croft is a shrewd woman," he finally said. "Let's leave it at that." He turned and continued on to the kitchen. Hopefully some servants were there. Blake would leave him alone in their presence.

But Blake stopped him again with a hand to his shoulder. "You think she did it for money!" He spun Leo around. "You're more heartless than I thought."

"How would you know her motives?" Leo hissed. "Do you know her well, do you? *Do you?*"

"Not very well, but—."

Leo shoved Blake's hand away. "Then don't lecture me. This conversation is finished."

Blake shook his head and held up his hands in surrender. "Truce. What I really wanted to ask you was how you got on at court this morning. Did you have any luck?"

Leo frowned. "Luck?" He was still thinking about Alice and what his brother was driving at, and now he had to talk about court?

"Gathering financial support for your mines."

"Of course." Leo tugged on the hem of his doublet. "Everyone's throwing money at me."

"Don't be sarcastic." Blake stepped closer and grasped Leo's shoulder. "Let me give you—."

"No! I don't want your damn charity, Blake. I don't want your money, your hospitality or your advice. My affairs are mine and mine alone. They are *nothing* to do with this family." He strode off. This time he couldn't hear Blake's footsteps following him. Good. He'd had enough of his brother's company.

But Blake, as usual, had to have the last word. "If that were the case then why are you trying to fix Lilly's life for her?" he called out. "You care, Brother. I know you do. Perhaps not about me, but about Lil. And Mother."

Of course Leo cared. That was the whole bloody problem.

CHAPTER 18

lice was glad to see Minerva Peabody in The Rose theater's tiring house in the morning. Since sleep had eluded her for much of the night, she'd set about making Min's wedding gown but without accurate measurements, she could only do so much.

"I adore it," Min said, handing back the sketch Alice had made of the gown. "It's so elegant and fashionable." She lifted her arms so Alice could measure her waist.

"I think it would look lovely in green velvet," Alice said, writing down the measurement beside the sketch. "Emerald green like..." Warhurst's eyes. She shook the image from her mind. "Like emeralds. With silk cuffs edged with silver and a matching ruff at the neck. Oh, and pearls on the sleeves, bodice and hem."

"Lovely," Min said dreamily. "But so much work. Are you sure you have the time?"

"Of course. Besides, it's not work when you enjoy it. I adore making beautiful gowns." And wearing them. Apart from Lady Dalrymple's crimson gown, she rarely got to try on gorgeous clothes before they were altered to Freddie's shape. "My sisters are eager to help too so it'll be done in no time."

"You have sisters! You're so lucky. I've always wanted sisters. And brothers. Lots of them."

Alice took Min's arm and held it out to measure its length. "You'll have one of each soon," she said. "I know Lilly loves you already and Lord Warhurst admires you." She leaned closer. "He thinks you're quite brave taking on his brother."

"Brave!" Min laughed. "I'm petrified. I might make a terrible wife."

Alice dipped the pen in the ink pot and wrote down the measurement. "I doubt that. Besides, I think it's the woman marrying Warhurst who needs all the courage. And a very large hammer." At Min's raised brow, she added, "To smash through all that pride to get to his heart."

Min giggled. "Blake—I mean Robert—doesn't think his brother has one."

"A heart? I think he has one but it's frozen solid."

"Then his future wife will need a hammer and a flame."

Alice smiled. "More like an entire forge."

"Alert all the blacksmiths to lock up their daughters! Lord Warhurst is in need of a wife." They collapsed into giggles until Roger Style walked past and shushed them.

Freddie, sitting on a stool in the corner of the tiring house, mimicked his master's sourness so perfectly that everyone laughed. Style stopped at the stairs and looked around. He snarled at Freddie who gave him an impish smile then belched loudly. Style clicked his tongue, huffed out a sigh, and continued up the stairs.

"He'll cut short your apprenticeship if you're not careful," Shakespeare said.

"Don't care," Freddie said, rubbing his crotch. "There's always good work for someone like me."

"Someone like you?" Henry Wells echoed. "You mean loud, ignorant, disrespectful and more irritating than a rash?"

Freddie sniffed. "Someone who's good at pretending. Someone who can do voices and copy how others walk and stuff."

"Who told you that?" Shakespeare asked. He put down his copy of the play and gave Freddie his full attention.

"Kit Marlowe."

Alice touched her bandaged arm, well hidden beneath the

sleeve. Marlowe was little better than pond scum but he was dangerous. If she'd gone alone to his rooms... She shuddered to think what would have happened if Warhurst hadn't been there.

"He must have been mistaken," Wells said.

"What d'ya mean?" Freddie asked.

"He must have thought he was speaking to someone with a brain."

The tiring house erupted in laughter. All except for Alice who'd not really been listening. "He is in need of a wife, you know," she said to Min when the laughter died and everyone returned to their tasks.

"Marlowe?"

"Warhurst."

"Oh." Min frowned at her. "Yes, of course he is. He's a baron." As if that explained the need to wed.

Well, she supposed it did.

"Do you know if he has anyone in mind?" Min asked.

"A widow. Someone he already knows. She's very rich." Alice sat heavily on a nearby stool and rubbed her temples.

Min sat on the stool opposite and touched Alice's hand. "Are you all right?"

"Just tired."

"Are you sure there's nothing else?"

"Nothing else," Alice said without much conviction.

Min didn't look like she believed her. "So this has nothing to do with you spending the night at Blakewell House?"

Tears welled and Alice looked away, only to find herself meeting Shakespeare's gentle brown eyes. He lifted an eyebrow. "All right?" he mouthed.

She nodded and turned back to Min. Dwelling on what she couldn't have served no purpose. Warhurst had given her more than anyone and she should be thankful—he'd given her a future with her own shop. She *would* make a success of it.

She smiled wanly at Min who looked at her with such tenderness. "I'm a seamstress," she said, her voice small. "He's a lord. I don't think there's any need to say more." She stood and arranged the forepart of her gown to display a neat triangle of underskirt beneath.

"Now," she said, pulling together the frayed ends of her nerves, "you need to speak to your betrothed for me. I've purchased the velvet and pearls on credit through one of Father's suppliers. If you would be so kind as to have Blake settle the account in short order, I would be grateful." She picked up her sketch of Min's gown and tucked it into the pocket of her skirt. "As soon as I've—."

Warhurst strode into the tiring house through the door leading directly outside, cutting short whatever she'd intended to say—not that she could remember anymore. Everyone stopped what they were doing and stared at him as if he were an oddity. With his black eye and swollen lip, he looked more out of place than usual. One of the hired men stood and bowed. Freddie smirked and received a withering glare from Warhurst which made the lad's face flare crimson and the smirk vanish without a trace. Warhurst spotted Min and came toward her. He didn't once meet Alice's gaze.

"Blake is looking for you, Mistress Peabody," he said with a nod of greeting.

She stiffened. "And who are *you* looking for, Lord Warhurst?" Min's voice was as blunt as the wrong end of an axe. Considering she was usually as sweet as honey to everyone, it was quite a shock for Alice to hear her speak to her intended's brother in such a manner.

Warhurst too seemed surprised. "I, I..." He glanced around the tiring house. "Is Master Croft here?"

"Upstairs," Alice said. "Why?"

For the first time since he'd entered, he looked at her. "You and I have business to discuss," he spoke so quietly that only the three of them could have heard. "I wanted to ask your father for his permission to speak with you outside. Alone."

She could put her hands around his throat and throttle him. At least he had the decency to once again avoid her gaze. "You've not been concerned about asking my father's permission before this. Why start now?" She strode past the actors to the back door. "Well? What are you waiting for? Let's go." She left the tiring house without turning to see if he followed her.

He caught up to her outside. "I wanted to do the right thing," he said with all the stiffness she'd come to expect from him.

"Why? You've not cared about doing the right thing before."

She'd not thought it possible for his body to become even more rigid but he managed it. "That is an unfair accusation." His brow lowered into a deep scowl. "I've never had any intention of doing anything without your father's knowledge."

"Oh? You wanted to inform him *before* you ravished me? How thoughtful of you. Although I'm not sure he'd thank you."

His mouth twisted into a grimace. "I'd prefer not to discuss that incident, Mistress Croft."

"By all means. Let's sweep it out the door with the dust and forget about it."

"Forget it?" He took a step closer and lifted his hand. She thought he would caress her cheek but he checked himself. Even so, all the coldness and disappointment were sucked out of her by the nearness of him and the sheer force of his presence. "I can't forget it," he said, voice rumbling deep within his chest.

The tears that had never been far from her eyes all morning pooled again. She reached up and touched a fingertip to the cut on his lip. Air whistled between his teeth and he leaned into her hand. Just a little.

Then he stepped back. "We have to forget," he whispered. "*Have* to. Otherwise..."

She wanted to know what that 'otherwise' was but she dared not ask. Dared not even breathe for fear it might shatter her.

He cleared his throat and looked to the sky. It had begun to rain. Perhaps it had been raining the entire time.

"Let's find shelter," he said, taking her hand. The soft leather of his glove was warm against her skin and she curled her fingers into his as he pulled her along.

When they reached the nearest inn, he let go and removed his gloves. He flexed the fingers that had been linked with hers then caught her watching him and stopped. He hailed the innkeeper and ordered ales.

There were few other patrons, still being morning, and she and Warhurst sat on stools at a table near the fireplace. Soon their damp clothes were steaming and her fingers warmed up. She'd not grabbed her gloves before leaving.

"Cold?" he asked, reading her mind.

"Not anymore," she said, staring at the flames so she didn't have to look at him.

After a long silence during which a serving wench delivered their ales, he said, "I'm sorry. For a great many things but particularly for what happened between us at Blakewell House." He cleared his throat. "I should have employed more control."

She shot him a glance. He quickly looked away. A muscle in his jaw twitched and he took a sip from his tankard. "We both should have," she said. That was all she would say. She would not apologize for something she'd enjoyed, something that had affected her so profoundly. Nor would she tell him she accepted his apology. For all his aloofness, she didn't believe he was truly sorry for making love to her either. He'd certainly not shown any signs of being sorry on the night and it was that unguarded emotion that she trusted, not the mask he'd worn before and since.

"Good," he said. "Now, Hawkesbury."

So that was the end of that. She forced herself to concentrate on their other task. "We must remove the letter from Enderby's possession," she said. "The sooner we do that, the sooner this will be over." And she will no longer have to endure Warhurst's coldness towards her. She could proceed with the rest of her life.

"Yes," he said, much louder than necessary considering she was sitting right near him. "I'll confront Enderby today."

"Confront him? No, you can't! That's much too..." Dangerous. "Foolish. Enderby is a blackmailer and that means he's a slippery, conniving fox. We have to use more devious methods if we want that letter."

Warhurst stared at her. "Devious." The corner of his mouth kicked up in a crooked smile. "That might work. Any ideas?"

Alice drummed her fingers on the table and stared at the flames dancing around a log. How did someone get into a house unnoticed? Who could move about a mansion without arousing suspicion?

A servant. Or a person of trade—like a seamstress. A plain one would be even better.

"I can do it," she said.

"No."

She told him of her plan. Even he, ox headed as he was, should see the logic in it. There really was no other way.

But when she finished, he thumped his first on the table, making the tankards jump. "No!"

"But—."

"I forbid it."

She straightened. "You cannot forbid me to do anything."

"I can in this. Lilly is *my* sister, this is *my* endeavor. We do it my way or I'll do it alone." He crossed his arms and rested them on the table. "In fact, I'll do it alone anyway. I don't want you involved in something so perilous."

She crossed her arms too and leaned forward. "You are *not* cutting me out now, Warhurst. Anyway," she said before he could disagree, "you can't do this without me. You're not the sort of person who can wander in and out of a house unnoticed, let alone Lord Enderby's."

"And you are?" He snorted. "Hardly."

"I am a seamstress."

"You might be a seamstress but unremarkable you are not." His nostrils flared and he regarded her with a challenge in his eyes, daring her to disagree.

Alice's heart swelled to twice its size and beat wildly against her ribs. "Nobody would take much notice of me if I said I was there to mend some clothes. I could pretend Lord Enderby has hired me to make something for his daughter."

"It's a foolish idea and it won't work." He held up his hand to stop her argument.

"Do you have a better idea then?" she asked. He nodded. "Does it involve me?"

He sighed. "I admit I can't think of a way of avoiding your involvement. But I will be there with you. I'll keep you safe."

She remembered how he'd kept her safe from Marlowe's blade. Warhurst had held her close then, gently tended her wound and used all his power to keep her from further harm.

Then, as now, her skin tingled at the mere thought of his touch. "Tell me," she said on a hush of breath.

He'd been watching her lips with a dark intensity but when she spoke, he appeared to shake it off and concentrate once more. "We'll need Enderby's daughter's help. You've met her— do you think she'd be willing?"

"Patience?" Alice chewed on her lip. "She loves Richard Farley enough to want to wed him and not Hawkesbury. I'm sure I can speak to her without raising the suspicions of anyone else in the household. What shall I tell her?"

"Tell her she's invited a friend of a friend over for supper. Or better still, for the night. She can tell her father you are newly arrived in London and have not yet secured yourself accommodation."

"And you?"

"Enderby knows me. I can't show my face to him but if I can avoid him then I'll—."

"No. If he knows you then it is too dangerous for you to come. I'll go alone."

"You will not! I'll pretend to be your brother or cousin. If I keep my head down and we tell Patience to treat me as your kin then I'll be safe."

She shook her head. "It would be better if you were my groom, that way you could safely stay out of Enderby's way. You could sneak out of the stables during the night and we can search the house together while everyone is asleep." When he began to protest, she put up her hand. "It's what I'm going to tell Patience so you might as well accept it. You do know how to act like a groom, don't you?"

He lifted one shoulder. "I'm good with horses."

She rolled her eyes. "You obviously haven't spent much time around players. You must *become* a groom if this is to succeed. You'll need to speak like one, walk like one and dress like one. I can help you with that part. There'll be a suitable costume at the tiring house. I'll tell Father it needs mending and take it home with me tonight." She smiled. This was beginning to sound like fun.

Warhurst, however, still looked like he wanted to argue with her. "And what about clothing for you?"

Her smile faded. "The clothes aren't the problem. As to how I sound and walk...I will have to muddle through as best I can."

Warhurst's eyes narrowed. "This is not something you can muddle through, Mistress Croft. If Enderby discovers your true identity—."

"He won't." She tilted her chin. "If Freddie can be a lady then so can I. I at least have the right shape."

His gaze shifted to her chest. She cleared her throat and he raised his eyes to meet hers. His face was flushed. "Then we're agreed," she said, standing. "I'll speak to Patience directly. And Min. I'll need her to publicly invite me back to her house tonight so that Father won't worry. I'm sure she'll understand when she hears what we're up to."

"Tonight?" he said. "Will you be prepared by then?"

"I'll have to be. The sooner we do this the better. For Lilly's and Hawkesbury's sakes." And for hers. It was time she severed all contact with Warhurst except by business-related correspondence. If she couldn't have him then she wanted nothing to do with him.

It was the only way.

CHAPTER 19

*A*lice couldn't believe how easily everything fell into place. Patience readily agreed to the plan, telling Alice she would prepare a story to satisfy her parents' curiosity about her new friend. Min played her part and asked Alice in the tiring house, loudly, if she would like to stay the night again so they could work on her wedding gown together by candlelight. John Croft gave his permission without demur. Before they went on stage for the afternoon's performance, Will Shakespeare and Henry Wells taught Alice to speak with the clipped accents of the gentry and even Freddie showed her how to walk as if she were born to privilege. Only Shakespeare asked her why she needed lessons in becoming a lady but he didn't press her when she gave a vague answer.

After the performance, she folded the costumes for herself and Warhurst and carefully placed them in a valise. She told her father they required mending and she'd do it at Min's since his eyes were too weak to work by candlelight. She then went to meet Warhurst behind the copse of trees to the east of the theater. He wasn't there so she changed into her costume but it was the devil's business to fasten the hooks at the gown's back.

"Allow me."

She knew that voice as well as she knew the fingers brushing the nape of her neck as Warhurst fastened her gown. Without speaking, she handed him the small ruff and he fixed it at her throat. His breath warmed her ear and rustled her hair as he bent to his task. When he finished, he stepped back and she sighed at the loss of contact.

"You wore that the first time we met," he said.

She looked down at the full crimson skirts. "So I did." It was the gown she'd tried on at the White Swan's tiring house. She'd adjusted it only a little for Freddie and it was still a reasonable fit although tight in the chest.

Warhurst's eyes were hooded but she knew he was watching her. She could feel the heat from their smoldering depths burning into the back of her neck. He still wanted her. Knowing that didn't help settle her nerves. She'd been looking forward to their adventure but now she wasn't so sure it was a good idea. Being anywhere near him wasn't a good idea anymore and tonight they would be alone again. The separation of their sleeping quarters would hardly be a barrier if he kept looking at her like he wanted to eat her.

"I have your costume in the bag." She bent and retrieved his groom's woolen hose and leather jerkin.

"You should call me Leo for the time being," he said, accepting the garments from her.

"Leo." It rolled nicely off her tongue.

"And I have something for you, my lady." He removed a small pouch from his doublet pocket and took her hand. He turned it palm up. "These belong to my mother but I haven't seen her wear them for some time. I doubt she'll miss them for one night." He emptied the contents of the pouch onto her palm.

She gasped. A pair of emerald drop earrings nestled beside an emerald pendant hung on a gold chain. She looked up at him, directly into another set of emeralds of the exact same shade as the gems.

"They're beautiful." She wasn't sure if she meant the jewelry or his eyes.

He grunted and turned away. "Don't lose them," he said, removing his riding cloak.

She put on the earrings and necklace—which didn't quite suit the red gown but were beautiful anyway—while he dressed then packed their regular clothes into the valise. When he turned around, he paused with his hat in his hand and blinked at her.

"Is something wrong?" she prompted.

"No. It's just that you look...the part." He didn't elaborate but picked up the valise and led her out of the trees to two horses tied to a post.

"I hadn't thought about transportation," she said.

"You thought of everything else. Anyway, as the groom it's my task to organize the horses." He strapped the valise to the big bay's saddle. Beside it stood the gentle mare she'd ridden to Crouch End. He must have hired it for her.

"You didn't have to go to so much trouble," she said, patting the mare's neck. "I could have walked."

"You need to arrive in style. I thought you might prefer a familiar horse." He helped her onto the saddle and gave her the reins. "Back straight," he said. "Not that straight. Relax a little. That's it. Now look down your nose at everyone."

She tried but it hurt her eyes.

"Not quite what I meant." He rubbed the mare's nose. "Just pretend you own her as well as those gems you're wearing. You even own me."

Their gazes locked until he turned away and mounted his own horse. She stared at his broad shoulders as he gathered the reins and guided the gelding to the road.

Imagine owning him...

She couldn't help smiling a little and squared her shoulders at the thought.

"Much better," he said.

Her horse plodded along behind his, content to follow the handsome devil prancing in front of her. Alice didn't mind in the least. She quite enjoyed the view of man and beast. Her hat slipped to the side and she straightened her head and raised her chin. It was time she acted like a lady and ladies didn't ogle their grooms.

They crossed the bridge and headed north then east along Candlewick Street. A gentleman walking by tipped his hat to Alice. "Good afternoon, ma'am," he said. He smiled at her and kept watching her long after they'd passed him. She knew because she turned in the saddle to see.

Good lord, how remarkable! That gentleman had just called *her* madam. His kind wouldn't normally see her let alone speak to her.

A moment later another gentleman did the same then another. She smiled at them both and bid them "Good afternoon" in her schooled accent.

When it happened a fourth time, Warhurst dropped back to be alongside her. "You don't have to acknowledge all of them."

"Why not? This is fun."

He grunted. "And I was worried about how you would pull this off," he muttered.

"I should go out in the troupe's costumes more often. I quite like the reaction."

"It's not just the clothes," he admitted gruffly. "Although you are very...striking in that gown."

Striking? Was that a good thing? "The jewels and horse help too of course."

"Is that what you think?"

She blinked at him. "Well, yes. Those are the only things that are different."

He kicked his horse into a trot until he was ahead of her again, leading the way through the late afternoon throng leaving St. Paul's. The booksellers who used the churchyard to trade their wares were closing for the day but a crowd still gathered to listen to the tales of sailors who'd defeated the Armada the year before, or have their forecasts read by astrologers or their humors balanced by charlatans. Servants looking for work begged Alice to employ them. Such a great lady must have need of a cook, maid or groom. Lads darted about posting handbills and the ones touting the new play by Lord Hawkesbury's Men gathered the most interest.

Warhurst's horse danced nervously but he kept it under control with what appeared to be minimal effort. Alice's mare maintained a steady pace but she was glad to leave the busy churchyard behind and head out through Ludgate, over the Fleet River and onto The Strand with its grand houses and fewer people. They stopped outside the gates to a mansion which wasn't as large as Lord Hawkesbury's further along but still impressive nonetheless with its brick façade, multiple gables and extensive glass windows.

"We're here," Warhurst said. He lowered his hat over his eyes and walked his horse through the stone arch, nodding at the gatekeeper. The servant must have been expecting them because he let them through without question.

The horses' hooves scrunched on the gravel drive and they were still several yards from the house when the front door opened and Patience blew out, a broad smile on her face. "Alice! I've been watching for you all afternoon. It's so good to see you."

Alice dismounted and allowed Patience to kiss both her cheeks and tuck her hand through her arm. She dared not look back at Warhurst. Er, Leo. Her groom. *Hers.*

"Come in, come in," Patience said, drawing Alice inside. "You look tired after your long journey." She turned to a liveried servant hovering in the doorway. "Bellows, take Mistress Croft's valise from her man then direct him to the stables. See to it he's taken care of tonight."

The servant hurried to do her bidding but Warhurst gave him the reins instead of the valise. "I'll take my lady's belongings to her room. Wait here."

Inside the house, Alice sidled up to him. "What are you doing?" she whispered. "You're not supposed to give orders and you're not supposed to be in the house. You might be seen."

"I want to see which room you'll be staying in. It might be important later."

Alice's heart skidded to a thudding halt. She swallowed. *Later.* He would come to her.

"Follow me," Patience said. "Quickly."

They followed her up the wooden staircase to the second floor and through a series of adjoining rooms to a spacious bedchamber. A small fire warmed the air and the smell of smoke mingled with a faint scent of lavender. "This will be yours for tonight, Alice," Patience said. She went to the window and peered down. Alice and Warhurst joined her. The room over-looked a small formal garden, an orchard speckled with late-season apples beyond it. To the side was a cobbled yard backing onto the stables and either a brewery or bakery.

"I should be able to climb up," Warhurst said to no one in particular.

Alice put her hands on her hips. "You will not try to climb up here! We'll let you in through a door downstairs." Patience nodded although she didn't appear too certain about that plan either. "That's if we think we need your help," Alice added.

"You'll let me in through this window whether you *think* you need my help or not," he said. "This is *my* family's problem and I'll give the orders."

"Nonsense. Don't be so obstinate."

Warhurst bent down to her level. "Do not let the role you are playing go to your head, Mistress Croft. You cannot order me about."

She forked an eyebrow and gave him a smile. He sighed and straightened. "Why do I think I'm going to regret this?"

"You won't regret it," she said.

He didn't look entirely convinced but launched into the plan for the evening. "You can lead us to your father's study," he said to Patience. "Hopefully the letter is in there. Mistress Croft, do you think you can locate Patience's bedchamber in the dark?"

"It's easy," Patience said, pointing to a door. "It's straight through our shared withdrawing room there. Wake me up when you're ready." She said nothing about letting him in downstairs. It seemed she wasn't as concerned about Warhurst falling and breaking his neck. Alice looked out the window again. Her room was a long way up.

"I'd better go." He doffed his cap and bowed but somehow managed to show not the least bit of courtesy or submission. "Until later," he said, and left the two women alone.

Later. There was that promise again. A shiver of pleasure swept across her skin before she forced herself to remember that they were there for one thing—to get Hawkesbury's letter. Their situation was dangerous and she needed to stay alert. Thinking about Warhurst must be strictly forbidden.

"Supper will be served early evening and I think you should rest until then," Patience said. "We both should. It might be a long night." She showed none of the cheerful familiarity she'd displayed on Alice's arrival but that was to be expected. It seemed she was a consummate actress as well. And here everyone thought only men made good players.

"You look better," Alice said. "Note quite so green."

"It's a good day." Patience lifted the gold pomander hanging from her girdle and put it to her nose. "The sickness comes and goes on a whim."

Alice squeezed her hand. "Have you received news of Richard Farley since Warhurst and I paid him a visit?"

A small smile flickered across Patience's lips and her face flushed. "He can't write to me here, of course. Father would confiscate his letters. But he found a way to send me a note. He says he'll be ready to wed me as soon as your plan bears fruit and I am free of Lord Hawkesbury." She pressed the pomander to her lips as if the gold filigree were her lover's mouth. "He's concerned that he can't offer me the sort of life I'm used to, but I don't care. As long as I'm with him, I'll not want for another luxury ever again. What's a big home and nice clothes when you're unhappy?"

Alice sat heavily on the bed. "I...I suppose so." She looked down at her beautiful crimson skirts. The velvet felt smooth against her skin and the embroidery was so delicate and intricate. But it was just fabric. She could make something like it in less than a week. Something Warhurst had said on their way to the Enderby house finally sank in—*it's not just the clothes.* Nor had it been the jewels or the horse that set her apart from everyone else and garnered her the acknowledgements from the other gentlemen.

It was her bearing.

A woman like Patience held herself erect and walked as if she had a right to be anywhere she wished to be. Without her beautiful gown and the golden pomander, she would still be a lady because she took it for granted that she *was* a lady, through and through.

Alice touched the emerald pendant at her throat. "I think you and Richard Farley will do very well together," she said.

Patience gave her a small smile and let the pomander drop. It swung from the girdle until it settled against her dark blue skirt. "Does Lord Warhurst know your gems match his eyes?"

Alice let the pendant go. "I'm not sure. He seems quite unaware how beautiful they are." *I'd rather the man with the eyes than the gems any day.*

Patience laughed, a gentle tinkling sound which she smothered with the back of her hand. "I'll leave you now but I'll return to take you down to supper. Mother is quite keen to meet you."

Alice froze. "But what should I say?" Oh God, she couldn't do this. Surely Lord and Lady Enderby would see straight through her awful acting.

"Don't fear. I've told them I met you when I visited an old friend last summer. You're from Essex and are traveling to your aunt in Surrey with a stop-over in London tonight. Your mother is quite dead and your father is at his wits end with a girl on his hands. He's sent you away for awhile in the hopes you'll be less of a burden. I'll guide you where I can but otherwise," she waved her hand, "just make it up."

Alice felt sick. "I'll do my best."

Patience squeezed her arm. "You can always plead tiredness if it becomes too much for you."

She left and Alice tried to rest but without luck. After a while she got up and looked out her window toward the stables but she couldn't see Warhurst. What was he doing now? Would he be with the horses or would he have found something else to do? As long as he was staying out of trouble she didn't really care. Hopefully Lord Enderby had little interest in horses and never went anywhere near his stables.

Daylight faded into darkness while she waited and finally Patience came to take her down to supper. They sat at a long table in a small, informal dining room rather than the large great hall which they must use only for grander affairs. Lord and Lady Enderby entered a few minutes later. The countess bestowed a cool smile on Alice but his lordship merely grunted a greeting and concentrated on stuffing a slice of mutton into his mouth as quickly as possible.

Lady Enderby asked polite questions about Alice's journey and her home and Alice gave short answers. Although she sounded as much like a lady as the women she sat with, she didn't trust herself when it came to make up believable responses. How did she know what a lady's house in Essex looked like or what she would do all day? Indeed, if she had servants to cook and clean for her, there didn't seem a great deal else to occupy her time.

"Tell me, will you be going to the theater while you're here in London?" Lady Enderby asked. "We're quite famous for our theaters, you know. Patience's betrothed, Lord Hawkesbury, is patron to our most famous company, isn't he my lord?"

Lord Enderby looked up, a piece of olive pie halfway to his mouth. "What?"

"Lord Hawkesbury's Men are one of the City's finest acting troupe's, don't you think?"

He grunted. "I hate the theater." He shoved in the pie and washed it down with the entire cup of wine.

"They certainly have the finest costumes," Patience said with a knowing smile at Alice.

Alice smoothed imaginary wrinkles out of her skirt. "Unfortunately I won't have time to go to the theater. I must leave tomorrow. Early." The earlier the better. She bit into her bread. She wasn't really hungry but if she kept eating then she wouldn't have to speak.

"What do you do to keep busy?" she asked Patience after supper when they were sitting in the small withdrawing room between their bedchambers.

Patience lifted one shoulder in a delicate gesture. "Embroidery. I like to read but Father's library isn't extensive. Mother and I go to the theater on occasion or visit friends."

"What do you do when you visit?"

"Talk. Sometimes we take our sewing or embroidery and work while we talk." Alice frowned. Patience laughed. "I'm sure it must sound dull to you but it's not all bad. When we're in the country there's riding and hunting. I like to visit our farmers and learn from them but Father discourages it. He thinks it's unladylike."

"That sounds much more interesting. I'm not sure I'd want to embroider all the time."

"Don't you sew all day now?"

"Not all day," Alice said. "And when I am, it's often at the tiring house and there's always something happening there. It's never dull when the actors are around and there's always half a dozen prancing about. They're quite amusing."

Patience sighed. "You're lucky. I can't go anywhere or do anything without a chaperone but you seem to come and go as you please. You lead such an interesting life."

"Interesting!" Alice laughed but it quickly faded to a thoughtful silence. "I suppose it is," she murmured.

Good lord, why had she not realized it before? Her life was certainly different. Roger Style could be tyrannical at times and her father tried to keep the conversations civilized, usually in vain, but on the whole the tiring house had been a fascinating place to grow up. Actors and playwrights came from all over the country and being natural storytellers, they had a way of enthralling her. Indeed, it was their stories that had encouraged her to seek out her own adventures.

But they were only stories. The reality was probably entirely different to the embellished version. Just like being a lady wasn't at all as interesting as she'd expected it to be.

Odd. She'd always thought she was bored with her life, but perhaps it wasn't boredom. Perhaps she only needed to know what else was out there, outside her world. Now that she did, she wasn't sure it was what she wanted after all.

She sighed heavily. "I envy you knowing what you want," she said.

"You do?" Patience blinked at her then laughed, but it was a sad laugh. "And here I envied you for your freedom."

"My freedom?"

Patience nodded. "To go where you want without a chaperone, for having something to do and meeting all those players and writers." She looked down at her clasped hands and fiddled with her pearl ring. "And for marrying whom you want."

Tears pricked Alice's eyes. "That counts for nothing when the man I want doesn't want to marry me."

Patience looked up. Her eyes softened and she leaned

forward to take Alice's hand. "Doesn't want to or can't? There is a difference."

"It amounts to the same thing." She sucked in a breath and shook her head, hoping to dislodge the melancholy that had settled over her. She refused to dwell on what she couldn't have. Not tonight. When this was all over and Warhurst had returned to his life in the north, she would wait and see how she felt. Hopefully time and distance would ease the pain and help her to think clearly. In the meantime, she would have her shop and a new determination to appreciate her life.

Patience smothered a yawn with her hand and Alice rose, drawing the other woman up with her. "You need your rest. Nothing will happen for some time."

Patience nodded. "Good night. And thank you." The candlelight picked out the shine in her eyes. "I know my own happiness is not your intended aim, but I will nevertheless reap the rewards."

"Do you think your father will let you marry Farley after we destroy his plans to wed you to Hawkesbury?"

Patience pressed a hand to her belly, still flat despite the baby. "I'll do everything within my power to make sure he does."

Watching her rise with such dignity, Alice was determined to do everything within her power too.

CHAPTER 20

$\mathcal{A}$lice awoke with a start but didn't know why. Her room was quiet, dark and empty.

Or so she thought.

A shadow split from the other shadows and crouched beside her bed. She wasn't alarmed. She knew it was Warhurst even though she couldn't make out his features. Had he been watching her?

"You're awake." He didn't whisper but his voice was low and quiet. He was so close his breath warmed her cheek. She couldn't even make out his eyes in the darkness but she knew he was regarding her with his usual fierce intensity—she could *feel* it. Perhaps he could see in the dark. It wouldn't surprise her. She was beginning to suspect he was capable of almost anything.

"I told you not to climb up," she said.

His white teeth formed a crescent in the darkness. She wished she had a candle to see him by—he smiled so rarely it seemed a shame to miss a single one of them.

"I managed not to break my neck," he said.

She reached up and touched the warm flesh at his throat. A pulse throbbed against her fingertips. "Good." She flattened her hand and cupped the side of his face. Her thumb swept across the arc of his cheek up to the corner of his eye. He turned his face a little, pressing his cheek into her hand.

"Why?" His voice was barely a whispered rasp.

"Because I want you here. With me." Always.

And because I love you.

She placed her other hand against his other cheek, gently because it was the one sporting a bruise, and would have drawn him down to her but he was already there. His mouth closed over hers, cut lip and all. His fingers dug into her hair. His tongue explored and tasted and he groaned against her.

He smelled like horses and leather and she thought nothing smelled as sweet. She clutched his shoulders and wanted to feel his bare skin, wanted to sink her teeth into his muscles. But he was wearing too much clothing. The black leather jerkin had to go. She tugged on the laces and managed to dive inside his shirt and press her palm against smooth, hot skin.

But not for long. He broke the kiss and sprang back from the bed. "Christ," he said. The only sound in the darkness was his gasping breaths, as if he'd been under water too long.

She wanted to ask him why he'd stopped, wanted to know what he felt, but didn't trust her voice. Her entire body shook, so it probably would too. At least he couldn't see the tears slipping silently down her cheeks.

"I'm sorry," he said after what felt like forever. "I shouldn't have watched you sleeping." His silhouette turned and walked towards the door leading to the adjoining room. "We should wake Patience. There's only a few hours until dawn."

She rose from the bed, still dressed in the crimson gown and his mother's jewelry. She hadn't wanted to take them off in case it made her less of a lady. It didn't work. Her behavior just now had been anything but ladylike.

She came up behind him, her body still humming from the desire coursing through it. Surely he must be able to feel it vibrating off her. But it was impossible to tell much in the dark except that he was big and formidable and she wanted him with every piece of her.

"This way," he said. His hand touched hers and she swallowed her gasp. Their fingers linked and she felt instantly more comfortable as his strength seeped into her.

They made their way through the withdrawing room,

moving around dark blobs of furniture to the next door which led to Patience's room. She was awake and wore a housecoat over her nightshift. A lantern on the mantelpiece cast a miserly glow through her room from its single wick.

"You made it." She took in Alice and Warhurst's linked hands. "In the dark?"

"Light is too dangerous," he said. "But we'll need one for the study. Are you ready?"

Patience nodded and picked up the lantern. "We'll have to be quiet. There's only a small sitting room between his study and bedchamber." She led the way through empty guest rooms across a landing and stopped at a door. She opened it, peered around and signaled the others to follow her. "I'll listen at the inner door," she said.

Warhurst went straight for the desk while Alice turned to the nearest coffer. It was locked. The second one wasn't but it only contained ledgers. If Warhurst didn't uncover a key in the desk then it must be elsewhere. She could only hope it would be somewhere in the study and not on Enderby's person or in his private rooms. She looked to Warhurst but he only shook his head. He was having no luck either.

He ran his hand beneath the desk so she followed suit and checked the undersides of all the chairs and lifted all the small statues lining the mantelpiece. No key. Warhurst got down on his hands and knees and searched through the rushes covering the floor. Alice knelt too then had a better idea. If she hid a key she would find something to sew it into. There were no tapestries lining the walls but the main chair situated at the desk had a cushion tied to its seat. She undid it and squeezed. Through the stuffing and stiff embroidery she could just make out something small and hard.

She joined Patience and held the cushion up to the lantern. Sewn into the taffeta was a small pocket of matching material with one side left unstitched as an opening. It was so tight she could only fit one finger inside but it was enough to pull out the key. Triumphant, she held it up to Warhurst.

He wasn't watching her. He cocked his head to the side,

listening. Then Alice heard it too. Footsteps. Fighting panic, she looked around for somewhere to hide.

But the heavy footsteps were already on the other side of the door.

It was too late to hide.

Patience hurried to the desk and Warhurst slipped his arm around Alice's waist. He pulled her back against the wall as the door opened. The heavy oak shielded them from the newcomer.

"It's you," said Lord Enderby. He sounded gruff, as if he'd just awoken. "Thought I heard a noise. What are you doing in here?"

"Just getting some more ink," Patience said casually. Alice marveled at the other woman's steady nerves—there wasn't a hint of fear or guilt in her voice.

"You should be sleeping."

"I can't. I thought writing some poetry might make me sleepy."

"Poetry." He yawned. "Ever since that bloody playwright turned out to be a woman, every silly creature thinks she can write."

Warhurst's arm tightened around Alice's waist and she leaned into his solidness. His face was just above hers, his lips level with her forehead. She could stand on her toes, tilt her head and kiss him. She remained still.

"Go back to bed, Father," Patience said gently.

"Did you find some ink?"

"Not yet but I know where it is. Good night."

He grunted and the door closed. Alice breathed again but Warhurst didn't ease his grip. For several minutes they all stood where they were, waiting and listening. The footsteps didn't return. They were safe for now.

Warhurst let Alice go and they knelt side by side at the chest while Patience listened at the door. Without speaking, Alice slipped the key into the lock and Warhurst lifted the lid. Inside were stacks of papers, some tied with ribbons, some loose. They rifled through each one until Warhurst signaled that he'd found it. He showed a thin, folded page to Alice. Lord Hawkesbury's name was clearly written on the front.

They silently stacked the other letters back in the chest,

closed the lid and locked it. Alice slipped the key back into its pocket and retied the cushion to the chair. All three of them crept out of the study.

When they reached Patience's bedchamber, Alice drew a deep breath, her first proper one since they'd entered Enderby's study. That had been close. Too close. If Enderby had moved further into the room, or if someone had made a noise... She shuddered. It didn't bear thinking about.

It might have been fun to pretend to be a lady and dress in fine clothes, but if she were discovered, she would be in a great deal of trouble. Enough trouble that Warhurst probably couldn't save her from a thrashing if Enderby called for assistance from his servants. As a child, having adventures had been exciting, but as an adult, some adventures were much too exciting for comfort.

"What does it say?" Patience asked Warhurst.

He shook his head and showed them the page. "I'll need time to decipher the code."

Patience groaned and sat heavily on her bed. She looked exhausted.

"Get some sleep," Alice said. "And thank you for all you've done. I'd leave now except it would only alert the household and arouse suspicions."

Patience took the hand Alice offered and squeezed. "Good luck. I'll be thinking of you both."

Warhurst guided Alice back through the adjoining rooms to her own bedchamber where he lit a candle and placed it on the table beside the bed. "Are you all right?" he asked, studying her face in the dim light.

She nodded. "I am now that it's all over."

"It's not over yet. I won't be happy until you're away from here."

"Me? Don't you mean us?"

"I, er, yes of course I do." He looked to the window. "I must go." But he didn't move. He took a step closer to her. "Are you sure you're going to be all right?"

"Yes."

"Good. You're not afraid?"

"No," she lied.

"You're shivering." He removed a blanket from the foot of the bed and placed it around her shoulders. His fingers curled into the edges as he clasped it tightly at her chest. The delicious scent of him filled her nostrils.

"You should go," she said, leaning into him.

"Yes." He regarded her through half-lowered lids.

"Yes," she repeated dully. The spicy scent of him muddled her wits, thickened her throat. "Yes." *Take me. Here. Now.*

Their heavy breaths sounded loud in the silent room. Warhurst's chest rose and fell like a bellows. He inched closer. Closer. His nose brushed hers, his breath was hot on her lips. His intense gaze stripped her of all remaining sense.

"I want you," he whispered. "God help me because I can't help myself. I want you, Alice Croft."

Still he didn't move. What was he waiting for? A sign from God? From her?

Piddle to that. She pressed her hands to either side of his face and pulled him to her. His lips opened without hesitation and he kissed her thoroughly. It would seem he'd got the sign he'd been waiting for.

She should resist, should grasp for any common sense still remaining, but she was hopelessly, desperately lost and she didn't care a wit. Warhurst was kissing her as if his life depended upon it and she adored every moment, relished the rush his kisses produced through her body.

His hands fluttered at her shoulders, caressed the flesh beneath her gown. His lips soon followed, leaving a trail of delicious destruction in their wake. She tipped her head back to expose her throat. *More. More. There, yesssss...*

"I can't stop thinking about you," he murmured against her raw, sensitive skin. "You are always in my thoughts....driving me mad with desire...my love."

Love?

She gasped. He withdrew suddenly, as if the madness had been slapped out of him. In the darkness she could just make out the roundness of his eyes, his parted lips.

"I have to go." Before she could protest, he was out the window.

She closed her eyes and dared not check to see if he'd made it down in one piece. She couldn't move anyway with her bones as weak as water and her heart pounding so hard it was difficult to breathe.

All she could do was lie on the bed and let the tears seep into the pillow. Warhurst would never allow himself to love her, not the way she wanted. He was much too proud to lower himself, and in too much control to abandon reason entirely.

She remained that way until dawn when the maidservant brought her breakfast and stoked up the fire.

* * *

THE JOURNEY to Charles Grayshaw's house was mercifully short. Leo had suggested they travel there immediately to see if he could decode the letter. It would also provide a place for them to change back into their own clothing without attracting notice. Thankfully Alice agreed, although with a slight nod only. She said nothing else as she sat on her horse. She didn't even look at him.

Perhaps that was just as well. He deserved nothing less than her cold shoulder, but an argument would have been preferable. He liked arguing with her. It made him feel alive.

They dismounted outside Grayshaw's house and he tied up the horses and carried their bag to the door. Being early, Grayshaw was home. He seemed surprised to see them although his first words were not a greeting.

"Remarkable gown, Alice," he said, eyeing her crimson dress when she removed her cloak.

Leo glared at him but the fool didn't seem to notice. He continued to give Alice a sickly smile. She shrugged back at Grayshaw in return but said nothing. She'd been quiet all morning. Not even the doffed hats and "good mornings" from the passersby had amused her as they had the day before. Leo didn't like this change in her. He much preferred the old Alice, the one with more fire in her belly than a forge.

He only had himself to blame. Stupid, idiot fool. Why couldn't he think with his head instead of his—?

"Is there somewhere I can change?" Alice asked Grayshaw.

"Certainly," he said, directing her to a small sitting room adjoining his study. "Sorry there's not fire burning."

She picked up the bag with her clothing inside and disappeared into the room, closing the door with a bang behind her.

Leo winced. Grayshaw raised an amused eyebrow at him. Leo clenched his fists. Hitting his old school friend would be quite satisfying but probably wouldn't do him any good. He needed Grayshaw to have his wits about him.

"I found it," Leo said.

Grayshaw's features instantly flattened into seriousness. "The Hawkesbury letter? Where was it? How did you get it?"

"It was at Enderby's." He didn't answer the last question and from the way Grayshaw glanced at the sitting room door, he suspected he didn't need to. "I want you to decode it." Leo produced the missive from the pocket of his jerkin and handed it over.

"I was beginning to think it didn't exist and we'd jumped to the wrong conclusion."

"Can you decipher it?"

Grayshaw opened the letter and scanned the page. There wasn't much writing, just a few jumbled letters and numbers. "I think so. It's an old code, not used anymore, but I recall the sequence." He sat at his desk and rubbed the stubble on his chin as he studied the missive. Leo hadn't taken much note of his friend's face but now he frowned at the unkempt beginnings of a beard. Grayshaw was usually so fastidious about his clean-shaven appearance.

After only a few short minutes, Grayshaw sat back and looked up at Leo. "Lord Hawkesbury is in a lot of trouble."

"What sort of trouble."

"The treason sort."

Leo's heart tripped. So Marlowe had told the truth. "The last earl of Hawkesbury was involved in a plot to assassinate the queen," he said heavily.

Grayshaw re-folded the letter and gave it back to Leo. "If I had to guess how he was discovered I would suggest he was tricked into hiring an agent of Walsingham's, disguised as an assassin. It's a method he's used before."

"Then why was he never tried for his crime?" Leo asked.

"Do you know when the old earl died?"

Leo frowned in thought. "Lilly mentioned Hawke inherited the earldom about ten years ago."

"That letter is dated June 1579. Ten years ago."

"So old Hawkesbury dies and the accusations are never made public. They were buried along with him."

Grayshaw nodded. "This letter must have been written just before his death and has only now come to light again."

Leo rubbed his forehead. It ached like the devil. "Marlowe discovers it, passes it to his superior, Enderby, who failed to hand it over to *his* superior, Walsingham."

"That's a dangerous thing to do in itself."

Leo couldn't help smiling. "Indeed it is." If Walsingham learned of the deception, Enderby could find himself in a lot of trouble with the powerful courtier. "Thank you," Leo said. He clapped Grayshaw on the shoulder. "Thank you very much."

"So we're friends again?"

"Were we ever not?"

Grayshaw glanced at the door to the room where Alice was changing. "I wondered if something had come between us, ever since you discovered...my past with Alice."

Leo's back teeth hurt. He unclenched his jaw. "What is past is past. As long as you stay away from her now, all is forgiven."

"Why do you want me to stay away? What business is it of yours?" Grayshaw didn't seem to be offended or angry, only slightly amused.

"I don't want her getting hurt."

"And I would hurt her?"

"Haven't you already?"

Grayshaw waved a hand. "If she'd cared for me more then perhaps you could say that. But she never did, she still doesn't, and so I would argue that I haven't hurt her in the least."

Damn him with his legal education. "Still, the way you look

at her...as if you..." *Would bed her or wed her or both.* Leo couldn't say it. The words stuck in his throat.

"I won't. She wouldn't have me anyway. She's in love with someone else." He clapped Leo so hard on the shoulder that Leo stumbled forward.

He recovered his footing and gave Grayshaw a glare which did nothing to wipe the smile off the cur's face. He had a good mind to tell him they weren't friends anymore but Grayshaw spoke first.

"She looked quite the lady in that gown," Grayshaw said. "Regal almost. She could easily pass for nobility with that haughty bearing of hers."

"Haughty?" Leo echoed without really thinking. Grayshaw was right, he realized with a jolt. No one had suspected Alice wasn't a lady. Not the people they passed in the street nor the Enderbys. She was a fine actress. The gown had looked like it belonged on her, and she had looked like she belonged on that horse with his mother's emeralds around her neck.

"She doesn't seem like herself today," Grayshaw said, snapping Leo's attention into focus. "You wouldn't have anything to do with that, would you?" All teasing friendliness had disappeared from his tone and he watched Leo with a sharp gaze and rigid jaw.

"What if it does?" Leo couldn't help asking. He had to know what she meant to Grayshaw, how far he was willing to go to protect her.

"If you did, I might have to challenge you to a duel and we both know I abhor violence."

"Only because you know the blood spilled would be yours."

Grayshaw sighed. "True." And with that, his stance relaxed.

They both looked to the door and it suddenly opened. Alice emerged dressed in her normal clothing of simple woolen gown, the cloak over her arm, the bag in her hand. She looked no less ravishing than she had dressed as a noblewoman.

Her chin was tilted forward and the spark that had been missing all morning was back in her eyes. She must have shrugged off the melancholy she'd felt after Leo's premature departure the night before. He wished he could shrug it off too.

Unfortunately he was destined not to forget his actions so easily. He'd give anything to turn back time and finish what he'd begun in the guest room of Enderby's house.

Almost anything.

Leo took the bag from her. She didn't look in his direction but listened to Grayshaw as he confirmed what was in the letter.

"No wonder Lord Hawkesbury didn't want the letter to come to light," she said. "Not only would his mother and sister be terribly upset, but suspicion would fall upon them all."

Leo nodded. "It's quite likely the old earl involved his son in his plans. Ten years ago Hawke was already an adult."

"Their property could be seized and the title stripped if the queen believed this evidence." Grayshaw pointed to Leo's doublet pocket where the letter was safely stowed once more.

"Poor Lady Hawkesbury," Alice murmured.

Leo nodded and bit the inside of his lip. Hawke had a very good reason for marrying Patience Enderby. If her father gave the coded letter to Walsingham, Hawke's family would be plunged into dangerous waters. Leo felt sorry for him, he even understood his actions, but that didn't mean he had to like him. Son of a traitor or not, he still got Lilly with child. If he'd only possessed enough self-control around her they wouldn't all be in this predicament.

Self-control...*Christ*.

Leo stared at Alice. She stared back, challenging.

Oh God, what a heartless wretch he was. A cold, selfish beast. He and Hawke were alike in the worst possible way.

He drew in a deep breath and let it out slowly. "Are you ready, Mistress Croft? I'll escort you home." It would give them precious minutes to talk. He had something to say to her. Something very important.

CHAPTER 21

*A*fter all she'd just learned from Grayshaw about Hawkesbury's predicament, Alice thought concentrating on that particular topic and not her own woes would have been easy. It wasn't. The London sun shone down on her and Warhurst as they rode the horses through the streets back to her house, or more specifically around the corner from her house. They couldn't risk anyone seeing them together when she was supposed to have spent the night at Min's.

As she rode, she tried not to think about the beautiful crimson gown squashed into the bag strapped to Warhurst's saddle. She tried not to notice the lack of greetings from strangers passing by, and tried not to think about that kiss and the way Warhurst had abruptly ended it.

She tried and failed.

She glanced across at him and was surprised to see him watching her. One corner of his mouth flicked up in what could almost be described as a smile.

"What is it?" she asked. "You have a strange look on your face."

"You're very...pretty."

"Don't humor me, Warhurst. Whatever it is, stop staring. I don't like it."

"I'm not humoring you. It's the truth. I don't know why you don't think you're pretty—."

"Because I'm not. My nose is too sharp, my lips too thin and I have no eyelashes to speak of."

"I like your lips." He flushed and looked away. "And your nose and eyelashes too of course."

What was he playing at? Why the sudden compliments? Could he possibly be regretting the way he'd unceremoniously treated her last night? If so then good. Hopefully he was consumed by guilt. She could cope with the resulting compliments if that were the case.

They reached the next street along from her house and dismounted. She passed the reins to Warhurst. He closed his hand over hers and didn't let go.

He cleared his throat. "Mistress Croft. Alice."

Alice? Good lord, he was definitely feeling guilty. She tried not to smile and show too much enjoyment at his discomfort.

He tugged on his ruff and cleared his throat again.

"Go on," she prompted, aware that her smile was breaking out despite her efforts. She was going to enjoy this apology.

"I will. I am. I mean...Alice, will you marry me?"

She removed her hand. Blood rushed from her head to her toes then back up again. It thundered between her ears. Her heart pounded against her ribs. She wanted to be sick. She wanted to scream. She wanted to faint.

Instead, she laughed, an awkward girlish laugh pushed out by all the emotions roiling through her.

Warhurst's cheeks turned as crimson as her borrowed gown and his knuckles went white around the reins. "I thought you'd be pleased," he said quietly. "I thought it's what you wanted."

Her laughter dried in her throat. "Oh. You're serious."

"Of course I'm bloody serious! When have you known me not to be?"

Her breath faltered and her heart seemed to cease working altogether. She knew she should say something, anything, but she couldn't think of the right words let alone trust her voice.

"Let's go," he said gruffly. "Will your father still be at home or would he have gone to the tiring house already?" He turned to walk off. "I want to ask him for your hand before I...before it grows late."

"Wait!" He stopped and forked one eyebrow at her. He didn't look like a man happily embracing matrimony. He looked like a man trapped by his own conscience. "What if I don't want to get married? I haven't said yes."

"You haven't said no either."

She sniffed. "I might."

He cocked his head to the side and waited. When she didn't say anything he gave a short bark of humorless laughter and strode off, the horses in tow.

Alice sighed and followed. This was not how she'd imagined a proposal of marriage. There should have been kisses and hand holding and he should have gone down on one knee. Having Warhurst on his knees before her would be a sight to behold but she knew, deep down, it would never happen. Not only was he not the chivalric sort but this wasn't a real marriage proposal, not in the true romantic sense. He was doing it out of duty because he'd bedded her.

On the other hand, lords took women of her ilk to their beds all the time and didn't offer marriage. So why had he?

"You don't have to do this," she said, joining him. She glanced at his face. It was set as hard as stone. He didn't blink but kept his gaze focused on the road ahead. "I don't think there's a code of honor that applies to the deflowering of seamstresses."

He stopped suddenly so that one of the horses nudged his back. He rounded on her. "First of all, you were not a virgin and therefore deflowering you was not my honor. Secondly, I absolutely do not take any woman to my bed lightly, no matter who she is, particularly seamstresses."

"Really? Why? I thought gentlemen kept women like me as mistresses all the time."

He started walking again, turning the corner to her street. She had to trot to keep up. "Some do."

"But not you?" she asked.

"No."

"Why not?"

"That's not important," he said.

"It is to me."

He remained silent.

"Warhurst, tell me why our situation is different. What makes me different, or you, or...something!" He was the most frustrating, infuriating man. Why couldn't he just admit there was a connection between them? That he liked her and wanted to be with her? Their kisses and lovemaking had not been light, meaningless affairs. A strong bond had developed between them, deeper than mere friendship. She felt it through her entire body, it ached like the devil and lifted her up at the same time. She was sure he felt it too.

Almost, quite, nearly sure.

"You can call me Leo now," was all he said.

A pox on him!

They reached her front door and Warhurst—Leo—tied the horses to the post. It would seem he would not tell her what had prompted the offer of marriage. Very well, if he was determined to wed her then she would accept. After all, it *was* what she wanted.

"I agree to marrying you by the way," she said.

He gave her a wry look. "I thought you might."

"And it's not because you're a lord or because we spent that night together at your house." She waited for him to ask her why she agreed but he didn't so her response died on her lips.

I'm doing it because I love you and I'll have a lifetime to convince you that you love me too.

She just wished she had the courage to say it out loud.

Her father wasn't at home. Her mother and sisters curtsied to Leo and murmured surprised greetings. Jane giggled behind her hand and elbowed Elizabeth in the ribs. Elizabeth didn't stop staring at Leo, her mouth open as if her jaw was unhinged. Their mother offered him ale and bread. He politely refused. Alice quickly ushered him out and they rode to The Rose theater.

She could think of nothing to say to him so they rode most of the way in silence. No, that wasn't entirely true. She could think of a great many things to say to him, she just didn't know how to say them without sounding like a silly female.

"Shouldn't we return my horse?" she asked as they crossed

the bridge. It was early but travelers were already out in great numbers, most crossing the river into the City but some heading the same way as Alice and Leo. It was market day at Eastcheap and farmers drove their sheep over the bridge, blocking traffic in both directions. Alice breathed shallowly but it did little to lessen the stench the animals left behind. "We have the mare for the entire day so we might as well use her," Leo said.

They rode in silence along Bankside, much quieter than the bridge with very few of the whores yet at work and the theater performances not starting for a few hours yet. When they reached The Rose, Alice finally thought of something important to ask him, something she would have thought to ask earlier if she hadn't been so distracted.

"You've been trying to get Lord Hawkesbury to marry your sister so that there won't be a scandal when news of her condition becomes public."

"You might be surprised to learn that I already know that."

She ignored his sarcasm. "The scandal it will bring to *your* name you told me."

"She's my sister." He shrugged. "Any scandal involving her will rub off on me."

"And you can't have scandal attached to your name because it will further ruin your chances of obtaining finance for your mines."

He dismounted outside the theater and held out his hand to assist her. She curled her fingers around his and slid out of the saddle. Their hands remained entwined with neither making an attempt to remove them. He watched her closely, his eyes lazily hooded but there was no laziness in his sharp gaze.

"What are you trying to say, Alice?"

"You're going to all this trouble to avoid scandal over Lilly, and yet you'll willingly create another scandal if you wed me. Which, by the way, will also end your chances of marrying a rich heiress who could fund your mines."

He snapped his hand away. "That's different," he said, tying up the horses.

"Why?"

"Lilly is with child. She deserves to have a husband to take care of her and the baby. She doesn't deserve the nasty things people will say about her, the banishment by people she's known her entire life."

He might have answered the question but he'd neatly side-stepped the bigger issue—why he was willing to give up his chance of financial gain by marrying her.

"Do you mean to say you're doing this for your sister's sake, not yours?"

He patted his horse's neck and after a long moment, inclined his head. "I suppose I am."

She wondered if that was the first time he'd admitted it out loud. Perhaps it was the first time he'd admitted it to himself. Finally she was seeing cracks appear in the tough shell he'd built around himself.

He turned to face her. A frown darkened his features. "How did you know about the mines?"

"Charles told me." She took a deep breath. "He also told me about the business difficulties that befell your father."

He swore. "Bloody Grayshaw."

"It's not his fault, I pressed him. Leo, you're not like your father."

"You never knew him."

"Nor did you. He died when you were young."

"I know what he was like," he growled. He strode towards the theater door.

She ran to join him and caught his arm before he could enter. He didn't shake her off but she felt his muscles tense. She tightened her grip. "So how will you get money for your mines now?"

This time he did shake her off. He wrenched the door open. "I'll get the money some other way," he flung back over his shoulder. "Don't worry about that. The Warhurst name will rise again."

Why did he say it with such viciousness?

She couldn't ask him because he was already inside, striding across the floor where the groundlings would pack in later. He avoided the stairs and vaulted up onto the stage, leaving her standing near the front door wondering if she'd been wrong.

Perhaps he didn't love her after all. He certainly wasn't

behaving like a man in love. More like an animal chained in the bear baiting ring with its freedom, and its life, at stake.

* * *

LEO SCANNED the faces of the men in the tiring house, looking for Croft. He wasn't among the players standing in a circle studying at a bound book or play on a table. He must have interrupted their rehearsal.

"Lord Warhurst!" Roger Style tossed his head so that the tall feather in his hat fluttered like a flag. "What a surprise." He broke from the circle and came over to Leo, a smile stuck to his face. He looked to have a crooked back but then he straightened and Leo realized he must have been bowing.

"Is Master Croft in?" Leo asked.

"Croft?" Style's smiled slipped. "What do you want with him, my lord?"

"He's upstairs," said the player named Shakespeare.

The young actor who performed the female roles flopped onto a nearby chair, sighed then belched.

Leo thanked Shakespeare and headed up the stairs. Behind him, Style yelled at the boy, Freddie. Freddie belched again. He didn't hear Alice's clear voice joining theirs. She mustn't have followed him, thankfully. She was too distracting with her beguiling face, challenging eyes and all those bloody awkward questions.

Why did she have to keep asking them anyway? She'd got her wish—they were to be wed. She wouldn't be asking pointed questions if it hadn't been for Grayshaw sticking his nose in where it wasn't wanted. So much for their friendship.

Alice had caught him unprepared outside, making him admit he wanted to avoid scandal for Lilly's sake. While that was true, he was doing it for his own sake too. He was. It was even more important for Lilly's condition not to become known until she was safely wed to Hawke now that Leo was to marry Alice. The mud that would get slung his way after his betrothal was announced would be thick enough, he didn't want it to be worse on Lilly's account.

Of course he was happy that Lilly would have what she wanted too—marriage to Hawke, even though she could do better. It made him very, very happy. Indeed, Leo was much happier than he'd been for some time, he realized with shock. Despite Alice's questions, despite the desperate situation his finances were about to be plunged into thanks to a marriage he couldn't afford, he couldn't stop smiling.

It must be because his sister's situation was finally about to be settled. After speaking to Croft, Leo would set the wheels in motion to release Hawke from his obligation to marry Patience Enderby. The world was beginning to steady itself after being tilted at a dangerous angle for several weeks.

"Lord Warhurst! What brings you up here?" asked Croft. He sat on the closed lid of a large coffer, a threaded needle in one hand, a white garment of some description across his lap. Several more coffers were pushed up against the walls and a large table sat square in the center of the room. It was covered with fabric, scissors, threads, beads and a long red wig.

Leo ducked under a blue cape hanging from the overhead beam. A dark patch marred the bottom edge of the fabric. It reeked of ale.

"Part of Freddie's costume," Croft said, nodding at the cape. "Sometimes he forgets to change before he goes drinking."

"I'd wager Style isn't very happy about that."

Croft's long white beard twitched with his smile. "Aye, you could say that."

Leo sat on the closed coffer lid beside Croft but he felt too low so he stood again, but then was too high. He couldn't ask permission to wed the man's daughter while towering over him, so he sat again. He stretched out his legs and crossed the ankles. Croft watched him out of the corner of his eye. His fingers fussed with the fabric but he seemed to have stopped sewing.

"I'd like to ask for Alice's hand in marriage."

The garment fell off Croft's lap and slipped to the floor, taking the needle and thread with it. He stared at Leo, mouth ajar. Leo picked up the dropped items and handed them back to the tiring house manager.

"Is that a yes?"

"Ummmmm..."

Leo gave him a grim smile. "I realize this has come as a shock."

"Uhhhhh..."

"I've come to know your daughter well." God, that sounded like he knew Alice carnally. It might be true but he doubted it was something a father wanted to hear. "We've become friends. I like Alice." It felt good saying her name, natural. Why had it taken him so long to say it? "I believe she likes me too. We want to marry as soon as possible."

Croft's beard shivered as he pressed his lips together. Leo waited. Croft frowned, shook his head and said, "But why?"

Leo sighed. This wasn't an auspicious beginning. If Alice's own father couldn't understand the union, how would everyone else react to the announcement? "I told you I like her, she likes me. Isn't that explanation enough?"

Croft flinched. "I, uh, yes of course, my lord."

"So are you giving me permission?"

The old man's eyes widened. "Do you need it?"

Leo couldn't help a chuckle escaping. He clapped Croft on the shoulder. "Of course. I may be many things but I am still a gentleman. Well? Do I have it?"

"Y, yes you do, my lord. Most definitely. Where is Alice?" Croft glanced at the door. "Is she here?" His gaze shifted back to Leo. "She does agree to the union, doesn't she?"

"Of course. Why?"

Croft sighed and resumed his sewing. "She can be a contrary girl. Who knows what thoughts rattle around that head of hers. She's always had grand ideas. She wants something more, she says, something else." He sighed deeply. "I'll never understand her. What's wrong with being my assistant? It's a respectable occupation for a girl."

Leo tuned out the prattle and swallowed hard. Panic rose into his chest like heartburn, scalding. "Something more," he echoed. "Like what?" *Would she agree to marry someone she didn't like to get what she wanted?*

"Like wanting her own shop. That's the latest scheme. Once

she said she'd like to be a tiring house manager in her own right."

Leo let out a long breath. The answer should have given him relief but it didn't. He'd always known the "something more" Alice wanted was his title and estate, he didn't need her father confirming or denying it. Leo just *knew*.

He extended his hand to Croft. The tiring house manager looked at it for a few heartbeats before taking it in a firm grip.

"Good luck to you, my lord," Croft said.

"Thank you." *I'll need it.*

* * *

ALICE HAD MANAGED to do the unthinkable. Render an entire company of players speechless. All the men stared at her, mouths open like dead fish.

"It's true," she said, unable to stop the laughter bubbling to the surface. They all looked so ridiculous, she couldn't help being amused. "He's asking Father's permission now."

Will was the first to recover. He took her hand and kissed it. "Congratulations, Mistress Croft. Or is it Lady Warhurst?"

"It's just Alice to you," she said. "It always will be."

Edward and Henry congratulated her. Roger stared at her and made a strange sound as if he was choking. Perhaps he was —choking on his snobbery.

"Bloody hell," Freddie said, hands on hips. He pursed his lips and openly appraised her. He studied her face as if seeing it for the first time and nodded. "I suppose you're pretty, but you're no beauty." His gaze shifted down and settled on her chest. He snorted. "Now I understand."

Henry punched him in the arm as Alice tried to think of something witty to say. She couldn't and fortunately Leo came down the stairs to distract them all from her breasts.

He stopped on the bottom step and narrowed his eyes at the troupe. "Why are you all staring? Of course he said yes."

"Of course," Edward muttered.

"He'd be a fool not to," Henry agreed.

Roger Style felt behind him for a chair, found one then sat

down heavily. "What's the world coming to?" he mumbled to no one in particular.

Alice patted his shoulder. "Never mind, Master Style, at least now Father can get himself a real assistant and not a silly female."

Will, Edward and Henry all bit their lips which did nothing to hide their smiles. Freddie snorted but Roger didn't seem to notice. He brightened. "I know just the lad," he said.

Alice didn't have the heart to tell him her father would probably ask her sister Elizabeth. At thirteen she was old enough to learn the trade.

"Congratulations," Will said to Leo. "You're a lucky man." He offered his hand and Leo shook it.

"Very lucky," Henry said. He too offered his hand but Leo hesitated before shaking it. His questioning gaze slid to Alice.

She knew exactly what the question was without hearing it—were these men more than mere friends to her? She rolled her eyes and shook her head slightly. Leo thrust out his chest and accepted the congratulations of the other men then he gently drew her aside. She smiled up at him because despite her misgivings, he really was very handsome and she loved him. Their marriage might have a rocky start but she was determined to not let him regret it.

He rubbed the back of Alice's hand with his thumb. Her fingers closed tighter around his and she blinked up at him. He watched her through those dark green eyes, so intensely that she wanted to melt into a puddle right there at his feet. He was going to kiss her. She was certain of it.

"I have to tell my family," he said.

She relegated any thoughts of kisses to the back of her mind. "You mean *we* have to tell your family."

"It's better if I do it alone. Mother can be...unpredictable."

In a way it was sweet that he was protecting her, but she'd have to face his mother sooner or later and she wasn't one for putting off the inevitable. "So can I. Let's go."

He sighed then shrugged and followed her out of the tiring house.

* * *

"AH, GOOD, YOU'RE SITTING DOWN," Leo said upon entering his mother's withdrawing room. Alice remained outside where he'd asked her to wait a moment. To his surprise, she agreed. She must be more nervous than she let on.

Lady Warhurst regarded him as if he were a fool. Perhaps he was. He seemed to be doing some remarkably foolish things of late. Except he didn't *feel* like a fool. He felt...strange. Like he'd never felt before—daring and adventurous and light-headed. More like Blake. The strange feeling had only grown on the short ride back to the inn where they'd returned Alice's horse then gone onto his brother's house.

"Of course I'm sitting," his mother said. "You don't expect me to read on my feet, do you?"

He tried to stand beside the fireplace but it was too hot and his limbs needed the exercise so he crossed the room. His mother swiveled to follow him. "Sorry, I'm just..." *Excited.* "I have two things to tell you, Mother. The first is that Hawkesbury will soon be released from his obligation to marry Enderby's daughter." He went on to explain about the letter, leaving out the detail of how he'd obtained it. "I'm going to confront Enderby this very day. I want him to see that now he no longer has the letter in his possession, he's in quite a predicament. He won't want Walsingham to know that he failed to pass on a very important missive."

His mother put down her book. "Is that wise, Leo? Lord Enderby is no fool. He won't like being forced into a corner."

"It's a corner of his own making. Besides, he will have no choice but to relinquish Hawke from his obligation to wed his daughter now that he has nothing to use as blackmail. If Hawke does love Lilly as you say, then I expect him to come to me and ask for permission to wed her instead. If he doesn't do it willingly—."

She raised a hand. "I know, I know, you'll force him. I hope this time it doesn't end in violence. You've still got the bruises from your last encounter."

He touched his cheek. He'd forgotten about the cuts there.

"You said there were two things you wanted to tell me. I take it the second thing isn't quite so dramatic?"

Leo swallowed and paced the room again. Lord but it was warm. "Why do you keep your fire so hot, Mother? It's stifling in here." He wiped the back of his neck above his ruff.

"I find it quite comfortable, thank you, now stop moving about. It's giving me back ache."

He stopped near the window seat and looked at the door. Alice was outside, waiting to be called in at the appropriate moment. When was that moment? Now? After he told his mother?

"Leo! The second thing..."

"Ah. Yes." He sat down. Perhaps it was best if Alice waited a little longer. One unpredictable female in the room was quite enough. "I'm getting married."

The book slid off his mother's lap. Her lips parted and an unladylike gasp slipped out. "Married? To whom?"

"Alice Croft." He swallowed. "The seamstress for Lord Hawkesbury's Men."

"I know who she is." She bent to pick up her book. "Well, that's a relief. I thought it was going to be to someone I didn't know."

He blinked. "A...a relief? You're...glad?"

She stood and came to sit beside him. "After she stayed here that night, I asked Lilly about her. I could see there was something between you. I admit I wasn't...enthusiastic at first. She's not the sort of girl I expected to catch your interest, but clearly she has. Lilly confirmed it. She said she liked her, that she was clever and capable and precisely the sort of woman you needed."

Needed? Alice? But he needed a woman of high birth with a lot of money. He could understand his sister might be going a little mad thanks to her troubles with Hawke and the baby but his mother too? She had no such excuse. "You're happy about the union, even though Alice is the daughter of a tiring house manager?"

She patted his hand and sighed. "I admit it would have been easier if you'd fallen in love with the widowed Finchbrooke girl which is why I encouraged you in that direction. Quite severely,

I fear, and I'm sorry if I seemed unfeeling. I've only ever had your best interests in mind and I thought wedding her would remove some of the financial burden from your shoulders. But no one knows more than I that the heart cannot be manipulated. If you're in love with Alice—."

"In love!" He scoffed and almost told her it was nothing to do with love and everything to do with duty to the woman he'd bedded but stopped himself. That was not a conversation he ever wanted to have with his mother. "I've told you before, I don't believe in love."

His mother began to say something but it was drowned out by a loud knock on the door. It swung open before she could tell the knocker to enter and Blake strode in, a mixture of horror, anger and desperation on his face. Alice was right behind him, looking paler than usual.

"Mistress Croft!" Lady Warhurst said, rising. "You're here!" She glared pointedly at Leo who rose too.

"Uh, yes, I was about to ask her to join us," he said.

"Never mind that," Alice said with an urgency that made everyone stare at her. "Your brother has something to say."

Leo almost corrected her out of habit and said half-brother but Blake spoke first.

"It's Hawkesbury. He's been arrested and thrown in the Tower."

CHAPTER 22

*L*eo's body went rigid as Blake told them how Walsingham's men had arrested Hawke for treason. He'd been taken by boat from his house to the infamous Traitor's Gate at the Tower where those accused of treason went.

"On what grounds?" Leo asked. But he knew. The letter. Someone had decided to break their silence now that the missive was no longer in Enderby's possession. His money was on Enderby himself, trying to save his own neck while he still could.

Alice came up beside him and placed her long, fine fingers in his. He closed his hand around hers and squeezed. "But you have the only evidence of Lord Hawkesbury's father's treason," she said.

"Which is why we can still stop this."

"They'll be looking into the case now," Blake said. "If they can't find any evidence then he might be released."

'Might' being the most important word in that sentence. Everyone knew the queen and her chief adviser could do as they pleased for as long as they pleased. If they thought Hawkesbury was a serious threat then they would keep him in the Tower and find new evidence.

"Her Majesty likes Lord Hawkesbury," Lady Warhurst said, twisting her fingers together in front of her. "I cannot imagine she'd detain him for long." She glanced from Leo to Blake then back again. Looking for confirmation? She didn't get it.

"We have to get him released as quickly as possible," Blake said, removing his hat and running a hand through his hair. "Lilly will be devastated when she finds out and her health is delicate enough as it is."

"We won't tell her unless it becomes necessary," Lady Warhurst said.

"I'll speak to Enderby," Leo said. "He needs to be made aware that his own freedom rests with me." He gave Alice's hand one more squeeze before releasing it.

Blake noticed, raised an eyebrow but simply said, "I'm coming."

Leo let him. Blake was the only person he wanted at his back in this kind of situation. There was none better.

"Mother, can you entertain Alice until I return?"

"Of course," she said with an absent smile. "I could do with the company."

"Forgive me," Alice said, "but I'll be needed at the theater. There's a great deal of work to be done tidying up the tiring house."

Leo thought the tiring house had looked quite orderly but he said nothing. He could understand the need to escape his mother. At least Alice hadn't requested to join himself and Blake. He didn't want to order her to stay away from Enderby or his daughter but order her he would. The Enderby house was a dangerous place for her to be now that she was connected to the Warhurst-Blakewell family.

He and Blake left the withdrawing room. Greeves handed him his hat, coat and gloves in the entrance hall. Blake still wore his. Together they strode to the stables and mounted their horses, both of which were still saddled.

"Let me do all the talking," Leo said as they rode as fast they could across the City. It was too busy with midday traffic to do more than a swift walking pace and Leo had to grind back his frustration. Blake looked far more composed. No doubt he saw this as yet another adventure.

Then Leo remembered his brother's face as he'd told them the news of Hawke's arrest and knew it was not an adventure he'd invited.

"You talk, I'll slice his head off with my sword," Blake said. So much for composed.

"That'll achieve a lot."

"It'll make me feel better."

"This is about making Lilly feel better, not you. She's my sister too."

Blake grunted. "Nice to see Alice Croft has brought you to your senses."

Leo shifted fully in his saddle to look at his brother. "What's that supposed to mean?"

"It means you've not only called Lilly your sister instead of half-sister, but you've finally realized this endeavor is about her wellbeing and not your reputation."

True, he had come to recognize both those things, however it wasn't Alice's doing. The idea that she could alter his opinion! Ha! Blake was becoming as bad as their mother with his ridiculous sentimentality. Yet another reason why Leo would never fall in love. He was far too sensible.

Still, he decided not to tell Blake he'd also been thinking of him as his brother and not the half that he was.

It was time to turn this conversation away from women and romance and start thinking about the task ahead of them. "Promise me you'll keep your sword sheathed, your fists at your sides and let me do the talking."

Blake *humphed* and urged his horse ahead. Leo had to wait for a cart with a dozen children and just as many chickens riding on the back to pass before he could join his brother. Neither spoke for the remainder of the journey.

* * *

ALICE BREATHED a sigh of relief when she found Grayshaw at home. She'd thought he'd be with Walsingham, doing whatever it was clerks did. He must have returned home for his midday dinner.

"Alice, my dear, so pleased to—."

"Enough, Charles. No more sweet words from you." They stood in his study, which she'd realized after changing in the empty sitting room earlier that day was the only room furnished to receive guests. "I think you know why I'm here."

"Ah." At least he didn't try to pretend otherwise. "Your guard dog not with you?"

"Leo's busy elsewhere." Busy barking up the wrong tree. As soon as Blake had told them about Hawke's arrest, Alice had guessed it was Charles who'd alerted Walsingham to the existence of the treasonous letter. Enderby had too much to lose by admitting he'd withheld it. Charles on the other hand had a career to forge and what better way to do that than make himself useful to the queen's spymaster.

"Leo?" he echoed. "Not Warhurst anymore?"

"We're going to be married."

His eyebrows almost shot off the top of his head. "Really? Well." He nodded slowly and sucked on his bottom lip. "I thought his kind kept your kind as mistresses."

"No, that's just your kind," she spat back.

He grimaced. "I suppose I deserved that."

He deserved much more but she couldn't afford to make him angry. She needed him. "You have to tell your employers that you made a mistake and the letter doesn't implicate any Hawkesbury, living or dead."

He snorted. "Alice, I adore you, I really do, but you're a naive girl if you think I'll do that."

She suddenly needed to sit and plopped down on the chair opposite him. He sat too and leaned his elbows on the desk. It was piled with papers and she could just manage to read what he'd written on the top-most one. It was a letter addressed to Sir Francis Walsingham, requesting an audience to discuss him returning to his employment.

Returning? Oh. Good. Lord.

"You no longer work for the crown, do you? That's why you're here in the middle of the day and not with Walsingham." Charles's gaze shifted. "What happened?"

"Nothing," he said.

"Were you caught reading Hawkesbury's file?"

He sighed and leaned back in the chair. "I was caught, yes, but not with Hawkesbury's file. Since I was already inside the storeroom, I took the opportunity to...check some other files."

"Why were you doing that?"

"I don't wish to discuss this with you, Alice."

"You were going to blackmail some other prominent families, weren't you? Like Enderby did. Hawkesbury's situation gave you an idea, didn't it?"

He crossed his arms and gave her a defiant stare. The nasty, devious toad! Why had it taken her so long to see through the flattery to the slimy creature lurking beneath?

"Now, if there's nothing else," he said, "I'm going to respectfully ask that you leave."

"And I'm going to disrespectfully tell you I'm staying until you agree to inform Walsingham you were wrong."

"Alice. Pretty, foolish Alice with stars in her eyes." He laughed and shook his head. "I'm pleased you're marrying Warhurst, I truly am, and I understand why you're willing to shackle yourself to that cantankerous bear but—."

"I'm marrying him because I love him."

"But," he went on as if she'd not spoken, "do you know he's penniless? He hasn't got a cent to his name, his house is a crumbling ruin and his estate is a patch of barren land in the middle of nowhere."

"You already told me that. What's your point, Charles?" She knew she shouldn't nibble at the bait he was dangling but she couldn't help it. Charles was leading up to something and she knew it was in her best interests to find out what, even if it was something she didn't want to hear.

"I also told you about his father's history, didn't I? How he left his high-born wife for his low-born mistress."

She tilted her chin. "I love Leo. I'm not marrying him for his money or title."

He snorted. "So why drag him down with you? Do you know what will be said about him when your marriage is made public? He'll be ridiculed at court. Do you know how vicious those people are to each other? They're like savage dogs. The scent of scandal drives them into a frenzy. But it'll be worse for

Leo. He hasn't been allowed to forget what his father did thirty years ago. Many of them are still angry that they were made to look foolish and these are the same people who think the apple doesn't fall far from the tree. Any chance he had of dragging the Warhurst name out of the mud is now gone by marrying you."

Alice's throat thickened. It hurt to swallow. "He doesn't care about court gossip. If you knew him at all you would know that."

"Ah, yes." He rested his elbows on the chair's armrests and steepled his fingers. He pointed them at her. "True. But do you know that court gossip will stop anyone from even contemplating investing in his mines? Not a single man will want to be associated with someone who's proving to be so like his wastrel father. They wouldn't risk it."

"Of course I know," she snapped. "Charles, I'm not here—."

"Do you know," he said loudly, "that no money for mines means his tenants will starve. They can't farm the land anymore, it's too barren, and there's no employment for them in the villages up there."

"No employment?" she said weakly.

"Nothing. Many country folk have moved to London or other centers but find they don't have the skills to get good work. They're no better off here than they were there."

"Oh." Those poor people. Charles may be many things but he wouldn't lie about hardship on such a scale. He'd known desperation when he was orphaned and wouldn't treat the subject lightly.

How could she have been so selfish to not see the whole picture? She'd been so wrapped up in her own drama that she'd failed to consider the people who relied upon Leo. People who needed him more than she did.

"By marrying you, he can't rely on a dowry to help him out of his financial woes, nor can he rely on anyone at court to invest. He'll have failed his people."

Oh God, oh God. Alice's stomach clenched and rolled as if she would be ill. It was awful, simply horrible. So many people...with nothing.

She shook her head, tried to make sense of it, tried to think.

Why would Leo wed her at all if so much was at stake? But she could only think of one reason.

Pride. Bloody senseless pride and honor.

A pox on him! By doing the right thing where she was concerned, he was putting his tenants in jeopardy.

"His family," she said, hearing the plea in her voice. "They have money."

"He's too proud to borrow a shilling off his brother."

"But surely for the sake of all those people..."

He huffed out a bleak laugh. "You really don't understand the depth of his stubbornness, or his sense of duty, do you? Let me explain it to you." He regarded her with amusement, as if he was speaking to a favorite child. "Warhurst's worst nightmare isn't destroying the lives of his tenants, or hearing the slurs against his name. His greatest fear is that he'll become like his father."

She shifted in her seat and thought about getting up and walking out altogether. Charles didn't deserve this attention from her. He was a petty-minded, greedy man who didn't value friendship or loyalty or the sense of duty he so derided. But she needed to hear this. He was offering her an insight into the man she loved—an insight she lacked. It was the key to unlocking the mystery that was Leo and she desperately wanted it.

Especially now she knew about the effect his marriage would have on his estate and tenants. *Something* must have made him propose marriage to her, something important.

"I don't understand," she said. "His father left his mother for an ordinary woman, a nobody. I'm nobody. If he wanted to avoid the comparisons then he's failed miserably on that score alone."

"The important part isn't your lack of noble birth, not to Warhurst anyway, it's the fact that his father dishonored his wife. He didn't just keep a mistress, he actually left his wife and son to live with her. Apparently he'd met this woman before he married and continued the relationship afterwards. Its rumored he couldn't forget her." He shrugged. "It was very scandalous at the time, and Lady Warhurst was humiliated."

"Are you saying Leo doesn't want to marry a noblewoman because he's worried he'll leave her for me? That's ridiculous. Leo would never break the sanctity of marriage."

"Wouldn't he?"

"He's far too honorable."

"Is he? In that case, if he's so honorable he wouldn't have taken a young woman who wasn't his wife to his bed, would he?"

He had her there. She stood, suddenly desperate for air. The fire might be low but the study was stifling with all those papers everywhere and the tart smell of ink. It clawed at her throat, her nose, and made her eyes sting.

"I have to go," she said, stumbling towards the door.

Charles was at her side, gripping her by the arms. He held her up, his face close to hers. Too close. She couldn't focus on his eyes. His breath was hot on her skin. It stank of ale. His lips brushed hers and she drew back.

"What are you doing?" she said, gasping for air.

"We were good together, Alice," he murmured. His fingers bit into her arms and she winced at the burning pain. "Now that you're to be wed we can resume our...fun. Remember the fun we had?" His mouth descended on her. She turned her head away and he kissed her cheek instead of her mouth.

She gathered all her strength and shoved him away. "Enough!" Her breathing came hard and fast but at least her mind was clear now. She understood what she must do. "You and I were a mistake then and we're a mistake now. Stay away from me or I'll tell Leo what you just did. I think you know him well enough to understand that he's a jealous man. Imagine what he'd do if he discovered his so-called friend betrayed his trust *and* tried to kiss his betrothed."

Charles wiped his mouth with the back of his hand, never taking his eyes off her. His icy gaze sliced through her. She shivered. "Good luck to you both," he snapped. "You'll need it." He jerked open the door. "Oh and when you see him, thank him for me. Now that he's to marry you the path is clear for me to open negotiations with his widowed neighbor."

The poor woman. Alice would have to think of a way to alert her to Charles' true nature.

But first she had to make another visit not too far away. A visit she didn't want to undertake.

* * *

LEO AND BLAKE had to wait for Enderby to return from a ride before they were received in his study. The same study Leo had raided with Alice only the night before to get the letter. The coffer that had contained it still occupied the same spot. It was locked, the key presumably inside the cushion pocket under Enderby's fat arse.

The steward introduced them then bowed out of the room. Enderby glanced up from his papers, waved at the chairs opposite then returned to his paperwork. Leo and Blake remained standing.

"Tell Walsingham you made a mistake," Leo said.

Enderby looked up, frowned. "What are you talking about?"

Blake rested his knuckles on the desk and leaned down. "You got Hawke arrested," he said, "now get him released."

Enderby's pen dripped ink over the page. He didn't notice. "Lord Hawkesbury has been arrested? Good lord, on what charge?"

"Treason," Leo said.

"Treason!" Enderby glanced at the locked coffer and paled. His jaw dropped then snapped shut then opened again. He looked like a large fish flailing on the dock. "How...? he whispered.

"Don't play the fool," Blake snarled, leaning over the desk.

Enderby backed away and dropped the pen. "It wasn't me," he said, eyeing the rapier strapped to Blake's hip. Blake never cleaned the end of it so it looked well used. He said it was a ploy to scare off attackers. Leo might be the only person in the world who knew Blake had only ever killed two men with it, and that had been in self-defense.

Enderby looked genuinely afraid. Leo's anger dissolved instantly. He was wrong. Enderby hadn't told Walsingham about the letter. His shock was too genuine and his fear too palpable.

So if Enderby hadn't told Walsingham, who...?

Grayshaw. Bloody Charles Grayshaw. Leo clenched his fists at his sides. So much for friendship. The arse licker was going to pay for this.

"Let's go," Leo said. "We're wasting our time."

Beside him, Blake seethed with anger for the fat, ruddy-faced man sitting behind his desk. "It might not have been him, but he started this by using that letter against Hawke." He rested his hand on his sword hilt. "Your actions have upset our sister greatly and we don't like seeing her upset."

Lord but he could be dramatic when he wanted to be. That was the problem with being around players and playwrights so much.

"Letter?" Enderby's gaze shifted to the coffer again. "What letter?"

"The letter implicating the late earl of Hawkesbury that is now in my possession. The one you didn't pass onto Walsingham but instead used to force the current Lord Hawkesbury into a marriage he doesn't want."

"Thereby upsetting our sister," Blake added.

"I, I..." Enderby's jowls began to shake and the ruddiness in his cheeks slowly began to fade.

"Check if you like," Leo said. "We can wait."

Enderby hesitated, glanced from one sword to the other, then stood. He removed the key from the chair cushion and unlocked the coffer. He rifled through the papers twice before sitting back on his haunches. "How did you get in here?"

Blake glanced at Leo. "We're wasting our time," he said.

Leo nodded. "He's no use to us."

"Shall we kill him?"

Leo tapped his finger on his sword hilt, enjoying the look on Enderby's face. He'd gone completely white and his eyes were huge, much like the rest of him. "There might be reprisals."

"Oh, I don't know," Blake said. "The queen can't possibly like him more than she likes me. She'd have to put us in the Tower as a show of authority but not for long and we'd be treated well. What do you say? Would you like to have first go?"

A strangled gurgle bubbled inside Enderby's throat. "You wouldn't," he whispered. Leo shrugged. Blake chuckled. "Pearson!" Enderby shouted. "Pearson, here, now!"

The elderly steward flung the door open and took in the scene. His eyes widened and his hands began to shake. "Be easy,"

Leo said to him. "We were just having a little fun at your master's expense."

"Father? Is everything—." Patience ran into the study but halted in the doorway when she saw Leo and Blake. "Oh, good day to you, my lord, Master Blakewell."

Close behind her stood Alice, peering over Patience's shoulder as if she were watching a play. What the bloody hell was she doing here?

"You," said Enderby, frowning at Alice. He must have been paying attention last night. "I thought you left..." His face cleared. The color flooded back into his cheeks and he blinked over and over. "*You* stole the letter. You...you *bitch*!"

Bright red light exploded behind Leo's eyes. Blood rushed between his ears, pounding out an erratic beat. He felt a hand on his arm, steadying—Blake's. He tried to step closer to Enderby but was held back. He was going to thump his brother, right after he made Enderby eat his words. "You do not speak to her like that," Leo ground out through his tight jaw. "Apologize."

Enderby snorted.

Blake's grip tightened. "This is nothing to do with Alice," he said quietly to Enderby.

"Nothing to do with her!" Enderby spluttered, sending spittle over the rushes. "She robbed me!" He turned on his daughter. "Explain yourself."

Panic seized Leo's heart where before it had been gripped by pure rage. This was all about to unravel and he had no control over it. He glanced at Alice. She looked remarkably composed as she watched Enderby square up to his daughter. Patience didn't back down, surprisingly.

"I had to do something, Father. I don't want to marry Lord Hawkesbury."

"Shut up, Child! You'll do as I say." He lifted his hand and Patience flinched and shut her eyes. Leo and Blake both grabbed Enderby's arm and forced it back to his side.

"You hit anyone here and I'll hit you twice as hard," Leo said.

Enderby stretched out his fingers but kept them at his side. "Explain yourselves. Who is she?" He nodded at Alice.

"I'm Alice Croft," she said, stiffly. "I'm nobody." A change seemed to have come over her since he last saw her in his mother's parlor. She held herself very erect, still almost, and she hadn't once looked in his direction.

"Not nobody," Leo said, watching her and not Enderby. He thought he saw her wince but he couldn't be sure. "She is my bride-to-be."

Patience gasped then took Alice's hand. "Congratulations," she said. "I knew it."

Her words were almost drowned out by Enderby's raucous laughter. "Married? To her? And don't try to tell me she's your wealthy friend from Essex, Patience. She might have fooled me last night but not today. She really is a nobody, isn't she?" He turned his shining eyes on Leo. "Congratulations, Warhurst, you've surpassed your father for foolishness. At least he married well."

Maybe the queen really would be lenient if Leo killed him. The realm would be a far better place without Enderby in it.

"Steady," Blake murmured in his ear. "He's not worth it."

He was right. All jokes aside, Her Majesty could not afford to overlook the murder of a peer. Pity. Leo would enjoy gutting the slimy fish.

"Thank you," Enderby said. "Thank you, thank you for making me laugh today, Alice Croft. Tell me, what does your father do?"

Alice lifted her chin. "He's tiring house manager for—."

"Tiring house manager! He works for a theater company?" Enderby tilted his head back and laughed loudly. Too loudly.

Leo grabbed Enderby's doublet and pulled him up straight. Then he landed a punch right on all three of his chins, making them wobble more. It wasn't a hard punch, just enough to wipe the smile off Enderby's face.

"Do not insult my betrothed again," Leo said, "or her family. They're good people. Better by far than you."

Enderby tried to shake himself free. In the end, Leo just let him go. "Are you going to do that to everyone who laughs at you?" he said, rubbing his chin. "Well? Because if you think I'm being cruel, just wait until the rest of the court hears about this."

"I don't care what they think."

"No? You don't care that you'll be compared to your father with his cheap whore of a mistress?"

Alice watched Leo carefully out of the corner of her eye. He seemed to be holding onto his anger by a few frayed threads. Thank goodness Blake was there to come between them if need be. The steward didn't look capable of stopping Leo if he flew at Enderby. In fact, the steward had disappeared outside.

"You're just the same as him," Enderby went on. Did the man not have enough sense to stop? Couldn't he see the black temper Leo was in? "You're just as selfish as he was. He didn't care what his actions did to his wife, his child, or his tenants. He was a hopeless husband, hopeless father and no better than a criminal, stealing from those of us who funded him. His people almost starved because of his foolishness."

Alice thought Leo might hit him again but he surprised her by not moving. His chest rose and fell with his hard breathing and his jaw could have been hewn from rock but he didn't attack Enderby. He took everything the horrible man said in his stride.

"Father, please," Patience said.

Enderby didn't acknowledge her, didn't seem to hear her. Alice wasn't sure why she'd come to her for help anymore. She'd hoped Patience could convince her father to end her betrothal to Hawke now the letter was no longer in his possession but it was clear that would've been a fruitless endeavor.

"Enough of this," Alice said. "Leo is not at all like his father. Everything he's done, he's done with his tenants at the forefront of his mind. A kinder landlord, a kinder gentleman, you could not find. You, Lord Enderby, are the scoundrel here. You've kept two couples apart for your own gain. Nobody is happy, your daughter especially—."

"My daughter is a dutiful creature," he growled. "She'll do as she's told."

Patience bowed her head but not before Alice saw a tear drip down her cheek.

"Let's go," Blake said. He gripped Leo's shoulders and steered him towards the door. Alice squeezed Patience's hand and tried to give her a look of hope. She doubted she'd succeeded because she felt nothing but a sense of hopelessness for all involved.

Including herself. Especially herself. She couldn't wed Leo now. Not when it had been made gravely clear to her the trouble she was causing him and his tenants.

Tears stung the backs of her eyes and clogged her throat. She glanced at Leo. He was watching her, his expression dark and dangerous, his eyes shining like polished emeralds.

Outside on the forecourt, Blake strode ahead in the direction of the stables. Leo remained with her but he was no longer looking at her. A small muscle pulsed high in his cheek and his fists were closed at his sides, the knuckles white.

"Leo," she whispered. She wanted to touch him. Hold him. Tell him everything would be all right and they would find a way to be together and save his estate and people. They could ask his brother for money...but then his pride would suffer and she couldn't force him to swallow that too when it was all he had left.

She wanted to help him so much, to make his life easier, and there was only one way she could do that.

Relieve him of his obligation to marry her. She only needed to find a way to tell him.

CHAPTER 23

*L*eo's night was a sleepless one. Burning anger kept him awake. Anger at Enderby for his senseless words, and anger at Grayshaw for betraying him and for not being at home when Leo paid him a visit.

But there was concern lurking beneath the surface too. Some of the concern was for Lilly. Their mother had told her what had happened to Hawkesbury and she'd retreated into herself again, refusing to eat and taking to her bed early. Most of his concern however was for Alice. She'd not spoken to him after they left Enderby's house. She'd uttered an excuse about helping her father then left before he could stop her. He knew she was lying about having work to do, or exaggerating at best. Something had changed within her. He could only assume Enderby's words had sunk in and she agreed with them—that Leo was a worthless piece of dirt, just like his father. If she hadn't realized the depth of his troubles before, she did now.

And she wanted nothing more to do with him.

He shouldn't think about it, not until after the business with Hawkesbury was resolved. Perhaps Alice simply needed time to digest it all. She'd soon return to the same conclusion as before— that Leo was titled, a landowner and that marrying him would see her rise in the world even if she wouldn't be wealthy.

Yes, that's all she needed—time. Good because he liked

having her near. Her practical mind and her biting wit brought brightness into his life. He was surprised to find that he was happy to be marrying her. Very happy. It felt right.

He would go to her after breakfast, directly after he paid Grayshaw another visit. No way was he taking her to that arse-wipe's house. He didn't want her to witness what he would do to his one-time friend, nor did he want to see the way Grayshaw looked at her—like he wanted to devour her.

Leo was the only one allowed to do any devouring where Alice was concerned.

But Leo never got to Grayshaw's house, or Alice's. A summons came from court. Leo, Blake, Lilly and Lady Warhurst arrived in the queen's audience chamber an hour later. As usual there was a large number of people waiting for their moment to beg a favor from their sovereign. The queen herself sat on her throne, her advisors flanking her, listening patiently to a gentleman plead for something or other.

As Leo and his family moved through the crowd, whispers followed them like drifts of smoke on the breeze.

"...Hawke's lover..." he heard one courtier say to another.

"...scandalous..." said a young woman.

"A seamstress!" yet another snorted. "She's got him wrapped around her finger."

"More like her..."

"Just like his father," said an elderly gentleman with a curl of his lip. Leo recognized him as one of his father's creditors he'd paid off years earlier.

"She'll lead him astray too," said the man's companion.

The whispers became murmurs then open discussion. The voices echoed around the audience chamber, filled his head, made it throb. All faces swiveled towards them, even the queen's. Leo stared straight ahead, concentrating on keeping his fists at his sides and not showing any emotion. He dared not glance at his brother, sister or mother lest he see their pain. He couldn't risk anything shattering the thin veneer of composure he'd wrapped around himself. He suspected his brother was just as frustrated that he couldn't challenge every man in that room to a duel. Their mother should not have to listen to such horse shit. The hurt she must have endured years earlier at the hands of his father had been lessened by her marriage to Blakewell, thank God, but it must distress her to hear such maliciousness dredged up again.

Leo stopped still. Lilly almost bumped into him. She looped her hand through his arm and gave him a pleading look.

"Not here, Leo," she muttered.

He kept walking, drawing her gently along with him. "It's all right, Lil, I won't make a scene. I've just realized I'm not as angry as I should be. Not for myself anyway, only for you and Mother."

She gave him a smile which might have been weak but was heartfelt, nevertheless. "You just called me Lil. You never call me that, only Robert does."

He patted her hand. "Let me know if you need to escape and I'll get you out. Blake and Mother can make your excuses to the queen."

"I'm well enough, Leo. But I'll be much better once I know Hawke will be released."

He winked at her. "He will be."

She squeezed his arm and whispered, "Thank you."

The queen signaled them to approach. Leo bowed low to her, as did his brother. Their mother and sister curtsied. He then nodded to Sir Francis Walsingham sitting on the queen's right. Her old advisor looked frail, his thin frame swallowed up by the black gown with its fur collar. He leaned forward on his walking stick, his long gray beard pooling in his lap, and regarded Leo with eyes as sharp as ever. He might be weak of body but only a fool would think his mind had diminished.

"Lady Warhurst, we are so pleased to have your company," the queen said, holding out her hand. His mother kissed the royal ring. "It's been too long. And your pretty daughter." She smiled at Lilly who curtsied again and kept her head bowed. "Such a jewel in your family's crown."

"She is, Your Majesty, and my greatest comfort."

The queen leaned forward and clasped Lady Warhurst's hand. The two women, once much closer, exchanged a meaningful glance before the queen let go and leaned back.

She crooked her finger at Leo. He stepped forward, bowed

again. "Welcome back, Lord Warhurst. Two visits to court in such a short time, we are truly blessed!"

He felt the color rise to his cheeks. "I could not remain away from Your Majesty's—."

"Spare us your pretty sentiments today, my lord." Her voice was clear and commanding and drew the attention of her audience as was no doubt intended. "We are informed that you have evidence that may help or hinder the case of Lord Hawkesbury."

"Yes, Your Majesty. My brother and I believe your advisors have been misinformed as to Lord Hawkesbury's situation."

"Misinformed?" She half-turned to Walsingham who inclined his head. Someone stepped out of the group of men standing to one side.

Grayshaw.

He didn't look at Leo but bowed to the queen, lower than Leo or Blake had with the addition of a flourish. Peacock. He rose and gave her a broad smile with a hint of intimacy in it. The same sort of smile Grayshaw had bestowed on Alice. It was lost on the queen, however, since she wasn't looking at him.

She lifted a finger and Grayshaw spoke. "Lord Warhurst asked me to decipher a letter for him," he said. "I did. It clearly pointed to the previous earl of Hawkesbury being involved in treason, Your Majesty. I thought it prudent to bring it to Sir Francis Walsingham's attention immediately. I would deeply regret any harm being done to—." He stopped when the queen held up her hand.

"Where did you find this letter, Lord Warhurst?" she asked.

"It was in Lord Enderby's possession," Leo said. Behind him, several eavesdroppers gasped.

"Enderby?" The queen glanced over Leo's head. "Is his lordship here?"

"He just arrived, Your Majesty," Walsingham said. He crooked a finger at the crowd. The short, barrel form of Enderby made his way to the throne. He bowed and paid his respects.

The queen rose. "Let us adjourn somewhere more private." Her ladies descended upon her like a flock of starving pigeons but she waved them off. She led the party through to another chamber and sat behind a large desk of polished oak. Leo, Blake,

Lady Warhurst and Lilly stood to one side, Lord Enderby a little separate. Walsingham came in behind them all, limping and leaning on his stick. He shut the door in Grayshaw's face.

"We wish to resolve this today," the queen said. "If there is insufficient evidence of the late earl of Hawkesbury's involvement in any plot then we shall release the present Lord Hawkesbury. However if there is sufficient evidence of guilt then we must detain him until we can ascertain what he knows of it. He was certainly of an age to have been kept informed by his father."

Enderby glanced at Leo. Leo gave him a smile. Beside him, Blake drew himself up to his full height. It felt good to have him there, sharing the family's burden.

"Well, Lord Enderby? Do you or did you possess such a letter?"

Enderby seemed unsurprised by the question. He must have come prepared with an answer. "I did, Your Majesty. The missive came into my hands barely a day ago and I was about to pass it onto Sir Francis. Unfortunately it was stolen from me before I could." He inclined his head at Leo. "Lord Warhurst here was the thief."

The queen's painted eyebrows rose. "That is quite an accusation, Lord Enderby."

"He was with a wench, a common seamstress who duped me and inveigled herself into my home. The two of them colluded—."

"Your Majesty," Lady Warhurst said sharply, cutting him off, "I believe you'll find my son's betrothed is a friend of Lord Enderby's daughter, Patience. She's no common wench, nor did she dupe anyone. Patience invited her to stay with the express purpose of finding the letter. The letter which Lord Enderby had in his possession for *several* weeks and was using to blackmail Lord Hawkesbury."

Blake must have told her everything he knew. She tilted her chin at Leo as if to say *he* should have kept her informed of the situation all along. He sighed. She was right. He'd know better next time.

"Blackmail?" The queen frowned but it quickly cleared. "Ah,

the marriage to the Enderby girl. Is that how you forced Lord Hawkesbury to agree to the union when he was clearly in love with another?"

No one could have failed to hear Lilly's intake of breath. Leo willed her to be strong, remain calm, when he felt anything but calm himself. This could all still unravel in the most dramatic way.

"I, uh... The betrothal will be broken of course," Enderby blustered. "My name *cannot* be linked to Hawkesbury's now that we know he comes from such stock that would dare harm Your Gracious Majesty—."

"Very well," the queen said with a wave of her hand. "He is free to marry Lilly Blakewell if he still desires the union. And *if* he is found not to have been involved in his father's crimes."

Enderby looked relieved. Lilly exchanged a glance with her mother. Leo could see they were both trying hard to contain their smiles. Neither seemed to doubt that Hawke would be released.

It was time to put the final nail in Enderby's coffin and give Lilly something to really smile about. "Your Majesty," Leo ventured, "I am not so sure the previous earl of Hawkesbury was involved in any plots. The letter Lord Enderby used to blackmail Lord Hawkesbury proves no such thing."

Enderby's jowls shook. "What!" he bellowed. "It certainly does. I saw it with—."

The queen lifted a hand and Enderby fell silent although his cheeks and chins continued to wobble. "Explain yourself, Lord Warhurst," she said.

Leo produced a piece of paper from his doublet pocket. "This is the original letter. It's in code but when deciphered, it clearly states something entirely different to what Lord Enderby is suggesting."

She took it, scanned the writing then handed it to Walsingham. While he positioned a pair of spectacles on his nose, she nodded at Leo. "How did *you* decode it?"

"I, uh..." Damnation, he needed to think of an excuse fast. To admit he learned the code from Grayshaw would give credence to the cur's story that he'd seen a letter containing treasonous information implicating Hawke. They needed to avoid that and discredit him as much as possible.

"I did it," Blake said. "We use codes all the time at sea. This one wasn't terribly difficult to decipher."

The queen glanced sharply at Walsingham. He squinted over the top of his spectacles at her. "That's why it's no longer used, Majesty." He shook the letter. "This is an old code. It went out of use years ago."

"Then it would be authentic?" Her Majesty asked.

He nodded and scratched his chin beneath his beard as he studied it again. Eventually he sighed and shook his head at Enderby.

Enderby's eyes widened, a hint of doubt in them. "But it points directly to Hawkesbury! His name is mentioned."

"Indeed it is," Walsingham said. He folded the letter and handed it back to the queen. "But there's nothing of a treasonous nature in it, merely a scandalous one."

The queen leaned closer. "Oh?"

"The message says old Hawkesbury had a mistress, a widow who is no longer with us but had quite a reputation I believe. It suggests the affair be kept secret from Lady Hawkesbury."

"What?" Enderby shouted. He held out his hand for the letter. The queen ignored him. "It says no such thing! Why in God's name would I keep a letter about Hawkesbury's bloody mistress?"

"Because you knew you could use it against the current Lord Hawkesbury," Leo said. "His lordship is a proud man and cares deeply for his mother. He wouldn't want her to learn that her husband kept a mistress. It would upset her. He was willing to agree to marry your daughter in exchange for your silence. Am I right?" Out of the corner of his eye, Leo saw Lilly staring open-mouthed at him. His mother frowned.

"No!" Enderby clasped his hands and went down heavily on one knee. "Your Majesty, this is false! The note I had in my possession and which Warhurst stole from me, clearly stated the late Hawkesbury was a traitor. You must believe me, I—."

"*This* is the letter you used to blackmail a peer of the realm," Leo said. "After all, I'm sure you would never keep a document pointing to treason from Her Majesty's agents." He tilted towards Enderby who was slowly heaving himself to his feet. "That would make you a party to treason too."

Enderby rocked back on his heels. He glanced from Leo to the queen and Walsingham and back to Leo. He was trapped. He could not admit to withholding important evidence any more than he could admit to blackmailing Hawke. Enderby had caused his own downfall, with a little help from Leo's own skill at writing in code.

The silence in the chamber stretched to snapping point as the queen and Walsingham both waited for Enderby to answer the accusation. In the end, he swallowed hard then bowed.

"I'll send a message to Lord Hawkesbury releasing him from any obligation to wed my daughter." He spoke quietly, his head tilted back, his chins thrust out. "It will be waiting for him upon his return home."

The queen dismissed him and he almost ran from her chamber, but not before he gave Leo a poisonous glare. Once the door closed on his back, Lilly released an audible breath. Leo felt like he could suddenly breathe too.

The queen turned to Walsingham and simply raised an eyebrow. He bowed his head. "My man gave me false information, it would seem. He shall be punished."

Leo hoped Grayshaw's punishment wouldn't be too painful. All anger he felt towards him had dissipated along with his fears that his scheme would blow up in his face and he would be thrown into The Tower alongside Hawke. Grayshaw wasn't a bad man, he was simply driven by a need to rise. Leo could understand that.

Thankfully, he thought differently now. All because of Alice. He couldn't wait to inform her of the new developments. She would be pleased. So pleased she might kiss him. All over.

"Poor Lady Hawkesbury," the queen said, tearing the letter in half. "She's such a gentle lady and she was deeply in love with her husband. She must never know of his betrayal." They all nodded. The queen handed the torn paper to one of her servants. "Have Lord Hawkesbury released immediately," she said to Walsingham. "He's such a charming man and so handsome. I knew the charges must have been false. He couldn't possibly think ill of me."

Walsingham nodded, apparently unperturbed by her change of heart. "I'll see to it at once, Your Majesty." He rose and began a slow, awkward walk to the door.

The queen held out her hands for Lady Warhurst and Lilly. They both went to her immediately. Lilly sat on the cushions near the queen's golden slippers. Leo thanked God his sister's condition was not yet showing. He wasn't sure if the virgin queen would be so considerate if she knew Lilly wasn't the virtuous girl she thought her to be.

"I expect he will ask you for your hand now," she said to Lilly.

Lilly blushed and bowed her head. "It would be my dearest wish," she said demurely. Leo smiled and caught his brother's wicked glance. Their sister was as good an actor as any of Lord Hawkesbury's Players. Demure she was not.

The queen spoke of the pending nuptials then dismissed them. They left through the audience chamber, even more crowded than before, and endured the same whispers and taunts. Leo didn't care in the least. Alice may be a seamstress but she was his and she was as much a lady as any of the women there. When she dressed in the finest clothes he could afford, they would see. The women would be jealous of her and the men of him.

"They won't forget so easily," his mother said when they were outside the palace walls and heading home on their mounts. "They'll talk about you behind your back for some time. Does that bother you, Son?"

"Not at all," he said, grinning at her.

She smiled back and breathed a heavy, contented sigh. "All my children to be happily wed. It's a mother's greatest wish."

"You have Leo to thank for that," Blake said, bringing his horse alongside theirs. "Good work by the way, Brother. I didn't know codes were a specialty of yours."

"Aha!" Lilly cried, then softer, "You gave her a false note." She giggled into her hand. "Leo, I never knew you to be so wicked."

"It is unbelievable," Blake joined in. "So much for being the honest one among us."

"I still am," Leo said, "but that's only because you and Lil are so wicked. You'll always make me look good."

Lilly laughed until she cried. "I'm so ridiculously happy," she said, wiping away her tears.

So am I, Leo thought, *so am I.*

"Where is the real letter?" their mother asked, ending the laughter abruptly.

"Destroyed," Leo said.

"Good. The information within it must never come to light."

"It won't," Leo said. "Do not fear, Mother, it's all over now."

Alice would be so pleased to know their hard work brought about a satisfying conclusion. He must go to her but first he would return home and change into something less elaborate. He hated court clothes with the ridiculous slashed, pinked and primped doublets, gaudy embellishments and short trunk hose. There was nothing practical about them.

They arrived at the Dowgate Street house and Greeves handed him a single sheet of parchment. "From Mistress Croft," the steward intoned.

Leo unfolded it and read.

Dear Lord Warhurst,

I apologize for the written message but I could not face you. I have deceived you and I am terribly sorry for it. I cannot marry you. It was not my intention to hurt you but I see now that we cannot be together.

Please accept my good wishes for yourself and your family. Do not try to contact me. This is for the best.

Regards,

Alice Croft.

He dropped the note and ran out of the house.

* * *

ALICE TOLD her father and the players that her marriage would not go ahead. Informing everyone might make it more real and make it harder for her to change her mind.

It worked because she didn't run back to Leo's house and tear up the letter. But it didn't make her in the least satisfied. Quite the opposite. She felt like she was being eaten away inside, first her heart and then the rest of her so that there was nothing left but a hollow shell. It was a miracle she didn't flop to the floor, boneless. It was a double miracle that she didn't cry.

She had the players to thank for that. At first they all stared at her when she made the announcement in The Rose theater's tiring house. They were preparing for a performance of *The Fantastical Life and Loves of Barnaby Fortune*, reading lines, checking costumes, but all activity ceased for what felt like an age after she told them. In truth it was barely a few thunderous heartbeats.

The first to break the silence was her father. "Oh," he said. "Sorry about that, Love. Never mind, there'll be other gentlemen." He patted her shoulder, gave her a sympathetic smile and handed her a cape that needed mending.

She sighed and took it. He really should have been blessed with sons instead of daughters. Perhaps by the time Jane was ready to marry he would understand women a little more.

Roger Style swept past her in a puff of powder he was using to whiten his hair. "So that's the end of that nonsense then, eh? Can't say I'm surprised," he muttered.

His brother, Edward, winced and mouthed an apology. Henry gave her hand a sympathetic squeeze and kissed the top of her forehead. "Are you all right?"

She nodded. "It was my decision so—."

"What?" Freddie yelled from across the room. "*You* ended it? Are you mad? He's a bloody duke or something isn't he?"

"Baron," Will said. "And shut up, Freddie, no one's interested in your opinion."

Freddie made a rude gesture with his fingers and tongue. "Come and get drunk with me after the show," he said, winking at Alice. "We'll have a bit of fun."

Her father pointed a needle at him. "She'll not go anywhere with you. Style, are you going to tell your apprentice to behave or do I have to put sand in his hose again?"

Style sighed then began to berate Freddie, listing all his faults. It continued for some time.

Will handed Alice a sewing kit. She looked down at the cape she was supposed to be mending and wanted to cry. Just when she thought her days of mending for others was over, here she was back at the beginning again. She'd not asked Leo to continue with his arrangements for her shop in her farewell letter. It hadn't seemed right to ask for it knowing the struggles he was going through. Hopefully he would just forget about it. Forget about her.

"Marriage is not an endeavor to enter into lightly," Will said. He rubbed the back of his hand across his high forehead and appeared to be warring with himself over something. After a long pause, he said, "I, uh, have a wife. She lives in our village with our three children."

"Three! Good lord, Will, you kept that close to your chest." She'd thought him a single man. He'd not once mentioned a family.

His smile was sheepish. "My friends know."

She couldn't help smiling at that because it meant he now numbered her among them. The quiet actor was certainly someone she wanted to count as her friend. She had a feeling she was going to need them around her for the next few days and months, and the long, lonely years ahead.

The tiring house door burst open and crashed back on its hinges.

"Take care!" Style protested. "That—." The rest of his sentence died on his lips as he saw who'd entered.

Leo.

Alice swallowed. She'd suspected he might come to the theater and she'd prepared herself for it. Or so she'd thought. But she was completely unprepared for her reaction. If she'd felt hollow before, she now felt full, with her heart taking up all the space inside her, its beat louder than a stampede of wild deer.

Leo filled the doorway, his hat askew, his eyes two green emeralds in his hard, angular face. He wore beautiful clothes that would have cost a lot of money to have made and clearly stamped him as a man of high birth. It was enough to whisk her breath away and have Style scurrying to please him.

"Can I get your lordship something?" Style said, bowing

hurriedly. "An ale? Sweetmeats? There's some bread somewhere..." He trailed off when he noticed Leo's attention was
focused entirely on Alice.

She shivered beneath that stare. It made her hot and cold and
breathless. She thought she knew him but she couldn't read his
expression. All she knew was it was as dark as a pit and she was
to blame for putting it there.

"Alice," he said, voice low but somehow still booming. "We
must talk."

She tried to think of something to say to avoid him, but no
inspiration struck her. Nor could she run past him, he was
blocking the doorway. There was always the back door leading
directly outside but he could probably run faster. Everyone's
gaze settled on her. They were waiting for her answer so she
gave the only one a sensible girl could give.

"Upstairs." She made her way up first.

"We're just going to talk," Leo said to someone. Her father?
Will? All of them?

He followed her up then closed the door when they reached
the room used for storing costumes and props. She moved to the
table in the middle of the room but didn't turn around. Looking
at him would make it so much harder to say what needed to be
said.

"Leo, you shouldn't have come. There is nothing more to be
said."

"Bollocks," he said quietly, ominously.

She half-turned and saw that he was leaning against the
closed door. He'd removed his hat and the jagged ends of his
hair hung over his forehead. Beneath it his eyes fixed on her,
stripped her bare and bore right through her. It allowed her to
see into him too and what she saw almost broke her resolve.

There was no anger in him, just a desolate bleakness. There
was confusion too. He opened his mouth to speak but closed it
again and simply shook his head. He blinked slowly, inter-
minably, and drew in two deep breaths.

He came to her, stepping gingerly across the floor as if she
was a deer and he the hunter and he expected her to flee if he
made any sudden moves. "Why?" he whispered. He stopped

before her and raised a gloved hand to her cheek but didn't touch her. The scent of leather filled her nostrils then was gone. He lowered his hand to his side. "Why?" he asked again, stronger.

"I...I just can't."

"That's not a reason."

She'd had the words in her head earlier. She'd repeated them over and over several times. Why couldn't she remember them now when it mattered?

"I explained in the letter."

"No." His shoulders rounded, deflated, and he closed his eyes. "Please, Alice, you owe me that much."

Oh God, don't do this.

He opened his eyes and pinned her with that intense stare of his. But there was no fury in it. If only he would be angry it would be so much easier. She hadn't expected this intimacy. He was supposed to be full of bluster and bravado, not pleading and...lost.

She needed him to be angry again or she would be undone.

She crossed her arms and stepped away. Drew in a deep breath to steady her erratic heartbeat. "I got what I wanted. A shop of my own. You will keep your word, won't you?" It hurt to say it but she had to. Had to do everything possible to get him away.

She'd rather have stuck a thousand needles into her flesh than see the shock on his face, the disbelief then finally the horror.

His jaw dropped. His breath came in short, sharp bursts as if he couldn't breathe. "Alice..." He shook his head, over and over. "What are you saying?"

She began to shake but willed herself to stop. She had to do this. For him. It was for the best. Absolutely, definitely for the best. He would thank her one day. "I'm sorry, Leo, I tried to save you this by leaving a note. You shouldn't have come."

"I...I don't understand." He reached for her but she stepped further back. "Does this have something to do with what people are saying? Because I don't care about the rumors and gossip. I don't care what people think. You're my... You're mine. Alice, no...stop. Stop moving away."

She shook her head quickly and put up a hand. "Don't come closer. Please, just stay there and listen to me. You and I getting married was a mistake. I duped you, Leo, just like I duped Enderby that night. I played a part, the part of a willing woman." She sucked in her bottom lip because it was threatening to betray her with a wobble.

Leo remained silent, still, watching. His nostrils flared and his breathing became deep and steady and Alice was almost relieved that he was finally getting mad. She deserved his anger, but most of all it was a sign that he believed her and would leave.

"All I wanted was the shop," she said, forging on while she still could. "And I'll have it if you can afford it. If you can't it doesn't matter. Now, please go."

But he didn't move, not at first. He merely stared and stared and stared. Then he spun on his heel and marched to the door. He opened it but paused, lifted his face to the ceiling, and shut the door again. Hard. A set of wings fell off their hook. Alice went to pick them up but he was there before her, lightning fast. He grabbed her wrist and forced her to face him. It didn't hurt, not as much as her heart.

"Tell me you feel nothing," he all but growled. "Tell me there is nothing between us, that you don't care for me, and I'll leave you."

It wasn't supposed to be like this. He was supposed to quickly capitulate and be relieved she'd released him from his obligation. His pride must be severely damaged by her rejection or he'd have left already.

Or he'd fallen a little in love with her after all.

It's for the best, for the best, for the best. Perhaps if she kept chanting that she would one day believe it and the ache would lessen. One day, many, many years from now.

"There is nothing between us, Leo," she said as loudly as she could, which was barely a whisper. "I care nothing for you." She bit the inside of her lip. The tang of blood filled her mouth.

The muscles in Leo's face worked, a vein in his neck

throbbed. He reached up with both hands, almost clasped her face. He was going to grab her, shake her, hit her or kiss her. She closed her eyes and waited. Her skin prickled, her breath and heart stopped. Nothing happened.

She opened her eyes just in time to see him striding toward the door. He slammed it shut behind him. She crumpled to the floor and let the flood of tears finally wash over her.

CHAPTER 24

*L*eo stopped at the nearest tavern—he didn't know its name—and got drunk. Wildly, blindly, couldn't-find-his-way-home drunk. If it wasn't for Blake, he would have spent the night...somewhere. He didn't recognize the lane he'd stumbled into to take a piss.

"Lucky you're a loud drunk," Blake said, his arm around Leo's shoulders, propping him up, "or I'd never have found you."

"Loud?"

"Did you know your language is worse than most pirates I've met when you've had too many ales?"

Leo looked at his brother but that caused him to stumble so he went back to concentrating on putting one foot in front of the other. It was bloody hard. "Who was I shouting at?"

"No one that I could see. Maybe your own demons."

"Ah, those." His demons had been friends to him for a long time. They'd disappeared there for a while, whenever he was with Alice... He groaned.

"I know." Blake squeezed Leo's shoulder. "I know, Brother." He sounded far away.

"You know what?"

"You said Alice just now."

Bollocks. "I hate her."

"No you don't."

"No I don't." Somehow they were already home. Leo shoved Blake away because he was damned if he was going to let his family and his brother's servants see him being assisted like an old man. Problem was, he couldn't grasp the doorknob. It kept moving. Blake reached passed him and gripped it on the first try. He opened the door and tried to take Leo's arm.

Leo shook him off. "I'm not a bloody invalid. Go fu—."

"Mother," Blake said smoothly.

Leo glanced up, right into the face of his mother. She stood beside Greeves who hovered close by, hands out as if he was about to catch something. Leo?

"You found him." She didn't sound angry. She didn't look angry either. That made a change. When he was younger and often used to drink to excess, she would berate him when he eventually stumbled home. But now her eyes were soft and full of unshed tears as she came towards him. She touched his cheek with her cool fingers. "My poor boy."

He reached down and hugged her. "Mother... Alice..." He couldn't continue. His throat closed and the words wouldn't form in his head.

She tightened her hold. "I know. I know."

It felt good to be held by her. She was warm and comfortable and it reminded him of when he was a boy and had scraped his knee. She would hug him and put something cool on his wound and he'd feel instantly better. Not this time. Nothing would make this fiery, piercing pain go away. Not ever.

He closed his eyes but that was a mistake. His stomach roiled and his head swam. He pushed his mother away and made it as far as the stairs before he retched.

"He was never a good drunk," Blake said on a sigh.

* * *

IT WAS ALMOST midday the following day when Leo awoke. He wanted to remain abed but his manservant came to tell him Hawke and Min were joining the family for dinner.

"Greeves had Sweet Mary make up a draught, my lord," his

man said. He handed Leo a small phial and Leo drank it down. It tasted like dirt but he knew from experience it would make his headache ease sooner rather than later.

The servant helped him dress then Leo joined his family in the dining room. They looked up upon his arrival, varying degrees of sympathy on their faces, even Hawke's. Leo wanted to turn around and walk right out again but he stayed and greeted the guests.

Hawke, standing as close to Lilly as possible without actually touching her, shook his hand. "I hope we can put the last few weeks behind us."

Leo wanted nothing more. He wanted to forget everything. All of it. If only that were possible. He could get drunk again but that hadn't helped much the night before. He'd still thought of Alice even when every other thought had become jumbled by the drink.

"As long as you wed my sister, all will be conveniently forgotten," he said.

"Leo," Lilly hissed.

"Agreed," Hawke said. "We're to marry as soon as possible. The bishop of London is a friend of mine and I've already petitioned him for a special license. We won't need to wait long."

Lilly smiled up at Hawke. He smiled affectionately back at her. Leo turned away lest he be sick again but he had the misfortune of focusing on Min and Blake who were also staring lovingly into each other's eyes. *Ugh.*

"Come sit down," his mother said, holding out a chair for him. She had that sympathetic glaze in her eyes again, the one that reminded him of everything he'd lost.

His heart clenched. "After you," he said.

She sat and indicated she wanted him to sit beside her. "I expect you'll want to eat quickly before you go out again."

He looked away, at his plate, the food, anywhere except at her and the others watching his every move. "I'm not going anywhere."

"I see."

He waited for her to say something more, because she rarely said, "I see" and left the conversation alone. Those two words were always a precursor to something else. But this time, she said nothing and he felt the words hanging over him like an executioner's blade.

They dined more grandly than usual on four courses. They ate oysters, beef pies, roasted lamb and capons, larks and tart, and spoke of nothing in particular. Not wedding plans or any such talk that would usually occur with two couples about to be married among the party.

Finally when the servants served fruit and cheese, Leo asked Hawke if he'd heard any more from the queen or Walsingham since his release from The Tower. Hopefully politics could distract him from thoughts of Alice.

"Of course," Hawke said, "but now is not the time for such talk."

"I disagree."

Hawke looked like he wanted to thump him. Leo almost wished he would try. He wanted to go toe-to-toe against a worthy opponent. Perhaps he could talk Blake into letting him mess up that pretty face of his later because Hawke didn't follow through on his threatening glare. He simply shrugged.

"Walsingham dismissed the clerk who brought the letter to his attention," he said. "To me that indicates he believes your version of the letter. If he didn't, he would have rewarded the fellow."

It seemed Grayshaw couldn't talk his way out of this mess then. "I should apologize for what I wrote about your father in the false letter," Leo said. "I hope you see it was necessary. I had to think of something scandalous enough for Enderby to black-mail you over, but not treasonous. It was all I could come up with at the time."

Hawke waved off the apology. "It was a good ruse and I don't think it will ever reach my mother's ears."

"Everything will be all right now," Lilly said, resting her hand on top of Hawke's. She spoke as if they were alone together, as if he was the center of her world.

Hawke brought her hand to his lips and kissed the knuckles. Leo looked away, straight into Min's sympathetic gaze.

"At least Patience will be taken care of," Min said. "Lord

Hawkesbury informed us she is to wed her lover and that her father has reinstated him as land steward."

Great. Wonderful. Another bloody happy couple. Leo was surrounded by them.

The room felt hot and close, his ruff too tight. He stood and waved off his mother's concerned questions. "I need some air."

He left but was dogged by his mother. "Leo," she said, somewhat breathlessly. He stopped and let her catch him. "Leo, are you going to see her?"

"Why would I do that?" he snapped. "She's made her point. She doesn't want anything to do with me."

"I don't believe that."

He laughed harshly. "You didn't hear what she said yesterday."

"No," she said quietly, "but I can guess."

"Can you? Can you, Mother?" He didn't want to have this conversation, not now, not ever. He stalked off towards his chambers but changed his mind. He needed a hard ride somewhere, anywhere, away from all the love in his brother's damned house.

"You know she's lying," his mother called after him.

He shouldn't listen to her. He should leave. He had things to do, a ride to take, and maybe some drinking afterwards.

But he stopped. He didn't turn around but he heard the swish of his mother's skirts as she came up behind him. "Did she tell you she only wanted your money? Your title? Is that why she agreed to marry you?"

If he remained very, very still, his bones might not shatter into a thousand pieces. He said nothing but inclined his head.

"And you, foolish man, believed her. I always thought you were the sensible one of all my children."

"Sensible," he echoed. His voice sounded thick, not his own.

His mother came round to face him but he refused to look at her. He focused on a painting of his step-father, Blake and Lilly's father. It stared back at him, austere, not at all like the real man who'd never shown anything but kindness to Leo growing up.

She took both his hands in hers but she didn't force him to

look at her. He was grateful. "Listen to me," she said. "There's something I need to tell you. Your father loved Belle."

He frowned. "Belle?" Oh. The mistress. "What are you trying to say?"

"I'm trying to tell you that he risked a great deal to be with her because he loved her. He never loved me, not like that. She was the daughter of a baker but he didn't care. He was besotted with her and I'm pleased they had some time together at the end." She smiled. "I can say that now. I couldn't then, not when he was still alive, but after I met your step-father, I realized what love was. It was nothing like what I felt for your father or he for me." She tugged on his hands. "Do you understand?"

He blinked slowly at her. No, he didn't understand. What did this have to do with Alice? "My father was a selfish man. I hate him."

She shook her head and clicked her tongue. "No, Leo, I never wanted you to hate him. I tried to get you to see—."

"He hurt you!" He wanted to swear but he didn't want to upset his mother any more than she already was. "My father hurt a lot of people. He stole from them and gave the money to his whore."

"She was not a whore, don't call her that. It was your father's choice to buy her things with other people's money. Of course he was a fool to use borrowed funds but he loved her, he wanted to give her everything. You understand that, don't you?"

"No!" He let go of her hands. "I don't. I want to give Alice everything that's in my power to give her, not borrowed promises that'll one day come back to strangle her when I'm not there."

"See, you do love her."

"What?" The conversation had taken a wild leap and left him behind. "What has any of this got to do with her?"

"You brought her name into it."

"I was using her as an example."

"No, you weren't. You love her. Admit it to yourself then go and fight for her."

He stalked back to his mother and took her by the shoulders.

She was remarkably small, not tall and willowy like Alice. "She doesn't want me, Mother. She's made it perfectly clear."

She sighed. "Oh, Leo, you're not terribly bright when it comes to women."

"You'll get no argument from me on that score."

"She loves you too, Son. Any fool can see it. She's just afraid of what her love will do to you, and what your love for her will do to yourself."

He threw up his hands. "Can you not speak in riddles?" He blew out a breath. "Mother, if you don't believe me, go and speak to Alice yourself. She'll tell you what she told me—that I meant nothing to her. I was purely a means for her to get the bloody shop she's always wanted."

"When did you promise her the shop?"

"What do you mean? I promised it to her upon her agreement to help me with Hawke's business."

"So at the very beginning. Before you developed feelings for her. Before you..." She cleared her throat. "Before that night she spent here."

"Yes!" He threw up his hands. "Mother, I don't see—." And then he did see. He saw very clearly, like sunshine after rain. It was so bright it was dazzling.

"She already had what she wanted before she agreed to marry you," his mother said. "Before she...before that night here. There was no need for her to lie and accept your marriage proposal. She accepted it because she truly wanted to marry you, which I might add is quite a feat considering the ill-temper you've displayed on several occasions."

His body felt heavy suddenly, his head numb and filled with wool, but his skin was on fire. His breath hitched, kicking his thoughts forward again. He licked his lips, tried to think it all through but it was so hard, so confusing.

"Then...why? I don't understand, Mother. Why would she end it?"

"Oh, my dear boy." She pressed her hands to the side of his face and drew him gently down to her level. Her thumbs rubbed his cheeks and she smiled gently at him. "Because she knows that marrying her will cause you a great deal of hardship."

"No it won't."

"Not for your heart," she said, letting him go and tapping his chest. "I know it's what you want with every beat of this. I'm not sure she does though."

He straightened. "You think she doesn't know I...I love her?"

His mother smiled. "Did you ever tell her?"

"N, no..."

"Then you should. Now."

"But...she made herself clear."

"Tosh! She thinks she's protecting you from scandal and money difficulties. She thinks you'll now be free to marry the Finchbrooke girl or some other wealthy widow. She thinks that's what you need."

Need. He needed *her*, Alice, not anybody else. If he had Alice he could weather any storm, financial or otherwise. Without her, life was going to be one long, lonely, straight path.

But what if his mother was wrong and Alice meant everything she said?

Something inside him shifted, smashing into his heart so that it bled and bled and bled. He squeezed his eyes shut, squeezed his fists closed, held everything in check lest it spill out of him.

His mother's hand on his cheek sent a jolt through him. "Go to her, Leo."

He didn't need to be told twice.

* * *

ALICE WENT through the motions of mending costumes and keeping the tiring house tidy. Her parents and sisters tip-toed around her at home, and the players did the same at The Rose. Even Roger didn't make snide remarks about her broken betrothal. She wasn't sure ignoring it was a good thing to do, but at least it kept her from crying. In truth, she was all cried out. She'd shed tears all day and night and she had no more left.

The door to the costume storage room where she sat alone opened but it was only Will looking for a sword. He smiled wanly at her, retrieved the sword from the table then left. Every time the door opened, her heart lifted with hope. Not hope that

Leo would walk in and beg her to reconsider, of course not. That would be foolishness beyond imagining. No, she expected to receive instructions about her shop, that was all. But he sent no word.

He would soon. He was a man who didn't back away from responsibility. She hadn't decided if she would accept it or not though. It seemed wrong when he needed the money himself.

In the meantime she would be a dutiful daughter and assistant. She would do her work without complaint and try not to think about him. If only she didn't feel like she was drowning in mud she would be able to enjoy the prospect of becoming a shop keeper.

The door opened again. "What are you looking for now?" she asked without looking up.

"The woman I love."

Alice pricked her thumb with the needle and squeaked. Oh God, she was bleeding all over the cape, and her father would throttle her, not to mention what Roger would do, and Leo was there and she wanted to run to him and cry and cry and cry.

She remained where she was, her bottom firmly planted on the chair, and didn't move, didn't look up because if she met his gaze she knew she would beg him to have her back again.

He knelt in front of her and she swallowed past the boulder-sized lump in her throat. He gently took her hand and sucked on the bleeding thumb. His hot tongue laved her, sending thrills shooting down her spine to her toes. She should remove her thumb, should scurry away from him, far, far away, but she couldn't. She was caught.

Just when she thought she couldn't stand the excruciating pleasure any longer, he withdrew her thumb and cradled it in his hand.

"My poor lady," he murmured. "My princess, my baroness. Let me take care of your wound." He put a finger beneath her chin and tilted her face up so that she had to look at him. "Let me take care of you."

He didn't smile, didn't gloat, didn't sneer and say "There, we're even, now goodbye." He simply watched her with those bright green eyes that had always sucked her into their depths.

This time she couldn't climb out of the whirlpool, no matter how much she struggled.

And she struggled. She tried to think of something to say, tried to recall what she'd told him yesterday that had made him believe she didn't love him. But she was hopelessly, utterly destroyed.

"I... You..."

"Shhh, my love, it's all right. I know what you want to say."

Oh. Good.

My love?

"I believed you yesterday," he said. "I believed everything you told me. But I don't anymore. I know you were trying to protect me." He kissed her nose. His lips were warm and impossibly soft. "And I commend you for it, in a way, even though your words were like a thousand stab wounds."

"I...I don't understand."

He caressed a strand of hair from her cheek and tucked it behind her ear. "I know. Let me explain it to you. Yesterday after I left you here, I got drunk. If I hadn't, I would have been back much earlier. As it was, I didn't speak to my mother until today."

Lady Warhurst? What did she have to do with this? But his lips were on hers, teasing and tasting, and she was rapidly losing herself in his kisses. She had to find herself again before it was too late.

She pulled away. "Leo, no. We can't. It's...this...us...we are not getting married. It's a terrible idea."

"We *are* getting married because I love you and you love me too."

Her heart plunged to the floor. She began to shake. "You...you can't."

He laughed at that. "I do. And I know you love me too, so stop denying it."

He loved her. He loved her. Oh God, it was so much worse than she'd expected.

"Love doesn't matter," she said, her voice pathetically small. "It's irrelevant to marriage."

He scoffed. "Of course it matters. It's all that matters. Mother made me see that." He took her by the arms and brought his face close to hers. He was going to kiss her again.

She could not allow that. Kissing him was like falling off a cliff. She would have no control left at all. She leaned back and he let her go.

"You can't marry me! Don't you see? It will ruin you, ruin your family, your people. They need you, Leo, they rely on you."

"And I need you." He wasn't soft anymore. His face had gone hard again and there was a hint of panic at the edges of his green eyes. "Alice, listen to me. Just listen. Without you in my life I will be useless to my tenants, to my family. I'll be unbearable. Ask them, they'll happily tell you." He wasn't laughing and she realized he wasn't joking. "You are my map, Alice Croft. You're the one who sets me on the right path. You're my conscience. You're the other half of me, the clever, sensible half. The best half. I can't rebuild my estate without you guiding me. I can't be the best landlord, the best son, the best brother or the best man without you. Alice, the money is not important. I'll get it. Hell, Hawke owes me a debt for extricating him from a future as Enderby's son-in-law, he'll lend me the money. Lend, not give, not like Blake would have. And you'll help me spend it in the best possible way to benefit our tenants."

Our tenants.

She swallowed. Hard. Her body tingled all over. She clutched the seat of her chair and held on lest she slide off and ended up on the floor in a puddle of skirts.

"Say something," he whispered. His face grew long, white. His jaw went slack. "Alice?"

"I...I'm so sorry."

He sat back on his haunches. His nostrils flared and his eyes faded to a dull shade of green. He glanced away.

"No." She captured his face and forced him to look at her. "I didn't mean that, I meant I'm sorry for yesterday. I wish I could take it all back. I hurt you, I hurt both of us. Oh Leo, I love you, and if you'll still have me—."

His mouth cut off the rest of her sentence. The kiss was hot and hard at first but it soon softened and she melted into him until they were tumbling together on the floor, laughing.

He rose above her and kissed her again, still smiling. She squirmed beneath him and dug her hands through his hair. His smile vanished and the kiss deepened and stole her breath.

"I take it you'll be marrying my daughter again?" came her father's voice behind her. She hadn't heard the door open. "Because I'll be forced to challenge you to a duel and I rather think you'd beat me."

Alice giggled. Leo scrambled to his feet, straightened his doublet and helped her up.

"If it's all right with you, Master Croft," he said in all seriousness, whereas Alice was going to burst with laughter. "I'm going to marry her as soon as possible."

"Good," her father said. "Do it before she changes her mind again. Women are fickle creatures, my lord. Remember that and you might survive marriage without going mad."

Alice should have been offended but instead she started giggling and couldn't stop. She was utterly, ridiculously happy.

"I will, sir, thank you," Leo said, clearing his throat.

Her father grunted then left. Alice jumped into Leo's arms and kissed his nose, his chin, his throat.

"Come here, fickle woman," he said, circling his arm around her waist and hoisting her against his body. "And kiss me properly."

She didn't need to be told twice.

Now Available

A FORBIDDEN LIFE

the 3rd Lord Hawkesbury's Players book

Read on for an excerpt

A FORBIDDEN LIFE

(AN EXCERPT)

About A FORBIDDEN LIFE

When assassin Rafe Fletcher returns home to London, he can't help falling for his brother's woman. For a man looking for redemption, it's the last thing he wants.

Lizzie Croft has feared her friend's brooding brother for years. She remembers him as cold, calculating and dangerous, the very last man she needs in her life. The very last man she can trust. But trust him she must when she becomes the prime suspect in a murder.

Protecting Lizzie and finding the real killer might be just the redemption Rafe needs…or it might be the path to more pain.

CHAPTER 1

"I'm going to prison," James said.

Rafe Fletcher thought few things could shock him anymore, but it took him a moment to gather his wits. After a seven-year absence, they were not the words of welcome he expected upon his return to the family home.

"Why?" he asked.

James groaned and buried his head in his hands, but didn't offer any more information. Rafe stretched out his legs and regarded his brother sitting across from him in the small parlor. James was seven years younger, but it might as well have been more. He seemed so childlike with his thin frame and innocent eyes, it was difficult to imagine him doing anything wrong. Assuming he hadn't broken any laws, there was only one reason why he could end up in jail.

"You're in debt, aren't you?"

James looked up. "How did you know?"

Rafe waved a hand, taking in the bare parlor. It was like an empty tomb with only two chairs and one small table. There was nothing in the way of comforts, not even a fire despite the chilly autumn air. It was vastly different from how their mother had kept it. Her embroidered cushions had adorned at least four chairs, a tapestry had hung on one wall, and the rushes had always been clean. James kept no rushes on his floor.

"I don't suppose you have any money saved to loan me?" James fixed Rafe with a wild-eyed stare. "I would pay you back as soon as possible."

"Not yet. I'm sorry." Rafe wished he'd saved the money from his missions and not given it all away in Cambridge.

But then he remembered why he'd given it away, and to whom, and he didn't regret it at all.

"I'll be starting a new job in a week and whatever I earn will go to your creditors, as long as I can stay here."

"Of course!" Relief flooded James's face. "Thank you. I'm sorry to do this to you. I didn't want to ask you for money…"

"Why not? We're family."

"Barely."

Rafe sucked in air through his teeth. He deserved that. They were half brothers, their mothers the same but their fathers different, and Rafe had been absent for a long time. He should have come home earlier, as soon as he heard about old Pritchard's death a year ago. James had been alone since then, struggling to survive on an apprentice's wage, and before that he'd had only the heavy-fisted Pritchard for company for six years. Without their mother to soothe the old man's tempers, and without Rafe to protect him, James must have lived on a knife's edge. It was no wonder he sometimes hated Rafe for escaping.

"What happened to your job?" Rafe asked. "Your last letter said nothing of problems with your apprenticeship."

James sighed again. "I lost it. Cuxcomb went into debt himself and had to close the shop. Tailoring apprenticeships are hard to come by. Times are difficult. And some consider me unlucky, having lost both my previous masters one way or another."

Rafe shook his head. Some people were ignorant, superstitious fools. Losing the apprenticeships wasn't James's fault. His father's death, while welcomed by almost everyone who knew him, meant James had needed to find another master, and Cuxcomb's debts couldn't be blamed on him.

"I put off my creditors for a while," James said. "But then they all called in the debts at the same time and I couldn't pay. I've been ordered to go to the Marshalsea prison until the debts are dissolved."

"It'll only be for a week."

"That'll feel like forever."

"I know," Rafe said heavily.

James rubbed his hands through his overlong hair, messing it up. "Is your new job a certainty?"

Rafe hesitated. "Almost."

"Almost?" James winced. "And how will you pay my debts off immediately upon starting? Your new master would have to be very generous to pay you in advance."

"I can only ask. And if Lord Liddicoat doesn't want to advance me some of my wages, then perhaps your creditors will agree to me paying off your debts in installments if I can prove I have secure employment. I won't let you starve."

"It's not the starving I'm worried about, it's the other prisoners. And the filth, the lice, and sickness. Have you ever been to a prison, Rafe? Have you seen the kind of base people housed in them?"

"They're not all base," he said. James didn't seem to notice his offended tone, which was just as well. Rafe didn't want his brother asking why he'd been in jail, because that would lead to questions about his activities over the last seven years. He'd told James he was a mercenary, and while that had been true at first, in more recent times he'd taken on a new role with a new master. Innocents like his brother didn't need to know what that employment entailed, especially now it had ended. Returning to London was the start of a new phase of his life, a fresh beginning. The past was better left buried.

Besides, he'd only been in jail twice and he'd escaped both times after a short stint. It hardly counted.

But his brother had a point. If the prison's conditions didn't get to him, the other prisoners might.

"Do you have any friends you could ask for a loan?" Rafe asked.

"One or two," James mumbled. "Well, just one."

"That's better than none. Who?"

"John Croft."

"The neighbor?" Rafe remembered the Crofts. They were good, respectable people, but Rafe had not had much to do with them in years past, distracted as he was with his own problems. "They have three daughters, don't they? The eldest married a lord a year or two before I left."

"Lord Warhurst. Jane, the youngest, is living up in Northumberland with them in the hopes of bettering herself. Lizzy still lives at home." His voice softened when he said her name and there was a ghost of a smile on his lips.

So Lizzy Croft meant more to James than merely being his neighbor. "I hardly remember her. A shy little thing, wasn't she? I don't think she spoke two words to me her entire life."

"She's changed. She's still a sweet-natured girl. Very good and kind. You'll adore her, Rafe. Everyone does."

Such a glowing recommendation. James clearly cared for the girl. "You're going to marry her, then."

"One day. There's an understanding between us. I can't afford to marry her until my apprenticeship finishes and that's some years off. If ever," he added gloomily.

"Then ask her father for a loan to pay your debts."

"I can't."

"Why not?"

"He's an old man now and doesn't work. He's still the tiring house manager for Lord Hawkesbury's Players, but in name only. Lizzy does all the work as his assistant. Her wages support both her parents."

"But surely the eldest daughter sends them money."

James shrugged. "I don't think Lord and Lady Warhurst have much either, what with their own family and their miners to take care of. The Crofts live as I do. If they have money, there is little to show for it."

Rafe struck Croft off his list, but not his daughter. "Why not see if there is work for you at the players' tired house?"

"Tiring house."

"If you can show you're working, your creditors might give you longer to pay them back."

"Perhaps."

"Perhaps? What do you have against the idea?"

James sighed. "I don't want to tell Lizzy what's happened. She might…think less of me as a man. I couldn't face her pity."

Bloody hell. Rafe hadn't expected his brother's pride to be larger than his fear of prison. "If she loves you, she wouldn't think less of you for a situation that isn't your fault." Love. What did Rafe know about love? It wasn't a sentiment men like him had the luxury of experiencing.

"Her company is prosperous but I wouldn't earn much as her assistant."

"It would be more than what you're earning now."

James's shoulders slumped and he lowered his head. "True."

"If you want to avoid the Marshalsea, brother, you need to ask her. And believe me, you want to avoid the Marshalsea."

He straightened. "You're right, I will, just as soon as she gets home from the playhouse."

"Glad to see you've still got some sense in that head of yours."

James gave him a withering glare. Rafe rose and clapped him on the shoulder. "I'm hungry. Got anything in your pantry?"

"There's bread, but that's it I'm afraid."

Rafe left him to inspect the provisions. He got as far as the kitchen when someone knocked loudly on the front door.

"Lizzy!" he heard James say upon opening it. Rafe smiled. He was curious to meet the middle Croft girl again after all this time. For the life of him, he couldn't recall what she looked like. It was shameful, really. He'd lived next to the Crofts for twenty-two years before leaving London, but Lizzy was faceless in his memory. He'd not even recalled her name until James mentioned it. Granted she would have been young when he left and he'd been an angry youth with burdens to bear, yet he felt some regret all the same now that she was to be his sister-in-law.

But first he'd leave the lovers alone for a few moments. It would give James a chance to ask her for work, then he'd join them to discuss what to do next.

At least, that was his plan. He abandoned it when Lizzy's voice rose above James's. "You *have* to marry me!" she cried. "And soon."

Rafe frowned when James didn't respond immediately. Then he sat down on the stool near the hearth. He wasn't going in there. His brother needed to sort this out on his own.

"James?" Lizzy prompted when he didn't answer her. "Did you hear me?"

"I...I..." James stared at her through dull, shadowed eyes that were usually a vibrant blue. "You look tired," was all he said.

This was his response? "I've been rushing about," she said, touching her hair and wishing she'd taken time to repin it beneath her hat before she left the Rose's tiring house. She wasn't sure how proposals of marriage should be given, but perhaps she would have received a better reaction if she'd taken extra care of her appearance.

James had not seemed to care upon seeing her in disarray before, except for the one time a chamber pot had been emptied from a third-floor window onto her head. He'd laughed. She'd been humiliated and stormed home in tears. His laughter had rung in her ears for hours afterward, until he redeemed himself by giving her a square of crisp white lawn to make herself a new pair of cuffs. They'd been thirteen, and he'd probably stolen the fabric from his father's shop, but she didn't care. She was just so happy to not be mad at her closest friend anymore.

She stopped fidgeting with her hair and said, "I'm aware women do not usually do the proposing, but time is running out. I'm desperate, James." She pushed past him and stood in the parlor, waiting for his sudden grin to light up the room and lift her heart.

It did not.

He glanced past her to the door leading to the kitchen area. She turned. There was no one there. Of course there wouldn't be. James lived alone.

"Lizzy, I'm glad you're here. I wanted to speak to you about something."

"One thing at a time. First we discuss marriage. Well? What say you?"

"I say why the sudden urgency?"

"Sudden? There has been an understanding between us for *years.*"

"Yes, but you've never pounded on my door until it almost shattered, then demanded I marry you. So what has changed?" A lock of brown hair tumbled over one eye, making him look younger than his twenty-two years. A flash of dimples would have completed the effect of youth, but he wasn't smiling.

Lizzy offered up a weak one in the hope he would return it but he merely stared at her from behind the curtain of hair and waited. She drew a deep breath. "Very well. Let me explain. I could lose my position with Lord Hawkesbury's Players. We all could. The new Master of Revels, Walter Gripp, is going to shut us down. He's already banned one play and has promised to continue until we are ruined. And if the troupe is ruined, what will I do? Who will employ me at such good wages? What will all my friends do? There isn't enough work for them here in London." She was rambling but couldn't stop herself. She felt hopeless, and Lizzy had not felt hopeless in a long time. Not since she'd grown out of her crippling shyness. "I can do nothing for them, but I can do something for myself. Marry you."

"I...ah..." He turned away and lowered his head. A few deep breaths later and he looked at her once more. "Lizzy, you're in a state." He took her by the elbow and steered her farther into the parlor. "Sit." He indicated the chair nearest the fireplace, the best position in the house reserved for favored guests. She felt honored, even though the fire wasn't lit. Perhaps his hesitation was because *he* wanted to do the proposing. She sat with her hands in her lap in case he wanted to get down on his knees and clasp them.

He didn't clasp them or get down on his knees. He sat too, not in the nearest chair, but on another far away. Indeed, he didn't even look her in the eyes at all, but looked again to the door that led to the kitchen, buttery, and pantry, then settled his gaze on the small ruff at her throat.

"Now, explain it again," he said. "Calmly."

She bit back the tears pricking her eyes. If she allowed herself to give into them, she could not be the calm woman he wanted. It wasn't James's fault that he wasn't reacting with the appropriate amount of sympathy. He didn't understand the seriousness of the situation. Very well, she must make him understand.

"Walter Gripp is the new Master of Revels and he hates Roger Style. Not a mild, passing hatred, but a vicious loathing that's grown deeper over the years."

James shrugged. "I can see how someone would dislike a pompous prig like Style, but *hate* is a rather strong word."

Lizzy spread her fingers in her lap and tried again. "Style stole Gripp's wife."

"*Roger* Style? Not his brother?"

She nodded. "Apparently they were secretly...you know... while they were both married. When Style's first wife died, Mistress Gripp left her husband to live with Roger."

"How did she get a divorce?"

"They didn't divorce." Despite old King Henry's precedent, one had to have a great deal of money and influence to obtain a divorce. "She lived with Roger for a few months, then left him too. Left London altogether apparently. He wed the current Mistress Style a year or so later. But Walter Gripp never forgave him. As far as he's concerned, his wife was a good woman until Roger corrupted her. He claims Roger seduced her with his *wicked theatre ways* as he calls it."

If it wasn't so awful, she'd laugh. It was impossible to think of Roger as a seducer, let alone the troupe being wicked. They were all respectable men from good families. Most of them anyway.

"Walter Gripp adored his wife by all accounts," she said. "He's been trying to hurt Roger ever since. He's threatened him with lawsuits and even placed his friends in our audiences from time to time to throw rotten fruit and jeer. Once he stormed in and announced he would ruin Roger by destroying the company. He was so angry he was foaming at the mouth and shouting like a madman. It was horrible."

"I'm sure it was. But if Gripp hates Style so, why doesn't he just challenge him to a duel?"

"Roger's too cowardly to agree to one."

"Run him through with his rapier in a dark laneway then."

"And be hanged for it? He's no fool. This way Gripp can ruin the troupe quite legally. Now that he's the Master of Revels, he *can* ruin us too." All new plays had to be read and passed by the Master of Revels before they could be performed. If he deemed a play too offensive or seditious, he could shut a production down. Doing that to every play submitted from Lord Hawkesbury's Players would cause the company to lose money like a cracked barrel loses wine. They couldn't keep rerunning old plays—the London theatre crowd demands fresh stories and would quickly grow weary of repeats. "It's awful. I'm going to lose my job and the only solution I can come up with is to wed you."

"Thank you," he said, wryly.

"Oh James, I'm sorry, that came out wrong. I do *want* to marry you."

"Lizzy…" He rubbed his eyes and blew out a breath. "Getting married isn't a good idea. Not now."

"Are you worried your wages can't support all of us?"

"Yes. Yes, of course. That's it." He looked relieved. "So you see the need to wait?"

"No, I don't. I have a solution. You can come and live with us and let this house to boarders. Or if you prefer, we could live here and let out Papa's house." It was only next door. Her parents could move easily enough, frail as they were. "The extra income will stretch if we live frugally until your apprenticeship is complete."

"You really have thought of everything." He sounded as if his doom was imminent.

"I'm sorry," she muttered. "Forget I said anything." She dropped her head into her hands and tried to suppress the sense of hopelessness welling within her.

"Now listen to me." He knelt in front of her and patted her arm. "Your company's plays are tame. With Lady Blakewell writing most of them, she's much too smart to put in even a veiled reference to dried-up old virgin queens who failed to put their country first and get an heir."

Lizzy glanced around out of habit although there was no one to overhear them. The royal succession was a sensitive issue. Any plays alluding to it never found an audience beyond the Master of Revels.

"It doesn't matter what our plays allude to, subtly or otherwise. If Gripp wants to hurt Roger, he will."

"Can't Style ask the Lord Chamberlain to intervene?"

She snorted softly. "Don't be a fool."

He sighed again. "I suppose not."

The Master of Revels came under the jurisdiction of the Lord Chamberlain's office, but the Lord Chamberlain was patron of a rival troupe. He had every reason to keep out of the matter.

"What about Lord Hawkesbury himself?" James asked.

"He won't want to interfere either." Lord Hawkesbury was rarely drawn into politics, even the politics of the theatre, unless the queen commanded it. If the troupe of players who bore his name ceased to exist, he would simply become patron of another.

Lizzy groaned. It was all so awful, so uncertain and terrifying! She'd grown up with Lord Hawkesbury's Players. The tiring house was as much her home as the house she lived in with her parents. She knew every costume in the storage room, every wig, every pin. She'd made friends with many actors and stage hands including some who'd become famous. She felt comfortable with them, not tongue-tied and awkward the way she often did around people. The players spoke the same around her as they did around each other. And that was how she liked it.

Yet it could all be destroyed by Gripp.

Her friends would scatter and there would be no wage to support herself and her aged parents. Without it, they would be destitute or have to survive on the charity of her sister's husband all the way up in Northumberland. So far from London and the people she loved. She would not burden Alice and Leo unless absolutely necessary. They had enough financial difficulty with a growing family and mines still in their infancy and not yet fully profitable.

No, Lizzy *had* to marry James to secure her future and remain in the city. There was no one else and besides, everybody knew they would one day wed. It was inevitable, so why not go through with it now to solve her problems?

James had sold his father's tailoring workshop after the old man's death, but creditors had pounced on the money from the sale, leaving nothing. He had found another master tailor to oversee the last years of his apprenticeship, but apprentices earned little since they usually boarded free of charge with their masters. James had insisted on remaining in his family home, but his wage had not been raised accordingly.

"I think you're overreacting," he said. "Gripp is hardly going to abuse his position because of an old feud."

She blinked at him. "Overreacting? James!" How could he say such a thing to her? "When have you ever known me to overreact?"

His gaze shifted sideways. "Well, there was that one time a chamber pot was accidentally emptied on your head."

"I was a child!"

He shushed her and glanced past her to the kitchen again. He stood and took both her hands in his. It had been what she'd wanted him to do earlier. So why did it turn her blood cold now? "You have such a temper," he said with half a smile. "But you only show it to me."

"That's because you're my best friend—the only person with whom I can truly be myself." Except that wasn't entirely true. She was herself around most of the troupe, she just found no need to get angry with them. None of them would ever accuse her of overreacting. Their very definition of it was probably vastly different from James's.

He bent and kissed her forehead. "You're right and I'm sorry. You rarely overreact." He sounded very serious all of a sudden. "So Gripp truly presents a problem?"

"If he decides to punish Roger, then the entire company will suffer. Including me."

He squeezed her hands and massaged the knuckles with his thumb. It was a soothing motion but there was nothing reassuring in his grave expression. He'd gone quite gray in the face. "You'll find work as a seamstress elsewhere. Your stitching is very fine."

"I wouldn't earn a tenth of what I earn now." The only way a seamstress could make a good income was to open her own shop and Lizzy didn't have enough money to do that, nor did she want to be a shopkeeper. The thought of conversing regularly with strangers made her gut churn.

No, the only way she could earn enough to support her parents and herself was to stay with one of the good theatre troupes and neither of the other two main London ones needed new tiring house assistants.

"I'll be without work soon," she said.

"When you say soon...how long do you think? Would you need an assistant in the meantime?"

"Of course not. Roger Style hasn't hired an assistant for my father before, why would he now when everything is so uncertain?"

"Yes. I see. I thought I'd ask anyway," he muttered, bowing his head again.

"Why? Do you need work?"

"A little extra would be nice."

No wonder he hadn't agreed to her marriage proposal. His lack of money must be playing on his mind. Perhaps he was poorer than he let on. She'd noticed that his fire was rarely lit of late, despite the cooler weather, and that the house seemed barer, yet she hadn't put the pieces together. Now that she looked, she could see his jerkin had more patches than original fabric, although it was difficult to pick them out, so good was the work. Lizzy felt terrible. She should have seen the signs earlier. Oh, James. Why hadn't he said something?

"You believe Gripp will force the company's closure?" he asked.

"Walter Gripp is a vindictive man and he has the power to do it. There is nothing and no one standing in his way."

"Want me to kill him for you?" The voice came from behind her. It was deep and low, quiet yet commanding. The sort of voice that belonged to men in control, respected men who didn't need to shout to get attention.

She recognized it although she hadn't heard it in many years. She felt cold through to her bones even as a warm flush crept up her neck.

"He's jesting," James said.

Lizzy didn't turn around but she could feel Rafe's presence the way an anvil feels a hammer's blow.

"Lizzy, you remember my brother," James went on. "Rafe. Rafe Fletcher," he added, perhaps to remind her that the brothers had different fathers. He'd left London suddenly on that terrible day when their mother died. Lizzy had no idea where he'd gone or what he'd been doing, because she'd never asked James and he'd never offered the information. Indeed, he rarely mentioned his brother at all and never discussed the incident that had led to his departure. But Lizzy hadn't forgotten him. Rafe Fletcher was not the sort of man a girl, or indeed anyone, could forget.

And now he was back.

She forced herself to turn, but she couldn't bring herself to look up at Rafe's face. She stared at his boots instead. They were good boots. Sturdy with scuff marks on the toes and…was that a bloodstain?

She suppressed a gasp but not a shiver.

"Light the fire," Rafe said. "She's cold."

James hesitated, then did his brother's bidding. Lizzy clasped her hands in front of her and kept her gaze down. Her insides roiled and surely her face must be the color of burning coals. It felt hot enough. She tightened her grip on her fingers.

"I doubt you remember me," Rafe said above her. Far, far above her. "You were still a child when I left."

Seven years ago, she'd been fourteen, hardly a child. She wished she could tell him that, but she just nodded instead. She'd tried so hard to leave the shy, speechless girl behind, yet here she was again with her flushed cheeks and twisted tongue. So much for all the practice she'd put in over the years. While the actors worked on remembering their lines, she'd studied them: the way they spoke to one another, what they said, when they laughed or teased or offered a sympathetic frown. She'd forced herself to imitate them when she'd rather have sat in the corner and hidden behind her sewing. Eventually she'd felt confident enough to put her observations into practice. Tentatively at first, then more often and with more people. It had worked. Old acquaintances commented on how she'd emerged from her shell, and new ones were none the wiser. None suspected the amount of effort and time she'd put into remaking herself.

But Rafe Fletcher had stripped all that hard work away as if it were merely a layer of the thinnest silk. And she hadn't even looked at him yet.

"So do you?" he asked. "Want me to kill this Gripp for you?"

"Rafe," James warned. "Stop teasing her."

"Who said I was teasing?"

Out of the corner of her eye, Lizzy saw a lit taper flutter into the fireplace and James's booted feet turn at the same time.

"Pay him no mind," James said. "He's not going to kill anyone."

"It's early yet."

From his light tone, she doubted Rafe was being serious, yet the thought of him killing someone wasn't a stretch. He'd also nearly killed his own stepfather. And Lizzy had seen the whole thing from the first spray of blood to the moment Rafe walked away.

"Lizzy, sit down," James said, taking her elbow and steering her back to the chair. It was much warmer with the fire blazing but not cozy with Rafe in the same room. Not in the least.

"There's something I need to tell you now that my brother is here."

She hazarded a quick glance from one to the other. James seemed distracted, his brow lined with concern, and he kept giving his brother what she could only describe as warning glares. Rafe, however, didn't seem to notice. He met her gaze with a mixture of concern and curiosity.

She blushed harder and stared down at her lap. Rafe Fletcher was as handsome as ever. He never had been boyish like James. There were no dimples, no big brown eyes, or errant locks. Rafe was all hard lines, dark shadows, and severely cropped black hair. If it wasn't for the friendly eyes, she would have frozen in fear.

That at least was different. The last time she'd seen him he'd been wound up like a tightly coiled rope, full of tension and threatening to snap. But he hadn't snapped back then, not entirely. He'd gone into his house and come out a few moments later with a pack slung over his shoulder. He'd sported a black eye, a bloody nose, and a distant, detatched expression. His stepfather, James's father, had lain half dead in the street.

That memory was going to be hard to shake loose, no matter how friendly he seemed now. Yet she could pretend, for James's sake.

She leaned forward slightly so that she looked interested and eager to speak to him. "Where have you been, Mr. Fletcher?" she asked in a strong voice.

"Call me Rafe like you used to."

She'd never called him anything. Indeed, this was the first time she'd ever spoken to him. "Rafe," she repeated dully. Then she attempted a smile. Smiles were a good way to make the other person feel comfortable. Not that Rafe looked uncomfortable. He looked remarkably at ease lounging against the mantelpiece, arms crossed over his chest, feet crossed at the ankles. Like he was the master and he was home.

"I've been abroad," he said, curt.

"How interesting. Abroad where?"

He lifted one big shoulder. "Here and there."

"How interesting." She winced. *You've already said that, fool.* "I mean, what did you do abroad?"

"This and that."

Right. So he didn't want to tell her. Indeed, why would he want to chat with *her*? He probably just wanted her to hurry up and leave so he could talk to his brother or get on with whatever business he'd returned to London to do.

"I think I should go," she said to James.

"Not yet." He put out a hand to stay her. "I still I have something important to say. I have to go away for a while."

She frowned. "Where to?"

"Out of London."

He must have taken avoidance lessons from his brother. "Why?"

He looked down at his knee, jigging up and down. He pressed his hand to it and breathed in. "I have business to conduct."

"Where?"

"A small village. In Dorset. You won't know it."

"I might."

"Doebridge," Rafe said.

James glanced at him and then at Lizzy before staring down at his jigging knee once more. "Yes, Doebridge."

"Is that far?" she asked.

"Far enough."

"Is Cuxcomb sending you?" And why was he sending his apprentice all the way to Dorset? Lizzy had once traveled through that county with her family to visit Alice and Leo. It had taken two days in good weather by wagon. With the recent rain, the roads that weren't too muddy would be full of potholes. James could be gone awhile.

"How will you get there?" she continued. "Is he making you walk?"

"It really doesn't matter," James said. His leg stopped jigging and he finally fixed his gaze on her. She chewed her lip, unnerved. James was worried. Not quite afraid, but certainly apprehensive. "The important thing is, I won't be back for some time."

"How long?"

James stood and strode to the fireplace to stand beside his brother. He was slender next to Rafe's broad-shouldered frame although they were of a height. Perhaps that explained why he looked the more approachable of the two, like someone you would stop to have a conversation with. Rafe looked liked someone you crossed the street to avoid.

"A week," James muttered. "Maybe more."

"That's not too long. When you get back we can discuss the future." She watched Rafe furtively as she said it but he showed no curiosity over her words which meant he must have heard her earlier. Wonderful. She'd had her marriage proposal rejected by her best friend as well as overheard by his brother.

"I've asked Rafe to take care of you and your parents while I'm away," James said.

He wanted his brother to take care of them? A man who'd almost murdered his own kin? Lizzy made a sound of protest except it came out a whimper.

Amusement shone in Rafe's pitch-black eyes. "So it seems you'll need to speak to me after all."

A FORBIDDEN LIFE is now available.

A MESSAGE FROM THE AUTHOR

I hope you enjoyed reading A TEMPTING LIFE as much as I enjoyed writing it. As an independent author, getting the word out about my book is vital to its success, so if you liked this book please consider telling your friends and writing a review at the store where you purchased it. If you would like to be contacted when I release a new book, subscribe to my newsletter at http://cjarcher.com/contact-cj/newsletter/. You will only be contacted when I have a new book out.

ABOUT THE AUTHOR

C.J. Archer has loved history and books for as long as she can remember and feels fortunate that she found a way to combine the two. She spent her early childhood in the dramatic beauty of outback Queensland, Australia, but now lives in suburban Melbourne with her husband, two children and a mischievous black & white cat named Coco.

Subscribe to C.J.'s newsletter through her website to be notified when she releases a new book, as well as get access to exclusive content and subscriber-only giveaways. Her website also contains up to date details on all her books: http://cjarcher.com She loves to hear from readers. You can contact her through email cj@cjarcher.com or follow her on social media to get the latest updates on her books:

facebook.com/CJArcherAuthorPage

twitter.com/cj_archer

instagram.com/authorcjarcher

pinterest.com/cjarcher

bookbub.com/authors/c-j-archer

www.ingramcontent.com/pod-product-compliance
Lightning Source LLC
Chambersburg PA
CBHW050147120726
47903CB00002B/521

* 9 7 8 0 6 4 8 8 5 6 1 7 7 *